SEVEN CARD SEDUCTION

"Well, it's early yet," Charity said. "Can't be much past seven. I don't suppose you've got a deck of cards?"

"No. My cards are outside in the saddlebags."

"Well then," she said pertly, as she reached into her pocket, "we'll use mine." She began to shuffle.

"Where . . ." Jake paused to clear his throat. "Where in God's name did you find a deck of cards?"

Charity riffled the deck, cut it one handed, and re-shuffled before she slapped it down in the small space between them. "Cut," she chirped. When he tapped the top with his index finger without looking at it, she said, "Same place you confiscated that little hatchet of yours. Got a bag of rock candy and a beat-up dime novel, too. It's a Buffalo Bill one, I think. If you're nice to me, maybe I'll read some of it to you later." She began to deal: two face down, one card up. "Seven card stud, nothing wild. They're not marked, in case you're worried."

Numbly Jake picked up his hole cards. Charity stifled a giggle. He looked at them, then at his face-up card. His lips pursed, and then he looked her straight in the eyes. It sent a flood of heat rushing through her. He said, "And what, Miss Caine, do you propose we bet?"

She took a deep breath. She had planned on being in control, but that look he'd just given her made her a little woozy. She said, quite softly, "I have the high card showing. Queen of diamonds. And the queen bets . . ." She slithered one slim, bare leg out from under the coat, exposing it to the knee. ". . . one leg."

Jake leaned back. He checked his hole cards again. "I see," he said with a grin that was full of purpose. "Well, that's really only half a leg, you know, but I'll accept it. And I'll see that leg." He tugged off a boot.

PHOEBE FITZJAMES

OKLAHOMA ANGEL

ZEBRA BOOKS
KENSINGTON PUBLISHING CORP.

ZEBRA BOOKS

are published by

Kensington Publishing Corp.
475 Park Avenue South
New York, NY 10016

First Printing: February, 1993

Printed in the United States of America

Chapter One

Indian Territory, 1877

Wearily, Charity Caine heaved another armload of wood atop the bonfire. Sparks gusted up against the midnight sky to mix with the gritty, relentless pelt of sleet.

As she stepped back and readjusted the ice-encrusted muffler that masked her nose and mouth, she wondered idly if, at long last, she resembled any of her relatives, the greater share of whom had spent much of their public lives aiming pistols at disgruntled bankers or stagecoach passengers. Gloved thumb up, she pointed her index finger at the flames. "Stand and deliver," she muttered into her scarf before she trudged back toward the corral to wrench free a few more boards.

The fire had been burning since late afternoon. Two cords of wood had been reduced to ash, and now the corral fence was going in. It seemed a shame about the corral, but the storm had been so fierce that she feared to scavenge kindling too far from the clearing. These hills were no place to be

5

lost in bad weather. Besides, there wasn't much need for a fence anymore: the goats were long gone, and the old milk cow had died ten days earlier. One horse and two scrawny hens were the only remaining livestock. They could stay inside the shed.

This latest storm had added no fresh drifts to those already pushing against the ramshackle buildings. The bitter wind gave it no chance. Flurries swept along the frozen earth, disguising it, layering it in a shifting blanket of moonlit white that mixed with the fresh fall to leave the world in a pale, frigid haze.

More boards on the fire. She stepped back again, squinting and shielding her eyes from the flare. The fire was a large one. It had to be, to thaw the ground deep enough to dig a grave.

The gale flapped Charity's heavy coat's tail, spattered her face with stinging granules, and carried the blaze's smoke and sparks away at sharp, swiftly shifting angles. Behind her, the little log house's shuttered windows leaked weak ribbons of warm golden light across the snow. *It almost looks cheery,* she thought. *You'd almost think someone was alive in there.*

A wave of shivers, unrelated to the weather, swept through her. She hugged her shoulders, gathered the too-big coat closer, and looked toward the skies. Through the flickering haze of sleet, the moon showed round and full and yellow for an instant before the clouds moved in again to slowly diffuse its light.

With gloved and clumsy fingers, she tucked a few stray wisps of straight, blue-black hair under her

6

scarf. In all her nineteen years, she had never been quite so tired or so cold. Or so alone. She rubbed at her eyes to brush away the ice crystals that fringed her lashes. Then, sighing, she picked up the charred pole at her feet and began, for what seemed the hundredth time, to stir and poke the bonfire.

"Dawn," she said to no one in particular, her words lost in the wind's lonely cry. "By dawn I'll be able to start digging."

When she woke, the storm's howl still leaked through the cracks in the door and rattled the shutters. Groggy and stiff, her hair in a long black braid that reached her waist, she rose and shoved cold feet into colder leather moccasins. She wrapped a threadbare quilt over her nightgown before she tiptoed, as she always had, to the tiny curtained room at the cabin's far end.

"Grampa?" she called, her breath rising in cloudy wisps. Still half asleep, she hugged the quilt closer and cowered out of instinct and long habit. The hearth's fire had gone so low that the narrow, dusty blades of afternoon light seeping through the shutters seemed almost bright. "Grampa Zeb, I didn't mean to sleep so late. I . . ." And then she remembered: his death, the bonfire, and how she had buried him as the sun rose.

She sat down at the little table before the hearth, bowed her head on folded arms, and wept: not from grief, but desolation. Even poor company had been better than no company at all, and now she was completely alone.

But was that such a bad thing? There was no one

7

to talk to; but then, there was no one to beat her, either. No one to order her around or to get drunk and smack her for no reason. No one to lock her up in the dark, under the ground, and forget she was there . . .

Her arms broke out in gooseflesh, and she caught herself glancing at the door, reminding herself that the bar was on the inside and that she could open it any time she wished. Silly. This house didn't even have a cellar, and it had been a long time since Grampa Zeb had pulled that trick. But even after all these years, she still had to remind herself that the door would open if she wanted.

She wiped her eyes roughly, grinding her fists into the sockets, telling herself there was no reason to cry. For the first time, she was free. She could get up when she wanted, go to sleep when she wished, and she'd never have to play another stupid game of chess as long as she lived. If it so pleased her, she could sing while she cooked or chopped wood, and there'd be no one to slap her for making noise. *Interruptin' my concentration again!* Grampa Zeb used to holler while he walloped her.

No, there was no reason to weep. But why couldn't she make herself stop?

It was a half hour before the numbness in her hands and feet reminded her to stoke the dying embers in the hearth. She fed it the last two logs in the bin, then dressed in boots, three pairs of breeches, and four flannel shirts. Two long, knitted scarves and Grampa Zeb's enormous bearskin coat went over the top. As she braced to open the door, she caught a glimpse of herself in the cracked mirror that hung near the sink.

Aunt Tildy, dead these past six years, had always said she was pretty: the prettiest Caine anyone could remember. But what peered back at her from the mirror looked more like a half-sized grizzly bear than a pretty girl. The only things to show she was human — or to show at all, for that matter — were her eyes: the irises whiskey brown, the whites bloodshot from crying.

"Not so pretty now, Aunt Tildy," she whispered. "And nobody to care one way or the other."

She opened the door and stepped out into the gale's icy blast.

It wasn't cozy inside the windowless shed, but it was more tolerable than she'd expected. The first thing she did after she lit a lantern was to tend the horse. It was an aged gelding, muddy bay in color and currently wooly with winter coat. Tall, hammer-headed, and thickly built, he was sweet-tempered but far from quick in mind or body, and seemed more suited for pulling a plow than bearing a rider. But Grampa Zeb — a big, solid man who needed a big, solid mount — had never used him for anything but a saddle horse. The Caines had little use for farming.

The horse was old when Grampa Zeb "found" him, and that had been at least eight years ago. Aunt Tildy had named him Number Ten, in honor of the last train Charity's Uncle Aaron had robbed. It was the last train, because about five minutes after he took up his "collection" from the first class passengers, he was shot through the eye by a Pinkerton man. The Caines were as famous for the way they died as the way they lived.

Charity mucked out Number Ten's narrow stall,

gave him a measure of grain, broke the skin of ice in his water bucket, and threw cracked corn and oats down in the aisle for the chickens. That done, she climbed up the rickety, crooked ladder into the tiny loft, pulled a thick flake of hay from the closest bale and dropped it into Number Ten's manger.

Next, she crawled behind the small stack of bales. Listening carefully, she began to rap the loft's rough plank floor. That was no good. She pulled off one thick, fur-lined glove and tapped bare-knuckled, stopping every few seconds to blow clouds of warm breath on her hand.

From below came a small sound: a scutter and squeak that hadn't come from the horse or chickens, or the trembling sparrows that sheltered in the rafters. She leaned back and craned her head to look. On the strawed floor below a thin rat scurried, intent on the feed she'd tossed to the hens.

Without thinking—or looking—she reached over her head to the low, slanted roof beam. Her hand found the hilt of the knife they kept there to cut baling twine. In one fluid motion, she pulled it free, flipped it once in the air, caught it by the tip of its blade and raised it overhead, poised to throw. But she didn't. She stopped herself just before the knife left her hand and, with a sigh, flipped it round again, caught it by the hilt, and stabbed it back into the wood overhead.

"Sorry," she said to the rat, whose grey, furtive head twisted up sharply at the sound. It stared at her with tiny, unblinking eyes turned red in the lamplight. "Force of habit." It snatched up a last crushed kernel of corn and scurried away, hugging the wall. "Come back any time," she said to the place it had been. "Rats have to eat, too, I guess. Just stay out of the house. And don't eat my chickens."

She blew on her hand again, then went back to tapping on the loft's floor.

At last she heard the hollow echo she'd been waiting for. Brushing away crumbling bits of hay, she ran her finger along the boards until she found a groove. The plank tilted up with no argument. She reached inside the shallow hiding place and withdrew a metal box: about ten inches square and four inches deep, dented on one side, spotted with rust and corrosion, and marked, on the lid, with a small, crude etching of a wolf's head. The lock had been broken off long ago. Its former position was marked by two small holes and a thin, crest-shaped skin of flaking rust.

Jamming the glove back over numb fingers, she tucked the strongbox under her arm, climbed down the ladder, and started back toward the cabin.

She paused at the grave site. She hadn't been able to dig it as deep as she would have liked: her arms and back had given out by the time she got down four feet. She didn't think Grampa Zeb would have minded, though. He had been a hard man, used to hard times and hard things. All the Caines were hard.

Now more than ever, she thought, an only slightly guilty smile twisting briefly at her lips. She wondered if he was frozen solid, down there under the ground. He wasn't completely alone, though. She'd thrown his damned home-carved chess set down there and buried it with him. Ever since Aunt Tildy died, he'd made Charity play him practically every other night; since his illness, they'd played every day. Charity didn't like the game to begin with, and she liked playing it with Grampa Zeb even less. If she made a move he didn't like, he'd slap her and call her stupid. She didn't see that it had mattered one way or the other what moves she made. Grampa Zeb always cheated, anyway.

It had started out straightforward enough, but as Charity got better at it and began to bring him into check in fewer and fewer moves, he began to freely augment the rules. "Durin' the full moon, rooks can take the diagonal if they's in line with a bishop," he'd intone, when he had use for that particular strategy. "Pawn goes sideways if a knight moves just afore it. That's a Kaintuck rule." Or "I'm buyin' my queen back with two'a your pawns and a bishop. That there's a Frenchman rulin'. Don't you know nothin'?"

Of course, if she tried to take advantage of his "rules," there would always be some newly created edict which prevented it. And if it seemed certain she'd beat him anyway, he'd simply upend the board with a grumbled, "Game's over," then stomp out cursing. Sometimes he'd backhand her before he left.

And so it had been with everything Grampa Zeb had ever taught her, drilled her on, or cajoled her into doing. He'd push her and push her and push her some more, mainly in order to find ever new reasons to belittle her. But Charity was nothing if not determined, and once she was able to rival—or better—his skill at whatever it was, he'd either change the rules or make up some new, impossible assignment.

The one exception had been what she now thought of, in retrospect, as the Year of the Knife. After countless hours of forced practice, after months of sinking blades into ever-diminishing targets that were always placed farther and farther away, she became so skilled that he had simply stopped making her do it. He'd also stopped turning his back on her, much to her unending, if secret, satisfaction.

She considered the grave wherein lay both Zebulon Caine and his blasted knights and rooks and pawns. It was ringed by a jagged circle of scorched earth, iced over. The earthen mound at its center was layered in ice as well, and the crude cross at its head was coated with frost that shimmered dull white and yellow and pink in the storm-muted light of the dying sun. She decided it looked almost pretty, even considering what lay beneath it.

She took an axe to the few pieces of fencing that hadn't gone into the bonfire and splintered them into smaller lengths before she gathered them up. They would last until morning. If the blizzard didn't abate before tomorrow mid-day, she'd have to start breaking up the furniture.

Inside, she set the box on the table and dropped the broken boards into the kindling bin. The cabin had warmed a little during her absence, and she peeled out of her clothing until she was down to one pair of britches and two shirts. She swung the kettle over the fire to heat, then sat down, opened the dented metal box, and lifted its chilly contents.

Besides the tiny cabin and rickety outbuildings, the things in the box were her only inheritance: faded photographs and tintypes, a lock of someone's hair; a Wanted poster featuring her late Uncle Odis, offering a $600 reward and neatly punctured, mid-forehead, by a bullet hole; about four dollars in Mexican pesos; a beribboned medal attached to a yellowed paper tag that read *Cletus Caine got this for Antietam;* a second medallion, its metal gone green, tagged with a faded and barely legible note that read *Zachariah Thaddeus Caine, Battle of Horseshoe Bend, 1814;* two fifty-dollar Confederate bonds; and a twenty-dollar gold piece. This last item she promptly bit, to make sure it was real. Her teeth made an easy dent. It was real, all right.

She stacked everything back inside the box, except for the photographs: these, she laid out before her like playing cards. She hoped to find a picture of one or both of her parents, Sam and Garnet Caine. They had both been killed when she was small, and she had no memory of their faces or the sounds of their voices. She hadn't even known this box existed until Grampa Zeb, sick for months and wasted from a monumental three hundred and twenty pounds to a feeble ninety-five, finally realized he was dying.

"Strongbox in the loft, gal," he'd whispered to her five hours before his eyes closed forever. After he told her how to find it, he'd said, "Ain't much, but you're a Caine. We got steel in our veins, iron in our will. You don't need much else to make a start. You can have my Henry. Old Reliable, too," he had added magnanimously, as if there was anyone else for him to leave them to.

She sorted through the pictures. Most were labeled on the back in Aunt Tildy's thick, wandering handwriting; others bore a script she didn't recog-

14

nize. Here was Aaron Caine, the uncle who had died robbing the Number Ten out of Wichita. He was posed before a painted scenic drape, six-guns in his raised hands, his smile cocky and mocking beneath narrowed, jet eyes.

There was no likeness of Aunt Tildy or Uncle Festus, but there were two pictures of Uncle Jabez. He'd visited them when she was seven and lived in some swampy place she couldn't remember the name of. She remembered Uncle Jabez, though, as he had made her a corncob doll. When she was about eleven, they heard he'd been drowned in the Salt Fork of the Brazos, while engaged in the business of herding some cattle that didn't exactly belong to him. His son, Dirk, then a little boy, was with him in one picture. Dirk was all grown up now. He had gone off to Arizona to seek his fortune, and ended up in the Territorial Prison at Yuma. He was probably dead by now, too.

There was no picture of Uncle Odis except the shot-up wanted poster, which was why, she supposed, Aunt Tildy had kept it. Uncle Odis had been hanged, up in Nebraska, ten years back. Aunt Tildy always said that's what a person gets if he goes around shooting marshals and doesn't have enough sense to own a fast horse.

Finally, Charity found what she was looking for: a picture of Garnet and Sam Caine. It was a small daguerreotype, bent at one corner. The date on the back of the plate was 1857. *The year before I was born,* Charity thought, and worried the image with her thumb, rubbing away a bit of dust.

It was not a good picture. Her mother's face, especially, was blurry and faded, as if she had moved slightly. She couldn't see that she looked anything like either of them, except for her father's dark, straight hair. Grampa Zeb's wife, Sweet Dove Caine, had been a full-blooded Choctaw, so Charity's father, aunts, and uncles had been halfbreeds, and she was one quarter native. Aunt Tildy called it their "wolf blood," said it made all the Caines crazy, made them want to howl at the moon.

"Didn't need any Indian blood to do that," Charity muttered to the whining wind, the clattering shutters. "Grampa Zeb didn't have a drop of Choctaw in him, and he was mean as a boar and crazier'n popcorn on a hot skillet."

Zeb Caine's "wild jags" were legend among the Caine clan, or at least, what was left of it. In his youth he'd been a hellraiser, and always claimed to be wanted in Louisiana on two counts of murder and one of larceny. "Done a lot more murders than that, even not countin' the Mexes and Creoles and a couple'a pistol-totin' octoroons," he used to brag, looking self-satisfied and nasty. "But them ones in Louisiana? They's the only ones where the witnesses got away on me."

Age hadn't done much to calm him down. Even after he'd been gored by an ox six years back and had to go around on crutches, he'd still been cranky enough to make Aunt Tildy tie him in the saddle and ride with him all the way down to Pandora, Texas, to stick up the Flyer, just to prove he could do it. They missed the train by about a half-minute, but he managed to put a few long-range rifle shots into the caboose and one through the conductor's hat.

Once, when he was in a particularly foul mood,

16

Charity had seen him drop a fractious horse with a sledge hammer.

Conversations in the Caine household consisted, almost entirely, of short bursts of bickering. Snide remarks and curt retorts were normal dialogue for Grampa Zeb and the rest; but willfulness, especially from the females of the clan, was not tolerated. The one and only time Charity had mustered the gumption to stand up to Grampa Zeb had been nine years ago, to ask if she could be sent away to boarding school, to Miss Jeanette Hildebrand's Academy For Young Ladies of Good Breeding in St. Paul, Minnesota.

They were living up in Missouri, then, and somehow they'd gotten hold of some old catalogs and magazines, most likely to use in the outhouse. But in one magazine she'd seen an advertisement for the Hildebrand Academy: an engraving of several beautifully dressed young ladies gathered around a forte-piano in a fine drawing room. The advertisement was torn out and hidden beneath her pillow to be stared at each night, and Charity dreamed and fantasized about music and dresses and real china tea cups for at least six months before she mentioned it, along with a string of what she considered to be unshakable arguments guaranteed to sway even the strongest opposition.

Grampa Zeb heard her out, all right. And his considered answer was to backhand her so hard the blow lifted her off her feet and sent her crashing against the wall.

"None'a that!" he'd snarled as she cowered in the corner, ten years old and crying and bleeding on her best shirt. "You're a Caine, remember that.

Tildy, this is your fault, teachin' her to read!" He would have smacked Aunt Tildy, too; but Tildy was a big woman, and just as strong and as mean as he was, and he knew she'd smack him right back: most probably with an andiron. "We ain't fancy people," he'd raged on. "We live on instinct and wiles. Foxes, we are. Smart and fast. Don't need no schoolin'. Slip in, steal the grapes, pluck the vine-yards dry, slip out."

Charity had remarked—under her breath, but just a hair too loudly—that it didn't seem to her that her parents and most of her uncles were too good at the slipping out part, and got smacked again for it. She still had a little scar, just below her lower lip, where her front tooth had punctured through.

She learned to keep her mouth shut that day, and had since kept her remarks to herself. It didn't ex-actly stop him from hitting, but at least he had never drawn blood again.

Being a Caine was not an easy occupation.

She had never been to a town. She had never lived within five miles of another person or family. Grampa Zeb moved around a lot. They had lived in Louisiana, Arkansas, and Missouri—at least, those were the places she remembered—before Grampa Zeb, Charity in tow, had decided to make a home in the Nations. They'd come across this place three years past and, finding no one in residence, settled in.

Aside from their personal things, their only civi-lized accoutrements were those that Grampa Zeb had supplied by holding up a freight wagon they met along the way. The load—which had been taken, wagon, oxen and all—consisted of two bolts of red flannel and two of calico; a case of bourbon whiskey; three ten-pound tins of soda crackers; a two-pound tin of green tea leaves; four fifty-pound sacks each of flour, sugar, and rice; half a dozen twenty-pound bags of cornmeal; two cases each of tinned peaches and tomatoes, another of dried apples and currants; plus odds and ends of everything from baking powder to licorice whips to vegetable seeds to percussion caps, canning jars, and paraffin.

Charity hadn't actually taken part in the robbery. Grampa Zeb had wandered off before dawn and returned to the campsite crowing over his booty and hollering at her to hurry up. But she supposed she was as guilty as if she'd been there when Grampa Zeb took the wagon and left the driver senseless in the road. She had, after all, been living off the spoils for three years.

She and Grampa Zeb made out well enough. He trapped a little, hunted when need be, and sometimes "found" stray livestock. Sometimes he'd disappear for a week or two at a time. She never asked him where he went or what he did, for fear he'd tell her; although he sometimes brought back things he needed, like shotgun shells or cartridges for his Henry. Or whiskey. For her part, Charity kept a little garden, canned, knitted, baked, played forced games of chess or poker, ducked when need be, and wondered what it might be like to be a normal person and not a Caine.

She used to pray for company: for someone, anyone, besides Grampa Zeb to talk to. But in all the time since they'd come to the Indian Nations

19

they'd had only two visitors. A couple of bedraggled trappers wandered through the previous spring and, glad for even unwashed company, Charity had fed them the biggest, fanciest dinner she could muster. She'd been surprised that Grampa Zeb seemed so cordial: he'd joked with them and traded stories and offered them liquor. The trappers departed the next morning amid much handshaking and companionable talk and back-slapping. A short while later, Grampa Zeb took down his Henry and set out to do a little hunting. He didn't bring home any game, but two days later, when Charity had occasion to visit the shed's little loft, she found several bundles of pelts.

After that, she prayed no one would come, and they hadn't. The nearest real town was a four-day ride over rugged territory, and few people were foolish enough to wander into this part of the Nations. It was too unforgiving, too inhospitable, and it was known to be a place where renegades and badmen lurked.

She'd never seen any of those rumored badmen; but she had known her Grampa Zeb, and he'd been a very bad man, indeed.

The wind picked up, its shrill screech gaining in pitch. Charity rubbed down the gooseflesh on her arms before she tossed a chunk of fence board on the fire and went to the cupboard. She took down several jars of home-canned vegetables, checking to make certain the seals were intact. One was bad, and she set it aside. Next she brought out a cast iron kettle. The good jars were opened and their contents — potatoes, carrots, peas — poured in before she opened the cold box.

The little door, set low into the back wall of the cabin, opened into a small above-ground cupboard that jutted out into the weather. Winters, she kept meat and leftovers in it, as well as butter, milk, and eggs when she had them. Several days earlier, she had brought up a venison steak from the meat house. She tested it with her finger. It was partially thawed, but still crunchy with ice crystals. She brought it to the counter and began slicing it into thin strips.

"Venison stew," she said to the air, to the gale, to the ghosts. "Your favorite, Grampa. Sorry you have to miss it, you wicked old son of a—"

She wheeled toward the door. The pounding came again, solid and not part of the storm.

Shaking, she snatched Grampa Zeb's well-used Henry from its rack. Her fingers trembled and she fumbled, almost dropping it before she swung its muzzle toward the door. "Wh-who's there?" she called over the wind. *Badmen,* she thought.

From beyond, from the storm, came, "Help . . . please let me . . ." And then a thud.

"Who's there?" She cocked the rifle, seated the butt against her shoulder, pressed her cheek to the stock, stared down the barrel. Her heart pounding like a sparrow's, she took a step closer. "What do you want? I've got a gun and I can use it!"

No answer.

Cautiously, her feet leaden beneath rubbery knees, she went to the door, then flattened herself against the wall beside it. "Who are you?"

Nothing.

I didn't hear it, she thought. *I'm crazy. I'm a crazy, wolf-blooded Caine, and I've gone all the*

21

way mad, just like Aunt Vena did down in Fort Smith right before she shot her dog in the head and drank poison.

"Who's there?" she called again.

Only the wind.

She took a deep breath. If she *was* crazy, she supposed she'd best find out sooner than later. Keeping to the side of the door, she opened the latch.

The door swung in abruptly. She jumped, as much from the blast of cold as from the slumped body that tumbled in at her feet.

It was a man: she could tell that much by the sheer bulk of him, although she couldn't see his face. She nudged him with her foot. He made no sound. She nudged him again, harder this time. He rolled onto his back, his head lolling to the side.

He wore a deerskin cape over his knee-length wool coat. Both were crusted with ice. His hair, shaggy and tangled, was as matted with sleet as his rough, reddish beard. His brows and lashes were frosted white, stark against the windburnt red of his cheeks and forehead. His eyes were closed.

Her teeth chattering, Charity leaned Grampa Zeb's rifle against the wall and bent to get a grip under the man's arms. At her first tug, his coat parted to reveal a bloodstained shirt. As, haltingly, she dragged him out of the doorway and away from the freezing blast, she muttered, "You'd better not be dead, Mister. I've got neither the strength nor the firewood for another funeral."

Chapter Two

Jake Turlow came awake slowly.

He was in a bed: a soft bed. The welcome warmth that had been his first sensation was provided by a scatter of soft furs, heaped over the quilts that covered him. "Laura?" he whispered, even as he realized, for the thousandth time, that Laura wasn't there. Wouldn't ever be there again.

He turned his head slightly, and one of the furs atop his covers tickled at his nose. *Wolf pelts,* he thought, then, *Where the devil am I?*

The bed in which he lay was pressed hard against the far wall of a narrow log cabin. Two feet from the bed was a worn curtain, hung on old harness rings from a slim, uneven sapling pole. The curtain was parted slightly, and he could see a raised stone hearth whose fire crackled comfortingly. Before the hearth stood a crude table and three chairs. *Two and a half chairs,* he corrected himself. The third lay on the floor, in scattered pieces. He could see part of its carved back slowly charring in the fireplace.

Above the mantel was a crude horizontal gun

rack. A Henry rifle rested in the lower position. Above it hung a double-barreled shotgun. Both looked well used and, from what he could see, well cared for.

To the left of the fireplace he could see a snatch of what appeared to be a kitchen area. At least, there seemed to be some sort of work surface with rough, warped cupboards above and open shelves below. But the curtain gave him only a slivered view.

Except for the fire's low pops and snaps and his own soft, slow breathing, there was no sound. He decided he was alone, at least for the moment. Without warning, his stomach growled noisily, and it was only then that he realized the air was wonderfully rich with the smell of baking cornbread.

His memory returned in grainy snips and patches. Cold: the cold and the blizzard. Seeing smoke against the sky and following it: this he remembered, too. And Claude Duval, sitting on that damn ghost-grey horse of his up on the hill, veiled in the blow of sleet, looking like an evil mirage while his boys cut down fourteen of Arkansas's finest.

All but me, Jake thought, as a wave of guilt washed through him. *I should have seen some sign, should have figured it for a trap. But Rex should have sensed it, too, damn it. We were both too stupid from the cold and tired from the chase . . .*

Rex Jeffords had been in the lead when they followed Duval's trail into the clearing. Ferret Rogan, the best man for two hundred miles in any direction with a Bowie knife, had brought up the rear. Ferret didn't get a chance to use his blade, and Jeffords didn't even have a chance to be surprised. Duval's mob of cowards had picked them off from the trees, starting with the ends and working toward the middle. It was only because Jake had been riding in the center of the party that he had lived.

At the first shots, they had all returned fire — at least, those of them that were still alive after the initial volley. But how could a man aim at what he couldn't see? He remembered yelling, "Scatter!" He remembered spurring his horse around the fallen bodies of his men. He remembered the snow, spattered bright red.

And Rex Jeffords — the friend of his youth, a man as brave and solid as he was quick to laugh — lying twisted and crumpled on the ground. "I'll get him, Rex," Jake said under his breath. "I swear it. They'll pay for what they did to you. To Laura."

He started to sit up, but the sharp twinge in his shoulder reminded him that if he had been the only one to escape the ambush alive, he hadn't gotten out unscathed. Gingerly, he pushed back the covers. His clothes were gone, and someone had bandaged his chest, likely the same someone who had baked up the batch of cornbread whose aroma was driving him crazy. He peeked under the bandage. The wound was healing: almost healed, in fact. The cotton pad, where it touched his skin, had been smeared with something that had a faintly herbal scent, not at all unpleasant.

He let his head fall back on the pillow. Dimly, he remembered a cabin. He had fallen off his horse, and . . . he must have made it to the door. That must be where he was. But for how long?

His stomach growled again. He tried to ignore it. He had to think. Duval wouldn't simply let him get away. He'd be on the march. *He'll never let me get back to Fort Smith alive if he can help it,* Jake thought, and rubbed wide fingers on his jaw.

The sensation startled him. Someone had shaved his beard, and quite recently. His face felt nearly as smooth as a baby's backside. His fingers went to his upper lip, and he sighed with relief. Whoever had barbered him had at least possessed the sense to leave him a little lip hair. Neatly trimmed, too, from what he could feel.

Odd. He knew he was still deep in the Nations. White folk were few and far between out here, and justly so—they had no right to be on Indian land. Of course, there were unofficial exceptions. Farther to the southeast and closer to the Arkansas border, old-timers like old Tink Maynard, the Widow Pritchard, and Big Nose Harry Hildermann lived in the same cabins they'd occupied for decades. Nobody bothered to order them out. They didn't cause trouble, they minded their own business, and besides, they were too obstinate to move. Additionally, their isolated homes were welcome islands of friendship, warmth, and trade for those who traveled the Nations, white and native alike.

26

But this place was more hidden than most. He supposed he'd just never been through this particular valley before. He figured the cabin must belong to a trapper or an Indian agent or, more likely, a squatter.

It crossed his mind that it might be the home of a family of Cherokee or Creek or one of the other Five Civilized Tribes; but he ruled out that possibility, though it was likely that such a family had originally built the place. Besides running their own businesses and newspapers and schools, many members of the Five Civilized Tribes had farmed — even owned slaves — before the War. But since Appomattox, they'd been shoved farther West, and their lands had been divvied up amongst more newly conquered and relocated tribes.

No, somebody was squatting where they shouldn't. Somebody white, by the looks of the photographs he had just noticed, propped up along the mantel. Somebody who had no business being out here.

But they shouldn't have to die for it, he thought. Duval's boys would be hunting him, and they were the sort who'd just as soon kill a man as walk around him. Whoever the fellow was who'd taken him in, Jake wasn't about to reward his kindness by bringing Claude Duval's minions to his doorstep. He resolved to get himself up and out and away as soon as he found his clothes. And had a little of that cornbread.

Charity was up in the north grove, not far from

27

the house, when she saw the riders. The worst of the storm had temporarily abated, and the driving sleet had changed to a gently falling haze of snow. Through it, as through a breath-steamed window pane, she counted four men on horseback. They traveled slowly, their horses struggling through knee-deep drifts frosted with fresh powder. It was a second before she made out the fifth member of the party. Mounted on a pale, dapple-grey horse and cloaked in a long white coat, he rode slightly apart from the others, taking no advantage of the trail they broke through the drifts. She blinked twice, just to make certain he was really there. *A phantom,* she thought. Beneath her heavy wraps, her arms broke out in gooseflesh.

She had a pistol with her, of course: she never left the yard without tucking Aunt Tildy's big old retooled Navy Colt in her belt or her deep coat pocket. This was wild country, and during a hard winter, the wolves and catamounts were apt to be bold. But the sight of those men frightened her more than the threat of any predatory animal.

She let fall the armload of kindling she'd already gathered, and began, with frustrating clumsiness, to half-slide, half-run down the slope, her coa ttail dragging a wide trail behind her. They hadn't seen her. She had the cover of the trees, and they were down below, in the narrow meadow. They were following the beacon of smoke from the cabin's chimney, and it wouldn't be more than a few minutes before they came to the end of the meadow and passed through a little stand of oak to enter the cup-shaped clearing that was home.

Five minutes, she thought. *Five minutes, the way the snow's slowing them. I can beat them.*

She ducked between the trees, skidded and fell once, shoved her way through drifts, forgot to mind the cold. Breathless, she raced into the clearing, crossed the yard and slammed her shoulder into the cabin's front door before she remembered to lift the crude latch.

Inside, she shoved the door closed again and dropped not only the latch, but the crossplank. She didn't take the time to remove her scarf or muffler. She ripped off her gloves and ran to the mantel, tripping over part of the chair she'd broken up for kindling the night before. She caught herself on the table, kicked a stray chair leg out of her way, and, swearing under her breath, snatched Grampa Zeb's Henry down and laid it across the table. Then, fingers shaking, she dug into her pocket and gripped the butt of Aunt Tildy's gun.

Just as she jerked it free, she heard, "You got trouble out there, Mister?"

She spun, the long-barreled pistol in both her hands and aimed straight out.

Her patient, unconscious for two days, was not only awake—he was sitting on the edge of Grampa Zeb's bed and leaning forward to part the curtains. Bandages still swathed his chest and shoulder. He snugged the quilt across himself, hastily covering his hip before he raised his hands, palms out. He said, "Easy, friend. Wouldn't make much sense to shoot me after all the work you did to fix me up. What's going on? You're thumping around like a herd of buffalo."

29

Over the muffler wrapping her mouth and nose, Charity stared at him. She had decided, once she had gotten him cleaned up and shaved, that he was a nice-looking man. Now that he was awake and his features were animated, she realized he was nearer to handsome. It was the first time she'd seen his eyes open, too. They were startlingly light: the color of robin's eggs.

Which, she quickly reminded herself, made him not one jot less dangerous.

Through the thick pad of muffler over her mouth, she growled, "Shut up."

She'd already decided he was an outlaw. He was no Indian agent. He didn't look like a trapper, either—wasn't outfitted like one. And the only other whites crazy enough to venture this deep into the Nations were on the dodge. Like Grampa Zeb. Like her whole family. *Like me,* she thought. These new riders might be outlaws, as well. But there were good outlaws and bad outlaws. "Just because two fellers is bankers don't mean they won't graft off each other," she'd heard Grampa Zeb say more than once, "and the same goes for folks in our line of business. Just because a feller's your own kind don't mean he won't knife you first chance he gets. I oughta know. I knifed my share."

She heard hooves crunching snow, then voices, low, out front.

The man had heard them too. He started to get up.

She cocked the Colt's hammer. He sat back down. Softly, he said, "You're just a kid, aren't you? Listen, I think I know who's out there and, trust me, you don't want 'em in here." When she didn't move, didn't answer, he held out a hand. "C'mon, son, toss me that pistol. Or the Henry. I don't care which, just do it quick."

Someone pounded on the door. They both jumped.

"Hello! Hello the cabin!" came the call.

"Briscoe!" The man spat it under his breath, like a curse, before he hissed, "The pistol, boy!"

She kept it trained on him, but turned her head toward the door. She barely noticed the little start he gave when she tugged the muffler away from her face and called, "Who's that making a ruckus in my front yard!"

There was a short pause before the voice came again, this time with a poorly disguised note of amusement. "Why, it's just peace officers, ma'am. Party of Marshals. Like to ask you a few questions."

The man was on his feet, clutching one end of the quilt loosely about his waist as he tugged the rest free of the bed. He started, on uncertain legs, through the curtain. She twisted toward him, waved the gun again, whispered, "Get back in there. And close that drape!" Then, loudly, she called, "How do I know you're lawmen?"

"Happy to show you badges and warrants, ma'am, if you'd be s'kind as to open this door. Mighty cold out here."

"Just a minute." In one motion, she slid the Colt to a chair with her left hand, snatched up the Henry with the right, then tore off her muffler

31

and dropped it over the Colt. A back-up weapon. Swiftly jacking a cartridge into the Henry's chamber, she hissed, "I said, close that curtain." He opened his mouth to argue, but she snapped, "Listen, Mister, this is my house and I've got the gun and that puts me in charge. Now, shut up and do it or I'll shoot you myself."

Glaring, he obeyed.

Charity went to the door. She lifted the crossbar and put her hand on the latch before she realized what a poor weapon the Henry was in this particular situation. Abruptly, she leaned it against the wall, returned to the rack and pulled down Old Reliable. Like the Henry, Grampa Zeb always kept it loaded and ready.

Three swift steps put her at the door again. Standing to the side, she lifted the latch, then stepped away: Old Reliable pressed to her shoulder, twin hammers cocked, her finger positioned to pull both triggers.

The closest man, his gloved fist poised in mid-air to knock again, took a quick hop sideways when the door swung open.

"Don't shoot, lady!" he said. A red plaid muffler was looped over the crown of his hat and tied under his chin. Wiping at his nose with one end of it, he moved off to stand behind his friend. "We're the law, ain't that right? Show 'er before she peppers us with that thing!"

The man he addressed, heavily built and black-bearded, stood about five feet from the door. He said, "Calm down, Toad. You'll excuse Toad, ma'am, he's the nervous type. I'm U.S. Marshal Jeffords. 'Preciate it if you'd set aside that scatter gun. Just want to ask you some questions."

She kept the muzzle steady, aimed chest high. "Questions about what? Where are your badges?"

Gingerly, he opened his coat. "If you'll allow?" When she nodded, he reached inside and slowly drew out a long black leather wallet, which he held open for her to see. A Federal Marshal's badge was pinned inside. Above it, *R.T. Jeffords* was stamped in gold. "Got my warrants in here, too, if you'd care to look 'em over."

She gave her head a slight shake. "No. Tell those others to stop milling around."

Behind him and beyond Toad, two more men stood in the yard. One was over by Grampa Zeb's grave, prodding its icy, lumpy mound with his boot. The other man lounged against the shed as he attempted to roll a cigarette without dropping the reins of their four horses. She didn't see the fifth man or his grey horse.

Over his shoulder, Jeffords called, "Don't be doin' anything rash, boys. Got a nervous lady here with a double-barreled shotgun."

The men stood still.

"Now, Miss, we're awful cold. If we could just come inside . . ."

"No. Ask your questions from where you stand. And after I answer, I'd be obliged if you'd set right out again."

He didn't look happy. He rubbed at his beard. "We're on the trail of a dangerous criminal. No tellin' what he might do. I believe you might be safer if I left one'a my boys here with you."

The one called Toad brightened slightly until she wiggled the shotgun at him.

"Ask and git."

The Marshal sighed. "Looking for a man what calls himself Jake Turlow. Sometimes tries to pass himself off for a lawman, but he's a hardened murderer. Sly as they come, and bad through and through. He was with a gang that stuck up the Curry-to-Hastings Express, killed the driver and an innocent widder-woman in the process. Got away with the Augustus Mines payroll. Five thousand dollars, give or take."

It was difficult, trying to hold his eye while she watched the others, too, but she managed. She said, "I don't know anything about any robbery."

"Like snot, she don't," said Toad, braver now that he was standing slightly behind the larger man. "You're part Injun, ain't you?"

She ignored him.

The Marshal leaned close and whispered, "'Fraid Toad's got a point, Miss." He lowered his voice even further, so that she had to strain to hear him. "We know Turlow's been through here. Fact is; you got his horse out in your shed. If he's in the house and told you a pack of lies, or if he's got a gun on you, you just jump aside. We'll settle him quick enough."

She held steady and spoke out clear and loud. "I've got two horses in my shed, Mister. One of them is my Grampa's, and the other belonged to a man that rode in here two days back, in the worst of the storm. Big man, with brown hair and a beard. Not a dime on him, let alone any five thousand payroll dollars. He was shot up bad and half-froze."

The Marshal stood up a little straighter. Toad stood on his toes, trying to peer over her shoulder and into the cabin.

"He's not in here," she lied. She did it quite gracefully. She hadn't grown up a Caine without absorbing a few skills.

Jeffords didn't look too sure, though. He said, "You mind tellin' me where he lit out to, then? And without his horse?"

"He lit out exactly nowhere," she said evenly, "except maybe to the Devil. One of your boys was just kicking at him a minute ago." She tipped her head in the direction of Grampa Zeb's grave. "And don't you go thinking about taking that horse of his. It's mine now. I earned it. Had to burn up near all my firewood and the corral fence to thaw the ground enough for digging. So if you plan to spade him up again, I'd appreciate it if you'd put the dirt back where you found it when you're through."

Although one man, at Jefford's order, chopped his way into the burial mound deep enough to make certain it was, indeed, freshly turned earth, none of them had been of a mind to dig any deeper into the grave, which was exactly as she had expected. She stood in the doorway and watched them leave. Her arms ached from the weight of Old Reliable, but she held the scatter gun up and ready until they moved out of range. At that point, she slid it to the floor and grabbed the Henry. She kept the back of the marshal's head in her sights until distance, trees, and soft snowfall erased the riders from view.

She decided that Grampa Zeb would have been proud of her. *Well, maybe prouder if I'd blasted them in the back and lifted their watches,* she thought as she closed the door and dropped the bar.

The click of a gun's cocking hammer reminded her that she had a long way to go before she was in Grampa Zeb's league. She'd been so busy watching the posse that she'd forgotten their reason for being there in the first place. And that reason, wrapped in a quilt, was sitting at her table and aiming Aunt Tildy's Navy Colt right at the center of her forehead.

Chapter Three

"Well, you're no boy, that's for sure," he said. "Put that rifle the rest of the way down and take a couple steps away from it, if you don't mind. Or even if you do."

She did as she was told. "You've got no call to aim my own gun at me, Mister Jake Turlow. I'm the one that dragged you in out of the snow and pried the lead ball out of your shoulder. Plus, I just saved your bacon from that marshal and his posse."

He eased the hammer down, but he held onto the pistol. "That was no marshal."

"Oh. I suppose these days they give those badges out for party favors back in Fort Smith. What happened to the five thousand dollars?"

"You should've asked those boys that just left." *That son of a bitch Briscoe has got Rex Jeffords' badge,* he thought. *Another reason to kill him.* None of the anguish he felt showed on his face. He only said, "Was there a man in a white coat? A thin man, rides a grey horse?"

Her eyes narrowed slightly. "Yes. No. I mean, I saw him before, when I was up on the hill. But he didn't ride in with them. Why? Who is he?" she asked, her eyes mocking. "The King Marshal?"

"He's Claude Duval, and you'd better pray you never meet up with him, honey."

"Don't call me that."

He felt one corner of his mouth twist into a grin. "Then maybe you ought to give me something else to call you. I don't suppose you've got a name?"

"I may be poor, Mister Jake Turlow, but I can afford that much," she said, pulling herself erect. "It's Caine. Charity Caine."

He rubbed a hand over the back of his neck: "Caine . . . Caine . . ." Something clicked inside his head. She was part Indian, judging by her high cheekbones and clear, almost poreless skin: a soft, understated copper kissed by soft blush. Her hair, at least what little of it he could glimpse while she was wearing that scarf, was black and straight. He glanced again at the photographs propped along the mantel and, pressed one finger against the small rough spot on the Colt's butt: a tiny wolf's head, carved into the wood. *I should have known it right away,* he thought. *My head must still be wooly with all that sleep.* He said, "You any relation to Odis or Aaron Caine?"

"They were my uncles," she said, half proud, half ashamed.

"Zebulon Caine?"

"My Grampa. That's him buried in the yard."

Of course. She'd shielded him from that "marshal" because she thought he was one of her own: a renegade, like all the Caines.

He said, "You alone out here?"

She hiked her chin in the air. "Don't go getting any ideas. I wouldn't feel a bit bad about shooting you."

He waved the gun at her and smiled.

"Don't know that I'd feel so bad about you shooting me, either," she added, levelly.

It occurred to him that she probably wouldn't mind one way or the other if she was mad enough at the time. The Caines were all crazy, and there were none more ruthless. One of the Caine women, a whore over in Fort Smith and likely an aunt to this girl, had gone berserk one sultry August night and killed herself and her black and tan coonhound for reasons unexplained. There had been five brothers that he knew of. He wondered which one had been her father, not that it much mattered. Festus Caine was said to have once lined up ten Chinamen in a row, roped together, to see how many of them he could kill with one shot from a Sharps carbine. Sam Caine, arguably the most level-headed of the clan, had at least four murders to his credit by the time he was lynched, in '59, by the citizenry of Nacogdoches, Texas.

But this girl had taken him in and patched him up, and she'd just stood off four of Duval's men, even if for all the wrong reasons. Those things said something about her nature; and if she'd been frightened, it hadn't shown. She was on his side, even if only for the moment, and he didn't see any point in disillusioning her. Only the Lord knew what she'd do if he tipped her the wrong way. Besides, he reasoned, he'd be gone soon enough.

His stomach rumbled again.

"You mind if I have some of that cornbread, Miss Charity Caine? I can sure smell it, but I don't know where you've got it hid."

She took a step toward him, then stopped. Her eyes flicked to the pistol in his hand before they came back to meet his. "You suppose that gun would go off if I got shed of this coat? I'm about to burn up."

"Thought you didn't care if I shot you."

"Shoot away, then," she said with a shrug, "but you won't get your dinner." She began to work at the closures.

Out of habit, he kept the Colt pointed in her direction until she shucked out of the heavy bearskin garment and tossed it aside. There was no gun beneath it, and he relaxed a bit.

But when she tugged off her head scarf, he had to stifle a gasp. Her hair, parted in the center, was glossy blue-black, absolutely straight, and fell in a sleek cascade to her waist. It was not ragged, but had been neatly trimmed and blunted at the ends.

She hung her coat and scarves on a peg by the

door, and then she began to unbutton her red flannel shirt. He said, "Hey, what are you doing?"

She scowled at him. It was a pretty scowl. He tried not to think about it.

She said, *"Now* what's wrong?"

He didn't answer.

She shook her head and went back to undressing, mumbling, "You'll get your belly fed soon enough."

He watched, fascinated, as she peeled herself out of three shirts and a pair of heavy woolen trousers. And when she finally got down to a faded calico shirt and a snug, worn pair of patched denim britches, the chubby, thick-middled girl had been transformed into a leggy, narrow-waisted, graceful young woman. And above that lithe, coltish figure, her face was elegant, finely chiseled and classically oval. Beautiful.

He wondered if she'd ever owned a dress, and what she might have looked like in it. And then he wondered what she might look like without a dress, without anything to cover her but that sleek, raven-black cloak of hair. Scrupulously clean and glistening with blue-purple highlights, it slid over her shoulders, swung lazily at her waist as she moved. He wondered what it smelled like and how it would feel in his fingers; how it would feel against his face, his chest.

Quite suddenly, he was glaringly aware that, except for the quilt, he was naked. And aroused. He shifted slightly and knotted a handful of quilt in his fist. *Jake,* he thought, *you have been way too long in these woods.*

She was staring at him. "Your shoulder hurt?" She looked genuinely concerned.

He cleared his throat. "What?"

"You look funny." Her eyes, thickly lashed, were the color of aged, smoky bourbon. Odd that he hadn't noticed until just then. When he didn't answer, she tilted her head slightly, and her hair swung softly to the side. "I said, does your wound pain you?"

"No, I'm fine, I . . ." He shifted again. "Just hungry."

Her mouth tightened almost imperceptibly with what he guessed to be impatience. She turned on her heel and went to the fireplace, kicking a stray chunk of broken chair out of her way. She said, "Will they come back?"

"I don't know." He honestly didn't. She had sounded convincing—and Briscoe had sounded convinced—but there was no predicting anything that Claude Duval's men did.

Her expression didn't change. He supposed she was ready for it, either way. She only said, "Don't founder yourself on this. There's something to go with it."

He watched her as, a rag wrapped round her hand, she pulled a shallow, rectangular pan from a warming oven built into the side of the fireplace. As she rested it on the counter and tested its content's golden crust with a gentle fingertip, he thought, *Keep your mind on your dinner,*

42

Jake, old buddy. The last thing you need is a lunatic Caine female messing up your life.

Apparently the cornbread was done enough to suit her, because she sliced it into squares. Then, stepping around the disassembled chair, she brought the pan to the table along with a pot of honey.

"It's not my best johnnycake," she said matter-of-factly. She slid a clean plate and a knife in front of him before she picked up a few pieces of chair—two legs and a spindle—and tossed them into the fire.

"Had to make it with powdered eggs," she continued, as if burning her furniture was something she did every day. "Have to make everything with powdered eggs. Hens stopped laying a month ago. Which is why," she added, as she opened the cold box door, "I'm about to give you leftover chicken stew. Maybe, after you get your gullet full, you'll tell me what you did with that five thousand."

By the time the stew was heated through and flooding the tiny cabin with its rich aroma, he had polished off all but two chunks of the johnnycake. There didn't seem to be much threat of his losing his appetite, though. When Charity filled his plate, she noticed that he sat with fork poised, as if he couldn't wait for her to move the ladle out of his way.

Earlier, she had made him let her check the

dressing on his shoulder. He hadn't stopped eating: he'd just dribbled cornbread crumbs on her while she worked. The wound was healing with almost miraculous speed: due as much, she suspected, to Jake Turlow's natural strength as to her herb poultices. The night he'd slumped across her threshold, her first look at his wound had told her he'd been carrying the slug for at least twenty-four hours. She'd been afraid the wound would go septic, but it had responded beautifully to treatment. Today the puncture was closed and scabbed over, and the skin around it was a healthy, healing pink instead of the angry red she had feared.

She sat back, watching him from the corner of her eye lest he look up from his supper and catch her at it. She decided she'd been right to leave the mustache when she shaved him. Bracketed by the deep dimples that slashed his cheeks, it complimented his square jaw and strong, slightly Roman nose. His skin was neither fair nor dark, but a sort of soft, warm gold. His shoulders were wide, but not so broad as to make him hulking in appearance. His upper arms were belled with muscle, his forearms hard, broad, and tapering to supple wrists that ended in strong, well-made hands.

A thick pelt of reddish-brown hair covered his chest. This had rather surprised her when she first undressed him. Grampa Zeb had been bedridden for months before he died, and in that time it had become second nature for Charity to care for an invalid. Changing sheets with a sick man still in the bed, rearranging limbs to prevent bedsores, bathing another person's body: these chores were nothing new to her. But Grampa Zeb had been scrawny and frail at the end, his skin white as parchment. And he'd had exactly four hairs on his chest: three white hairs and one black, all four of them hard and kinky. Until she had peeled Jake Turlow's limp form out of his clothes and Union suit, she hadn't realized that men were capable of such a luxuriant crop of chest hair.

She'd seen other parts of him, too, parts she couldn't see now as he sat across the table from her, helping himself to another plate of stew. She felt color rise in her cheeks just thinking about it.

She bit at her lip and made herself concentrate on above-the-waist things. Forgetting, for a moment, to guard her eyes, she began to study the way he ate.

He didn't slurp his food, the way Grampa Zeb had. Neither did he hunch over his plate and use his fork like a shovel. That was the way the ill-fated trappers had eaten. Instead, she thought, he ate like a civilized person, the way Aunt Tildy had taught her was proper. Not that she was certain Aunt Tildy had known much about civilized table manners. But this man, unlike the slurpers and shovelers and plate-rattlers she'd known, was a pleasure to watch.

The kettle whistled, and she tended to it. As

she poured hot water over the tea leaves in the chipped pot and set it aside to steep, Jake Turlow looked up from his plate long enough to say, "Aren't you going to eat?"

"Why?" she asked, without turning around. "You afraid it might be poisoned?" She regretted it immediately. She couldn't seem to be nice to him, no matter how much she wanted to be. Her life with Grampa Zeb had left her without trust or faith, or even smiles of more than a split-second's duration. As much as she wanted to be civil to this man, all those years of stored-up backtalk and temper had started to tumble out, and she couldn't seem to stop the flow.

She reached to the shelf and, out of habit, brought down two of the everyday tin cups. Both were dented and dinged. One had a bent handle. She bit at her lip. She hadn't looked at these mugs, really *looked* at them, in a long time. She replaced them on the shelf and went to another cupboard. There, at the back, she found two white-glazed earthenware mugs, the best she owned. One had a small chip at the rim, but the other was perfect. Carefully, she clamped them between her fingers, then carried them, along with the pot, to the table. She put the best mug in front of him, the chipped one at her place. She sat down.

He said, "I just wondered why you weren't eating, that's all. What's that? Tea?"

"There's no coffee. And I'm not hungry." That was the single largest truth she'd told all day.

46

Her appetite had been stolen by fear: not of Jake Turlow anymore, but of the posse. When she'd faced them at the door, she'd been so terrified that her knees had clattered beneath her coat. It had taken every ounce of her self-control to keep her voice from quavering. Although studying Jake had distracted her for the last few minutes, her anxiety over the rider's possible return had stolen any inclination she might have had toward dinner.

Jake Turlow didn't seem worried, though. Or if he was, it didn't show. He ate the final bite of his stew, laid his fork across the plate and leaned back in his chair, stretching his arms without favoring the injured shoulder.

She said, "There's more if you want it."

"Take you up on that as soon as I let this first batch settle. It's good cookin'. I don't suppose you'd know where my clothes have got to? And my pistols and rig?"

"Your clothes are in there," she said, tilting her head toward the ancient chifforobe that stood against the far wall. "Your hand guns, too, though I don't know why you're in such a big toot to have them back." She pointed at Aunt Tildy's Navy Colt, which was still on the table, at his elbow.

"Had a rifle in my saddle boot, too," he said. He poured himself a mug of tea. One for her, too. She didn't think he noticed the chip.

"Your Winchester's under your bed, along with your packroll and saddlebags. Now that

47

you know where all the firearms are, you can go ahead and murder me anytime."

He frowned slightly. "Haven't you figured out that I . . ." He held up his left hand, snatched up Aunt Tildy's Colt with his right. "Do you . . . ? Did you hear . . . ?"

Wood exploded with a boom and crash. Abruptly, he lunged across the table and knocked her sideways to the floor. The plates went sailing. Her good mugs shattered against the hearth. Even before the kettle hit the floor and sprayed the air with scalding tea, he was firing.

The riders were back, and they were coming through the windows. One shutter was already bashed through. It hung in splinters, and a man, blood spurting from the bullet hole Jake Turlow had just put through his neck, was draped through it. Somebody else was out there in the dark, shooting through the window, using the corpse for a bunker.

She heard Jake yell, "Stay down! Stay down!" at the same instant he tipped the table on its side and began firing over its rim.

On hands and knees, she scrambled to the door. It shook and groaned, as did the shuttered window on its other flank. The Henry and Old Reliable were leaned against the wall, right where he'd made her leave them.

She seized the shotgun just as the far window's shutter gave way. A man's torso thrust through the opening and she fired both barrels.

Simultaneously, there was a shrill, short scream and an explosion, not only of sound, but of flesh. The shotgun's kick knocked her flat. Even before she hit her head on the floor, blood, nearly vaporized by the blast, misted down to freckle the floorboards and her clothing with pink, then red.

She felt her stomach lurch, but she made herself drop the spent shotgun and grab the Henry. She had it cocked before she realized the battering at the door had stopped. So, too, had the gunfire.

Panting, she crouched against the wall. She glanced toward Jake, but she couldn't see him. Dead or alive, he was behind the upturned table.

She whispered, "Mr. Turlow? Jake!"

"Quiet!" His hand popped into view, waved at her to stay down and wait, then disappeared again.

A moment later, they heard horses milling, then galloping away into the distance.

Jake stood up, slowly.

"We've got to get out of here," he said.

She slumped all the way to the floor and laid the rifle down. She stared at her hands, at the blood. "I can't," she whispered. She started to turn her head, to look at what was left of the man she'd killed.

"Don't, Charity!" Jake bellowed. "Look at me. Right now! Do as I say!"

Numbly, she complied. She was accustomed to

obeying men who shouted. Grampa Zeb had seen to that.

He started toward her, then remembered himself and snatched up the quilt, wrapping it quickly about his waist before he stepped out from behind the table. He went to her, bent, and took her by the wrist. He hauled her to her feet and gave her a shake.

That snapped her out of her stupor. "Let go!" she said through clenched teeth. She wrenched her arm away.

"Better," he said. "Throw some food in a sack while I get dressed. Then we're heading out."

"I'm not going anywhere with you! This is my house! And this is all your fault."

"Listen, honey, you've—"

"I told you not to call me that!"

His jaw clenched slightly. "All right, *Miss* Caine. This is your house, and this is my fault. But that doesn't change the fact that you've got dead men hanging through both windows and another one out in the yard. And you've also got Sam Briscoe riding as fast as he can to bring back a larger force of men."

"Who's Sam Briscoe?"

"The one who claimed to be Marshal Rex Jeffords."

"What?"

He rolled his eyes, curled his free hand into a fist, and thumped it against his thigh. "Jesus, girl! Will you just do what I'm telling you?"

Chapter Four

It was hard going.

The weak moonlight reflecting off the drifts fell just short of casting enough light to clearly see their path, and the blowing snow that covered their tracks also served to impede their progress. Jake had tied a long rope between Number Ten's bridle and his own horse: to prevent their being separated in the dark, he had said, but Charity knew it was to keep her from running away. Jake rode in front, breaking a crude trail through the snowy crust for her. Charity had to cling to the saddlehorn to keep from pitching off Number Ten whenever he lost his footing, which was frequently. Number Ten was steady, but he was hardly nimble.

Aside from the soft drone of wind, the crunch of hooves in brittle snow and an occasional snort from one of the horses, the only sound was the dull clanking of the pots and tins inside the gunny sack tied to Charity's saddle.

There was no conversation. Charity was too furious to talk, and she supposed Jake was too busy navigating the landscape to say much. She split her time between being angry with him and wondering whether, along the way, he planned to pick up that five thousand dollars the Marshal had claimed he'd stolen. She wondered if she could manage to relieve him of it. It seemed only fitting. After all, he'd ruined her house. And wasn't she a Caine? She already had a reputation. It was time she lived up to it.

Of course, she had no idea what she'd do with the money even if she could get her hands on it. And what good was money to her, anyway? Money was something a person needed in town, and she'd never been to one. Her notion of "town" was nebulous at best. Towns were civilized places populated by nice people who wore fancy clothes and spoke softly and went to church, and who would certainly never have anything to do with a Caine.

No, she didn't belong in town, and she had no use for money. But that didn't stop her dreaming about it, or about all that cash. If nothing else, it filled the time.

They rode silently through the night, Jake steadily breaking the trail and Charity following and silently plotting. At last, just after the cold grey break of dawn, Jake held up one hand and said, "Let's give it a rest."

Chilled through and bone tired, Charity was grateful. Her empty stomach had gone past growling to hurting. She could barely feel her legs from the knees down, and she'd grown weary of inventing always more fantastic ways to steal the money from Jake if and when he picked it up. She slid off Number Ten, landed on numb feet and stumbled, catching herself at the last moment by grabbing the stirrup leather.

She looked up quickly to see if Jake had noticed, but he was busy loosening his horse's girth strap. Charity took a deep breath. *Can't let him see you're weak,* she thought, then snorted softly. *Idiot. He's already got your guns away from you, wrecked your house, dragged you out into the frozen middle of nowhere on the end of a tether line like a six-year-old, and you're afraid he'll think you're weak?*

Jake turned toward her. "You say something?"

She pulled herself up straight and stamped her feet to get the circulation started again. "I'm glad you finally decided to call a halt, Mister Jake Turlow, but you sure picked a bad spot. The wind whips right through these trees. There's no decent shelter, unless you plan to hack down a few saplings and build a windbreak."

He took a nosebag from his pack, shook it out, measured in a few handsful of grain, and strapped it over his horse's muzzle. "Don't plan to camp here. Feed your gelding, and then get us some grub."

A new flush of anger sent hot adrenaline through her. Suddenly steady on her feet, she

53

stepped away from Number Ten and gave a sarcastic little bow. "Oh, yes sir, Mister Turlow, sir. Yes sir, right away, sir!"

He glared at her. "Listen, you little snip, I'm trying to save your life."

She pulled down the sack that contained Number Ten's grain. "Really? Seems more like you're trying to freeze me to death."

Two long strides put him right in front of her. "Only if I'm lucky," he growled, and snatched away the feed. "Now get us some chuck. And no fires."

She flinched, Jake realized as he snugged the feedbag over Number Ten's nose. He was surprised. He hadn't thought she had it in her to be frightened. But she had flinched. No, more than flinched. She had almost ducked, as if she were afraid he was going to hit her.

She'd recovered immediately, pulling herself erect and glaring at him murderously before she turned on her heel and began to dig through the provisions. At the moment she was crouched a few feet away, her back to him as she pulled tins and small packets out of the gunny sack and dropped them in the snow.

Fine, he thought. *You pretend you didn't do it, and I'll pretend I didn't see.* She must have some kind of pride, all right. And somebody must have slapped her around. Probably a lot more than once, he realized, knowing what he did of the Caine clan. He also realized that he was suddenly angry: angry that anyone would have hit that girl; and angry that she'd think, even for a split second, that he might be capable of such a thing. And then he was angry with himself for being angry with her.

"Jesus." He thumped himself in the forehead with the heel of his hand. He had more important things to worry about.

"What?" She had twisted to look at him. She looked annoyed, although on her the expression was distractingly attractive.

"I said, I'm hungry." He made himself stare at the middle of her forehead instead of into those whiskey eyes.

"Everything's half-frozen," she said, "except the last of the stew you had for dinner. It was next to Number Ten's shoulder. There's a lot of it and it's not slushy or anything, but it's still pretty cold."

He looked past her, through the denuded, snow-frosted trees. Claude Duval was out there somewhere, likely closer every minute. "It'll do," he said. "Hurry up.

She batted at her face, for a moment still in the dream, wondering how Aunt Tildy could throw a snowball at her in the middle of July. And then she came full awake, and the dream

55

of warm summer vanished. She brushed away the rest of the clumped snow that had fallen from a limb above, then looked about to get her bearings.

She had fallen asleep in the saddle—just when, she wasn't certain—but the slant of the sun told her it was coming on late afternoon. The thickly treed terrain was more gently sloped than hilly, and after a moment she realized they were near the area Grampa Zeb referred to as Whiskey Ridge. It was still snowing feebly, just a few big soft flakes drifting down. Not enough to cover their trail unless it picked up.

Her captor (or savior, if she were to take his word for it) still rode ahead, breaking a trail through the snow-clotted passages between tree trunks. The long rope was still strung between his saddle and Number Ten's bridle, but he had taken in some of the slack to prevent Number Ten from going the wrong way round a tree and fouling the line.

Charity tried to wiggle her toes inside her boots. She thought they moved a little. She slipped her boots from the stirrups and began to circle her ankles. Grampa Zeb had once "entertained" her with the story of one "Demon Dan" MacMurray, who, one icy Kansas winter, had frozen his feet so badly that they had to be sawed off. Grampa Zeb was there for the sawing and thought it was quite a sporty spectacle. Demon Dan had thereafter gone around on crutches, and wore a pair of walnut feet on Sundays, "just for show."

She didn't want to end up like Demon Dan.

"Hey!" she called loudly, although Jake was only a horse-length ahead. He didn't answer her. He didn't even flinch. For a moment she wished she had a good tossing knife. Inside her glove, her fingers twitched slightly in minute imitation of the familiar motion she'd make as the blade left her hand. *Whack!* she thought. *Right in the back of the neck, just the way Grampa Zeb taught me. That ought to get your attention, you kidnapping muskrat!* But she didn't have a knife, so instead she yelled again. "Hey you! Jake Turlow!"

On the second shout, a flock of crows suddenly took to the air from their overhead roosts. Whether it was Charity's voice or the crows' raucous complaints that got his attention, Jake jerked slightly and straightened. Only then did she realized that he, too, must have dozed off. She glanced quickly over her shoulder at the trail behind. It was reasonably straight, considering the saplings and trees that had to be piloted around. She wondered how he could navigate so well in his sleep. She wondered if his shoulder hurt him. She wondered where he'd stashed that five thousand in train robbery money.

She wondered if he'd have to saw off her feet.

"I said, *hey!*"

As she rode up even with him, he reined in his horse and twisted in the saddle, the cold leather creaking almost painfully.

"Heard you the first time," he muttered. His words rose in a foggy plume. His brows, lashes, and mustache sparkled with tiny scattered ice crystals.

She was half-tempted to reach over to brush them away, as she had the night he first stumbled into the cabin, but she kept her hands down and said, "Maybe you don't care if you freeze me to death out here, but I'd think you'd be kinder to these poor horses."

He didn't argue with her. Grateful for even this short break, both animals stood with sagging heads, their weary eyes half-lidded.

Jake said, "I know they're in bad shape. But we need decent cover. Some sort of windbreak big enough for us and them both. I don't ever remember a winter this bad in this part of the Nations, and I've seen some bad ones. Looks like it's going to blow up again tonight, too." He pointed out through the splinters of naked branches toward dark, threatening clouds. "I know where there's a shack, but that's another day's ride in this weather."

"A lot of good that is," she sniffed.

He frowned. A bit of crusted snow fell from one of his brows and stuck to his cheek. He brushed it away, adding, "A deadfall of timber would do. Something to hold the wind back

58

. . ." He looked out through the trees, distracted.

Charity followed his gaze, but didn't see a thing. Neither, apparently, did he, because after a moment he turned back, saying, "You have a better idea?"

She sat up as straight as her saddle-weary back would allow. "Well, thank you very much for asking, *Mister* Turlow."

His jaw muscles clenched before he said, "I wish you'd just drop that 'Mister'—"

"Because if you had asked me," she continued, cutting him off, "I could have told you that there's a nice big cave not a half mile from here. There are caves all through these hills."

"I know that," he replied testily. "Most of them are just about big enough for a bear, if it backs in."

"Well," she said, pressing her knees to Number Ten's weary sides and taking the lead, "this one's big enough for six bears and all their cousins."

Her legs were so numb that she had to hang on to Number Ten with one hand while she helped Jake break a hole through the frozen brush at the cave's mouth. The storm Jake had forecasted was already descending. The sky was prematurely dark, and the wind had risen again to lash them with sleet. More than anything she wanted to pry off her boots and put her bare feet dangerously close to a nice hot fire.

They made a opening just big enough to lead the horses through, single file: Jake in the lead, holding a lit match in the air. As she came up beside him, it burned too close to his fingers. She smelled scorched glove as he shook it out, immersing them in total darkness. Funny, she thought, how you could sense a person standing three feet away from you, even when you couldn't see him.

She heard the *pop* as he scratched a new sulphur-tip, saw it flare as he held it up. The small, pale orb of light played gold off his hat rim, flickered softly over his cold-ruddied features. He whispered, "You sure nothing's in here?" He wasn't afraid, she knew, just curious.

"If you didn't see any tracks outside, then no, because I didn't either. Course, there might be a catamount or two holed up on that ledge right over your head." She covered her mouth with a gloved hand when his head jerked slightly to the side, then snapped back to glare at her. "But if there were," she continued dryly, "I think we'd likely already be dead."

The match had burned halfway down. He twisted it higher in his gloved fingers, then held it aloft. "How big is this place, anyway?"

Charity stamped her feet a few times, then braved letting go of Number Ten. Her feet were still numb. It felt like she was walking on stilts and she wobbled a little, but she didn't think she'd fall over. She said, "You'll need more light than that to see it by. There used to be a stack of kindling over here somewhere . . ."

She stepped away from him just as his match went out, and began to feel her way through the darkness by memory. One, two, three careful steps. She stopped and tapped ahead with one boot. The toe contacted something solid—a wide, chair-high upthrust of limestone that gave her bearings. She heard Jake strike another match, but she was too far away to be helped by its light. She stepped two paces to her left before she started forward, toward where she knew the woodpile should be. One step, two steps; three, four . . .

She tripped and fell forward, arms out. Her forearms hit the stacked kindling, breaking her fall and scattering the wood in an deafening racket, magnified tenfold by the cave's stone walls. She knew, even as she landed, that she wasn't hurt. Besides keeping out the cold, her old bearskin coat made substantial padding.

As the last echo faded, she heard Jake choke back a chuckle, then clear his throat. She twisted to see him standing over her, holding a match aloft. "You, uh, you find it, did you, Miss Caine?"

Jake built a small fire toward the rear of the cave, once she showed him where the stone roof was cracked and would vent the smoke. She was happy to huddle over the flames, melting snow for the horses, melting more snow to make tea, heating the last of the stew. She would have liked cornbread or grits—and she had the fixings—but she was too bone tired to fuss with it.

Outside, the storm continued to build. She could hear the rush as it alternately shoved and sucked at the tangle of limbs and brush at the cave's mouth. Wind lashed over the fissure above, the whistle and sharp whine of it changing pitch every few seconds as it pulled the fire's smoke—and too much of its precious heat—up and away.

While she worked, sitting so close to the fire she was practically in it, she watched Jake tend the horses. He took great pains with them, the way she did when Grampa Zeb hadn't been around to cuff and scold her for "treatin' critters like babies" and "makin'em soft." Well, she didn't see—had never seen—why treating an animal with respect for its needs would make it "soft." It was only decent, to her mind.

And, it seemed, to Jake Turlow's. After he stripped the horses of their tack (which Grampa Zeb might have done, if he could be bothered) and fed them (which Grampa Zeb certainly would have done, although mainly because a dead horse can't carry you anywhere), Jake Turlow commenced a series of procedures that Charity deemed commendable, and which

Grampa Zeb would have denounced as outright pampering.

First, he took a fistful of rags and rubbed both horses down from nose to tail. The snow had melted into their shaggy winter coats, and both animals steamed as he worked. He then unrolled his bedroll—which consisted, she saw, of two wool blankets—and draped one over each horse. Next he fished a hoofpick from his pack and proceeded to clean out what snow remained balled up under their hooves. And then, when she was certain he was finished, he brought out a bottle of emerald-colored liniment, took off his gloves, and rubbed down their legs.

He worked so expertly and swiftly that the entire procedure took him no more than twenty minutes; but by the time he joined her at the fire, she was worn out from watching him.

"Thank you," she said. The way he'd tended the horses didn't make up for the misery he'd brought into her life, but for the moment she was too tired—and too grateful to be out of the blast—to be angry with him. She handed him a mug of strong hot tea. "I've got more snow melted for the horses if you want it."

He shook his head. "They're fine for now."

Interesting, she thought, the way he held the mug close to his face, letting the steam rise up and bathe him: his eyes half-lidded, unguarded for a moment. His hands—strong, beautiful hands—were so large they dwarfed the mug, the mate of which seemed huge in her own. She knew he was letting the first sharp warmth of the metal seep into his fingers, work toward his bones. She could almost feel it with him, for she had done the same thing not many minutes before. She had just never realized a man would care so much about a thing like comfort, about good sensations. Or admit it, if he did. Grampa Zeb never seemed to care one way or the other if things were scratchy or soft or too hot or too cold. Burlap or silk, it was all the same to Zeb Caine.

She felt badly about having been snippy with Jake. Not that he didn't deserve it for introducing so much turmoil into her life; but he had been good to her, too. It was just that after a lifetime of never being able to talk back or even voice an opinion—except under her breath—there was something about snapping at Jake Turlow that made her feel independent and strong, even when she was wishing she wasn't doing it.

She handed Jake a plate of stew and a fork. He nodded his thanks and began to eat. She joined him, although, despite her hunger, she paid more attention to him than the food on her plate. Even in a cave, crouched on cold rock with no table in sight, he still ate . . . *nice*. That was the only word she could think of to describe it.

She wished he'd talk to her again. She liked the sound of his voice, when he wasn't ordering her around.

"You rub down your horse's legs every night?" she said, immediately wishing she could have thought of something brighter.

He looked up, apparently surprised at the question. Those pale blue, darkly fringed eyes were staring at her, crinkling at the corners; and for a split-second she imagined she was falling, falling into them . . .

"When he's worked hard," he said, and it took her a moment to realize what question he was replying to. He fell silent. He stared at her legs. He said, "I know it's damn cold in here even with the fire, but you're about to catch your boots on fire."

He was right. The leather on one boot was already scorched from the heat, and she hadn't felt it. She tried to pull her feet away, to tuck them up under her, but her legs, cold and numb before, were now cold and numb and stiff. The best she could manage was a choppy, ineffectual motion that jerked both her feet no more than six inches to the left.

He put down his plate. "Take those boots off," he said quietly.

Charity stuck her nose in the air. "Why should I do that?"

"Get 'em off." That time it was more like an order, and she found herself automatically obeying: sitting forward and reaching down . . .

She couldn't make her knees bend, and she suddenly realized she couldn't feel her feet at all. "Oh, God," she whispered, "please don't make me have to have walnut feet."

Before she realized it, he had come round the fire and was gently easing off her right boot.

"No, don't! I'll be even colder without my—"

"Hush."

He dropped the boot and began to peel off her socks, and when he finally got down to bare skin, she could feel the warm pressure of his hand, but just barely.

"Am I . . . ?" She swallowed hard. "You won't have to . . . ?" All she could think of was Demon Dan and the wooden feet. And the saw.

He pushed her foot forward, forcing her knee to bend. "Does that hurt?"

She was trying not to cry. "I can't feel it much at all."

He pulled the leg straight again, then flexed it again. "How about that?"

"I don't care if they're solid ice!" she blurted. "I'd rather be dead than have wood feet."

He look up and smiled oddly. "Wooden feet? Where'd you get an idea like that?"

Gently, he drew her leg out straight, put her foot down and began to slide the second boot free. "It's not frostbite," he said, "but you came damn close. I think we can get you fixed up."

Relief washed through her—along with gratitude that her immediate future didn't include any amputations — and so, when she snapped, "What's leaving me barefoot in the middle of winter got to do with fixing me up?" she was surprised at herself. She wanted to take it back immediately, erase it with something nicer. *Thank you,* for instance.

But all Jake said as he pulled the last stocking free was, "Can you get those britches off by yourself, or you want me to do it?"

Chapter Five

"My *what?*"

"Your britches," he repeated.

"I won't!"

He turned his back and started for the kindling pile. He'd wondered why she hadn't built the fire any higher while he was seeing to the horses, and now he knew the reason: she simply was too stiff and cold to walk that far. He doubted whether, after sitting still for the past half hour or so, she'd be able to stand up at all now, much less walk or mount a horse. If he didn't get her thoroughly warmed and those muscles relaxed, she'd likely be in worse condition come morning. It was a delay they couldn't afford.

"Fine," he said, scooping up an armload of kindling. He carried it back and dropped it on the stone floor, then squatted next to the jumble and began feeding branches and sticks to the fire. "They're your legs." He shrugged noncommittally, never looking at her. If it took a little stretching of the truth to get her to do what was needed, then he'd have to stretch it.

There was a small pause before he heard her say, "What do you mean, *they're your legs?*"

He looked up and said, "Well, for the time being. I just thought, what with you having saved my life and all, that it'd be only decent if I returned the favor."

A look of horror on her face, she stared down at her bare, red feet, and whispered, "I'll die?"

He realized he was likely pushing it too far, but the expression on her face was so sweet and perplexed that he couldn't help himself: he hadn't had anybody so pretty to tease since poor Laura died. Of course, with Laura it had been different. . . . And besides, Charity really did need attending to.

"Answer me!" she said, a bit louder, still staring at her feet. "Am I going to die?"

"Oh, not right away," he said solemnly, and poked the fire before he added a few more sticks to the blaze. "You'll likely linger a bit. Seen it before. But if your modesty's more important, well, it's your decision." He shook his head slowly and risked a quick peek out of the corner of his eye to see if it had worked.

It had. She was fumbling with her belt.

He stood up and started toward the horses and his saddlebags. He didn't allow himself a soft chuckle and a smile until his back was completely to her.

* * *

Charity unbuckled the belt, then fumbled her way down the row of flat buttons on her britches. Although she didn't have much control over her numb legs, she managed to worry the pants halfway over her hips before she started to unbutton the pair underneath. *Demon Dan didn't die from cold feet,* she was thinking, *but maybe he did later on, after Grampa Zeb left Kansas. Maybe they just had to keep cutting off pieces of him, higher and higher, until there wasn't anything left to cut anymore . . .*

By the time she was unbuttoned down to her longjohns and had several pairs of trousers bunched around her hips, Jake was at her side, crouched down and rocking on his heels. He had two bottles: one was clear glass and half-full of the green liniment he'd used on the horses; the other was a dented silver flask. He unscrewed the cap on the latter, then held it to her lips.

"Take a couple good swallows of this," he said.

She pushed it aside. "Don't want to. That's liquor."

He sighed and rested the flask on his knee. "I'd never heard the Caine women to have anything against drink."

She almost told him that most of the Caine women were rather fond of it, actually, except for her. When she was twelve, she'd sneaked a whole coffee mug full of Grampa Zeb's corn whiskey out of the house and swallowed it straight down. She had never been so sick in her life, and since then the mere thought of alcohol was enough to make her bilious.

He shoved the flask back under her nose. "I said drink it. You need warming on the inside, too."

Before she had a chance to push his hand away again, he tilted the flask. Whiskey—cold in temperature but warm and sweet in taste—filled her mouth.

She swallowed, and almost immediately she felt heat trickling through her body. And although she didn't think liquor-drinking was something she'd ever be inclined to make a habit of, whatever he'd given her was certainly smoother than raw moonshine out of a tin cup.

"What is that?" she asked, her voice thick from the drink, after he'd made her take a second swallow.

"Kentucky bourbon." He stood up and stared down at her. She was still bundled in that enormous coat, and she was sitting up, her back propped against a stony hump in the cave floor. He said, "This isn't going to work."

She watched as he unrolled her two blankets and shook them out, then laid them both over his deerskin cape on the other side of the fire where the floor was most level. When he was satisfied with this "mattress," he came back to

71

her, bent down, and quite easily scooped her up into his arms.

"Your shoulder," she said, for the moment feeling almost kindly toward him again, and blaming it on the whiskey.

"You're not that heavy. This old coat of yours likely weighs more than you do." He laid her down on one side of the blankets, then squatted over her legs and started to pull her trousers down and off, one layer at a time.

At last he pinched a knee-side fold of her Union suit. "These, too."

She had put up with the boots and she had put up with the britches, but this was too much. "I can't take them off," she said indignantly. "They go all the way up!"

"Then you'll just have to strip, won't you?"

He said it so offhandedly that she wanted to slap him, even if it meant wooden feet and an early grave.

"I will *not*," she said, and clumsily crossed her arms.

"Your choice," he said with a shrug; and quite calmly stood up, walked round the fire, sat down, and proceeded to finish his dinner.

He was reaching for what meager seconds remained before she finally broke down. The man was infuriating, totally maddening, but he was the only one who could help her. She made herself unball her fists and unclench her teeth, and then she said, "All *right*, damn it.

But you'd better turn your back, and don't you *dare* look until I say!"

While she disrobed, Jake walked to the cave's mouth and peeked through the brush he had reassembled against the weather. It wasn't snowing much out there, but the wind was bad, and he was sure it had grown too cold to snow or sleet any more tonight. It was certainly freezing where he was standing. He took a couple of steps back, away from the cave's entrance. It helped a little, but not much. Behind him, he could hear the rustling sound of Charity fighting her way through all those layers of clothes.

Well, he'd promised, and he couldn't turn around and go back toward the blaze. *That's what you get for being a gentleman,* he thought, and blew on his hands before he clamped them under his armpits. He still had his coat on, but he'd left his gloves back at the fire. He hoped that son of a bitch, Duval, and his murdering cohorts were sitting out in the smack dab middle of an open meadow, freezing to death.

"Don't suppose you could hurry it up, Miss Caine?" he called into the air. "It's cold over here."

"It's n-not exactly toasty here, e-either, Mister T-Turlow. J-Just hold your h-horses."

From the sound of those chattering teeth, Jake figured she must be right down to her skin, and he was sorely tempted to take a peek over his shoulder. He didn't, but he couldn't help wishing that he had even a little scrap of mirror to angle *just so* . . .

"Don't put your coat back on," he said suddenly. "Just pull it up over you, like a blanket. Fur side in."

There was a short pause, and then he heard her say, "All right, you can turn around."

After he pulled the Union suit the rest of the way down over her legs for her, he had poured out a few fingers of liniment into one of the tin cups, then added the same amount of bourbon from his flask. "Got to cut it with alcohol," he'd said. "Too strong, otherwise. Might burn your skin." The odor had been past pungent, and when she wrinkled her nose, he'd quipped, "Not many ladies in the Nations get their perfumes custom-mixed."

Charity thought he was perfectly dreadful, even if he did have the most beautiful eyes she'd ever seen.

She lay on her back, her head pillowed on a roll she'd made of her flannel shirts—and longjohns, after he threw them aside—and stared up at the cave's roof while he worked. He was rubbing her left calf at the moment, having already kneaded and massaged the right leg from her toes to halfway up her thigh, and she could already feel her circulation coming back.

It felt quite wonderful, in fact, to have someone minister to her. Ever since she could remember, she'd always been the one to take care of everybody else when they were crippled up or sick, and never before had anyone touched her with the sole purpose of making her feel better.

Jake's touch was firm but gentle, and she could tell he was taking care not to hurt her or be too rough. It was as if he knew where all the muscles were and which way they lay, and just the right way to coax them back into pliancy. It made her feel warm all over, even if it was still so cold in the cave that she could see her breath each time she exhaled. And she was glad he'd told her to pull up the coat like a blanket, with the warm fur next to her skin. Of course, he had pushed it half-way up her thigh so he could work; but everywhere else, the thick, coarse fur alternately tickled and scratched faintly at her bare skin in a rather wonderful way.

A few times she peered down at him when he wasn't looking. Maybe he wasn't so bad. Maybe he was really all right. He was certainly good-looking, and he made her feel so . . .

"Can you turn over?"

She almost jumped. "I think so," she said, surprised when her voice emerged throaty and languid.

As she rolled onto her stomach, she realized that she could not only feel her feet and lower legs again, but that they felt almost better than when she and Jake Turlow had started out. But when he went back to her right calf and began to massage it again from this new angle, she didn't tell him to stop. She closed her eyes. She was beginning to think she wouldn't mind if this went on forever.

Unfortunately, it didn't. Less than fifteen minutes later, Jake gently folded up the bottom of the makeshift blanket mattress to swaddle her feet and lower legs, then pulled the coat's hem down over that. He stood up and stretched.

"Are you done?" she asked, half-asleep and a little disappointed.

"Should take care of it." He stood up. "You just stay put. Got to water the horses and fetch the rest of the firewood, then I think we'd better turn in."

Her eyelids heavy, her body warm and relaxed, she watched as he fed the fire again, stirring it and piling on enough fuel to keep it blazing till morning, then walked back to check the horses a last time. Groggily, she wondered where he planned to sleep. Between her mattress and the horses, all the blankets were in use.

"Move over a little," he said as, with a thud, he dropped his saddle next to her pillow.

"What?"

"You're taking your half out of the middle." He pulled off his coat, tossed it down on top of her and her bearskin cover, and sat down beside her on the blanket.

"But you can't!" she said, suddenly coming awake enough to remember she was naked.

"Yes, I can. It's cold out there and it's going to get colder. We're going to need both these coats for cover, and all the shared body heat we can get."

"Keep your coat to yourself and I'll keep mine," she snapped, and snaked a lean arm out into the chilled air to shove his coat away.

"Sorry," he said, without expression, "but I'm not going to freeze to death on your whim. That coat of yours is enough for three people, and mine is hardly big enough for me. Plus, you're already using my cape for a mattress pad."

"I'll move over, but I won't have you under the covers with me, *Mister* Turlow. Use your own coat."

He was too tired to argue with her. He swore under his breath before he snatched up his coat, tugged it back on and snarled, "Well, scoot over, then."

She did, making sure to glare at him the whole time.

"And you make sure to keep your hands to yourself!" was the last thing she had said to him. In answer, he had simply crossed his arms over his chest and closed his eyes. He didn't understand how any female could be so beautiful and so cantankerous all at once. Well, not cantankerous *all* the time: every once in a while

77

she was downright pleasant. And when she was like that . . .

She's a Caine, Jake ol' buddy, he reminded himself. *A Caine. And if you make a move on her, she's just as liable to knife you in the ribs as give you a kiss.*

He sighed. Next to him, Charity was asleep, her breathing slow and regular. She must have been completely exhausted. He was, too, but the knowledge that Claude Duval was out there on their trail wasn't too conducive to slumber. Besides, he was too cold to sleep. Quite softly, he said, "Charity? Miss Caine?"

When she didn't answer, he sat up, took his coat off again and very gently draped it over the top of hers. Then, teeth chattering, he lifted the edge and slipped beneath it, next to her.

Much better, he thought. There was plenty of room under the fur, and her body heat, trapped by the bearskin, had created a wonderful island of warmth. He took care not to actually touch her as she slept. He didn't want to wake her and have to listen to the fit she'd pitch. Additionally, he knew what his own physical reaction would be if he were to touch her, accidentally or otherwise.

He already knew, from massaging her legs, what he had already guessed from looking at that heavenly face: her skin was as smooth and flawless and soft as a baby's. And if the rest of her looked as he imagined . . .

78

He shifted uncomfortably. *Don't think about it, Jake,* he reminded himself. *Got plans to make.*

He slid his arms from under the fur and cocked his elbows back, lacing his fingers behind his head on the saddleseat pillow.

He was thinking that if they started out by seven, they'd make old Tink Maynard's cabin well before nightfall, even with the snow slowing them down. Tink might not be there, but he never minded visitors so long as they didn't steal him blind, and the cabin was tight against the weather and had a good wide, warm hearth. And a bed. Jake twitched slightly, trying to get comfortable. Even with a deerskin cape and two blankets to buffer it, a stone floor was a stone floor.

Beside him, Charity murmured something in her sleep and stirred; and then, to his consternation and surprise, she rolled over and snuggled against him.

He froze, daring to move only his eyes. Her head was pillowed on his chest, her arm slung across it under the cover; and he could feel the soft press of her breasts against his ribs and side.

Lord have mercy, he thought, when he felt her leg slide on top of his and come to rest: her foot between his knees, the inside of her knee pressing gently atop his groin.

Immediately, he felt himself swelling to push insistently against his trousers, and he ground his teeth. *Take it easy, Jake,* he thought. *You're in charge of this situation, not your Johnson.* . . . And then, forcing himself to stare at the ceiling, he started counting backward from thirty.

By the time he got down to five, there seemed no improvement. He started over again, this time at one hundred. He had to stop and start over once when she wiggled in her sleep and rubbed her breasts against him, but eventually he was back in control. Very slowly, he unclasped his hands from behind his head and brought his arms, now freezing and cramped, down and under the cover. The only place to put his left arm was around Charity, and that was where he put it, although carefully.

She didn't move.

He took a deep breath and closed his eyes, trying not to think about how warm and silky her back felt under his hand. He found himself sliding his hand slowly lower, down the velvet ripple of her spine, into the hollow of the small of her back, toward the soft swell of her buttocks . . .

He stopped himself. Although the temptation was nearly irresistible, it wasn't right. Not only was she sleeping, and therefore unconsenting; she was a Caine. It was becoming more and more difficult for him to remember that.

He removed his hand and laid it flat on the blanket behind her. The angle wasn't as comfortable, but it was safer. He started counting again.

He was nearly asleep when she squirmed again, squeezing him with her leg and pressing even closer.

Mercy, he thought, and stared at the stone ceiling again. *One hundred. Ninety-nine. Ninety-eight. Ninety-seven . . .*

Chapter Six

Her nose was cold.

It wasn't until she instinctively snuggled her face against the covers that she realized how deliciously warm the rest of her body was. She opened her eyes, just slightly. She was lying on her side, facing the dim glow of the dying fire, and she could hear, distantly, a soft howl of wind. Gradually, she began to remember the rest of it: the gun battle at the cabin and that freezing, endless flight through the snow; the cave, how cold and stiff her poor legs had been . . . and Jake Turlow.

No light filtered through the brambled windbreak at the cave's mouth, so she knew it was not yet dawn. She wiggled her toes, happy to find that they seemed in perfect working order; and it was only then that she realized she was not alone under the fur. Her bare back was pressed quite firmly against something that could only be Jake Turlow's body. And his arm, his hand . . .

Gingerly, she lifted the edge of the cover and peeked inside to confirm what she already knew to be an unsettling fact: his arm was not only curled around her torso, but his hand was very gently cupping her breast.

She was, quite suddenly, totally awake. She swallowed hard and fought the urge to shove his hand away and ram her elbow back into his ribcage. But living with Grampa Zeb had taught her you didn't wake a man suddenly—if you did that to Zebulon Caine, he was likely to pound you flat into the floor before he realized who you were. And this Jake Turlow might not be as strong as had been Grampa Zeb, who, in his heyday, had weighed as much as two men and fought like four; but Jake Turlow was a man, and men were strong. That was just the nature of it.

So she held still. She could feel the insolent bastard's breath on the back of her neck as it filtered through her hair in warm, humid clouds. His breathing was slow and metered: he was still asleep.

Seething, she tried to decide what to do. *What bald-faced audacity!* she fumed. *If unmitigated gall was measured in acreage, Jake Turlow'd be Texas!* The more she thought about it, the madder she got. She was about to throw caution to the winds and give him that elbow in the ribs—and a good piece of her mind—when it struck her that maybe more had gone on while she was asleep than a little fondling.

Was it possible? Could he have done something to her without her waking? She didn't think so, but then, having no experience, she couldn't be certain.

It was not that she was ignorant of the facts of life. When she was eight, Aunt Tildy had marched her out to the old rattletrap barn and made her watch a bull Grampa Zeb had "borrowed" breed their milk cow. "There," Aunt Tildy had said. "That's how it gets done. It'll get done to you, too, when you're older. Gets done to your Aunt Vena five, six times a day. Double on weekends."

Aunt Tildy had sounded vaguely disgusted with the proceeding, but Charity had been as fascinated as if Aunt Tildy had just explained a magician's trick. Since then, she had witnessed or overseen the breedings of sheep and goats and horses and hogs, and never thought much of it. But it had seemed to her a reasonably violent proposition in many cases. Surely a woman would know, or at least wake up . . .

But perhaps it was different with people. Maybe it could be done in a way a woman wouldn't notice if she was tired enough. Once, she'd heard Grampa Zeb brag that the Caine men could "knock up" a female in their sleep, though at the time she thought he was talking about the menfolk being asleep, and hadn't thought he meant it literally. What if he had, though?

The possibility that Jake Turlow might

have been "at" her made her even more angry. She considered that she could grab one of the pistols, shoot the son of a skunk, and then get on back home and forget the five thousand dollars. She didn't really think this Duval man was trailing them, anyway. Even if he was, they'd ridden through a whole night and day: surely there had been enough snowfall during that time to cover most of their trail. And as for that Marshal Jeffords or Briscoe or whatever his name was? Well, she could handle him. She'd been drilled all her life that the law was the enemy; and, if nothing else, Grampa Zeb had taught her how to deal with enemies. While it was true that she'd never exactly implemented any of Grampa Zeb's examples, she was certain that if that Marshal came round again, she could do what had to be done. She'd be scared for certain, but she'd been scared before and she'd come out all right.

But then . . .

What if Jake Turlow really *had* done it to her? What if she was pregnant? Of course, Aunt Vena had never had any babies, and to hear Tildy tell it, Vena'd practically had a turnstile at her bedroom door. But still . . .

All the more reason to shoot him, she thought. She was about to twist toward him and reach for the gunbelt she felt pressing into her hip when he moved slightly in his sleep. Along with the small shift his legs made, his arm curled more snugly about her and his hand moved just a little on her breast, his thumb momentarily brushing across the nipple.

She froze as a thin cascade of shivers—completely unexpected and decidedly pleasant—spread through her.

She decided she might put off killing him. For a minute or so.

Jake came bolt awake, as usual, at exactly six-thirty. Laura had always said that at six o'clock you could pound on his head with a rock and he wouldn't even mumble; but come six-thirty you couldn't keep him down with ropes. He was halfway rolled onto his back and about to stretch his arms before he realized that he had just taken his hand off someone's breast.

At the precise moment it all flooded back in on him (along with the realization that, in their sleep, he and Charity had likely come to a new and vastly more interesting sleeping position), Charity leapt up. She took the covers along with her and left him suddenly wrapped in nothing but his clothes and icy air.

"You weasel!" she snarled. She pulled the bearskin more tightly around her, and Jake's wool coat dropped away. He sat up and snatched it out of the air. He was most of the way into it as he jumped to his feet.

"What?" he shouted as innocently as he could.

"You know perfectly well *what!*"

"Miss, I—"

"Don't you 'Miss' *me!*"

He fastened the last button on his coat. "I wish you'd make up your mind, lady. First it's, 'Don't call me honey!' Then it's 'Don't call me Miss!' What the hell *do* you want me to call you?"

She snapped, "You know what I mean!" and he wouldn't have been surprised to see little flames flicker from those whiskey eyes.

He surreptitiously patted his holster to make sure his pistol was still there. He didn't want her armed when she was this mad. "Lady, I don't know what you're so het-up about, but if I were you, I'd get into my clothes and start some breakfast. I want us to be out of here in an hour. Less."

She balled her hands into fists and beat them against hips. "Quit changing the subject! You know perfectly well—"

He had already turned his back and started toward the horses, hoping that if he ignored her she'd just shut up. He also hoped she wouldn't launch herself at him. Once, down in some woebegone west Arkansas hamlet, the whore-girlfriend of the cutthroat he was trying to arrest had jumped him from behind, locked her legs around him in a death grip, and commenced to beat on his head like a bass drummer in a marching band. He'd had a devil of a time getting untangled without scuffing her up, and he'd been deaf in his left ear for the next two days.

He was halfway through feeding the horses before he chanced a glance in Charity's direction. She wasn't beside the fire and neither were her clothes. For a second he thought she might be even crazier than he'd suspected, and that she'd hightailed it: the hell with her horse and her britches and freezing to death. But a little flutter of movement at the edge of an outcrop toward the very back of the cave told him she hadn't fled: she was only getting dressed. He watched a slender hand poke from behind the rock, jab quickly through the shadowed pile of clothes at its foot, and angrily jerk away a pair of britches.

She's sure not happy, he thought, *but at least she's quiet*. He made a quick visual inventory of the weapons. *And she can't shoot me.*

As the horses placidly ground their grain, he prepared to saddle up. But as he slid the first saddle into place and threaded the cinch ring, he found himself pausing to cup the air in his hand, trying to recapture exactly the feel and shape and size of the warm flesh it had held as he woke.

He caught himself and curled his hand into a fist. *Jake,* he thought, *just saddle the damn horses.*

She didn't speak to him during breakfast, or after it. They broke camp, tore down the frozen brush at the cave's mouth, and set out in silence. And although she looked as if nothing would please her more than to see him hanged, shot, stabbed, and trampled by a cattle stampede all at the same time, he had more pressing things to worry about.

He was trying to figure out just how much of their trail had been covered by snowfall, and when. A great deal depended on how far away Claude Duval had been when Briscoe and the others attacked the cabin, and whether Duval and his boys had started right out when Briscoe brought them the news. He hoped Duval had been a couple hours ride away, and that he'd waited till morning to begin the chase.

No, Jake thought. *I'm not that lucky. Duval was likely a half-hour's ride up the valley, at most. And he wouldn't have waited for dawn. Even if he lost us in the storm, he has to know I'd head for Fort Smith to report in and put together a posse . . .*

In any case, the carnage Duval and his remaining men would find—*had most certainly already found,* Jake reminded himself—was bound to stir them up. He had checked the bodies before he and Charity rode out. The late Chico "Toad" Potter and Red Billy Byrnes were both draped through the windows, and half of Red Billy's face had been blown away by Charity's shotgun. In the yard, Poot Purdy lay dead in a twisted tangle of limbs. All three were wanted on numerous charges, including murder; and if they'd been captured alive all three of them would have been sentenced to die. But Jake didn't suppose for a second that Duval's men were going to see any justice — sideways or otherwise — in their companions' premature demises. No, they'd want vengeance, and they'd want it as soon and as bloody as possible.

He couldn't outrun them, not through these drifts, though he took some solace in the knowledge that they weren't going any faster than he was; and, when he got right down to it, just keeping a decent distance ahead of their pursuers was his — and Charity's — only hope. He certainly couldn't out-gun them: he figured Duval had about eight men left, maybe ten. And he didn't think it was possible to outsmart Duval: in the past, any man cocky enough to try it had ended up dead. Duval was the sort you gave as wide a berth as possible, unless you were sure the odds — and manpower — were two-to-one in your favor. If he and Charity kept pushing, kept riding as long and as fast as they could each day, they just might hold steady the interval of distance between themselves and the outlaws, and beat Duval to the Arkansas border.

Arkansas. He missed it, and the comfort of town. He fell into thinking about the little house in Fort Smith where he and Laura had lived. It was just four rooms, but it had seemed big enough, even with Laura's pet rabbits and tame squirrels and the stray dogs she kept collecting. They were all gone, now, all given away. Laura was dead, and he was never there long enough to take care of any livestock. Just four little rooms had never seemed so empty.

He took out his watch, telling himself he wanted to check the time, but knowing it was only the same old excuse. He fumbled with the catch, and when at last it opened, he didn't look at the clock's face, but at the inside of the lid, and the little picture of Laura.

He felt himself slipping back into a deep and familiar grief, and, snapping the watch closed again, reordered his thoughts. *Got to think about good things,* he drilled himself, and added, *Warm things, too.*

It was still too cold to snow. He hoped that situation would change by mid-day. As much as he hated having to plow through these drifts, another inch or two would go a long way to obscuring their trail.

He risked a quick peek over his shoulder. Charity's horse was still plodding along behind him at the end of the tether rope. Charity sat hunched in the saddle, that ridiculous, oversized coat draping her and half her horse like an enormous furry tent. The clouds of her exhaled breath were slow and regular and her eyes were closed. He decided that if she really was asleep, she had terrific balance.

He reined his horse around an ice-sparkled thicket and pulled his collar closer. At this moment, he would have given a year's wages to be back in that little house in Fort Smith: a bourbon in his hand, chest-deep in hot water in the big old tin bathtub, with the snow falling outside the windows and the hearth blazing . . .

At the corner of his eye, a trace of movement.

He reined his horse hard to the side, at the same time reaching toward his rifle boot. Before his horse finished the half-spin, the rifle was up and ready.

It was a small party of Indians, a family group. On foot, they were just trudging over the gentle rise. The motion he'd seen was the top of the leader's head as it bobbed over the crest of the hill. He let himself breathe again and lowered the rifle, although he didn't slide it back into its boot.

The Indian in the lead, an old man dressed more white than native, shaded his eyes against the snow's glare before he waved. "Greetings, Turlow!" he called.

Jake waved back. "Good morning, Thomas! How goes it?" He put his rifle away.

"Some good, some bad," the old man said as he walked closer. His family stayed at the crest of the rise. "Too much snow," he added, when he came to a stop ten feet away. "Two Turtles, she complain all time." He poked a finger over his shoulder, toward a chubby, thickly bundled woman who had just let drop the poles of a heavily laden travois.

If Charity had been asleep before, she was awake now. She reined her horse alongside Jake's. "Who are they?" she whispered.

"Thomas Lightfoot and his wife and sons," he replied, without looking at her. Then, louder, "Maybe one of your boys could spell her with that load, Thomas."

The old man snorted, as if he found the suggestion beneath consideration.

"Are you keeping on to the west?"

"Yes, Turlow," Thomas said. Behind him, his wife sat down atop the travois with a thump. His two sons simply stood and waited. They looked bored and surly.

"We go home, now," Thomas continued. "We traded for supplies. Most times wait for spring, but we had a bear get in, wreck everything. Had to trade now. Not much to barter, though. Weather too cold to get much fur. The winter kill them before we get chance. Except for that bear," he added, as a tiny hard smile flickered across his face.

Jake nodded sympathetically. "I should warn you, Thomas, I've got some bad ones on my trail."

"How bad? You gonna take them Fort Smith, Turlow? Put in jail?" His smile widened hopefully. "Hang 'em, maybe?"

Jake shook his head. "Not this trip, Thomas. Next time."

Beside him, Charity hissed, "What does he mean, 'Are you going to put them in jail?' "

He ignored her. "Just keep cutting due west, Thomas, and you should miss them."

He felt Charity poke his leg with her fist.

"What does he mean?" she asked again, this time a bit louder. "I thought they were going to put *you* in —"

"Who this, Turlow?" Thomas cut in. He had walked a few steps closer. "You have woman, now? She has own horse?" He reached out and put a fur-mittened hand on Number Ten's shaggy neck. "You trade for this horse?"

Charity hauled on Number Ten's reins and backed him up two steps, and she looked so affronted that Jake had a hard time not to laugh.

"Thought you were all traded out, Thomas," he said.

"Trade you my woman for your horse." Thomas tipped his head back toward long-suffering Two Turtles. "Horse pull better. You already have one horse, Turlow, and your woman too skinny. You need fat woman. That skinny girl fatten up some with Two Turtles to share work. With two women, you be richest marshal in Nations."

Jake heard a small, very angry sound from Charity's direction, but he declined to look her way. Instead, he said, "Sorry, Thomas. Two Turtles is a fine woman, but the horse isn't mine to trade. I thank you for the generous offer, though."

Thomas shrugged. "Not generous. Only fair. I have other wife at home. Younger and fatter. Better for pillowing."

Jake gathered his reins. "Then you'd best get on home to her, Thomas. And be careful."

Thomas signaled to his family. With a grunt, Two Turtles hauled herself up and hefted the travois poles. "You take care, too, Turlow," Thomas Lightfoot said. "Much more snow tonight."

"Believe you're right," Jake replied as he tipped his hat and urged his horse forward. He didn't look over his shoulder at Charity. He knew she was seething, but he hoped the talk of trading her horse for Two Turtles had distracted her from the mention of the word "marshal."

They moved on through the snow, and once Thomas Lightfoot and his family had trudged out of sight and earshot, the only sounds were the steady crunch of hooves in snow, the thin complaints of cold saddle leather, and the occasional scold of a jay. It was so quiet, in fact, that after a few minutes he took a quick look behind to make sure Charity was still on her horse.

She was. She sat stiffly upright. Her arms were folded across her chest, and she looked mad enough to bite off his head. He wondered how anybody that intent on glowering could still manage to look so pretty. If she'd been any girl but Charity Caine, he would have told her so. Instead, having been caught looking, he said, "Let's rest the horses and eat. It's about noon."

He reined in his horse and dismounted. Without any guidance from Charity, Number Ten had stopped as well, but she didn't dismount. She stayed in the saddle, glaring.

He unhooked the heavy food bag from her saddle horn and opened it eagerly. She had made johnnycake for breakfast, and he knew she'd fried up the extra batter into corn sticks. "If you're not going to eat," he said, avoiding direct eye contact in hopes of keeping at least a temporary peace, "you might want to get off your horse. Loosen his girth for a few minutes."

He heard her dismount, but she still didn't speak. *Fine,* he thought. *Let her sulk. It's better than yelling.* He found the packet of fried corn sticks and opened it. His stomach rumbled.

He lifted out a stick and bit into it, then held the packet out as he rose. "Sure you don't want—"

She had the Henry, and she was pointing it at him.

"You son of a bitch! You're the law! Don't bother to lie to me anymore, Mr. Turlow. Oh, excuse me. That should be *Marshal* Turlow, shouldn't it?"

He straightened. *Idiot!* he reproached himself. *You let your guard down.*

She was mad, all right: her breath was coming in short, shallow, angry spurts, her eyes were dilated with rage, and her face was flushed. Fury radiated from her in almost palpable waves, and he knew she was so completely immersed in anger that she was on the brink of hysteria.

As calmly as he could, he said, "Put the rifle back, Charity."

She didn't move. "You lied."

"No, I didn't. I never told you I *wasn't* a Marshal. And, if you'll remember, I told you Sam Briscoe wasn't the law. That badge he showed you belonged to my best friend, Rex Jeffords. I told you that, too. Briscoe stole it after Duval's boys ambushed us."

"There's no five thousand in train loot, either, is there?"

"Oh, there's five thousand, all right. Or there was. But Duval's boys stole it, not me. Probably already divvied up and spent most of it." He paused, waiting for her to say something. When she didn't, he added, softly, "Charity, I'm not your enemy. I'm sorry you got into this, but all I'm trying to do now is get you out in one piece. You've got to believe that."

She was still pointing the rifle's muzzle at his chest. She didn't say a word. She didn't look like she planned to.

"If you're going to shoot me," he bluffed, "go ahead and do it." He kept his voice as level as he could. "But remember, Charity, I'm your best chance to get out alive. If Duval's gang catches you, they won't care that you got into this by accident. They won't care that you're a Caine. All they'll care about is that you're a female, and after they've finished with you, they'll . . ."

It hurt him to think about it, hurt him to say it out loud, hurt him more than this wild, whiskey-eyed girl could imagine. Unbidden, a picture of Laura, the way he'd found her, came into his mind. It was too horrible to bear, and he pushed it aside. What replaced it was an image of those fat, swaggering Rooney brothers: filthy, mossy-toothed animals. They'd be back there with Duval. It wasn't going to happen twice. He wouldn't let it.

"And after they're done with you," he managed to say, his voice breaking, "they'll leave you to die."

The rifle's muzzle lowered an inch. Charity's expression softened slightly, and he thought he'd gotten through to her. But then she straightened again.

"I can take care of myself," she spat. "You do whatever you have to do, Marshal. I'm going home. Now ease your pistol clear of the holster — slow — and drop it on the ground."

He did as she asked.

"Kick it away."

He did.

He watched as, keeping the Henry up and against her shoulder with one hand, she reached toward his saddle and slid her shotgun from beneath his packroll. "Aunt Tildy's Colt," she said, once the shotgun was free. "I want that, too."

"In my saddlebag."

She let the shotgun drop to the snow at her

feet. Then, still aiming the Henry, she twisted to fumble with the saddlebag's buckles.

Jake leapt forward, ducking at the same time he swept one arm up and to the side. His forearm hit the barrel just as she pulled the trigger. The rifle went sailing even as the blast of its discharge rang in his ears. He heard a sharp, splintery *crack* as the bullet severed a limb somewhere to his left, and the rapid beat of wings as startled birds took to the air. With a shriek of "No!", Charity bent to bring up the shotgun, but he planted a boot on it first.

She launched herself at him, beating at his face and chest with her gloved fists, cursing wildly and screaming like a catamount.

It seemed to him that she had suddenly grown three extra arms. No matter how he blocked her, she kept landing punches; and although the body blows were muffled by her gloves and his coat, the punches that connected with his face hurt like hell.

He kept trying to block her, trying to push her away, trying to tell her to calm down; but every time he managed to get half a word out of his mouth, she punched him in it. And when she landed an especially effective blow to his nose and he felt hot blood trickle down over his lip, he gave it up.

He hit her just once, square in the jaw.

She stared at him blankly for half a second, and then she collapsed.

He caught her before she hit the ground, and

carried her to her horse. He felt terrible, and not just from the hammering she'd given his face or the throbbing nose which dripped bright blood down his coat front. This girl had likely been slapped around and beaten on a regular basis for most of her life, and he had thought he'd be the one to show her that the rest of the world didn't operate that way: the Caine way. Well, he'd certainly done a good job of it.

As he lifted her and gently slid her across her saddle, belly down, he whispered, "I'm so sorry, honey, so very sorry."

She couldn't know how much.

Chapter Seven

For a moment she thought Grampa Zeb was thumping her in the head again, but then she remembered where she was, and why. Besides, Grampa Zeb had never thumped her so half-heartedly. She opened her eyes and craned her head up. That time the gently swinging stirrup missed her. Snow-patched tree trunks went by on a sick angle; but when she grabbed the stirrup leather and hoisted herself halfway up, the world turned right again.

Jake Turlow was still ahead, leading her along on a rope like so much baggage. And he had hit her! She'd thought she was done with that when she buried Grampa Zeb. Her jaw didn't hurt too much, but she wondered if there was a bruise.

She reached up, grabbed the cantle with her free hand and squirmed, trying to pull her torso over the saddle and swing her legs back at the same time. But she was stiffer than she'd thought, and the coat was too bulky. She only succeeded in shoving herself off Number Ten and landed in the snow, flat on her backside.

Jake whoaed his horse and turned around. "You all right?"

She got to her feet and brushed herself off.

"I said, are you all right, Charity?"

She twisted her features into the most dangerous expression she could muster, and snarled, "As if you care! You're no better than a stinking bounty hunter, and you're not a very smart one at that! Aren't you afraid you'll do yourself out of your blood money by leaving those boys' bodies to freeze out in my yard? Maybe we should go back. Maybe you ought to chop off their heads and haul them back, packed in salt or whiskey so they hold together long enough to get identified. I've heard your sort does that."

"Look, Charity, I—"

"And what do you want me for, anyway? There's no bounty on my head." She slapped crusted snow from her sleeve. "At least not yet."

Jake thumbed up the brim of his hat and crossed his wrists over the saddle horn. "Meaning, I suppose that if I let you near those guns again, there *will* be."

She stuck a foot in Number Ten's stirrup and mounted. "Maybe you're not as stupid as you look."

He didn't answer. He simply turned away from her and nudged his horse back into a walk.

Her satisfaction at having bested him—if only

marginally, and only in conversation—dropped away, and she was left feeling childish. But then, why should she feel that way? He'd practically demolished her home, dragged her out into the cold, frozen center of no man's land, and, for all she knew, raped her in her sleep. *He might be decent-looking,* she thought, *and he might have saved me from that Briscoe man and wooden feet, but if it weren't for him, I wouldn't have that gang* or *the cold to worry about!*

She decided she'd been hasty in trying to use force. In fact, she didn't precisely understand what had come over her. She'd been standing there one minute—scared and mad, but calm enough to remember to get her firearms back—and the next second. . . . When he slapped the rifle from her hands, something else took over: perhaps it had been simple overexcitement, or perhaps it was finally her Caine blood kicking in. Whatever it was, she hadn't liked it.

She rubbed at her jaw. It was only a little tender, and when she worked it from side to side, it moved just like it always had. There was no permanent damage. She had noticed, however, that the front of Jake Turlow's coat was stained with dark lines of frozen blood. She wondered if she'd done that. She didn't remember its having been there before.

She sighed, and a cloud of steam rose to tickle at the fringe of ice crystals on her eyelashes. She rubbed a gloved hand across her face as a group of chickadees, high overhead, chirped and scolded. "Oh, shut up," she muttered.

She stared at Jake's back. It was clear that she couldn't overpower him, but it was just as clear that she had to get away. He was the law, and that meant he was her adversary. Maybe he *had* been nice to her when she had given him a chance. Maybe he *was* handsome. And maybe he had the most pleasant voice she had ever heard come out of a man. Maybe, this morning, when she had found his hand cupping her breast, she had liked it, just for a second. And when his finger had grazed her nipple, maybe it had felt more wonderful than any other sensation, ever. And maybe she'd never meet anybody else in her whole life with eyes that color: eyes that laughed even when his mouth didn't, but the sort of laugh that was kind and warm and not at your expense . . .

She added up all those "maybes," but even though the list of reasons to go with him was long, the one item on the list of reasons to leave was stronger. *The law is the enemy.* It had been pounded into her over and over, from the time she could understand the words. Lawmen were bad. Lawmen chased your Grampa, hounded your family, killed your uncles.

Grampa Zeb's visage came into her mind. *Don't you never have no truck with the law, Charity Caine, or you'll be sorry.* The belt was in his hand.

She chewed at the inside of her cheek and took stock of her surroundings. The wind had picked up some, and snow was falling softly. Judging by the angle at which the sun's glare cut through the needley branches to the west, she guessed there was about an hour of daylight left. Jake was leading her along the eastern bank of a deeply cut creek bed. It would be two, maybe three strides and one downward jump away for Number Ten. If she could untie the lead rope without Jake noticing, she could vault the creek and be up the other bank before he could wheel his horse.

She nudged Number Ten ahead a bit, so that there was plenty of slack in the rope. Jake would be less likely to notice it dropping to the ground if it was already sagging low.

She pulled off one glove, stuffed it in her pocket, and reached for the rope, which was tied around Number Ten's neck and threaded down through the throat latch and curb strap. She was able to slide the loop about halfway down Number Ten's wooly neck before it caught.

After she paused to blow on her freezing fingers and make certain that Jake wasn't paying her any mind, she began to work at the knot. She had to stop four times to warm her hand, but the knot wasn't tied hard and at last she got it free.

Slowly, keeping an eye on the back of Jake's neck and holding the distance between them, she began to feed the rope forward, through the bridle.

At the moment the frayed end of it slid through Number Ten's curb, she sank her heels into him as hard as she could—which was just about hard enough to get his attention—and reined him sharply to the right. Two long strides took her to the edge of the bank, and when Number Ten leapt straight down to the frozen gravel below, she was ready: leaned hard back in the saddle, her legs stiff in the stirrups, braced.

Number Ten slipped when he landed, and for one horrible second she thought he would fall. But he caught himself, hopped over the creek, and scrambled up the far bank with Charity crouched low and clinging to the saddle horn.

Free! she thought as she urged him toward the trees. *Free!*

Something hit her from the side. She went spinning, her coat flapping about her like a tent in a tornado. Her arms and legs ineffectually jabbed the air for what seemed like forever, and then she hit: face down in a drift.

Slowly, she pushed herself up on all fours, clambered to her feet and wiped at her face.

"You hurt?"

It was Jake Turlow. He had already caught Number Ten, who must have stopped, she thought, about two strides after she fell. Jake dismounted and waited for an answer.

She didn't give him one.

He finally said, "Sorry to dump you off that

106

way. I was trying to grab for your reins, but Tico slipped just as I pulled even, and we bumped you."

"Who's Tico?"

He looked at her as if she'd just asked who the President of the United States was. "My horse. Who else did you think?"

She crossed her arms and glowered at him.

"I guess you're not hurt, then," he said. He gathered up the rope that trailed from Tico's saddle horn, then took a small knife from his pocket and opened it. As he began to cut off the last yard of rope, he said, "We were going to have to cross the creek pretty soon here, anyway. Course, I'd planned on waiting for the ford . . ."

He gave a final sawing tug to the rope and put his knife away. "All right," he said. "Give me your wrists."

"I will not!"

"Lady, I've had it with you. I'm cold and I'm tired. If you had any sense, you would be, too. It's only about another half hour to Tink Maynard's place, and I don't intend to be shot at — or run away from — anymore today. If you make me, I'll get the handcuffs out. But I warn you: that cold metal's going to be a lot more uncomfortable than this nice soft rope."

She hid her hands behind her back. "Just leave me here! Just go away and leave me alone!"

He grabbed her arm and quickly looped the

rope around her wrist. She tried to fight him, but he was stronger and this time she didn't have the advantage of surprise or the strength of hysteria. In the end she let him tie her hands before her and boost her back on her horse.

Tink Maynard wasn't at home. His cabin was built in the shelter of a small bluff, and looked long-deserted. The log walls were tightly chinked against the weather, though, and when Jake started a fire in the hearth, the flue was clear.

"You stay put," he said as he went to the door. "I'm going to take the horses down to the shed and settle them in."

Charity, who had refused to speak to him since they left the creek, extended her bound hands.

Jake shook his head. "No. Just sit down and wait."

The moment he closed the door, she tugged her gloves off with her teeth and went to the cabin's dusty little cupboard. *There has to be a knife,* she thought, although her thoughts leaned harder toward freeing herself than any damage she might do to Jake Turlow.

But the cupboard shelves contained nothing more than two dented cans of tomatoes and a few cobwebbed, empty pots. She went back to the center of the room, sat down, and looked about her.

The log house was barely fourteen feet

square. At its center sat a scarred table and two straight-backed chairs. The table's frayed and chipped edges looked to have been used for a good bit of idle whittling. Her saddlebags and Jake's, as well as the food sack and packrolls, were piled on top of it. There was no use sorting through his saddlebags for Aunt Tildy's Colt. He had removed it and stuck it in his belt before he brought the bags into the house.

Against the windowless rear wall stood the small cupboard and a makeshift cooking area, with a work counter, tin basin, and two rickety wooden shelves. A frayed curtain was hung at an angle across one corner, marking off a tiny privacy area. At least, that was what she assumed it was. She could see the spider-webbed edge of what looked like what Grampa Zeb had called a thunder mug, and what Aunt Tildy always referred to as "the night convenience."

To her right was the fireplace. It was small, but it would warm a cabin of this size with no trouble. The empty gun rack above its mantel was cobwebbed, as was the wide, worn rocking chair at its foot. Before her was the front door, bracketed with two tiny shuttered and barred windows.

The bed was to her left. It was a good wide one: perhaps not so big as Grampa Zeb's, but big enough to sprawl in. She wondered what kind of mattress it had. She had a cornhusk mattress at home, and she supposed it was comfortable enough. But Grampa Zeb had the goosedown mattress, and Lord help anyone who so much as thought about sitting on it. She would like to have slept on a feather bed, just once.

She was about to go and poke it, just to see what kind it was, when the door banged open and Jake strode in with an armload of firewood. He dropped it into the bin beside the hearth, then went back, reached around the corner and produced his rifle as well as her Henry and shotgun. "Don't get excited," he said. "I unloaded them." He barred the door.

"Snow's really coming down," he said, taking off his gloves. "That's good news for us. And don't worry about the horses. That shed is good and tight, and it'll warm up in a hurry with the both of them in there." He dropped his hat on the table, and unwound the muffler from his neck. "Hungry?"

"Untie me."

"Not yet," he said with a smile, and she wanted to slap him. "Not until I have every gun and knife and potential bludgeon in this house nailed down, Miss Caine. Is it all right to call you that? Miss Caine?"

She snorted and turned away.

"I guess not," he said, and picked up the food bag. "All right then, Charity, what all have you got in here?" He carried it to the counter top and carefully tipped out its contents. "Venison? Looks like venison, anyhow. And canned potatoes? And peas? Miracle those jars aren't

110

broken. Let's see . . . salt, sugar, tea, flour, cornmeal, hominy. . . . Good Lord. No wonder this thing weighs a ton!"

"Are you enjoying yourself?" she sniffed.

"Certainly," he replied with a grin. His dimples cut deeply into his cheeks. "Aren't you?"

Even though he had practically kidnapped her, even though he had tied her up and refused to untie her, his grin was so warmly teasing and, well, *affectionate,* that she felt herself starting to smile. Hot color rose in her cheeks. She turned her head away and bit at her lip.

When she dared to look at him again, his back was to her and he was merrily banging skillets and pots. "This venison is hard as a rock at the center, Charity."

She heard a knife: *chop, chop, chop* on the counter.

"I'm going to carve off the outside and simmer it up in a little stew and leave the rest out to thaw. We'll cook it in the morning and have it for the trail."

She heard the slushy *plops* as he dumped the half-frozen contents of a canning jar into the pot. "Sound good?" Without waiting for an answer, he said, "Yes, I thought it would. You getting warm, honey? I am."

He turned toward her and pointed with a wooden spoon. "Your coat, I mean."

In truth, the little fireplace did an admirable job of warming the cabin. Between her coat and the multiple layers of clothing beneath, she was beginning to perspire.

"I'm hot," she said, and held her wrists up again.

He shook his head, although he kept smiling. "Not yet. But we can ease up the situation a little, I think."

He gave a last stir to the pot, carried it to the hearth, and hung it over the fire before he shucked out of his own coat and draped it over a chair. Then he knelt before her. His fingers went to her neck, and she flinched.

He pulled back, his brow furrowing for a moment. "The button," he said, and brought his hands up again, this time more slowly.

He freed the four big buttons on her coat front, and then, as she angled her arms up and out of the way, opened her coat as far as it would go. And all she could think of the whole time was that he might accidently brush his arm against her breast. She was hoping he would. She wanted to know if it would feel the same as it had that morning.

But he didn't, although it seemed to her that he knelt in front of her a little longer than was necessary, and that, just before he stood up, his last look into her eyes was a little more lingering than she had expected. And when he at last got back to his feet, he cleared his throat a bit too gruffly.

He looks embarrassed, she thought, when he turned his back on her and made a point of stirring the stew a great deal longer than was necessary. *Now isn't that the strangest thing?*

By the time their dinner was ready, Jake had melted enough snow to make a pot of tea, a bucket of wash water for them and another of drinking water for the horses, which he carried down to the shed. When he came back up the hill and entered the cabin, it was too dark to see much of the outside world but, by the amount of powder on his hat and coat, she knew it must be snowing briskly.

She was grateful for the blast of cold air that came in with him. She was still bound, and so warm that the sweat trickled down her temples and her clothes were plastered to her back.

Jake shucked out of his coat and ladled stew onto two plates. He slid one in front of her, along with a fork and a mug of hot tea.

"Eat up," he said.

Once again, she held up her wrists.

"Oh," he said. "Just a minute." He pulled her Colt from his belt, unloaded it and stuck the cartridges in his shirt pocket before he laid the pistol on the table. "There. The only loaded gun in this place is the one in my holster, Charity. It'd be pretty silly of you to try and get it away from me, wouldn't it?"

A bead of sweat trickled down to the tip of her nose and hung there. She growled, "Just untie me."

Smiling gently, he began to work at the knots, muttering, "Nag, nag, nag . . ."

When he freed the last one, she jerked her hands away, tossed the rope aside and rubbed at her arms.

"And what do we say?" He was teasing again.

As much as she might have liked to go along with it, as much as she had always wanted someone to tease her and do for her and smile at her and worry over her, she said, "Shut up."

His face fell, and she immediately wished she could take the words back. Despite everything he'd put her through in the last two days, he'd been nicer to her than anyone she'd ever known. But every time she opened her mouth, Grampa Zeb's nasty old ghost seemed to be speaking through it. Sighing, she shrugged out of her coat, thankful to be rid of its hot bulk. She lifted a forkful of stew and put it in her mouth.

"Good," she mumbled, surprised.

Jake didn't smile back this time. He said, "Maybe I should avoid talking to you altogether and just cook. And why don't you get rid of those extra layers. You're sweated through." His eyes went back to his plate.

She stood up and quickly peeled down to the final shirt and trousers. She would have liked to be shed of those, too, as they, and especially the longjohns beneath, were sodden with perspiration. Maybe after she ate she could go behind the curtain and change. She wondered if he'd let her. Maybe he'd be afraid she'd try to bang him over the head with the chamber pot. For a moment, she actually considered it, but decided it was likely too heavy. And besides, she was too tired to run away tonight. Maybe in the morning.

"More?"

Without realizing it, she had scraped her plate clean. "No. I want to change my clothes."

He smiled and leaned back, crossing his arms over his chest. "Sure. Go right ahead."

She frowned at him and poked her thumb toward the curtain. "Back there."

Feigning disappointment, he said, "Oh, all right. But what do you plan to change into?" He reached over and sorted through the pile of damp clothing she'd left on the rocking chair. "You bring anything else?"

She had to think for a moment. It seemed like weeks since she'd hurriedly packed and fled into the night. "Two extra shirts, a pair of britches, and a nightgown." She didn't mention the spare Union suit.

Jake nodded and handed over her little satchel. "I vote for the nightgown," he said. "Going to be plenty warm in here. You can take the bucket along and wash up, if you want. You probably feel pretty sticky."

She considered it. It didn't seem quite right, wearing a nightgown—right out in the light and everything—in front of a man who was practically a stranger. But then, he'd already slept under the same cover with her when she was buck naked. Wearing a nightgown in his presence seemed fairly tame after that, especially considering where she'd found his hand when she woke up.

She pulled out the gown and unfolded it, fingering its coarse, flour-sack fabric. It was the closest thing she had to a dress. For a moment she thought that maybe she could pretend it really *was* a dress, and that Grampa Zeb had let her go away to boarding school all those years ago, and that she was a real lady who wore pretty clothes and sat in front of the evening fire with her husband: a husband who didn't curse her when the supper was five minutes late, or hit her for humming while she worked. A lady who never had to worry about being a Caine.

"All right," she said and, clutching the nightgown, went behind the curtain and pulled it closed.

She heard him moving around out there, and when she emerged, washed and feeling fresh in a clean gown, she found him draping her damp things over the chairs and mantel.

He stared at her for a moment, swallowed hard, then wordlessly took the clothes from her arm and hung them with the rest. "Won't take but a few minutes to dry," he said finally. He picked up the rope again. Softly, he said, "Wrists."

"But—"

"I want to get cleaned up, too."

She took handfuls of her nightgown and held it wide. "You think I'm going to try and run away through a blizzard in this?"

"Maybe not," he said, and took her arm. "But there are too many things around here for an inventive gal like you to whack me over the head with. I'd like to shave in peace, if you don't mind."

Hands tied again, Charity perched on the edge of the bed, which she decided, with some disappointment, was probably mattressed with a cornhusk pad. Jake had gone behind the curtain, but she caught glimpses of his shoulder and arm as he undressed. When he unwrapped his chest bandage, it fluttered to the floor like a wilted ribbon.

He was humming. It was a nice sound. She closed her eyes and scootched farther back on the bed. She opened her eyes again. Whoever stuffed the mattress had been a miser with his cornhusks. She hopped down and started toward the table.

The curtain jerked to the side and Jake's head popped out. "What are you doing out there?"

Charity snatched up her fur coat and sniffed, "I have a cannon hidden under the table, and I was just aiming it at you."

He stared at her for a second, then grunted and tugged the curtain back into place.

As she dragged the coat back to the bed and clumsily began to arrange it, she could hear Jake splashing water and humming. She sat

117

down again, more comfortably this time, and tried to rekindle the image of herself as a fine lady who wore dresses and played the pianoforte and slept on a soft mattress. And who didn't have a rope tied round her wrists.

"Your grampa," he said from behind the drape. "I noticed he put that little wolf's head mark of his on the underside of your saddle. Burned right into the saddle tree. Didn't notice it until tonight. It's carved into all your firearms, too."

She didn't reply.

"I suppose he carved or burned it into everything he owned."

Her head jerked up. Automatically, she tried to clasp her own forearm, but the ropes made it impossible. Damn him, anyway. "Are you asking if he branded it on me, too?" The venom in her own voice surprised her.

There was a pause, and then he muttered, "No. I . . . never mind. Just trying to make conversation."

He sounded hurt, and she wished she hadn't snapped at him. If their roles had been reversed and he had tried to kill her, she would have done worse than punch him in the jaw and tie him up. He had actually been incredibly patient with her, she supposed, and gentle: more gentle than anyone else would have been, especially Grampa Zeb. And he couldn't possibly have known about that business with the wolf's head, and how Grampa Zeb had gotten drunk and. . . . *No,* she thought. *He's trying his best to be nice. I suppose, the way he sees it, he's doing right by me. He's dead wrong, of course. He should have just left me be. But I'm here. I can't go anyplace tonight. So I might's well try to act like a civilized lady.*

At last he emerged, dressed in a clean pair of britches and nothing else. He had shaved, and was just tucking a folded straight razor and a small mirror into his saddlebag, which he dropped on the floor along with his dirty clothes.

He began to untie her hands. He smelled like soap and fresh air, and as he loosened the knots and slid the rope away, she stared at his damp, pelted chest. Somehow he seemed much bigger than he had before. She wanted to slither her fingers through all that reddish fur.

"Good girl," he said when he stood up, the rope dangling in his hand.

"You talk to me like I was a bitch pup," she snapped, immediately wishing she could take it back. All those good intentions, and she couldn't say one nice word.

He sighed and shook his head. "Look, I'm sorry, okay? I'm sorry for everything. I'm sorry Duval's men followed me to your house. I'm sorry you got shot at. I'm sorry I had to drag you along with me." He paused, and a smile teased at one corner of his mouth. "I'm sorry the sun came up this morning, okay? Blizzards, tornados, the fall of the Roman Empire, Sher-

119

man's march to the sea, flash floods, hurricanes, those little brown mealy bugs that get in the flour—all my personal fault. I apologize. I beg your pardon. *Mea culpa*. Enough?"

She knew he meant it. His eyes were sincere, despite his teasing tone and the fact that those dimples were deepening into his cheeks. She wanted to press herself against his chest, to feel his arms about her. She had a sudden yen to kiss his shoulder. She wanted to say something sweet, something homely, something that might trip from the tongue of a lady in a dress: something like *Certainly, Jacob, your apology is accepted,* but what came out was, "You can go to the devil."

With a snarled, "Jesus!" he hurled the rope to the floor. His eyes, so direct and ingratiating seconds before, were suddenly narrowed, the last shred of gentle humor gone. "Do you think I like dragging you all over the Nations? Do you think it makes my chances any better, having to stop every five minutes so you can take a shot at me or go for a canter? You seem to think this is a game, Charity. It's not. I don't play games with my life. Or anybody else's. Not even yours."

The anger she had tried so hard to wall away suddenly broke through to smother every other emotion. She jumped to her feet, not caring if he hit her for it. "Not even mine? Not even a lowly Caine?"

"Christ. Charity, I didn't mean—"

He put a hand out, but she slapped it away.

"I know exactly what you meant. You'd save me like you'd save a cur dog. That's all the Caines are to you lawmen—vermin and trash. Well, you're *less* than vermin to us! Less than trash!"

He took a step closer. "Charity, I—"

"You go around killing people's relatives or throwing them in prison to rot, and who's left to mourn over it? Nobody but me, and now you've got me, too! What're you going to do with me if we get to Fort Smith? Toss me in jail on some trumped up charge? Hang me for the hell of it, so you can brag to all your lawmen buddies that you put an end to the Caines forever?"

He reached to take her shoulder. She shoved his arm away.

"Don't! I don't want you touching me! I don't want to wear dresses for you! I don't want to kiss your shoulders! You're the law and I hate you!"

She slapped him across the face as hard as she could. And when he didn't respond, when he only stood there staring, his hands balled into fists at his sides, she slapped him again. "Bastard!" she cried, too angry to wonder why he didn't hit her back. "Filthy murdering low-life skulking bastards, the lot of you!"

Her hand came up to slap him again, but this time he caught her arm and held it. And when,

121

with a squeal of rage, she swung at him with the other, he caught it, too.

She stood, captured: her arms held fast and out to the sides; her breath coming in short, sharp bursts; adrenaline flooding though her. She didn't notice that his breath, too, had quickened, and that the line of his mouth was set in a peculiar and determined fashion. But she did notice, in that split second, that his eyes were the color of sky and wind.

"I hate you," she breathed.

"No, you don't," he said, and kissed her.

Chapter Eight

She twisted against him ineffectually, his hands holding her struggles down to wriggling squirms. His mouth covered hers, holding back her protests.

The kiss was in no way brutal, the way she had always suspected kissing might be. It was soft and warm, and his lips were firm but pliant against hers. She found herself forgetting to fight, forgetting he was her enemy. And when he released her arms and pulled her close, only one last breathy "no" escaped her before she molded her body to his. Unbidden, her fingers rose to his shoulders, then higher to touch the thick curls at the back of his neck. His arms came about her, his hands traveling her nightgowned body as his lips learned her face, pressed softly against her eyelids, her temples, and brushed greedy, possessive kisses over her brow.

She sought his mouth this time, hungrily; not really understanding where all this was leading, and not caring. Somehow, her anger had been transmuted into something more consuming and compelling than any rage.

His hands were in her hair, then floating down her back, then sweeping over her hips in firm, lazy circles. The pressure and heat of his hands, transmitted through the fabric, seemed to sizzle her skin. And when she felt the tip of his tongue dart between her lips, the unexpected intimacy of it made her dizzy.

She swayed in his arms as new and increasingly wonderful sensations fluttered and burned through her body in a fevered confusion. Her skin tingled everywhere their bodies met, caught fire everywhere he touched her. She forgot where she was and why. She forgot that she had ever tried to escape from this man, that she had ever *wanted* to escape.

And when he at last lifted the gown over her head and tossed it aside, she shivered: not from cold, but from the strange thrill of her own nakedness and the heat of her need.

He scooped her into his arms, hugging her briefly against his chest and kissing her again, deeply, before he gently settled her on the bed's edge and knelt before her. Her arms were around his neck, her forearms resting on those wide, strong shoulders as his knuckles stroked her cheek, her hair, and skimmed tingles up and down her throat. Her fingers laced through his hair, soft and thick and wavy, as he delicately traced the concavities of her collarbones, then feathered warm gooseflesh across her shoulders. With his palm, he rubbed a slow circle over the upturned crown of one breast. She gasped softly and felt herself arch forward, into his hand.

His lips left hers, then, and she heard him whisper, "Charity, oh Charity, so beautiful . . ." He began to trail kisses along the tingling path his hand had traveled. And when he reached her breast, he took the already-tingling nipple into his mouth.

The bliss she had felt before paled beside this new miracle, and she tightened her fingers on the unruly waves at the back of his head, urging him on, demanding more.

Mesmerized by delight, she barely noticed that he was easing her down, gradually turning her to lie back along the fur-covered length of the bed. Her head came to rest upon the pillow, his lips at her breast never ceasing their gift of pleasure, and she whispered, "Yes."

His hand came up to stroke her cheek; and she kissed his wide palm and the pads of his fingers as his lips moved to take the other breast. His fingers trailed down her face, down her throat, briefly captured the nipple his mouth had already warmed and moistened, then slipped lower to slowly glide down the length of her body. Down her side it traveled, warm and strong and so large, the fingers moving, stroking, massaging, leaving heated gooseflesh in their wake. Over her belly his hand crept, then outward to cup and cradle the swell of her hip, then lower, to slide like a heated whisper along her thigh.

"Oh," she breathed, the sound half-catching in her throat as his lips returned to hers. Her arms went round him to discover the taut muscles of

125

his back and commit to memory the tensed, uncompromising angles of his torso. His body was so solid, so sleek, so lean. His skin smelled faintly of soap and something wonderfully alien and male, and felt like hot satin stretched over fluid steel.

As she explored him, she felt his hand slowly slip to the inside of her thigh, then up along its tender inner surface. His kiss deepened at the precise moment that his fingers touched her where, without knowing it, she had most wanted to be touched. Her hand moved to cover his just as he parted her to pet a place so secret and so sensitive that, for Charity, the rest of the world ceased to exist.

"Jake," she whispered thickly, "Jake."

"I know," he murmured as he took her lips again.

He ached to be inside her, loving her, and it required all the control he owned to keep the pace slow for her sake. He knew she needed him as badly as he needed her, and he also knew he couldn't hold back much longer: but he wanted to make certain she was completely prepared. She had been hurt enough: by her family, by the world, and by him. He would not hurt her again.

Gently, as her hand still rode upon his, he slipped his finger more deeply within. She was wet silk, and when she gasped and raised her hips to meet his hand, he knew it was time.

He undressed quickly, fumbling with his buttons as he looked down at her: her hair fanned darkly across the pillow, her lips slightly swollen, barely parted. Her posture was at once languid and expectant, and her half-lidded eyes were filled with wonder and unashamed desire. The firelight danced over her skin with the intimacy of a lover, playing flickering shadows over the silky, sculptured tautness of her face and throat, the lush, darkly tipped globes of her breasts, and the gentle swell of her hips; Jake found he was almost jealous of the light.

As he lay beside her on the fur and kissed her again, he felt her fingers skim down his side, over his hip, then between their bodies. Tentatively at first, then rather brazenly, she took him into her hand. He was surprised but delighted, more so when she gasped, then murmured a throaty, "So big . . ."

But the sensation of her hand upon him, the simple fact of her fingers curled about him, motionless, was more than he could bear. He moved over her and pressed his knee between hers.

Charity clutched at him. For her, there was no storm, no cabin, no world: there was only Jake, only this moment. His hardness strained against her fingers and nudged her belly, and the thick curls on his chest teased her aching nipples. As he hovered above, his eyes locked to hers, she raised one knee and slowly slid her thigh up to his hip, the coarse fur on his leg tickling and gently abrading her sensitive skin.

"Honey?" she heard him whisper, his head down, his lips at her ear. "Honey, you have to let go."

When she realized what he meant, she reluctantly uncurled her fingers, and as she drew her arm from between them and wrapped it about his torso, he dipped his head to kiss her again. As their lips met, she felt him part her to position himself.

When he slowly entered, she gasped with both joy and surprise: joy at the ripples of tingling heat that emanated from his slightest shifting movement; surprise that she had never known, until this moment, that she was so empty.

He rocked within her with steady, shallow, almost hesitant motions, kissing her face and throat all the while, whispering her name, telling her that she was beautiful and perfect and that he loved her, that he would always love her. And she believed: believed every word, every syllable, every breath and touch. And then his words became as much a blur as the rest of her surroundings. Heat and texture and scent and flickering firelight combined into one mysterious and swiftly intensifying sensual whole.

And just when she thought she could bear no more and would surely perish from joy, he drove forward to fill her completely, perfectly. There was a tiny stab of pain, immediately swept from memory by a rushing wave of sensation that lifted her so high she thought she might touch the angels.

Sated, Charity drowsed in his arms, her eyes veiled. Jake cradled her protectively, whispering kisses over her brow. He had never known another woman to respond to him quite as Charity had. Not that he hadn't had plenty of others, and not that they hadn't been pleased with the proceedings; but there had been no artifice in Charity's responses, none of those silly social games that he'd found women insisted on carrying with them, even to the bedroom. But not Charity: she had been all instinct and honesty and unabashed heat. He pulled a stray tendril of silky black hair away from her face, then dropped his fingers to her mouth, tracing a tiny scar below her parted lips before he kissed it.

He no longer cared that she was a Caine. She had a temper, all right, but she wasn't crazy. She was a passionate woman in all respects: passionate in her loyalties and her anger, and now passionate in love. In her, he had decided, her clan's madness had been transmuted to something else—something fiery and quick to flare, granted, but something wholly sane. And wholly desirable.

He had hoped she was a virgin, and been gratified when he saw the twinge of discomfort flicker across her face. It wasn't that he took pleasure in causing her pain, or even that he had needed to be her first: he would have wanted her if he had been the second or the twentieth or the one-hundredth. But he was glad no one had hurt her in that way. She'd been shut up with her grandfather for years, and from what he knew of the Caines, there was no sort of sick mischief beneath them. He kissed Charity's temple and rested his forehead against hers. *Thank God old*

Zeb drew the line at that, he thought.

Charity stirred, and he cuddled her a bit closer. "You all right, sweetheart?" he whispered. "Cold?"

She snuggled against his chest. "What you . . . what you said. That you . . . did you mean that?" She bit at her lip and dropped her gaze, and looked, at that moment, very much like a little girl.

He gave her a squeeze and rubbed her back, then let his hand come to rest on her fanny. "Yes, I did, every word," he said, quite seriously. "And the Spanish Inquisition was my fault, too."

She smiled and colored a bit, then ducked her head. "No. No, I mean . . . you said you—you loved . . ." Barely a whisper, with a tiny squeak at the end.

Gently, he lifted her chin until her eyes met his. "I do, Charity. Despite the fact that you keep waving guns at me."

A grin, totally open, bloomed on her face. It was the most beautiful smile he'd ever seen. And then, quite suddenly, she blushed hotly.

"What's that for?" he said, brushing her cheek with his thumb.

"I was so stupid," she said softly. "The other night, at the cave. When I woke up and your hand was on my, uh . . . I thought that during the night, while I was asleep, you . . ." She flushed again and looked down.

It took a moment before it dawned on him. "You thought I—" He was taken by a sudden urge to laugh out loud, but he managed to hold it down to a soft chuckle. "Charity darlin', when I make love to a lady, she knows she's been made love to." He chuckled again. "Least, I hope so!"

She smiled, her face still tucked against his chest. "I'm sorry I was so snippy with you. Earlier."

He grinned. "Which time?"

She dropped one arm and, her smiling face still tucked against his chest, gave him a half-hearted punch in the side. He gave her a squeeze. "Ouch!"

She looked up, grinning devilishly. "I mean, when you asked me about Grampa Zeb. His mark." The grin faded. "You were right. He put it on everything. When I was seven, he . . . he . . ." She shivered.

Jake's breath caught in his throat and he held Charity tighter as a sick picture came into his mind: Zeb Caine, burning that damned mark of his onto a little girl, a tiny seven-year-old girl who couldn't get away, who could never hope to escape from a three-hundred pound devil. "Oh, honey," he breathed. "You don't have to tell —"

She shook her head. "No, it's all right. Aunt Tildy saved me. He was drunk and he had a bottle of ink and a sewing needle, and I fought him so bad he finally tied me up and stretched my arm across the table. That's where he was going to put it. But Aunt Tildy heard the ruckus and she hit him over the head with a poker."

She smiled again, faintly. "Bent the poker. When you asked if he marked everything, it made me remember that. It made me mad. It made me

131

feel sort of . . . I don't know. Helpless. And kind of ashamed. I don't know why. But that made me mad, too, and then everything you said made me madder."

He smoothed her hair. Was it possible that she had grown more beautiful within just the last few minutes? "I'm sorry," he said, and rubbed her fanny. "Not mad anymore, I take it?"

"Not even slightly."

"Or helpless?" He brushed his lips over her forehead. "I, for one, Miss Caine, am at your mercy."

"Not helpless, either. Although I'd feel better about it if you'd at least pretend to suffer a little more." Beneath his arm, she sighed. "I'm sorry I called you a bounty hunter, too. I guess if those polecats had killed *my* friends and then tried to kill me, too, that I'd feel pretty good about collecting the rewards on them."

He rubbed her back. "I won't be keeping the money for those boys, Charity. Don't get me wrong. I've put in vouchers for a few in my time. But those men back at your house, and any other of Duval's gang that I can round up when I bring a new posse out? That money goes to the families of the men they murdered."

After a moment, she looked up, her eyes shining. "I think I believe you. No, I know I do."

She kissed him.

This time their loving was slow—a gentle, unending waltz danced by partners born to move together in perfect synchronization. Her body was poetry and fire and music all at once, and he

132

covered her in kisses. He nibbled at her collarbones, suckled at her earlobes. With his tongue he ringed her nipples, dark pink flushed to deep rose, and nuzzled at the plump undersides of her breasts before she took his face in her hands and brought him back to her lips.

Her arms were about him, her hands ranging his back and shoulders as kisses and murmurs and sighs mingled with the soft pops and crackles of the fire.

They shifted on the mattress, slowly, without being conscious of the movement. First they lay side by side, stroking, petting; and then she sprawled atop him, her breasts pillowed on his chest, her fingers in his hair, as his hands swept over her back and buttocks, and then slid between their bodies to touch her.

Quite naturally, she brought her knees up so that she was crouched above him. And when he positioned himself, she needed no coaxing to ease down and back upon him, sighing softly as she slowly took him into herself.

With a languid, graceful motion she brought herself erect, lacing her fingers though his when he reached out to support her. She began to move—not with greedy rapidity, but sinuously, fluidly. Her hips swirled like lazily eddying water. Her hair swung over her shoulders, curtaining then revealing her breasts and torso as she swayed: eyes closed, lips parted, as if she moved to the lilt of a snake charmer's flute.

Spellbound, Jake forgot that he was supposed to take the lead, and then he forgot to think entirely. Neither of them had charge of the other, neither ordered their movements or choreographed their rhythms. There was no thought or plot or logic to it. They became as one being, instinct incarnate: loving for the sake of loving as one breathes for the sake of breathing.

And then he was above and she below, neither of them remembering how it came to be, but only conscious that the fiery dance had kindled past any control. Faster and faster they moved, both slick with sweat. Each thrust was met, each nuance answered. Her nails scraped his back, her teeth nipped his shoulder. Tiny primal sounds bubbled at the back of her throat, voicing her pleasure, urging him on. His lips were at her ear, whispering things meant to be words.

And then it happened for both, as one: a dizzying release that washed them clean, made all things new, and left them clinging to one another; still joined and not imagining, at that moment, that they had ever been or could ever be parted.

Chapter Nine

As quietly as she could, Charity fed another log to the dying fire and prodded it toward the back of the grate. Jake was sleeping soundly — so soundly, in fact, that he barely stirred when she slipped from his arms. She didn't know what time it was, but she knew it was early, for no light peeped through the tiny cracks in the door to announce the dawn. But she felt rested and terribly alive, and ready for whatever might come next.

Rescuing her nightdress from the floor, she dropped it over her head, then began to fold the clothes she'd already plucked from the chairs and mantel. She piled them on the table before she eased into a chair, one leg tucked beneath her.

As the flames crackled softly behind her, she watched their warm, wavering light bathe Jake's face and body. He was quite beautiful, if a man could be called that. Days before, when he had been hurt and unconscious and tucked into Grampa Zeb's feather bed, she had seen his body many times. At least, she'd seen portions of it as

135

she shifted the linens to wash him or change his bedding. But during those days he had seemed less a person and more a series of body parts that had to be bathed and bandaged and rearranged to prevent bedsores. There had been neither the time nor the inclination to observe him as an object of either art or desire.

It seemed to her a luxurious thing to sit in the warmth of the fire and gaze at him, naked and sprawled, the most perfect of animals. The warm light washed over him, casting shadows—now deep and dramatic, now ebbing and subtle—over the sculpted ridges and valleys of his body. He slept on his stomach, his head pillowed on one forearm. She watched the light lave shades of gold and pale orange over his broad back and the solid swell of his buttocks and thighs, their hard potential relaxed in slumber.

With her eyes she learned him, this strange and exotic man-beast. She memorized the curve and knit of his muscles as they tucked toward the creased center of his back. She studied the swelling bell of his biceps when he moved his arm slightly. The subtle shadows of his ribs where muscle wrapped them; the thick curve of his calves, covered in a haze of reddish-brown fur; his hands, massive and delicate all at once: all this she learned.

He had said he loved her.

A warm shiver ran through her, and she hugged herself. Love. The most beautiful of words. One she had never expected to hear from anyone, one which she would never have dreamed would come from the lips of an officer of the law. It went against everything she had been told, everything Grampa Zeb had pounded into her. But Grampa Zeb was dead, and he'd been spiteful and mean, and wrong about so many things: chances were he was wrong about lawmen, too.

It occurred to her that she might even be able to stand a game of chess with Jake Turlow, if he played. *I'll bet he wouldn't try any of that "rook moves double on Ground Hog Day" business on me. I'll bet he wouldn't roll the dice to get his queen back on the board or draw for high card on a rigged deck to break a stalemate. I'll bet he doesn't slide cards up his sleeve at poker, either. I'll bet he doesn't cheat at all, at anything.*

She had always wondered what it might be like to love and be loved. She wasn't really certain she had known, *really* known, what the word meant. But love this must be, for no one had ever made her feel the way Jake Turlow did.

She closed her eyes and, for a brief moment, almost recaptured the way it had felt: the glory of him inside her, of being perfectly joined. But there was more to it than the way her body soared when he touched her. She had come to realize that the rage she had felt toward him was a mask for something just as intense, yet completely different. Yes, he had made her feel things, physically, that she hadn't known were possible — things she was already yearning to feel once more. But she didn't think that was the "love" part; or, at least, it wasn't the core of the matter. No, "love" was what made her want to be

137

near him, to hear his voice and see him smile. It was what made her feel safe and cared-for. The miraculous act of taking of him into her body was what sanctified it somehow, solidified it for them both.

She knew now that she had never really wanted to run away from him. It was her own fear she'd tried to escape: the fear of needing another person, of not being totally self-sufficient and self-contained. But now it seemed she'd passed through that fear, and found it wasn't a frightful thing at all.

He loves me, she thought, and hugged herself again. "And he knew all along I loved him, too," she added in a whisper, when she saw his gun-belt, casually left on the floor and peeking from beneath his saddlebags. *He knew I wouldn't shoot him*. A tiny furrow creased her brow. "Cocky bastard," she muttered, then smiled again. She guessed she liked cocky bastards. Loved them. At least, she loved this particular one.

She sat for another half hour, watching him and feeling, for the first time in her life, fortunate. She had no illusions that he'd marry her. She was a Caine, after all, and he was an officer of the law. He probably had friends in high places and could go anywhere he pleased and fit right in and be respected. She knew all too well that it would ruin him to marry her, and she wouldn't let that happen. But it was all right. The Caines, historically speaking, hadn't much truck with the sanctity of marriage, anyhow. She doubted her parents had been spoken over by any Justice of the Peace, and Aunt Tildy had told her that Grampa Zeb was never legally married to Grandma Sweet Dove, at least in the white sense.

But even if he couldn't marry her, Jake did love her. He had said so, after all; and although he might have left a few things out here and there, he'd never actually lied to her. She had no reason to doubt him. Maybe, after they got to Fort Smith, he would get her a room somewhere and come to visit her. Maybe he'd even take her out in public, to a show or a play. She'd always wanted to see a real play. Maybe he'd teach her to dance.

She shook her head and sighed softly. It was asking too much. Caine women weren't the sort to be admitted to in public. She'd have to settle for private times with him. She would have to be realistic.

The idea of Fort Smith was somewhat frightening to her. What would it be like to carry out her life elbow-to-elbow with so many people? She supposed she would have to find a job of some sort, though not the sort at which Aunt Vena had toiled. Before she went crazy and drank poison, Aunt Vena had been a whore, plain and simple: something upon which the rest of the family made no judgment, moral or otherwise. It had always seemed a rather nebulous profession to Charity. Mentally, she formed pictures of every grown man she had ever seen or met, few though they were, and Jake Turlow was the only one she could imagine making love with. He was certainly the only one she had ever really yearned to be near. And somehow she knew he was the only one whose voice she'd long to hear and whose touch would thrill her. No, she couldn't follow in Aunt Vena's footsteps. Not for all the money in the world.

She supposed that, for Aunt Vena, being a whore had been all right. *But if you love somebody,* Charity thought, *how could you let anybody but him.* . . . She shivered and rubbed down the gooseflesh on her arms. The thought of being with any man but Jake gave her the collywobbles. Perhaps, she decided, if Jake hadn't come along for her, if she had never cared for him, the act of love would never have been special for her. Maybe Aunt Vena had never loved anybody.

Suddenly, she felt more sorry for Aunt Vena than she'd ever felt for anybody.

At last her thoughts returned to planning. Whoring was out of the picture, of course, but she could always be a laundress or a scrub woman. *I suppose I could cook someplace, or wash dishes,* she thought. *Or wait tables.* She doubted any town job she found would be harder labor than that in which she'd so far spent her life.

Jake rolled onto his side, turning his back toward her. She sighed softly. It would be so nice to be something other than a Caine: to be able to marry and live in a house where you could talk to your neighbors across the fence without them spitting on you. Nice to be welcomed at church and be called "Mrs. Turlow," nice to bear children who could go to school and hold their heads proudly. . . . But those were things she couldn't have. She would find a room and get a job, and Jake would come to her two days a week or three, whenever he could. She would cook for him and make love with him and watch him sleep. She would pick flowers and fill her rooms with them, and make the table pretty. She would wear dresses for him and wait for his knock on the door, and she would miss him when he had to be away. But it would be all right. For a Caine woman, it would be the next thing to heaven.

Jake made a sound, a sort of soft grunt, and then he opened his eyes. He smiled at her.

"What're you doing clear over there?"

She went to him and perched on the edge of the bed. "I was chilly. I fed the fire. Did I wake you?"

He lifted her hand and kissed the palm. "Must be six-thirty. Always wake up at six-thirty."

She glanced at the door, searching for slivers of early morning light in its cracks. "I think your clock's off."

He pulled her down, and she snuggled against him. She wished she hadn't put her nightgown back on.

"I may make mistakes about a lot of things," he said, "but I always know when it's six-thirty. Probably because it's my body that knows it and not my head. Give me a kiss."

She gave him one, then two, and then she lost count; and just when she was ready to slither out of her nightdress and climb atop him, he sat up.

"Charity, m'love, as much as I'd like to stay right here in this bed for the rest of my life, we've got to get moving."

"Yes, Jake," she said softly, aching for him but knowing he was right. So much had happened to her in this one night that she had forgotten the reason for their flight. Reluctantly, she got to her feet and tried to think about cooking breakfast.

He was on his feet, too. He followed her to the fireplace, then took her wrist and turned her to face him. "Hey!" he said with a grin, "I sorta expected you to put up at least a little fight!" He kissed her again, at the same time lifting her gown to her waist. Cupping her buttocks, he lifted her off her feet.

Her arms went around his neck and her knees came up to grip his thighs, more to balance herself than in any expectation. And when he lifted her even higher, she slid her legs higher to wrap about his waist.

Their kiss unbroken, he lowered her slightly, tucking her hips toward him, and she felt him nudge against, then enter her. She let out a long, breathy sigh and let her head loll back as he kissed her throat and began, slowly, to slide her up and down upon himself.

She built to her culmination with almost frightening swiftness, and when the release came, she clutched at his shoulders, her nails pressing crescents into his flesh. Just as she slumped against him, he jolted up into her one last time and crushed her to him.

142

Her head was on his shoulder, the damp from her brow mingling with his. She relaxed her legs, but he caught her thighs before she could slide free. He took one step to the chair and sat down, Charity straddling his lap, still impaled.

"You all right, honey?" he said after several long minutes. His hands were beneath her gown, stroking her back.

She kissed his ear and whispered, "I thought you were in a hurry, Marshal Turlow."

He chuckled softly. "I was. Guess you were, too."

She flushed, feeling the color rise in her cheeks, and kissed his shoulder. She was thinking how wonderful it would be to simply spend eternity like this: Jake inside her, already growing hard again; his arms about her, cloaking her in strength and safety and unspoken promises of forever.

He turned his head to kiss her temple, and when she lifted her face he kissed her lips quite sweetly. She could feel him swelling within her, pushing slowly higher as he deepened the kiss, only to break it off.

"This has got to go," he said, and deftly lifted the nightgown over her head and off. "Better," he said. He slipped a hand between them to fondle her breast before he gently rolled the nipple between his fingers.

Her voice throaty and not her own, Charity said, "But shouldn't we be going?" It wasn't that she wanted him to stop, but it seemed to her that someone should say it.

143

"I suppose," he said, rather absently. "But it was snowing like Christmas last night. Our tracks are covered good and deep. We can afford a few extra minutes." He dipped his head and nuzzled the deep V between her breasts. "However," he added with a devilish grin as somehow, in one movement, he managed to stand up and take her with him without breaking their union, "this is absolutely the last time this morning, young lady!"

He laid her across the table, yesterday's clothing for her pillow, and lifted her legs so that her knees were supported by the crooks of his elbows. And then, as she watched every gliding, firelit thrust, he slowly brought her to shuddering fulfillment.

Afterward, there was little time for the cuddling and whispers they both would have liked. Jake dressed quickly as Charity prepared the venison left from the night before. She set the pan on a rack in the fireplace and, humming softly, began to sort through her own clothes. It seemed she couldn't stop smiling.

Jake tugged on his boots and shrugged into his coat. "Smells good," he said. "Hand me my gunbelt?"

She reached into the pile and tugged it free, giving it over before she smiled to herself, marveling at how much things could change in just twenty-four hours.

"Awfully quiet out there," he said as he slung

144

the belt round his waist and threaded the buckle. "Can't hear a lick of wind. And I can't figure why it's so dark. No light coming through the door at all."

She jabbed a fork into the frying venison and turned it. It spat and sizzled. "I told you. I think your clock's off."

He grinned at her. "Impossible. I'll prove it to you." He patted his pockets. "My watch. Must be over there in my other shirt. On the saddlebags."

"I'll get it."

Still smiling softly and humming an odd little tune, she sifted through the clothing until she found the hard shape of it. She turned it over in her hand. It was not an expensive piece. Its un-adorned nickel case was scratched from years of being nestled against coins and other pocket detritus. She'd seen it before, but had never bothered to inspect it. Now she found the catch and popped it open.

"I take it back," she said. "It's fifteen past seven." As she cupped the watch to close it, she noticed a photograph on the inside of the lid. She turned the image toward the light.

It was a young woman. Her face was soft and round and big-eyed. Her light, glossy hair was parted in the middle and coiled at the sides of her head. A faint, teasing smile tugged at the corners of her bow-shaped mouth.

Charity stopped humming. Her smile disappeared. She stared at the image. Who was this woman? Why did he carry her picture? Was this a rival, a wife perhaps?

Her open hand turned to a fist, the watch snapping shut within it. Anger, liquid and volatile, swept through her. She twisted toward him. "Just who the hell—"

Her words were drowned. For, as Jake lifted the crossbar, the door suddenly swung in and knocked him to the floor.

"Jesus!" he shouted as he scrambled his way out from beneath the snow that had avalanched into the cabin.

There was no sky outside, no world. The snow that had tumbled in to fan over the planks accounted for only a pocket in a frigid wall that blocked out the sun.

Jake had already unbuckled his gunbelt and tossed it to the bed. "Damn it," he muttered, pushing his hand experimentally into the white wall. "Of all the lousy timing . . ."

Charity dropped the watch, forgot about it. She stared numbly at the blocked doorway. She felt her mouth move to silently form the word *trapped*.

Chapter Ten

As Jake began to tunnel through the packed snow, Charity made her mind focus on capping the well of her panic. *Do something,* she told herself. *I have to do something or I'll scream.* She made herself move. She dressed quickly, then shoved the table to one side to make room for the snow she scooped out of Jake's way and into the center of the cabin. She paused in this only long enough to feed the fire, and to rescue their belongings from the pool which formed on the cabin floor, and which was draining too slowly through the cracks between the floorboards.

She kept herself moving, laboring, forcing her mind away from the hysteria she felt pushing at the back of her throat and the top of her head. The fire kept them warm enough and kept the snow melting; but not as fast as Jake dug it, or as quickly as Charity pushed it atop the mound. The room was soon centered by a heap of slush several feet high, and within an hour Charity could hardly move around it to tend the fire.

By then it didn't much matter, since they were out of firewood. Jake solved this problem by flipping the table over and snapping off its legs. These he swung against the stone hearth until they splintered into shorter chunks.

"There," he said, handing an armload of broken lengths to Charity before he sat down on the piled snow and mopped at his forehead. Even in the relative cold of the tunnel, he had worked up a sweat. "If those run out before we're clear, we'll toss in the chairs. Wish there was an axe in here."

He stomped the floor with one boot. Cold water, pooled on the floor, splashed up and spattered his face. "Good thing that's a raised hearth," he said.

Charity, bent low and poking the new fuel into place, didn't answer. She had not, in fact, spoken a word since he started the tunnel. She was afraid that if she opened her mouth, she'd scream.

"Honey?" he said. She was still hunched down, her back to him. "Charity? Are you all right?"

She didn't turn, but one hand came up as she braced herself against the mantel. She took a deep breath, tried to choke back the taste of fear. "We're . . . tell me the truth. We're going to die in here, aren't we?"

He went to her and took her in his arms. "Of course not," he said softly. "This is just slowing us up a little, that's all."

She began to sob silently, shaking against him.

"Charity, darlin' . . ."

Choking, she mumbled something into his lapel.

"What, sweetie?"

"We're . . . we're buried alive." She wanted to explain to him about the cellar, and how Grampa Zeb had locked her in it when she was nine and then gotten drunk and forgotten her and left her for two days: alone in the dark and damp, with nothing but her own tears for comfort. But she couldn't form the words. She'd already told him about Grampa Zeb and the tattoo, and he'd looked at her with such sympathy; but it was his love she wanted, not his pity.

But he didn't question her fear. He acted as if it were natural. "It's just a big drift," he said soothingly, and stroked her hair. "Now that I've dug a ways out, I'm going to start angling up higher. I might have to go another ten feet, maybe only two. But we'll get out. It's not all the snow in the world. Though I'll venture it's more snow than the Nations have seen in the last five years put together. This is some kind of March, all right. The damned stuff is packed so tight you'd think an elephant had sat on it." When she didn't stir in his arms, he added softly, "That was supposed to be funny."

She looked up, her face wet with tears she was afraid to explain. "It's just . . . I don't like being shut in."

"Sweetie," he said softly, "you were closed in last night and it didn't bother you."

"But that was different," she sniffed. "I knew I could open the door . . ."

His brow knotted quizzically for just a moment, but then he smiled at her again. "We'll get out, don't you worry. Why don't you build that fire up a little higher. Concentrate on that, and I'll get back to work."

She hugged him tighter, then made herself step back. *I'll get through this,* she thought. *I have to get through this. Jake will make it all right.* "I'll be fine." She intended it to be the truth, but as he turned away she realized she was shaking again. She wished he could chop through the snow and hold her all at the same time. She bent to the fire and tried not to cry.

"Do you hear that?"

On her haunches, she swiveled toward him. Jake was in the doorway, peering intently down the tunnel. Charity stood up, edged around the pile of snow and joined him.

She could hear it, too: the faint, muffled sound of somebody whistling.

Jake's hand was on her shoulder. "Get my gun," he hissed.

She skinnied around the melting heap of snow, grabbed his gunbelt, and tossed it to him.

Just as he caught it, there was a crash and a *thud,* and sunlight broke through, reflecting bright off the white tunnel walls. It flooded the

the change in topic. "We ran across old Thomas Lightfoot and his family on the way."

Tink threw his head back and laughed. "That old reprobate? Say, there's a character for you. Never could stand him. He still got that big Two Turtles woman with him? Now there's a female a man could get to admire. They was by here not too long ago — musta been last spring — and I swan, but that woman do make the best squirrel and kidney bean pie I ever slid lips around. Mended up some shirts a'mine, too, without bein' asked. Don't say much hardly a'tall, but she's got a way with her. Known her since she was a little bit of a mite. Would'a wed her myself, 'cept her daddy sold her off to Lightfoot back in those years when I was trappin' up the Canadian River. Say, I ever tell you 'bout the time me and Red Hawk Mayberry was up the Dog Holler? We come across the biggest — "

Jake held up a hand. "Tink, I'd admire to sit and jaw, but Charity and I are in a fix. Got to head out fast. I've got Claude Duval's boys on my track."

"Well, why didn't you say so?" Tink took the opportunity to climb and slither over the slush to rescue his rocking chair, which was clotted with melting snow. He picked it up and handed it across to Jake. "That Briscoe an' his crew still riding for him?" he added, panting a little.

Jake nodded.

Charity said, "Jake, who is — ?"

"Bad trouble, them boys," Tink broke in. "Sam Briscoe's sharp, even if he is mean as a stove-up badger, but them boys'a his is dumber than dirt and vicious by way of a hobby. I reckon you best get a-movin', then."

Before Charity had a chance to ask about Laura again or mention the picture in the watch, she found herself down at the shed, helping Jake tack up Number Ten and Tico. She also found herself feeling more angry and hurt with every passing minute. She had finally found someone to trust, someone to love. She had made love to him, given him her virginity. She had planned a life with him. Without consulting him, to be sure; but she'd planned it nonetheless. She'd pictured herself dressed in pretty skirts, and arranging flowers on the table for him. Making dinner for him. Making love with him.

Who was this Laura person? Laura! Probably his girlfriend, maybe his wife. *The sonofabitch probably had six kids and a pet dog, too,* she thought; and he'd had the bald-faced audacity to look her in the eye and tell her he loved her!

She'd been so sure he meant it. Her every instinct had told her it was true. But now?

Laura. Maybe Laura wasn't the girl in the watch. Maybe Jake Turlow had a whole string of women. Maybe he told each and every one of them that he loved her, loved only her. But

154

his eyes . . . she hadn't seen a lie in his eyes.

By the time she cinched up Number Ten's girth, she was almost more angry with herself than with Jake. If there had been a lie, it was her fault for not spotting it, for trusting too much. And for still loving him, either way. That—the unshakable fact that she loved him anyway—was the hardest to take.

If he has a wife, she thought, *I'll be his mistress. Maybe that's what he had planned all along. He could be married to Laura and still love me, couldn't he? Maybe Laura is mean to him. Maybe she never loved him. Maybe he never loved her.*

By the time she finished tying her things behind Number Ten's saddle, her movements were less quick, less angry. If Jake had noticed she was upset, he hadn't let on. He even handed back both Old Reliable and Aunt Tildy's Navy Colt, then slid the Henry into her rifle boot without remark, although he paused to give her shoulder a little squeeze. Tink Maynard had plopped his rocker down in the yard and was presently ensconced in it, creaking back and forth in the snow as he watched them load the horses.

"What'd I tell you?" he said. "Not more'n four inches of powder out here, but ain't nothin' to show'a that cabin but the chimbley."

He was right. A huge drift had swept up over it. If it hadn't been for the curl of smoke drawing attention to the topmost chimney stones, one never would have known there was a house there at all.

Jake gave her a boost up on Number Ten. "This isn't good," he said quietly. "I don't know if there was enough snow to cover—"

"Headin' back to Fort Smith, then, would you be?" Tink was on his feet again.

"Fast as we can," Jake replied. As he stepped up on his horse, the cold saddle leather complained loudly.

"Well, if you stop by the Widder Pritchard's give her my best, if she ain't run off again. Woman's always findin' herself some young buck to bundle with. Don't know how she does it. Ain't enough people out here to throw rocks at, but she keeps a'conjurin' up beaus."

Jake evened up his reins. "You sound jealous, Tink," he said with a grin. "And here I thought it was Two Turtles Lightfoot you were admiring."

Charity took a breath. Even if he'd told her God's own truth, even if he really never had loved anyone but her, she still had to ask. Through clenched teeth, she said, "Who's Laura?"

"Ain't jealous over that widder—none a'tall, Jake," Tink remarked loudly, as if she hadn't spoken. He walked toward them.

Behind Tink, across the clearing, she saw a flock of birds rise hurriedly, black against the sky. "Jake?" she said softly, her hand on the butt of Aunt Tildy's Colt. "I think there's—"

156

"Just miss her preserves," Tink went on. "Always used to trade her my fresh-shot game for blackberry preserves. But when she's out gallivantin', I—"

Abruptly, Tink staggered and fell. He hit the ground a half-second before Charity heard the rifle report. She started to dismount, intending to run to Tink, but Jake grabbed her arm. He shoved her back into the saddle, yelled, "Go!" and quirted Number Ten across the rump.

He bolted so quickly she almost went off backwards, but she grabbed the saddle horn in time to catch herself. She hunched low in the saddle, cold wind in her face. She was too stunned to think of reaching for her gun or reining in her horse. She twisted her head as the cracks of a volley of rifle shots reached her ears. Jake closed the distance between them. Tink lay far away in the snow, his rocking chair tipped backwards beside him.

When she screamed, "We can't leave him!" the icy air nearly pushed the words back down her throat.

"He's all right!" Jake yelled. "They don't want him!"

He quirted her horse again. Number Ten picked up new speed, a speed with which Jake's Tico seemed to travel easily.

"Get up the rise!" Jake shouted, and pointed to the trees.

She dug her heels into Number Ten's flanks, wishing she wore spurs but knowing it wouldn't

157

make any difference. She and Jake breasted the slope together and entered the trees. When she risked a glance over her shoulder, she glimpsed Duval's men through the black bars of tree trunks. Seven men had already crossed the clearing and passed Tink, who had pulled himself up on one elbow. They galloped through the snow, closing the distance all the while, firing as they came.

Jake pulled ahead of her. She clung tightly to the saddle horn with one hand as she tried to follow the weaving trail he broke for her between the trees.

The icy wind lashed her face. Her heels beat against Number Ten's ribs, in futile demand of a speed and agility he didn't have. She could tell Jake was holding back so that she could keep up. She forgot about Laura and the watch. She forgot everything, except that she loved him.

She wanted to scream at him to leave her, to veer away, that they should split up so he could save himself. It didn't occur to her that for the first time in her life she had valued another person's safety over her own. She only knew, on some completely visceral level, that if Jake lived, part of her would go on forever.

A bullet-shattered limb crashed down upon her, its black, brittle twigs tangling in Number Ten's fluttering mane. She tore it away and flung it aside, crouching low again.

Please God, she thought frantically, *please let*

us live, please let us be all right. Jake yelled something, but his words were drowned by the whip of wind and the blood pounding in her ears. She wondered why he didn't shoot, and then she realized she was in his line of fire.

Just then she burst from the cover of trees onto a sharply sloped, narrow hill, strewn with boulders and fenced by forest on either side. Jake was already halfway to the crest. His rifle was out, and he was motioning her to hurry.

She kicked Number Ten again, for all the good it did, and headed toward him. He waited until she came even with him, then he yelled, "Get to the top and cut right, toward the rocks!"

She slapped Number Ten with her reins, forcing him to struggle ahead through the deepening snow. Behind her, Jake held his ground, firing down into the trees.

She reached the crest and hauled her horse to the right just in time to avoid blundering off the edge of a cliff. Thirty feet below, the rapids roared.

Jake was moving again, twisting to fire random shots down the hill as Duval's men left the safety of the trees to pursue him. "The rocks!" he called, "Get behind the rocks and get down!"

She saw the place immediately: a high upthrust of stone hugged by boulders, with just enough space between it and the cliff's edge to ride three abreast. She headed for it and was out of her saddle, the Henry in her hand, before Number Ten skidded to a grateful halt.

Charity skittered upward over the slippery stone, tripping over her coat and cursing. Jake was nearly to the hill's crest, but Duval's men were closing quickly. The thin echoes of their rifle reports peppered the frigid air. She ripped off her gloves and raised the Henry, sighting down on the first man in the pack. She squeezed the trigger. It clicked.

"Son of a bitch!" she breathed. He'd given her back her arms, all right, but he hadn't reloaded them and she had never thought to check. She shoved herself backward, sliding, half-falling toward Number Ten and cursing all the while. Just as she reached him and began to fumble with the saddlebags, Jake gained the top of the hill and turned, heading for her at a snow-slowed gallop along the cliff's edge.

She got the buckle free and began to dig hurriedly through the jumble within. Jake was moving closer, but everything seemed so slow. It seemed forever before her fingers curled around the box. She yanked it out, spilling half of them in the snow. As she cracked open the Henry and began to stuff cartridges inside, there was another volley of shots.

Jake wasn't on his horse anymore.

He hung in the air, unsupported, his arms out wide and the deerskin cape fluttering like ragged and broken angel's wings; and then he disappeared over the cliff.

He didn't scream or call out.

She supposed he was already dead.

Tico, riderless, thundered toward her. He was almost upon her before she managed to look away from the empty air where Jake had hovered. Abruptly—and just in time—she held out her arms, waving at Tico to slow him down. As he slid to a stop beside Number Ten, Charity forced herself to move, to shove the cartridge box into her pocket and scramble back up the rocks.

Dead, she thought. *Dead, you bastards. My Jake, my life.* Tears pushed hotly at her eyes, but she blinked them back. By sheer strength of will she forced her limbs to stop shivering. They'd killed him, murdered the only good, decent thing to ever come into her life.

She raised the rifle, seated it against her shoulder. *I'll show you what happens when you mess with a Caine, you murdering vermin.*

Her grief momentarily shoved aside and overtaken by the cold competence of vengeance, she began to fire down the hill. Her second shot knocked one man off his horse, though he was not so badly wounded that he couldn't scramble for cover along with his friends. They fanned out across the slope, shooing their horses away and dropping behind rocks.

She fired toward them ruthlessly, first to the left, then the right, then the center. Sometimes she'd catch a glimpse of a jacket or pantleg as a man moved from one place of concealment to

161

another, and once she heard one let out a yelp when she winged him. Bullets sang past her, chipped at the rocks about her tear-streaked face, stung her cheeks with tiny shards of stone shrapnel. She barely noticed. She meant to kill them all, and never considered that she might fail. It did not cross her mind that she might run out of ammunition before they did and have to run. She was in unfamiliar country, and knew no routes for escape. She didn't care. There was only this moment, this act of revenge. This hatred.

She kept firing.

When she exhausted the box of cartridges, she remembered the ones she'd dropped. She slipped back down to the ground and began to search. The horses' hooves had packed them into the snow and she had to dig, but she quickly rescued enough ammunition to half-fill her pocket. She started up the rocks again, trying to reload the Henry as she scurried. She was nearly into position when hands closed on her shoulders and jerked her off her feet.

The Henry went sailing. She screamed, kicked backward, twisted, tried to turn and scratch or bite or hit.

She heard a voice, coarse and too near, mutter, "Scrappy bitch, ain't you?"

And then something hard connected with the back of her head. There was pain, sharp and bright, and then there was nothing.

Chapter Eleven

Her head felt enormous. Her skull ached and pounded. Blood pulsed hotly at her temples. She realized she was upside down: once again, she'd been thrown over a saddle like a sack of grain. For a split second she was furious with Jake. But then she remembered. Jake was dead. She wanted to be dead, too. It wasn't until she tried to put her hand to her temple that she realized she was bound hand and foot as well.

She didn't open her eyes. She listened first, pushing back her pain and grief as she strained to separate the low tones of conversation from the sounds of travel.

"—do with her?" Someone was saying. The voice was twangy and the words came out slightly garbled, as if spoken around a lipful of tobacco.

"Don't get your hopes up," came the answer. She recognized the speaker. It was the man who had come to her cabin and introduced himself as a marshal. Sam Briscoe. "She's Duval's unless he tells you different. You keep that dinky pecker a'yours to yourself, Wilford."

A shiver swept through Charity as another man, somewhere behind her, laughed. She couldn't make out what he said, but the one called Wilford shot back, "How the hell would you know 'less you been admirin' it, Sam?"

"Know what?"

"How dinky it—"

"Sh-shut up, willya?" Stammered a new voice. "I already g-got enough p-pain with this slug that bitch put in my leg. And I ain't g-gonna make it worse by listenin' to you fiddle-b-brained Rooney boys yammer at each other." He grunted as if he were adjusting his wounded limb, and added, "What you think Duval's gonna do next, Sam? Now that we got T-Turlow outta the way, I mean? Don't see no need to c-cut down into T-Texas now . . ."

Charity had begun to cry, and although she kept her eyelids squeezed tightly together, she knew her tears were spilling down into the snow. *Oh, Jake,* she thought, *Oh, Jake. . . .* The image refused to leave her mind: that horrible split second when he hovered in mid-air above the brink of the cliff. She bit at her lips to hold the sobs in.

Briscoe said, "You been ridin' with us long enough to know there's no tellin' what Duval's gonna do, Arnie. But I can tell you right now that he's not gonna be so glad as you think that Turlow's out of the way. He wanted him alive. Jesus, it seems like that bastard's been doggin' us forever."

164

"He were just stupid," said Wilford. Charity heard him spit before he added, "You'd'a thunk he would'a backed off after me an' Bertie took care'a that gal of his."

"Shut up, Wilford," Arnie snapped. "Ain't g-gonna listen to that story ag-g-g . . . anymore. You Rooneys is nothin' but animals."

Wilford laughed. "You're a fine one to go callin' us names, Arnie. You had you a turn, too. You ain't no angel."

Arnie ignored him. "Mr. Duval's gonna be tickled pink I got him shed of that pesky marshal, you wait and see." There was a short pause before he said, "I believe I'm losin' a lot of blood, Sam. You d-dig this slug outta me when we g-get back?"

Wilford wasn't done yet. He said, "Well, we didn't cut up that yeller-headed gal'a Turlow's that bad. And when we got done, we kilt her clean."

The other Rooney brother, Bertie, said, "She shore did buck some, didn't she Wilford!" and giggled. It was all Charity could do to keep from vomiting.

"Oh she did!" added Wilford with a laugh. "Believe she might'a hurt us if'n we hadn't'a had her bound up s'good. This'n looks even scrappier to me. Never figured Turlow to take himself a breed, though. They's wilder than the full-bloods. Mebbe take three of us to hold her down." Raising his voice slightly, as if he were speaking to someone farther down the line of riders, he said, "How 'bout you, Toots? You want in?"

She heard a grunt, then, "Only if I's first. All you Rooneys has got Cupid's Itch."

"Hell," spat Wilford. "You'll likely get it from her, anyways. She's a breed, ain't she? They's all got it."

A rider had come up even with Charity's horse. She could hear the creak of his stirrup leather a few inches from her ear. She kept her eyes squeezed shut. She knew the rider was the one called Arnie when she heard him, very near, stutter, "Ain't all of 'em g-got it."

She felt him grab her scarf and yank it away. As her hair tumbled down, he took a handful of it and hauled her head up, the angle painful. "She's a looker," he said. "Shame to w-waste her on you Rooney scum. You can have this p-piece'a shit horse'a hers, though, with my blessin'. Looks t'me like he'd make b-better eatin' than ridin'."

In that second, Charity's anger overtook, then smothered her fear. Her eyes popped open. "Ouch! Let go of me, you pig!"

Arnie, a heavily bundled man with crooked teeth and long, coiled tangles of greasy black hair sticking from beneath his misshapen hat, jumped a bit. But he didn't let go. Still holding her head up by the hair, the angle shifting slightly with every step their horses took, he laughed. "B-breed's awake!" he called to the others, before adding, "Feisty little p-piece, ain't you, honey?"

Charity shook her head in an attempt to pull free, but only succeeded in causing herself more discomfort. When she tried to move her bound hands again, she discovered they were not only tied securely to each other, but to Number Ten's girth strap. She couldn't raise them more than a few inches. She jerked again, but her struggle only encouraged Arnie to haul her head even higher. He leaned down, laughing, his face bobbing only inches from hers, his sour breath bringing new tears to her eyes. "You g-gonna wiggle like that when it's my t-turn, Breed?"

Charity craned her neck to the side. She spat in his face.

Immediately, his leer twisted into a furious grimace. He jumped off his horse without bothering to stop it, then yanked Number Ten to a halt. Still holding Charity by the hair, he backhanded her upturned face.

Her mouth was filled with the salty, slightly metallic taste of blood, and she spat at him again. This time her spittle marked him — a dark pink splat dribbled down his stubbly cheek.

"B-bitch!" he barked, and pulled his arm back a second time.

"Hit me again, go on!" she shouted, barely aware that the others had stopped, too, and were gathering round. "Big brave badman, beating on a hogtied girl! Hit me again if it makes you feel like a man. I've been hit by better than you, you sorry son of a bitch!"

She braced herself, too angry and shot through with adrenaline to feel pain, and waited for the blow.

Instead, she felt someone pull the rope that secured her hands to the girth. Someone else grabbed her legs and yanked.

She skittered backward, her belly sliding off the hard saddle seat, her chin thumping it as she was pulled off the horse and down to the ground. Somehow, she managed to land on her feet.

They were all around. Their clothes were filthy, their faces dirty and unshaved, their eyes dull but dangerous. *Why did I have to open my mouth?* she thought frantically, panicking as reality suddenly overtook her. She tried to run, but her feet were bound and she fell.

No one bothered to break her fall. She landed, her coat jumbled about her, on one hip. Snow clotted her hair.

A short, extremely stout man with watery blue eyes and sparse blonde chin whiskers poked her thigh with his rifle. The barrel was sheathed in a fringed leather scabbard. A human scalp dangled from its tip. He poked her twice, the scalp flapping against her horribly, then flipped back the hem of her coat. The rifle's fat owner pursed his lips and spat out a stream of tobacco juice that cut a steaming hole into the snow inches from her face. Charity knew he had to be the one called Wilford.

"Mebbe we don't need to take her back to Duval," he said. One of his front teeth was missing. The others were calcified at the gums and stained to a buckskin color. "Reckon mebbe she tried to escape. Reckon mebbe we had to shoot her." He nudged her with the rifle again, this time running it over her trousers, up her thigh, between her legs.

She twisted abruptly on her hip, kicking at his shins with both feet. "Get away, Trash!" she shouted.

Wilford jumped back. The others laughed. "You little breed slut!" he snarled. He tossed his rifle to one of the others and, before Charity could roll out of the way, he threw himself on her.

His hands ripped at her coat, pulling at its voluminous folds of fur until he found the front and yanked it open.

She struggled and twisted under his weight, pulling up her knees, using her bound hands like a club against his fat-cushioned ribs. It was so fast, so violent: she couldn't see the others, just their boots crowding round in the snow. She heard them laughing, cheering him on. She felt a boot toe connect with her back, and then somebody called, "Git 'er Wilford! Make 'er squeal!"

He was ripping at her shirt, popping off the buttons, tearing the fabric, pulling at the next layer. She bucked again, corkscrewed her torso, and fastened her teeth on his ear. When he yelped and jerked away, she bit down hard.

He leaped to his feet. The hand clamped to the side of his head did nothing to stop the blood that ran between his gloved fingers to stain and spatter his scarf and coat.

The others were still laughing as, with a snort, Charity spat out his earlobe.

Besides Wilford, who was busy howling and cursing, one man did not laugh. He had to be the other Rooney, Bertie. He was no fatter than Wilford, but he was shorter by a good bit. Like his squalling brother, he had a minuscule pug nose and rheumy, narrowed blue eyes, and looked as if he had never bathed. He kicked at her, and if she hadn't rolled to the side his boot would have caught her temple.

"What'd'ya hafta go an' do that for?" he cried. "Dirty bitch! Dirty, dirty breed whore!"

He bent toward her just as Arnie, her blood and spittle still staining his cheek, limped forward and caught his arm. "Hey B-Briscoe!" he called. "You reckon she's g-give him the hydrophobics?"

Wilford Rooney, still bleeding profusely, pulled his sidearm. "Stand clear, Arnie," he said.

"Aw, p-put it away," Arnie said. "You want to ruin ever'body's else's fun?" A ratty scarf cinched his pants just above the right knee, forming a tourniquet. His pant leg was dark with frozen blood where Charity's bullet had struck him.

I hope it hurts, she thought. *I hope it goes septic and he dies like a dog.*

Wilford's dull brow creased with a scowl. "I said get outta my way. You ain't my boss, Arnie."

"Well, I am." Briscoe's voice. She couldn't see him. "Put the damn gun away, Wilford. Toots, you get her feet untied."

The one called Toots knelt at her legs, and Charity resisted the urge to kick him in the head. When he pulled the rope free, she heard Briscoe say, "Get her on her feet."

Hands grabbed at her, hauled her up. Only then did she actually see Sam Briscoe. A muffler covered most of his black beard. He was still on his horse, and he held Old Reliable in both hands. He rubbed a thumb over the stock's butt.

He looked her in the eye. "Where'd you get this shotgun?"

Her only answer was a glare.

Quite casually, he said, "Arnie . . ."

Hands grabbed her from behind. Fingers closed around her throat. She couldn't see Arnie, but she heard his voice in her ear. "You b-better answer him, B-breed."

She struggled, but he redoubled his grip, cutting off her wind.

"I asked where you got this shotgun." Briscoe again.

This time she tried to answer. It came out as a choked cough. Arnie relaxed his grip a bit.

171

She managed, "My grampa's," before she took a big gulp of air.

"And your grampa's name?"

She glared at him again.

Arnie's fingers dug into her windpipe as he shook her. His whisper a foul, steaming fume against her hair, he said, "D-don't say a d-damn word, honey. I'd purely admire to shake your b-brains out your ears."

"Zebulon." A hoarse whisper.

"Thought so," Briscoe said, fingering the stock again. He turned the shotgun, flipped the butt out so the others could see. "Wolf's head carved in the stock. 'Bout as big as my thumbnail."

Behind her, someone muttered, " 'Bout as big as Wilford's pecker." Several men snickered.

Briscoe ignored it. "Only one man I ever knew of did that. Zeb Caine's mark."

Immediately, Arnie let up the pressure on her throat and Charity gratefully filled her lungs. Even Wilford seemed impressed by the invocation of Zeb Caine's name. He took his hand away from his injured ear and stared at it, as if the blood staining his glove had somehow taken on mystical meaning.

"Ain't seen Zeb for a coon's age," Briscoe said. He slung the shotgun over his shoulder. "Where's he got to?"

Charity locked her eyes on his. "He's likely coming after me right this minute. He's likely going to put you no 'count nickel and dime boys in a mass grave for messing with me. You ought to do yourself a favor and let me go. And if you're halfway smart, you'll tuck your miserable tails and ride out of the Nations before he has a chance to think it over."

The speech, though hoarsely spoken through a bruised throat, had the desired effect. Behind her, the outlaws were muttering. "Jesus Lordie," she heard one man whisper. "Zeb Caine." Boots shifted nervously in snow.

Briscoe's eyes never left hers. "I don't think so, Missy," he said. "I think ol' Zeb finally kicked, elsewise why would you have took up with Turlow? No, I think that was Zeb's grave we was pokin' at back at your place."

Charity held his stare, her gaze unwavering. "You go ahead and think what you want," she said flatly. "It's none of my nevermind if it gets you killed. I'll enjoy watching it. My Grampa Zeb doesn't do anything by halves."

Behind her, one man offered, "But there's just one'a him. There's lots of us."

Without looking his way, Charity said, "There were eleven in Blazer Coogin's bunch."

A new wave of nervous mutters broke out behind Charity, and she was gratified. They had heard the story, too, of how Zeb had taken his revenge on Blazer's gang—after learning that Blazer had cheated him out of twenty-five dollars on a rustled cattle deal—by stealing to the shack where the gang was sleeping, barricading the doors, then setting fire to it. Grampa Zeb had liked to tell her how he sat outside, drinking Blazer's own 'shine, while they screamed and died.

Briscoe grunted, then turned in his saddle to slide her shotgun back under his saddle pack. "I think you're lyin'," he said. "I think Zeb's dead as dirt, Blazer Coogin notwithstandin'." He motioned to the others to put her back on her horse—this time on the saddle instead of across it.

She noticed they were a good deal gentler boosting her up than they had been pulling her down. It was the first measure of respect she had ever received solely for being a Caine, and for a moment she liked it. Almost reveled in it.

Don't go getting cocky, she told herself. *Look at their murdering faces. Stupid and cruel, the lot of them. So what if they make me Queen? I'm still roped up and half hogtied. What does that make me—Queen of the Pigs?*

Briscoe was still staring at her.

She glared right back and gave her head a toss to get the hair out of her eyes. Very calmly, she said, "Grampa Zeb owes me a favor. I believe I'll call him on it. I believe I'll ask him to kill you first."

"As long as we're believin' all over the place," he said, "I do believe you're a Caine. Ain't nobody else 'cept kin of Zebulon's can lie with that calm and flat a eye. Arnie, tie her hands to the horn. Bertie, you get her reins and lead that bear-bait she calls a horse. And watch her. She gets to yammerin' again, gag her."

* * *

An hour later they were still plodding through the snow, although the path they traveled was not a new one, being already tramped by hoof marks headed in the opposite direction. Charity decided that they must be taking her back to a camp they'd already established.

The one called Toots, a cadaverous blond who appeared to be trying to coax less than a dozen chin whiskers into forming a beard, was leading Jake's horse. Charity tried not to look at him. Every time she saw Tico's empty saddle, she started to cry.

She determined that Arnie's slap hadn't loosened any of her teeth. What bleeding she'd done had been from a cut inside her mouth, where the blow had driven the edge of one molar into her cheek. It was not serious, and had stopped bleeding almost immediately.

More serious were the after-effects of the blow she'd received back at the cliff. She wondered if she had a concussion. Once the initial, intense wave of anger had waned, she found herself fading in and out of mild spells of dizziness and nausea. Once she almost fell from her saddle.

All in all, though, she was much better off than Wilford Rooney. He had wrapped his head in a scarf but he was still bleeding, if not with such gratifying profusion as before. The scarf was soaked with blood where it covered his ear.

He kept pressing his hand to it, and turning in his saddle to shoot Charity quick looks that wavered between menace and awe.

The day was drawing to a close, but the outlaws showed no signs of stopping to make camp. They held the same steady, plodding pace. Toots broke out a pint flask of whiskey, and the men passed it up and down the line. Charity made herself rotate her ankles and wiggle her toes every few minutes. If her feet froze up again, nobody would bother to rub them down for her. She wouldn't want them to. She'd rather have wooden feet than have any of these vermin touch her.

When the trail led them out of the woods and along the edge of an old beaver meadow, the sun was almost down and streaming long, pale orange fingers of light between the darkly shadowed tree trunks. Ahead, Wilford laughed and said something to his brother. She couldn't make out what he said, but when he pointed out across the meadow, she turned her head to look.

Three bodies — or what was left of them — were sprawled in the snow. Crows roosted on the bodies, pecking at exposed flesh. Other scavengers had been at work, too, and one man was partially dismembered. Another, judging by the roil of snow that trailed behind him for twenty feet or so, had been dragged by powerful jaws — likely those of a wolf or catamount.

It was impossible to tell with the one that had

been so badly torn apart, but it looked as if the other two had been scalped.

Arnie rode up beside her, blocking her view long enough to scowl at her and grumble, "That's what we do with d-dirty Injuns, Miss Fancy B-breed. Even if they *is* p-part Caine."

Ahead, Wilford lifted his rifle, swinging the scalp that hung from it. He let out a trio of high, almost girlish *whoops,* and laughed.

Arnie spurred his horse and cantered ahead, just in time for Charity to glimpse a travois poking from a drift on the far edge of the meadow. Just in time for her to realize whose bodies lay, like discarded dolls, in the snow.

Dear God, she thought as she felt a tear spill down her cheek. *Thomas Lightfoot and his family. I should have let Jake trade Number Ten for his wife. If they'd been able to travel faster, they might not have met up with these animals.*

Quickly, she rubbed her face against her shoulder, scrubbing away the hot salt in thick bear-fur. If they'd had to kill Jake, she was glad he'd gone over the cliff, where they couldn't get at him. At least they hadn't been able to scalp him, the way they had the Lightfoots . . .

Her stomach turned over and she held her breath. She willed herself not to vomit.

Just as they re-entered the trees and the meadow was lost from sight, she realized she hadn't seen a woman's body.

What then, she wondered, had happened to Two Turtles?

Chapter Twelve

The roiling current carried Jake a quarter-mile downstream before he managed to work his way near the bank. Clinging to an icy boulder with one arm, he shoved himself around it, to the sheltered side. His boots hit pebbly bottom. Shivering, he made his way from rock to rock, hanging on, fighting the current until he was able to crawl out on the snowy, debris-scattered bank.

The slug had grazed the back of his skull and, although his head pounded, he knew the wound was superficial. It had been enough to knock him off Tico and over the cliff, though, and he realized it was a miracle he hadn't been killed. But fate hadn't let him off entirely. Soaked through and freezing, he stumbled to his feet and lumbered up the bank. His wool coat, which normally had some natural water repellency, was soaked through, and he labored under its weight. He also cradled his left arm.

It wasn't the first time he'd dislocated that shoulder, and he knew how to put it back in.

But that didn't make it hurt any less, and it wouldn't make its repair any less painful.

He stumbled upstream along the water's edge, toward an outcrop of rock. When he reached it, he paused to lean heavily against the stone. At last he stood erect. Gently letting go of his bad arm, he used the other to feel along the outcrop at about shoulder height. When he found a smooth place, he carefully pulled the useless arm free of his coat. Squinting against the pain, he manipulated the shoulder to determine the relative positions of the dislocated ball and socket and thereby judge the angle needed to put them back in working order.

The last time this had happened, Rex Jeffords had been handy to give his arm a good yank and pop it back into place. But Rex was dead. Charity probably would have been strong enough. *She'd have the nerve, too,* he thought to himself, smiling briefly despite the bright pain in his head and his arm, and the icy cold that was already sending paralyzing tendrils into his bones.

It came to him in that moment that if she wasn't dead, Briscoe and his thugs had her. And in that split second of realization, he simultaneously took an enormous gulp of air and twisted hard, lunging forward at an angle to crash the point of his shoulder into the stone.

Along with a *pop* he felt more than heard, came the relief of those muscles that had been stretched too tightly, and intense pain from the

179

flesh he'd just crushed against the stone face.

He gripped his arm and fell to his knees, muttering, "Jesus, Jesus . . ." It was bad enough having to put it back in like that, but it was the same shoulder that Charity had dug a slug out of less than a week before. Tears clouded his vision. His breath came in sharp pants and rose in a series of ragged puffs from between his chattering teeth.

At last he pulled the sodden coat closely over his soaked and already ice-stiffened clothes, and forced himself back to his feet. His movements leaden, every step a consciously forced effort, he began to search the steep banks for anything resembling shelter. And as he stumbled over the rocks, he remembered to reach down every few steps and pick up a length of dead branch or limb. He had to do it as he went. There might not be time later.

He was lucky. Less than two minutes upstream — and about three minutes before he might have lost his battle with hypothermia — he came upon a cavity, about ten feet wide, in the rock. Little more than a scoop in the living stone, its floor was at roughly his knee height, and it went back about two and a half yards. There wouldn't be room for him to stand, but he wouldn't need to.

By then he had gathered a small armload of kindling and some long, twigless branches, along with part of an old bird's nest. The nest had been several feet away from the river's flow and looked to be dry on the outside surfaces. He prayed it was dry on the inside, as well.

He dropped the wood and bird's nest just inside the cave's mouth, then quickly gathered several smooth, fist-sized river stones. These he spread in a single layer beside the wood before he stooped and entered the cave. Quickly, he stripped out of his clothing and gear—trembling, bluish fingers fumbling with buttons, pushing numbly at buckles—until he was down to his skin. Then, just as swiftly, he put on his coat again. The woolen outside was soaked through, but it was lined with an old duster he'd cut down, and the duster was waterproof. It would be relatively dry next to his skin, if a little scratchy. And though the coat's outside was already stiffening with ice, it would provide insulating bulk.

He folded his deerskin cape into a pad. He sat upon this, cross-legged; tenting the wool coat about him and tucking his bare feet inside. The deerskin was wet and cold under his legs and backside, but it was better than bare rock.

Next, he reached toward the scatter of kindling and rescued the bird's nest. Hands shaking, he broke it in two and placed the halves before him, on one of the larger stones. There were ice crystals within the tangled weave of grasses, twigs and stems, but he thought it was dry enough.

He wrested his shirt from the pile of wet clothes. It was already partly frozen together, and he had to peel one cuff away from the pocket, which he proceeded to pry apart. *Match tin, match tin . . .*

It wasn't there.

He reached for his trousers, aware that his movements were becoming more sluggish with each passing second. He felt a nearly overwhelming desire to forget about the fire: to simply lie down and have a nap. A nap from which he'd never wake.

No! He punched himself, hard, in his bad shoulder.

The stimulation proved enough to enable him to drag the trousers close and pry apart the freezing fabric of the pockets.

On the first try, he found his pocket knife, compass and watch. On the second, he found his matches. The tin was undented, and the sulphurtips inside were dry. His fingers were almost too numb to hold the match, but he managed; and at last the scraps of bird's nest sparked, then caught.

He cupped his hands about the feeble, infant blaze, gently puffing on it as he added the smallest pieces of kindling. Gradually, as warmth seeped into his hands and face, he nursed it into a small but steady fire. By the time he had added all but the longest, most sturdy branches, it was crackling and healthy. He had built the fire within two feet of the cave's lip, and so far the smoke was going up and out, thanks to a slight concavity of the cave's upper rim. He hoped the wind wouldn't decide to change.

The shallow cave warmed rapidly, and his shirt, trousers and longjohns were already steaming as he draped them on the longer branches he wedged between the cave's floor and sloping roof. He turned the tops of his boots toward the blaze, squeezed all the water he could out of his socks, and laid them between himself and the fire.

Next he unloaded his Colt. He put the pistol to one side and, using a damp sock, wiped away as much of the moisture as he could from the five cartridges. It was his practice to keep the hammer chamber empty, and had been since his nineteenth summer, when he saw a cowhand catch the hammer of his holstered gun on his own rope and shoot himself in the thigh.

He repeated the wiping process with the ammunition he slipped from the loops in his gun belt. And when all the cartridges had been dried as well as possible and placed in a pile behind him, where the cave floor was high enough to stay dry, he opened his knife. Using the blade as a screwdriver, he removed the Colt's wooden grips. These he wiped down and set aside before he hung the pistol over the fire.

There was nothing left to do but wait. If he tried to track Briscoe and his boys before his clothing was completely dried, he'd freeze to death before he walked half a mile.

"Charity." He whispered her name without

meaning to. *Dear Lord,* he thought, *please don't let her be another casualty of this. . . . This what? This private war.*

So far it seemed most of the casualties had been on his side. Twenty years ago, his father, a town marshal in Green Mule, Missouri, had run into Claude Duval. Duval was just beginning his career that day: the last day of Jake's father's life.

Duval had entered the sheriff's office with three other men, their intent to break out one Clifford Beedle, who was awaiting escort to St. Louis and a murder trial. Duval hadn't stopped with breaking out his friend, or with gagging and binding the eleven-year-old Jake back-to-back with his father.

The pictures of it were ever in Jake's mind: Duval, silent, leaning casually against the wall as his cohorts broke open the rifle racks, ransacked the desks and files; Duval, lighting a slim cigar and uttering, with matter-of-fact and chilling softness, the only words he would say that afternoon: "Dis what we do wit lawman marshal, *cher,* wit all lawman marshal fella. Boy child remember dat." He had signaled one of his men with no more than an offhand crook of his finger. And then came the explosion: the gun firing too near his own ear, the impact as his father's head, already lifeless, whiplashed to impact with Jake's.

And the blood.

Duval had been right about one thing: Jake

184

never forgot. When he grew up he went away to war, but when he came back, he became a marshal himself, working out of the courts that oversaw the Nations. That was where Duval lurked. It was where Jake would hunt.

He'd taken his badge seriously. Among his peers he was well-liked and respected. And it was common knowledge that he was the first assigned to any case that might involve Duval.

Duval had become more slippery through the years. Always sly, he'd grown crafty as well. Among certain outlaws, he was the stuff of which legends are made. Some said he wasn't human; that he'd been summoned forth from the Louisiana swamps by a voodoo priestess, and could vanish and reappear at will. Some said he had Cajun magic, that he could read the future in cards or water or bones and could summon the Devil. Or that he was the Devil.

Others, Jake included, claimed those rumors were window dressing and flimflam, and that Duval was nothing more — or less — than brilliant, and willing to let his minions believe whatever they liked, so long as he maintained his hold over them. In any case, his men feared him, but they'd die for him. Three times Jake had nearly snared Duval. Three times the Cajun had slipped away. And Duval's revenge for these attempts was just as intense as Jake's hatred of him.

Laura.

He refused to let the image linger in his

mind. It was too gruesome, too paralyzing. And it had been personal: Jake knew Duval had let the Rooney boys loose with her for no other reason than to hurt him. *Hurt me? Dear God, it nearly killed me. Oh, my Laura!*

He felt the tears well, and took a deep breath. He couldn't let it overtake him again. Not here, not now. He leaned forward and rearranged his clothing, turning steaming sides away from the fire and shifting sopping surfaces toward it.

Cotton Beutel, his first partner, dead six years ago at Sam Briscoe's hands, by order of Duval; three friends tortured to death on the Canadian River two years after that. And the last massacre that left so many friends dead, Rex Jeffords among them. For not the first time, he wondered if Duval had let him ride free of that blood-drenched valley on purpose. *The sick son of a bitch won't give up the game.*

Logic told him that Charity was most likely dead. *But I don't believe that,* he thought. *I can't believe it. If she were dead, I'd feel it. I would have felt her pass.* He shook his head. *You're a fool, Jake. You still don't really feel like Rex Jeffords is dead, either, and you saw him lying on the ground, covered in blood . . .*

"No!" he said aloud, so sharply that he startled himself. "She's alive. She has to be alive."

The only problem was that if she was still living, Duval had her. Which meant she didn't have long.

But he won't kill her yet, Jake thought, and reached to rearrange his shirt before the sleeve could scorch. *Duval likes his games. He likes to play cat and mouse. And right now, I'm the mouse. Maybe he'll use Charity to bait the trap.*

He knew Briscoe and the others had seen him go over the cliff. Did they think he was still alive, or did they assume he'd been killed when he went off his horse?

He reached for his gun, swearing softly when the metal was hotter than he'd expected. It was already dry, and he began to screw the grips back in place. If Briscoe and his boys thought he had survived the fall, they'd be working their way along the banks, searching for him. He needed to be ready. He reloaded the pistol, leaving the sixth chamber empty. He hoped they thought he was dead. He was in no shape to shoot it out with them.

I'm dead, you bastards, he thought. *Convince yourselves of that. Because if you think I'm dead, I can come up on you like a ghost and spirit Charity away. Somehow, I'll do it.*

But then a thought struck him, chilling him more deeply than any plummet into icy water. If they believed he was dead, what reason would Duval have to keep Charity alive?

Just as the setting sun's final rays withdrew from the land, Briscoe and his men, Charity in tow, rode into the outlaw camp.

187

It sat in a high place, halfway up a rocky, scantily treed hill. There had once been a cavern here, but many years ago the foremost portion of its roof had collapsed, leaving the back third of the cavern intact, but shallow. The front two thirds of the cave, now roofless but still stone-floored, formed something like a veranda. This stone shelf, backed on the north by what was left of the cave, was also sheltered, on the east, by a steep embankment. The other two sides were open. To the west was a sharp drop, below which was a meadowed valley. To the south was the sloping timbered land through which they had come.

It looked to Charity like a place of long time, if infrequent, habitation. Whatever small debris had once littered the "veranda" had been cleared. Large slabs of rock had been piled on one another and on boulders too big to move to form several makeshift benches, now frosted with snow. Stones had been stacked in a circle at the yawning mouth of the cave to form a crude firepit. Smoke curled up from it, half-obscuring a haunch of venison that was spitted across the top. A rain barrel sat just at the cave's lip, where Charity supposed the water must flow the heaviest when it rained. At the moment, it was iced over but chunky-looking, as if the ice had been broken frequently, only to freeze again.

A rope was stretched from rusty spikes driven into either side of the cave's mouth, and from it drooped several balding deer hides and a dirty blanket. At the moment, the hides and blankets were all shoved to one side, and Charity could make out a portion of the cave's shadowy interior. Two men, both scruffy and unkempt, were just rising from their seats: wooden crates, upended around a three-legged table, which rested at slightly off-kilter angles on the uneven floor. The two men brushed past the dangling deer hides. One went to the fire and gave the spitted venison a half turn. The other walked past, staring hard at her before he struck up a conversation with Toots.

"G'down."

She'd been so busy orienting herself that she hadn't noticed Briscoe. She waited until he backed off a step before she swung down off Number Ten. The others had dismounted, too. The younger Rooney brother, Bertie, led all the horses toward a picket line back in the trees. Charity doubted Number Ten and Tico would have such good treatment tonight as they'd seen the previous two.

Briscoe put his hand on her shoulder and gave her a little shove. As she stumbled, he grunted, "Inside."

"Quit pushing!" she snapped.

With the speed of a striking snake, he grabbed the neck of her coat and yanked her toward him.

"Listen, girl," he said, his voice a whispered growl, his face so close to hers that his bushy,

189

foul-smelling beard scratched her face. "I don't give a solid gold goat turd if you're related to Zeb Caine or Dan'l Boone or the goddamn President of these United States. You fiddle with me, you try to run off, you try anything smart, and I won't think twice about bashin' in that pretty face of yours. I won't take no pleasure in it, but it won't bother me none, neither. I'll just do it. You got that?"

Charity held his eye. She willed down the old fear and kept her face stony and her eyes unblinking. Until a few days ago, she hadn't known that Sam Briscoe existed, but she had known that tone of voice—and similar threats—all her life. She felt herself immediately fall into old habits, old patterns. Without emotion, she said, "I understand. Please let go of my coat."

"Better," he said, and let her go. "Now get inside."

As she stepped into the cave, she considered that she might just swing around and punch Sam Briscoe right in his ugly nose. But she was exhausted, and he was too much like Grampa Zeb. She knew he wasn't bluffing; he'd hurt her badly if she gave him enough excuse.

She could now see that the firepit was only walled high with rocks on its outside curve. The side facing into the cave was low, so that the outer, higher wall reflected both heat and light back into the cave. Not very much of either, though: she could see the outlines of parcels and crates and sacks piled haphazardly along

190

one craggy wall, but couldn't make out any real details; and she was still cold.

Outside in the twilight, Wilford Rooney chopped at the iced-over rain barrel with the butt end of a rusty branding iron. He kept stealing nervous looks at her from the corner of his eye. He appeared no less disgusting than the first time she'd seen him—he seemed even more so with that bloody scarf wrapped round his head. He was still somewhat in awe of her or, at least, her name. She hoped he stayed that way.

"Don't dawdle." It was Briscoe. He took her arm and led her to the back of the cave, where the firelight did little to permeate the gloom. He pushed her down to the floor. She landed against something soft that moved. Briscoe said, "Stay put," and walked off.

Whatever she had landed on stirred again. And groaned. She squirmed to one side, wishing for more light, and tentatively reached out with her bound hands.

"What's that?" she whispered. "Is someone there?" She could make out a shape in the shadows, but it was nothing more than a vague hump on the floor.

Her fingers touched a blanket. The blanket moved. "Crikey," said a man's voice, soft but thin, as if he were speaking through clenched teeth. "You landed on my leg."

"Who's that?" Charity whispered. She snatched her hands away.

The shape on the floor shifted, then stiffly sat up. "Might ask you the same," came the answer, soft and drawling. "If you're a friend of the Rooneys', you might like to know that the last dove they brought out here went over the cliff by her own choice. That's the rumor, anyway. Course, if you're a friend of the Rooney boys you're probably crazy anyway and wouldn't care. I don't suppose you'd have any laudanum? Or better yet, a pistol?"

Charity squinted. Her eyes were growing used to the dim light. She could tell he was fair-haired, and she could almost make out his features. "I'm no friend of the Rooneys or any of this other bunch. And I've got a pistol. A shotgun and a Henry, too. But they took them."

"They're good at that." The man readjusted his position slightly, grunting as he did so. His legs looked unnaturally stiff beneath the blankets. "You didn't tell me who you are."

"I—"

There was a burst of laughter from the front of the cave, and Charity twisted to squint into the light. Toots, the Rooney brothers, and Arnie were gathered in a knot beside the cook pit. Firelight washed up over their grimy faces. Arnie, still laughing, turned toward Charity and called, "We was j-just sayin' as how we ain't had nothin' but venison for a spell. I got real fond'a horse meat d-durin' the War. Mebbe we'll b-butcher out that cayuse a'yours tomorrow, have us a feast."

Now you can get Heartfire Romances right at home and save

Heartfire Romance

Get 4 Free Heartfire Novels. A $17.00 Value!

O GET YOUR
4 FREE BOOKS
MAIL THE COUPON BELOW.

FREE BOOK CERTIFICATE

Heartfire Romance

GET 4 FREE BOOKS

Yes! I want to subscribe to Zebra's HEARTFIRE HOME SUBSCRIPTION SERVICE. Please send me my 4 FREE books. Then each month I'll receive the four newest Heartfire Romances as soon as they are published to preview Free for ten days. If I decide to keep them I'll pay the special discounted price of just $3.50 each; a total of $14.00. This is a savings of $3.00 off the regular publishers price. There are no shipping, handling or other hidden charges. There is no minimum number of books to buy and I may cancel this subscription at any time. In any case the 4 FREE Books are mine to keep regardless.

NAME

ADDRESS

CITY _____ STATE _____ ZIP

TELEPHONE

SIGNATURE

(If under 18 parent or guardian must sign)
Terms and prices subject to change.
Orders subject to acceptance.

HF 110

GET 4 FREE BOOKS

HEARTFIRE HOME SUBSCRIPTION
SERVICE
P.O. BOX 5214
120 BRIGHTON ROAD
CLIFTON, NEW JERSEY 07015

AFFIX
STAMP
HERE

"And maybe you won't live that long," she snapped without thinking. "My Grampa Zeb'll be here before you have time to get hungry again. You'd better let me go, if you know what's good for—"

"Shut up, the both'a you!" It was Briscoe. "Zeb Caine's dead and buried. Ain't no shade comin' to your rescue. And if you don't keep your trap shut, I'm gonna put my boot in it. Arnie, if you're gonna do any butcherin' don't announce it, just get busy." He turned on his heel and walked away.

"Aw, hell," Arnie muttered. "I ain't that hungry . . ."

She was still staring after Briscoe when she felt a hand on her arm. The man said, "Zeb Caine? Your grandfather?"

She gave her head a little toss without meaning to. "You want to congratulate me or spit at me?"

He leaned back. "Neither. I guess that explains why you're mixed up with this bunch."

"It doesn't explain it like you think it does, Mister. I didn't get mixed up with them. They got mixed up with me. I never . . . they—they killed . . ."

The tears, too long denied, rushed forth; the more she tried to stop, the harder she wept. The man put one arm around her and cradled her head against his chest with the other. "Shhh," he said. "It's all right. Cry it out."

At last the worst was over, and she sat up

again, blowing her nose into a kerchief which he pulled off his neck. By then, someone had lit a lantern and placed it on the makeshift table. It didn't serve to brighten the rear of the cave to any great extent, but enough light filtered back that Charity could finally make out her companion's features, if dimly.

"That's better, honey," he said. "You have a first name to go with the Caine?"

He was not a particularly handsome man, his nose being a bit too hooked and his brow a tad too wide, but he had an honest and trustworthy look about him. She said, "I'm Charity."

"Pretty," he said. He reached to take back the kerchief and groaned as he did.

"Is your leg hurt bad?"

"Not leg. Legs. They broke both of them, after I tried to kite out of here five days ago. Held me down and went at me with a sledge hammer. They let me splint them myself, though, the big-hearted bastards. Not that there was much left to splint. Got a slug in my side, too, from a few days before that. Hurts like hell, if you'll pardon the expression, but I don't think it hit anything important. Just bled a lot. My legs aren't so bad anymore, though," he added. "Sometimes I don't feel the right one at all . . ."

He paused a moment before one corner of his mouth turned up in a rueful smile. He lifted a hand to the back of his head. "Had a goose egg the size of a powder biscuit, too. Guess my horse must have kicked me in the head when I went off him. They tell me I didn't wake up for a day and a half. Concussion, I reckon. Couldn't figure out why they didn't kill me at first, like they did the others. I guess they're plannin' on something more interestin'.'"

Charity pulled the blanket away from his legs and studied the splints. The splinting itself was a decent enough job, although the legs were so crushed and misshapen that she couldn't imagine how he'd gotten them as straight as he had. She couldn't find anything she could do to better it, but a peculiar odor wafted up from them. Both were discolored and swollen, the right leg the worst. She knew what that meant. When she looked up, she realized he knew it, too, but his eyes told her he didn't want to speak of it.

She pulled the blanket over his legs again, and said, "What do you mean, they're planning something more interesting?"

The man eased back on his elbows. "Don't think me rude, Miss Charity, but I'm going to have to lie down." He groaned softly, and it was a moment before he spoke again. "See, these boys work for a fellow named Duval," he began, "and Duval has a little feud going with a friend of mine. I expect the plan is to get their hands on him, and make him watch while they finish me off. Not that there's much to finish off, but it's Duval's style. To tell you the truth, Miss Charity, I wouldn't mind so much if only I could take out those peckerwood Rooneys before

I go. Excuse my language. But I tell you what else. My friend's too smart for Duval. I think he hotfooted it back to Fort Smith and roped together a posse. He's likely on the track this minute. We'll both get out of this just fine, honey. Jake's a good man. The best."

Charity felt the blood drain from her face. She whispered, "What . . . what's your name?"

"Rex Jeffords," he said. "U.S. Marshal, at your service."

"Marshal Jeffords," she said softly, as a single tear spilled to trail down her cheek, "I don't think I ever felt so sad in all my life."

Chapter Thirteen

Jake's pocket watch told him it was only a little after eight, which meant he'd been trudging through the snow for less than two hours. *Seems more like twenty,* he thought grimly, and pushed forward, ignoring the painful growls in his stomach.

He had made himself wait until his clothing was bone-dry before he dressed and left the cave, but his ragged deerskin cape was still stiff, and his coat was heavy with ice. He stopped again to work the wool back and forth, cracking powdery fragments and crystals from its weave.

He'd climbed up the steep embankment and backtracked to the place where he and Charity had been overtaken. The signs of a struggle were there, and also enough spent cartridges to reveal the fight she'd put up. There was no body, though, and that flooded him, to his surprise, with more anxiety than relief.

The trail was easy to follow, even in the half-clouded moonlight.

He trudged on.

* * *

Briscoe had untied Charity's hands, having decided she wouldn't try to run away, and Charity and her crippled companion were given food. Jeffords's venison had been thrown to him, as if he were a dog. The younger Rooney brother, Bertie, had brought Charity hers on a dented tin plate and doffed his hat when he held it out, saying nervously, "This here's for you, Miss Caine, ma'am." But other than that, little attention was paid them.

Charity was relieved, but she wondered if the outlaws' indifference had less to do with their reverence for the Caine name than with some other influence.

The men, Briscoe included, had assumed an anxious air once the moon had taken over the sky. They were jumpy, starting at even the smallest sounds, and they talked little among themselves. Even the Rooneys were subdued. They huddled at the tilting table with Arnie and a balding, bearded man they called Scud. They played poker for matches, but paid scant attention to the game. Others busied themselves by fussing with bits of harness or whittling, stopping every few minutes to blow warm steamy breath over ungloved hands. Briscoe loitered outside, his back to the fire. She could see his profile as he rocked on his heels and rolled, then smoked, cigarette after cigarette.

Beside Charity in the cold shadows, Rex Jef-

198

fords was silent. He'd been deeply shaken when she told him about Jake. At first he'd tried to make light of it and attempted to convince her that Jake Turlow had more lives than a barn cat; but they both knew he was trying to persuade himself more than her. Finally he had turned away, and he hadn't spoken since. She hoped he was sleeping. Once her eyes had adjusted to the light enough to really see his face, she had found it grey and sickly, and etched with tiny lines caused by the pain in his legs and side. He looked like a man who had not long to live.

· Too tired and still too frightened and sad to sleep, she sat nestled beneath the warm tent of her coat and watched the outlaws. Their behavior puzzled her. Jake was dead, so there would be no one on their trail; it wasn't ambush they seemed in fear of, for only two sentries had been posted. She wondered if, back in the old days, Grampa Zeb had roosted in a hideout similar to this. Had her uncles known secret places in the forests? Had they lived like these animals, dirty and unkempt and vulgar?

It seemed strange that until she met Jake and thereby had her first glimpse of honesty and goodness and selflessness, she would have thought her present surroundings—and companions—not at all unusual. These men, after all, were cut from the same cloth as her family; this life, far from civilization except when one neared it in order to plunder, was her birthright.

These men should have been her brothers-in-arms. She should have been their compatriot. Or their willing whore.

But because of Jake, because she had known him and because she had loved him, any sense of kinship she once might have felt for Briscoe and his cohorts was replaced by revulsion — a revulsion she would have to master, she realized; without Jake, she was back to the beginning. This existence, or one very much like it, was destined to be her way of life, and she was already falling into old habits, old patterns. Do what you're told, speak when you're spoken to; whether you're beaten with a fist or cut by words, try never to show the pain.

After a while, disguising the pain would come easy to her — the cloak of hopeless numbness she had lived beneath all her life was already shrouding her again. Only with Jake had she been able to lift it, and now he was gone. She had no hope of better things, or any reason to want them. She had no reason to wish for anything, except possibly to live. And she wasn't certain if she really wanted that.

"I believe we're to have an audience."

"What?" She turned toward Rex Jeffords, who had propped himself on one elbow.

"They're waiting on him," he said softly. "Duval, that is. He never stays here, but he's always near. Somewhere."

"I wondered. I've seen him once. I told you — when I saw them riding to my house. He was

200

off a ways in the snow, and riding a grey horse. I thought he was a ghost."

With effort, Jeffords pushed himself up into a sit. "You may be right, Miss Charity. But even ghosts can be exorcised."

She was about to ask what he meant when they heard hoofbeats on the rocks outside. Briscoe, then the others, snapped to attention. The steady, flinty click of hooves on stone and ice came slowly closer. And then, through a curtain of sparks and smoke, she saw the horse's head and front quarters, its dapples turned orange-grey in the firelight. It stopped with a steamy snort and a slow, faintly jingling shake of its head. Leather creaked. There came the muffled jangle of a spurred boot alighting, then another.

Claude Duval stepped into the light.

He was a tall man, and thin. He wore a pale grey hat and a heavy white duster, the hem of which nearly brushed the ground. A thick mustache, grizzled and mostly silver, bisected his narrow blade of a face. He did not speak.

The others made way as he came forward. His spurs, small but sharp rowels that gave off tiny clanks with his every step and sparked on the stone, were the only sound. He did not stop to greet or even acknowledge any of his men, but came directly toward the rear of the cave, stopping inches from Charity. The hem of his duster brushed her knee, and she shivered.

He struck a match and held it out. Towering above her as she crouched on the floor, he seemed a giant. In a modulated bass voice that surprised her with its resonance, he said, "What dis girl child?"

From behind him came Briscoe's voice. "She was with Turlow. Says she's Zebulon Caine's granddaughter. I believe her. She's hellcat enough for a Caine, anyway. Bit off half'a Wilford's ear."

Without expression, Duval continued to stare at her. She found she couldn't take her eyes from his. They were grey, and cold as tombstones. He said, to her this time, "What be your fadder's name, *cher?*" His voice was so deep it almost made the rocks rumble.

"Sam. Sam Caine." She hadn't wanted to answer, hadn't wanted to give him the satisfaction, but she couldn't keep herself from speaking.

He stared a moment longer. "Think not," he said, and shook out the match. She felt the hot stub bounce off her cheek as he walked away.

She gave her head a shake as if to settle her brain back into working properly. Maybe it was his voice, or maybe it was the way his eyes pinned you, sank into you, read the story of your soul; whatever it was about him that gave him such a paralyzing mastery over her, it seemed to have the same effect on his minions.

He stood in the center of the cave, his men clustered about him. "Where Turlow has got to?" he asked Briscoe.

"We k-killed him, sir," Arnie offered proudly, his hat in his hands. "G-got him up on the ridge. I done it, sir. Was my bullet what took him."

Duval considered this for a moment before he said, "You bring his body?"

"Well, it was at the t-top of the ridge, Mr. Duval. He sorta went on over the edge."

"You not go down, look around see?"

Arnie began to twist at his hat. "Well, I, uh . . . he c-couldn't'a lived, I mean, it was a thirty foot d-drop, maybe f-f-f . . . maybe more. And the river was g-goin' fast below."

Wilford Rooney bellied his way forward, his round bandaged head nodding. "Mebbe forty," he offered, his voice cracking. "That's right, Mr. Duval, sir. Mebbe fifty! Water was ragin'! That Caine gal bit off my ear, sir, jes' like Sam said. You reckon that's good luck, her bein' a Caine and all? I'd hate to think I lost it and it weren't even no good luck."

Duval ignored him. So softly that Charity could barely hear, he said, "You kill him dead all de way, Arnie?"

Arnie nodded vigorously. "The current finished him off if'n I d-didn't. We couldn't get to him, cause'a that b-breed. She's T-Turlow's squaw. She done this to me." He pointed to his blood-stained trouser leg. "Lead's still in there, p-pains me somethin' awful."

Duval was unconcerned. "You positive sure it your slug kill Turlow?"

Arnie nodded again.

Duval said, "Briscoe?"

Briscoe crossed his arms over his chest. "I told 'em just what you said."

Duval pursed his lips. He opened his coat and dipped fingers into his shirt pocket. The other men looked at each other nervously, but he ignored them. He drew out something shiny and golden: a small lady's locket on a fine chain.

Beside her, Charity heard Rex Jeffords curse beneath his breath.

Duval let the locket dangle from his fingers, watched it twist and sparkle for nearly a minute before he palmed it and turned back to Arnie. As if there had been no break in the conversation, he said, "You know my orders, but you kill him anyway. Why you do dat? You bring me disappointment. You deserve get shot up by girl child, should have been much more worse. You know I want dat marshal man here. I want him breathin' air in lungs, eyes wide and starin', brain workin'."

"B-but I figgered—"

"You go back in mornin', find Turlow. You find pieces, whole corpse, livin' flesh; you bring back what dat you find. You listen me straight up, ears open? You un'erstand?"

The blood had drained from Arnie!s face. "Y-yessir."

"You go now and you on knees pray, Arnie. Pray Christ Jesus a bad shot you are. Dat Turlow man dead, or he alive and you kill him on de way, I find you. I bring down de obeah on you. You know 'bout obeah magic, Arnie?"

The others shrank away. Arnie stood his ground, but only because he seemed too frightened to move. "Y-yessir."

Duval considered him for a moment. "No, you know not very much, Arnie, or you be pissing yourself in pants right now dis minute."

"What's obeah?" Charity whispered, her hand cupped to her mouth so that only Rex Jeffords could hear.

"Swamp magic," he replied. "The coloreds brought it up from the islands."

"Real magic?"

"Hush."

Duval didn't stay long. He and Briscoe, who seemed the only one of the gang not terrified of him, went outside. They exchanged a few terse words by the fire, during which Duval gestured once in Charity's direction. Then he got back on his ghost-grey horse and rode out. She wondered if he had a camp near by, or if he just melted into the atmosphere.

It was nearly midnight when the trail led Jake out of the trees and along the edge of the snowy beaver meadow. He grew more concerned about Charity with each passing minute. An hour earlier, he had come upon signs of a struggle: the snow was roiled and marked by imprints of boots as well as hooves. There had been blood, too: not a great deal, but enough to make him quicken an already fast pace.

The drifted meadow, blue-white in the moonlight, seemed an oasis after so many hours of slogging through the woods. Exhausted and cursing the cold, he stopped to catch his breath. *At least it's not snowing,* he thought. *That's something to be grateful for.*

Judging by the tracks he followed, the riders had kept an easy pace. He surmised they would have passed this spot late in the afternoon, which meant he might gain their camp within a few hours; they wouldn't have traveled far after dark. He was about to move on when he heard a faint rustling, and a low growl that could only have come from a wolf.

He slipped free his gun and warily turned toward the sound. Wolves, unless they were rabid, were normally too timid to attack a man. But a hard winter like this might create a starving—and therefore foolhardy—lobo.

The wolf was not alone. Except for the plumed tails that bobbed occasionally above the crest of a low drift about fifty feet from where he stood, he couldn't see them, but he could make out the low tussling sounds of leisurely feeding.

Two hours ago his stomach had stopped nagging and moved on to insistent hurting; at the thought of meat his mouth suddenly filled with saliva. The pack had likely brought down a whitetail. It was not a new kill—the wolves were feeding too politely for that—but in this weather it took a very long time for a kill to go bad.

He listened closely, and determined it wasn't a big pack. He guessed three animals; four at the most. It wouldn't be too difficult to spook them away long enough to hack some frozen meat from the carcass. He had no time to cook it even if he could have risked the fire; but raw meat was better than nothing. He'd need strength when he caught up to his quarry.

One or two shots would have sent them scurrying, but he could afford the noise less than the fire. He took off his cape. That it was stiff with ice was suddenly in his favor, for as he charged the wolves, whooping and waving the cape, it cut the air like a misshapen sail.

There were only three wolves after all, and at his first shout they leaped away, loping out about twenty yards before they turned—necks and tails bristled, heads lowered—to watch him.

He scrambled over the low drifts, slipping and sliding, catching quick glimpses of the dark shape at which they'd been feeding. He kept the cape swinging as he shouted, "Hi! Hi!" His gun was still out and pointed toward the wolves, although for the moment they appeared too jittery to attempt to reclaim their meal.

Within yards of his goal, he tripped and skidded face first, the cape lost but the pistol still secure in his hand as he slipped toward the snowy kill. It stopped his slide when he landed against it with his bad arm. He let out a yelping curse, which he repeated when he had to twist on the same shoulder to face the wolves.

They held their distance, heads low and hackles raised, as they paced in tight circles.

"Christ Almighty," he hissed, quickly rubbing his shoulder before he dug out his pocket knife and turned, for the first time, toward the frozen carcass.

It was not a deer.

Nausea overtook him immediately, but he had nothing to bring up. He crouched on all fours, convulsed with dry heaves.

At last he stumbled to his feet. The wolves had ventured closer, but backed off again after he picked up his cape and gave them another wave and a hoarse, half-sobbed shout.

It was Thomas Lightfoot there in the snow. The clothes were shredded, the limbs and torso mangled. But there was enough left of the face and clothing: just enough to show him whose body this was, and that Thomas had been scalped.

Jake's stomach lurched again, and he turned away. *The Rooneys,* he thought. *Those goddamn Rooney animals! Dear God, don't let Charity end like this . . .*

He looked about, searching for more grisly shapes in the drifts and hoping he wouldn't find any. In the end he discovered only one other body: the mutilated horror of it was frozen into place, but what remained was enough to tell him it was the younger Lightfoot boy. He, too, had been scalped. There was no sign of Two Turtles or the older boy, but he did find signs of a body being dragged. The trail led off the meadow, and the cougar tracks dimpling the snow along its course told him what had done the dragging.

He found the travois halfway across the meadow. Behind him, the wolves had returned to feeding. He waved his cape at them and shouted, but by this time they considered him merely a harmless, if noisy, nuisance. They skittered about, watching him nervously, but they did not leave the carcass.

It nearly killed him to do it, but he turned his back on the carnage. There was nothing he could do to stop it, short of shooting the wolves and hauling the remains up a tree. And even that wouldn't stave off the other scavengers for long.

Hurriedly, but with an ear to the wolf pack, he began to sort through the wreckage Briscoe's men and the elements had made of the Lightfoots' travois. The outlaws had requisitioned most of the Lightfoot family's provisions, but they'd made a mess of it. Chunks of twine and packing material were scattered every which way. There might just be a scrap of food — or a box of cartridges — they'd overlooked.

He worked quickly, and in the end came up with a smallish blue-cloth sack of peppercorns, which he tucked in his pocket rather absently; a scrap of jerky; which he immediately made himself eat despite the lingering nausea; and a small tin box containing a hundred count of percussion caps. Without powder, lead, and brass casings, the caps would do him no good; but he stuck the tin in his pocket anyway.

He took one last look backward, breathed, "I'm sorry, Thomas," and turned away.

The wolves feeding quietly behind him, Jake started back along the trail that would lead him to the outlaws and Charity.

Chapter Fourteen

She was dreaming about Jake, dreaming of firelight and warm furs and safety, dreaming of his arms about her. *I love you, Charity.* There was no danger, no fear. *I love you, too, Jake.*

"Wake up, b-breed."

Lurching out of a light doze, Charity twisted away from the boot as it jabbed her midsection a second time. She landed against Marshal Jeffords. He moaned, but did not stir.

She pulled herself into a sit, drew her legs double beneath her coat, and looked up into Arnie's stubbly face. His nose and cheeks were ruddy from drink, his mouth slack. One pantleg, just above his knee, was thick with the bandage beneath it—Briscoe had dug out the bullet and dressed the wound not long after Duval's departure. The liquor had been broken out in honor of the surgery, and most all the men had shared Arnie's "anesthesia." A bottle, nearly empty, was in his hand.

"Go away," she hissed.

"Been lookin' at you," he slurred. Behind

him, Wilford Rooney and Toots snored drunkenly around the table, their shaggy heads pillowed on their arms. Toots, she had discovered, was the second man she had winged from the rocks; although in his case the damage had been restricted, unfortunately, to a nick on his arm. Men, curled beneath blankets and snoring, were scattered about the cave's perimeters. Several were missing, Sam Briscoe among them. She made out a man's form, standing against the darkness on the other side of the fire, and thought it was he.

Arnie's boot connected with her side again, and she smacked his calf with her open hand. "Leave me alone."

He didn't seem to notice the swat or to hear her. "After the War . . ." He paused to take a swig. Most of it went down his coat front, adding to the previous stains. "After the War, I rode me a spell for Festus C-Caine afore Talon Joe Tyler gutted him up on the Elkhorn River. That Festus, he was one mean bastard."

He managed a sloppy but purely malevolent grin. "My yes, he was mean. Short and fat and ugly, too, and he didn't look one little tiny b-bit like you. Not one whit. You ain't no C-caine. Why you wanna go an' lie t'me? Why you wanna go an'. . . ." He grimaced lopsidedly and pushed at a cord of greasy hair that had fallen over his shoulder. "Why you wanna go an' f-f-fib like that?"

Charity scowled at him. He must really be

afraid of the Caine name if he was trying so hard to refuse her right to it. She wondered if he had cowered and slunk in the presence of her Uncle Festus the same way he fawned at Claude Duval's feet. She said, "Shut up and go away."

He reared back and waved the bottle at her. Whiskey sloshed wildly and a few drops cleared the neck to spray the air. "You qu-qu-qui—stop talkin' to me like that! You're nothin' but a stinkin' no-name Breed, tha's all you are. P-prob'ly stole them guns off'n poor Zeb's c-corpse." He swept off his hat and slapped it dramatically over his heart. "May he rest in p-p-p. . . . May he rest."

"Shut up, I tell you!" She was on her feet before she realized it. They had taken away her home and they had taken away Jake. The only thing she had left was her name, and she'd be damned if she'd let them take that, too, shabby as it was. "You don't know what the hell you're talking about! Bunch of trashy riffraff living in the back woods! The whole of you put together aren't half as smart as a box of rocks, so don't you go trying to tell me who my family is!" Then, by way of punctuation, she kicked him, as hard as she could, in the shin.

He jumped back and dropped the bottle. It exploded on the stone floor. Arnie yelped and began to hop on one foot.

"Shut up back there," someone thundered drunkenly.

"Shut up yourself!" Charity shouted. She

hadn't felt this good all day. "And I'll tell you something else, Arnie," she went on. "That slug in your leg? I was aiming about a foot higher. Next time I get hold of a gun, I'll—"

A hand took her shoulder and twisted her hard about. She staggered, only to be met with an openhanded blow that knocked her to the ground.

Briscoe stood above her. "It's near sunrise, Arnie, and blind drunk or no, it's time you headed back and fetched that Marshal's body. You wake up Wilford an' Little Teddy. Take 'em with you." When Arnie hesitated, Briscoe lowered his voice to a growl and snarled, "Move." Arnie did.

Briscoe turned his attention to Charity. Very quietly, he said, "You're about to wear me out. I hear one more peep outta you and I'll put a bullet between your eyes, Duval's orders or no. We understand each other?"

She opened her mouth, but felt Rex Jeffords's hand weakly clasp her wrist. She kept quiet.

"All right, then," Briscoe said, then walked away. Across the cave, Arnie was busy kicking Wilford awake.

Rex Jefford's hand was still on her arm. Softly, he said, "You're shaking."

Charity ground her teeth. She was watching Sam Briscoe's silhouette recede on the other side of the fire. "That pig, Arnie, said I wasn't a Caine. How the hell would he know?"

"Would it be so bad if you weren't?"

"Well of course it would! If I'm not who I am, then who am I?" She rubbed her cheek, where Briscoe's blow still burned. "That sounded stupid, didn't it?"

He smiled. "Not really."

He was paler than the last time she had looked. She put a hand to his forehead, then his cheek. He was terribly cold to her touch. Immediately, she wiggled out of her coat.

"Here," she said, "you need this more than I do."

He put up a hand to wave it away, but couldn't sustain the effort for more than a few seconds. Charity tucked the fur around him, then slid away his topmost blanket from beneath it.

"See?" she said. "I'll trade you. The blanket'll be plenty for me."

"If you're sure," he whispered. He already looked more comfortable, although his condition had deteriorated greatly within just the last few hours. She wondered if he would live until the morning.

"Don't know that I could pick it up to give it back to you, anyhow," he continued. "Kind of embarrassing. Used to be able to hoist a yearling steer. Jake and I, we used to . . ."

He turned his head away as his words trailed off. Charity couldn't tell if he was losing consciousness again, or if it was the strain of talking about Jake. She knew how he felt. Just the mention of his name made her throat tighten

215

with grief. She said, "Marshal Jeffords? Are you all right?"

He looked at her again. "Sorry. I thought maybe you'd rather not talk about him."

From outside, past her range of vision, she heard low voices and the sounds of boots crunching in snow as Arnie and the other two readied their mounts and saddled up. It was Jake's poor body they would bring back. She tried to blink back the tears. *Oh, Jake . . .*

She hugged the blanket about her shoulders and stared at the floor. "He was the only truly good thing that ever happened to me. I miss him. I miss him so bad . . ." She felt the tears coming again, and neither of them spoke until she had herself under control. "I want to talk about him," she said at last, and meant it. "I want to know all about him."

Rex Jeffords obliged her. Haltingly, in quiet tones, he told her about the death of Jake's father at Duval's hands. There were good things, too: boyhood tales of swimming holes and schoolyard pranks; and later on, tales of adventure. Jake had been the first to wear a badge. Rex had joined him later. "Of course," he continued, "when I finally got round to coming to Fort Smith, Laura was still with him."

Charity swallowed hard, but she didn't speak. She kept her features passive. She had forgotten all about Laura and the watch with the picture.

"They had this little cozy bit of a house," Jeffords said, smiling. "Laura kept a vegetable garden in back and a flower garden in the front, though they never lasted long, what with all the pet rabbits she had penned in there. She used to take in every homeless critter that crossed her path. What a soft heart she had! She was nine years younger than Jake, and he indulged her terribly. She couldn't put a foot wrong as far as he was concerned; as far as I was concerned, too. You couldn't help but feel that way about Laura. She was springtime. One smile from her and you'd give her over your immortal soul."

He made a small, choked sound, and Charity leaned toward him. He was crying, and turned his head away.

"Is it your legs?" she whispered, almost glad that his pain had changed the subject, and ashamed of herself for it.

He shook his head. "This damned war between Jake and Duval. It killed her, killed our Laura. She was on her way north. Going to visit some old schoolteacher of hers who'd been taken ill. Laura was always mending something hurt, be it human or otherwise. She was at a stage stop when they took her. Ran into her by accident. But when they heard her tell another passenger about her brother, Jake, the marshal. . . . She was so proud of him. Of both of us. She was always talking us up."

He stopped again, and Charity didn't press him — she had been taken with a sudden and violent wave of shivers. *Oh, Jake,* she thought, *she was your sister, your baby sister. I should have known it was true when you said you loved me, and that there wasn't anyone else. I should have known you wouldn't lie. I'm sorry I doubted you, I'm sorry I was ever jealous . . .* She bit at her lip, glad when its tender state—the result of Briscoe's slap—gave her pain. *I deserve it. I'm such a fool, such a stupid fool.*

A few moments later Rex Jeffords cleared his throat. Almost flatly, as if he had managed to somehow dampen his emotions, he said, "I'll tell you what those animals did to Laura. They took her out into the Nations. They did . . . they did badly by her, and then they killed her. And they left her for me and Jake to find. It was the Rooneys that did it, but Duval was around."

"How do you know?" Charity whispered.

"There was a note. A note pinned to her. It said, 'Black king takes white queen.'" He covered his face with his forearm. "Oh, Laura, my Laurie. Why did they do it, Laurie? Just two more weeks, and you would have been my wife. Oh, Laurie, Laurie . . ."

Gently, she put her hand on Jefford's arm. He was shaking with silent sobs. She whispered, "Laura was going to marry you?"

Jeffords rubbed at his eyes. "She was my life. And Jake is—was—like my brother. He was more father to Laura than brother. You've never seen any two people so close. After their mother died, Jake raised her. He was seventeen then, and Laura was eight. Laura was only twenty when they . . . when she died." He paused a moment, then smiled sadly. "You'd think that after two years, it wouldn't hurt so bad. But it still seems so fresh. And now they've finally killed Jake."

He closed his eyes for a moment, and Charity reached to touch his face, worried that he had lost consciousness, or worse. When her fingers brushed his cheek, his eyes fluttered open. He said, "Sorry. I keep fading in and out. Suppose it's just as well. My legs are gone. Nothing to do to save them now. Haven't been able to feel anything below the right knee for days. The left one's gone now, too, and the rest of me's poisoned with it. I'm dying, Charity, we both know that, even though you've been kind enough not to mention it. But it's only a matter of time. Doesn't make much difference, really. I guess I've been dead inside since I lost her, anyhow."

He took a deep breath that seemed to catch in his throat. He coughed once, his face twisting, then said, hoarsely, "But I'm not alone in it anymore. We're both going to die, Charity Caine. When Arnie comes back with Jake's body, they'll have no more reason to keep us around. I'm sorry to tell you that, but it's the truth. Would have been a time not so long ago that I would have fought like hell to keep it from happening, but now . . ."

He made a feeble wave toward his dead and useless limbs. "Might's well go to be with Laurie and Jake. Only two people who ever really made me happy, anyhow. You tell me that Jake loved you, Charity, and I believe you. I can tell you loved him. So please—for Jake, for yourself—get yourself a chunk of that broken bottle, and before they have a chance, you . . ." He motioned, drawing a shaking index finger across the opposite wrist. "I should do it for you, but—" He coughed again, his body convulsing with it. "But I'm close to the end, Charity," he rasped. "And I find that when it comes to taking your life, even to spare you, I'm a coward. Be brave for both of us, Charity. Don't give them a chance to hurt you. Cheat the bastards."

She took his hand and tried to think of something comforting to say, something to persuade him to want to live. But since she felt much as did he, she kept her mouth shut. Anything she said would be a lie, and Rex Jeffords would know it.

She held his hand until he went to sleep, and then she gently tucked his arms beneath the bearskin cover. Taking care to avoid the broken glass from Arnie's whiskey bottle, she quietly scooted a few inches away from the Marshal, then hugged her knees up under the blanket and propped her chin on them.

Carefully, she plucked up a large sliver of amber-colored glass and laid the shard against her wrist, considering it.

Jeffords said that when he died, he'd go to be with Jake and Laura. He probably would, too. But where did Caines go? She doubted it would be the same place God sent U.S. Marshals and beautiful girls who, by the simple strength of their sweetness and purity, could make every person they met fall in love with them. No. She'd probably end up in some squalid, windowless corner of Hell, with no company but Grampa Zeb's cantankerous ghost.

She put the piece of broken glass aside. Then, quite carefully and by turn, she began to study each man in the cave: his position in sleep, whether or not he was armed, and just how easy his sidearm or knife might be to take from him.

If I'm going to the Caine end of Hell anyway, I might as well go there for a reason other than an accident of birth, she thought. Then, with her thumb and index finger, she flicked the shard of bottle far away. It made a soft staccato note when it landed and broke.

She turned to look at Rex Jeffords's pale, sleeping profile, and muttered, "We may be set to die, Marshal Jeffords, but we will not die alone. And that's a Caine promise, no matter what that fool Arnie says."

She glanced outside, searching the stony yard beyond the fire. Arnie, Wilford, and the one they called Little Teddy had long since ridden off, but Briscoe stood beside the fire, his back to her as he gazed out over the valley below. She saw him turn his head slightly and put a hand to his mouth. He whistled: a low-pitched, three-note *whippoorwill* call. A moment later he

221

repeated it. She heard it faintly answered, then answered again from a different quarter. The sentries, checking in. Quickly, she tried to identify the few men that remained in the cave. Bertie Rooney and that ugly Scud were missing. It was likely their whistles that she'd heard answering Briscoe's.

Briscoe turned his back once more. She saw a brief glow in his cupped hands when he lit a cigarette, and then he walked off into the trees, and she couldn't see him anymore.

Charity returned her attention to the cave. She picked a man she'd heard called Porter. He was curled against the sloped wall, about halfway between the cave's rear and its mouth. He was snoring softly and evenly, and his blanket had worked up over one hip to expose the tip of his pistol's butt. Its narrow metalwork caught the low firelight, and gave off pinpoint sparkles of pale orange.

Very slowly, her gaze flicking between that exposed bit of Colt and the woods into which Briscoe had disappeared, she began to inch toward that tiny sparkle that might mean freedom. Or, at least, revenge.

Jake Turlow lay on his belly, just off the crest of a low brushy ridge. He was up to his chin in snow, but at the moment he was more concerned with cover than comfort. To his left, a thin wavering line of smoke rose, pale against the night sky, to mark the site of the outlaw camp. Just ahead of him and about twenty yards farther along the ridge's crest was a sentry.

The sentry was one Scud Jackson, wanted on two counts of murder, three of armed robbery, and numerous petty larceny charges. Scud sat propped against a tree. He had fallen into a light sleep, his head sinking forward, his ragged beard fanning jaggedly across his chest.

Jake inched forward again, then froze and held his breath as Scud roused and shook his head, then twisted from side to side as he looked down and out through the trees before closing his eyes again.

Over the last hour and a half, this ritual had been repeated more times than Jake could count. Scud would doze and Jake would creep forward on his belly. Scud would lift his head, and Jake would flatten himself in the snow and hold his breath. The dawn would arrive in less than an hour, and if he didn't take out Scud and find the other sentries—of which he was certain there were two, judging by those *whippoorwill* calls they circulated every half hour or so—he would have little chance at getting into the outlaw's camp. *Not that you've got much chance under the best of conditions, Jake ol' buddy,* he reminded himself.

Scud's head drooped lower on his chest, and Jake moved forward, careful to keep from snapping the hard, needley branches that scratched his face as he crawled beneath them. This time he was bolder—or had an easier path through the leafless scrub—and managed to close the gap by about ten feet before Scud showed signs of rousing again. He waited through the ritual headshake and headswivel, and when Scud looked to be drowsing peaceably again, he moved forward.

He was within three yards of the sleeping sentry when he felt his knee connect, beneath the snow, with a dead branch. Before he could shift his weight, it gave him away with a muffled *crack.*

Scud's head snapped up, but before he could haul himself to his feet or bring his rifle around, Jake was on him, riding his back and forcing him to the ground.

It was quick. One hard backward twist to the head, a muffled *snap,* and Scud Jackson was dead. Jake rolled off the body, panting and wiping at his face. As he reached for Scud's rifle, he heard the whistled call from down the hill.

He pursed his lips to answer, but nerves and the scuffle had left him so dry-mouthed that nothing came out. He swore and shoved a handful of snow in his mouth, spitting out half of it. The call came again.

Whippoorwill!

This time he answered it, mimicking Scud's breathy rendition. The third call followed directly. He placed its origin at about one hundred yards ahead, along the same line of hills and ridges.

Quickly, he searched the dead outlaw's body for cartridges, and found some. He jammed them in his coat pocket next to the peppercorns and the tin of percussion caps, then unbuckled Scud's gunbelt, slid it off him, rebuckled it, and slung it over his own shoulder. He had roughly a half hour to take out the other sentry and get down into the camp. If he took longer, the first sentry would know something was wrong when his whistles weren't returned from the right places, and in the right order.

He stood up, tilted Scud's rifle over his shoulder, and started toward the source of the third whistle.

He had not taken four steps when he heard the scream.

The third sentry forgotten, he turned and began to half run, half slide down the hill, the rifle held wide for balance. He tripped and fell, tumbled, regained his feet and kept running as the scream sounded again, and all he could think was, *Charity!*

Chapter Fifteen

Charity's fingers crept over the pistol's butt.
Slowly, hardly daring to breathe, she slipped it
from the snoring outlaw's holster. She held her
breath until the gun was clear, then tucked it inside her blanket as she began to inch away.

Suddenly, she was lifted into the air and
jerked backwards. It was Briscoe, and he had
her by the hair. She screamed, more in surprise
than pain. As she dangled, toes barely touching
the ground, he backhanded her with such force
that it spun her in a half-circle. She screamed
again, this time with frustration. She swiped at
him with her hands, her fingers curled into
claws; but he held her at arm's length, and her
hands barely brushed his coat. Growling, he
smacked them away almost effortlessly.

The stolen pistol slipped from beneath her
blanket and clattered to the cave's floor. Briscoe
gave it a savage kick toward the man from
whom she'd filched it, and then began to drag
Charity outside.

"Let go! Let go, you bastard son of a pole-cat!" She knew every hair on her head was going to rip free at any moment. Her scalp was shot through with the worst kind of fire, and her mouth was filled with the taste of blood. She grabbed for his pantleg, tried to gain her feet, but he only kicked at her and kept on dragging.

Her blanket fell away as she struggled, but she was too angry to sense the cold. Her boots scrambled and scraped the floor, searching for traction; but every time she found it and started to pull herself up on her feet, Briscoe jerked her to one side and knocked her off balance.

Past the stone fire pit he pulled her, and out into the pre-dawn gloom. In the center of the stony yard, he stopped and yanked her to her feet. At last he let go of her hair, only to put his meaty hand atop her head and shove her down to the icy ground. She landed, with a skittering thud, against one of those crude benches made of piled rocks. She lay there panting, too angry and terrified to think of what to do next.

Every man was awake and on his feet. Bertie Rooney, rifle balanced before his jostling belly, came skidding breathlessly out of the trees, shouting, "What's happened? Who's killed?" Men poured out of the cave and clustered around her, fencing her in a forest of legs. They were talking too fast for her ringing ears to make out any of the words, but the general tone of it didn't sound too promising. She began to wish she'd taken Rex Jeffords's advice and used that sliver of broken glass on her wrists.

Someone kicked her. More from reflex than anything else, she grabbed his boot and yanked it toward her and up. The boot was attached to Bertie Rooney, and he fell flat. Somebody laughed. The crowd shifted. Charity tried to dive through a gap, but was immediately seized by her hair and hauled back against the stone bench.

It was Briscoe again. He pulled her head around and made her look up into his face. He said, "I warned you." And then he turned to Bertie, who was just standing up and brushing the snow off his belly and backside, and said, "I don't care no more. You boys do what you want with her."

Bertie brightened immediately, but Charity saw Toots and the others hesitate, saw something flicker across their dull faces. They were still leery. She remembered the hold that Duval held over them: simply, it seemed to her, with vague, supernatural threats and the mere tone of his voice. They might be cutthroats without conscience, but they were a stupid, superstitious bunch. She might be at their mercy, but she was still a Caine, and it worried them.

Willing her voice to a low, unwavering pitch she knew she couldn't sustain for long, she fixed her gaze on Toots and said, "My Grampa Zeb is coming for me. He's coming now."

Beside her, his hand still snarled in her hair, Briscoe spat, "Zeb Caine's dead."

She kept looking straight at Toots. "It doesn't matter," she said quietly. "He'll still come."

Toots swallowed hard. Two men backed away, their heads twisting quickly from side to side as they looked out into the night. Briscoe gave her another shake. Her scalp hurt so badly that she wouldn't have been surprised if blood began to course down her forehead and into her eyes, but she'd be damned if she'd cry out again and give him the satisfaction.

Briscoe shook her again, this time so hard it rattled her teeth. "This is flesh! Zeb Caine was flesh!" he said to his men. "Zeb Caine's dead and gone, he's no haunt, no spook! Got no flesh left to harm you!"

Charity made herself hold back tears of pain, forced herself to keep her gaze fixed on Toots. Softly, she said, "You hurt me, he'll find you."

Bertie Rooney didn't back away, but he stared down at his feet.

Briscoe let out an exasperated groan. He slapped Charity across the face, and she felt a new trickle of blood welling inside her lip and spill, in a thin, hot line, down her chin.

"There! You see the ghost of Zebulon Caine comin' after me?" Briscoe smacked her again. She took a swing at him, but he blocked her fist, catching it in his and shoving it away. "Look at this puny girl. Caine ain't nothin' but a name. She's got no magic. Zeb didn't have no magic. He was just the meanest sonofabitch west of the Blue Ridge, and now he's dead and gone to Hell and he ain't comin' back."

The men looked at each other. They didn't back away, neither did they come forward.

Briscoe snapped Charity's head from one side to the other. "You see Zeb Caine anywhere around? You see him comin' for me? You see—"

A rifle shot split the darkness. Briscoe let go of her abruptly and grabbed his shoulder as Charity tumbled to the ground. She heard shouts of "It's Zeb! Zeb Caine!" and saw the men scatter as she fell.

Briscoe's gun was out. He staggered but kept his feet. He swore as he fired up into the trees above the cave. The other men had retreated inside. Cursing them for fools, he followed them, leaving Charity alone outside.

She huddled against the icy stone bench, her head burning and throbbing all at once, her jaw pounding. Her mouth was filled with salty liquid, and when she spat, she saw her own blood, black against the snow. She stared up into the dark trees but could see no one.

Two more shots sounded.

She heard wood pop and crack as the lead hit branches in the woods behind her. Shivers swept up her spine. Was it possible?

She whispered, "Grampa?"

Inside the cave, the men were engaged in rapid argument. Briscoe, gun in one hand as he gripped his wounded shoulder with the other, worked to browbeat his men into action.

"That's no ghost," she heard him shout. "That's one man. One flesh and blood smart ass bastard with a rifle. You gonna let some two-bit bounty hunter send you scurryin' like a bunch'a kids chased by a widder woman's lap dog?"

One of the others mumbled something she couldn't make out, and Briscoe hit him across the side of the head, none too lightly, with his gun barrel. The man staggered and gripped his skull as Briscoe yelled, "Dead! Dead, I tell you! Duval's done a job on you boys, that's for sure!"

"Grampa Zeb?" Charity whispered again. If any single person could rise out of Hell by the sheer force of will, it would be Zebulon Caine. But why would he put all the effort into coming to her rescue? He hadn't even liked her much.

You idiot! she scolded herself. *You're as stupid as those pigs, believing your own stories like that. Grampa Zeb's dead and buried. You buried him with your own two hands.*

Something light-colored sailed out of the trees above and landed solidly on a patch of snow not five feet from the bench against which she cowered. She blinked hard. Then, keeping low to the ground, she scrambled toward it and snatched it up. It was a scarf, wrapped tightly around something heavy.

Another volley of shots, five this time. They all missed her — almost purposely, she thought —

but she dove back into the shelter of the bench. Fingers trembling, she unwrapped the scarf.

It was a pistol, and it was loaded, except for the hammer chamber.

Three more shots came from the trees, chipping harmlessly at the rock around her.

Inside the cave, Briscoe had managed to bully his men into bravery. Guns in hand, they crept nervously forward. Toots and Bertie edged along one far wall, two other men along the opposite wall, the others behind them. All were looking up, as if they could will themselves to see through the cave's roof. Whoever her savior was, he was up there, and they knew it.

The man whose sidearm she had stolen earlier poked his head out. She raised her pistol and fired. The shot clipped his arm and he jumped back with a shout.

Briscoe's gun came up. She ducked just in time. His shot sang off the top of the stone bench. Rock chips and tiny shards of ice spatted into her hair.

She peeked around the end of the bench just in time to see another object sail in a graceful arc from the trees above. It was smaller than the first, squarish, and metal; and it looked vaguely familiar, as if she should recognize the shape. It went directly into the firepit, landing with a small metallic thud that sent up only a tiny flurry of sparks.

Someone said, "What in the name'a—"

It was not a large explosion. It didn't even

unsettle the stones that formed the high back wall of the fire pit. But the pit's construction served to aim the force of it—cinders and bits of burning wood and metal shrapnel—back into the cave. It sounded like a colossal string of firecrackers and lit the whole place bright for several seconds, and then the men started to scream.

Toots ran out blindly. His face was peppered with specks of blood and his hands clutched at his throat. A scorched and jagged chunk of metal protruded from between his fingers, and blood spurted around it. He fell ten feet from Charity, and he was dead before he landed. Another man, unbloodied but terrified, bolted toward her, waving his gun and shouting, "I didn't do nothin'! I didn't touch her! Don't hurt me, please, don't hurt—"

There was a shot. He dropped to his knees on a patch of snow, then fell forward. A tiny round hole pocked the back of his coat. Briscoe, behind him in the smoke-filled cave, still aimed his gun at the dead man. "Coward!" he shouted.

All of them were shooting, then. It was as if they didn't know what else to do, and fired out of reflex. There was no living target at which they could aim, and they fired wildly. Charity risked three more shots, but for the most part stayed curled behind the bench. She risked a quick glimpse up into the trees, but whoever—or whatever—had been there before wasn't there anymore. Or if he was, he wasn't firing.

And then Bertie fell. He was knocked backward by the bullet's impact, so she knew it had been fired from somewhere behind her. She twisted round and tried to see into the trees. Something sailed toward her and landed against her boot. Head low, she reached and plucked it up. It was a tiny blue cloth sack. She yanked open the drawstring top. Inside were cartridges, with a few peppercorns mixed in.

Well, whatever this spirit was, it wanted her to shoot. She did. She couldn't see into the cave very well without offering herself as a target, so she fired, without really aiming, over the top of the bench. She kept her shots fairly high, though. She was mindful that Rex Jeffords was in the back of that cave and helpless.

And then she realized no one was returning her fire. For the third time, she knocked the spent cartridges from her pistol and reloaded. And then she waited. The only sounds were that of her breathing, and the soft sigh of wind playing over the fire.

At last, Briscoe's voice. "Who's out there? I know you ain't no ghost."

Charity opened her mouth to answer, but before she could, another voice spoke from the trees behind her.

"Morning, Briscoe," said Jake Turlow. "You boys having a little hurrah?"

Briscoe grunted. "I should'a known you wasn't dead, you sonofabitch."

Frantically, her eyes brimming with tears of

relief, Charity strained to see him. "Jake?" she called, half whispering, half afraid that this wasn't true, that she'd been terribly wounded without realizing it and was hallucinating.

Softly, an answer came. "I'm here, honey. Stay put." Then louder, "You best come on out, Briscoe. You're all alone in there. Sun's going to be up any minute, gonna slant its rays right in there sooner or later. Won't be long before you make a nice, easy target."

"Oh, I'm not so all alone as you might suspect, Turlow," came Briscoe's reply. "Got a friend'a yourn in here with me."

He moved forward, into the dim firelight. Rex Jeffords was with him, although Rex wasn't traveling under his own power. His frail body was completely supported by Briscoe, who carried him upright, against his chest, as if he were a man-shaped shield. Jeffords's dead, splinted legs stuck out on a sick angle, stiffly thumping the ground. He looked terribly weak. He looked as if he were barely alive. But he was smiling, despite Briscoe's gun, which was pressed to his head.

Charity gasped. For a moment she considered that she might try to wing Briscoe, but she knew she wasn't that good a shot. She'd be more likely to hit Marshal Jeffords. She held her breath.

Dragging Jeffords with him, Briscoe emerged to stand even with the fire pit. He called, "Come out where I can see you, Turlow."

Charity heard the snap of a twig behind her, and turned to look. Jake stepped out of the trees. He had not put his gun down. It was still pointed toward Briscoe.

He came forward until he was even with her hiding place, and then he stopped. She wanted to leap to her feet and throw her arms around him and kiss him and tell him a thousand things; but she waited, crouched and trembling, afraid to touch even the hem of his pantleg lest it distract him.

"That breed'a yours. I want to see her, too."

Jake motioned with a twitch of his fingertips. Slowly, Charity stood up. She kept her hands — and the pistol — behind her back.

Grunting, Briscoe hoisted Rex Jeffords a bit higher. Jeffords's head flopped back against Briscoe's shoulder. Briscoe's pistol was cocked, and he lowered the barrel, so that it jabbed against Jeffords's jaw, just under his ear. He said, "Lay down your arms."

Rex coughed, then said hoarsely, "Don't, Jake. I'm dead already."

Jake ignored him. Scowling, but never breaking his eye contact with Briscoe, Jake dropped his rifle.

"No!" Rex croaked. "Just shoot him! Shoot *me!*"

Jake dropped his handgun. As unobtrusively as she could, her hands still behind her back, Charity sidestepped until she was right beside and slightly in front of him. The moment he tossed down his pistol, she turned toward him, threw one arm about his neck, and cried, "Oh, Jake!"

She could hear Rex. His voice rattled as he said, "You always were a bullheaded bastard, Jake. You remember that time when you—"

Briscoe told him to shut up.

Charity knew Jake felt her slip her gun into his coat pocket when he gave her a little squeeze and whispered, "Good girl."

"Quit that!" Briscoe hollered.

Charity stepped aside.

"She had a gun, too. Get your hands out where I can see 'em, Breed."

Charity complied.

"Gun! Where is it?"

She shrugged and inclined her head toward the bench. "I left it there."

"Go kick it out into the open. I wanna see it. Now!" He pressed his weapon more firmly into Jeffords's neck. Rex moaned and brought his hands up to his throat.

Jake said, "Never mind." He started to reach for his pocket.

"Christ, Turlow," whispered Rex Jeffords. "You've always got to do everything the hard way." And then, his hands suddenly equipped with more strength than Charity had suspected he owned, he grabbed at Briscoe's gun. Briscoe tried to twist it away from him, but Rex's fingers were already where they needed to be. Smiling, he pushed down on Briscoe's trigger finger.

Charity screamed.

Before Rex's body slipped to the ground, Jake fired. Briscoe tried to get off another shot, but by the time he managed it, he was already falling. Jake's shot took him in the throat, and he was dead when he landed on his knees and fell, sideways, against the fire pit's high rear wall.

As one, Charity and Jake ran to Rex. Jake dropped to his knees and scooped the lifeless body into his arms. He was weeping and muttering, "Damn, damn, damn . . ."

Charity knelt beside him and put her arms around them both. She held them for a very long time.

Later, Charity reclaimed her coat. Jake broke the ice in the water barrel and washed the blood from her face. "You're not cut on the outside, honey," he said, holding her a little too closely to facilitate the wash-up. "You must be cut inside your mouth."

She nodded. "Two places. But not bad. And he didn't loosen any of my teeth." She worked her jaw from side to side again, just to reassure herself that it wasn't broken. "It doesn't hurt," she added, even though it did.

She hoped her face wouldn't bruise. She didn't suppose Jake would think she was too pretty if she had a black eye. It was an odd thing for her to consider, when she and Jake were surrounded by death. They had, in fact, turned their backs as they stood at the water barrel, as if by simply not looking at the horror behind them, they could make it disappear.

At least it seemed to be helping Jake. As he wiped the last of the blood from her chin, he seemed slightly less grim. She wanted to keep him distracted as long as possible. She'd seen his face when he gunned down Briscoe, and what she'd seen there had frightened her.

"Percussion caps," she said suddenly.

"What?"

"That's what you threw in the fire, wasn't it? It scared me at first, and then I remembered this old story Grampa Zeb used to tell. About when he and some other man . . . oh, I can't remember who it was, but he and Grampa—"

"It was Mingo Taylor," Jake said with a trace of a smile. As strained as it was, just that hint of the old, joking Jake made her heart beat a little faster.

"That's right! How did you know that?"

"I met Mingo about fifteen years after it happened. Not socially, mind. I was escorting him to prison. He and Zeb took out the Flood boys with that trick. Climbed up on top of the roof and dropped a tin of percussion caps—primed with a tad of black powder—down the chimney. Flood boys didn't know what hit 'em. Zeb and Mingo picked them off when they came running out the door."

"I suppose there's a kind of justice in it," Charity said. "One of Grampa Zeb's dirty tricks gets used against—"

239

"Dirty tricksters. Well, this is the last of them. Except for Duval, that is." Jake took off his hat and ran his fingers through his hair. "I don't suppose anybody has that much luck."

Charity said, "Oh, God. It's not the last of them, Jake. Three of them rode out about an hour before you got here. Duval left orders for them to go back and find your body. I don't know how far away they were. What if they heard the shots?"

Jake stiffened. His expression, all too human only seconds before, was suddenly as icy as the air. "That's where Wilford Rooney is, then. I wondered, when I didn't find him here . . . all right. Even if they didn't hear the shots, they'll be back anyway when they can't come up with a corpse. Damn it!"

She wanted nothing more than to just hold him and kiss him and forget about this horrible mess: that, and the expression Jake's face had held when he pulled the trigger on Briscoe. Hatred, that's what it had been. Cold, pitiless hatred. Jake had every right to hate Briscoe and the others. If Grampa Zeb had been in Jake's place, he would have been less merciful. But still. . . . It was hard for her to reconcile the merciless killer with the man she'd fallen in love with.

The Jake she'd thought she'd known was kind and considerate, gently teasing, and tender, yet passionate. Perhaps passion was the key to it. Through Jake, she had learned that her own hatred was a cloak for passions that ran deeply within her. And through him, she had learned to slip the mantle away, and found that the emotion it covered was more powerful by far than the disguise. In the beginning, she'd hated Jake because she had been taught to hate the law. But now she realized that, compared to the icy malice on Jake's face when he gunned down Briscoe, she had never really hated at all.

Charity shivered. It was too much to sort out. It was too frightening.

Jake had taken his arm from her shoulder, and stepped away to stare out into the distance. The first hint of morning grey lapped at the eastern horizon, and in its granular, silvery light, she studied Jake's profile. At the moment, she could see no emotion whatsoever playing there.

Well, what do you expect? she chided herself. *He's just seen his best friend die—and for the second time! Did you think he'd sweep you up, right here in the midst of all this carnage, and make love to you? Did you think he'd start planning what flowers to put in the window boxes?*

She gave her head a shake. Well, he was just attending to business. His manner was only sane and logical. She'd been wrong. It hadn't been hate on his features at all. She'd imagined it, mistaking self-preservation—or perhaps just skill at his job—with something else. Yes, that had to be it.

He said, "Duval's out there somewhere. For all I know he's watching us right now."

Charity followed his gaze. There was nothing out of place in the meadow below or the woods beyond. Except for the first early morning bird sounds, everything was still. But she knew Jake was right. Duval was out there somewhere. She wondered if he were casting some of that obeah magic.

Jake got down to business. Taking Rex's body along would slow them down too much, he told her; Rex would understand.

They laid him against the stone bench and speedily built him a cairn. The rocks would protect him, Jake said, until a posse could return to collect the body, as well as whatever remained of the others. He didn't bother to touch them except to identify the corpses, although Charity noticed that when he stood over Bertie Rooney's body, it seemed to be taking all his will not to kick it.

At his request, Charity gathered food from the cave while he made a quick search for reclaimable booty from the gang's most recent jobs. There was no cache of money, although he requisitioned a small hatchet and several boxes of ammunition. He tried to talk her into leaving Number Ten behind in favor of Sam Briscoe's gelding, which he pointed out was faster and a great deal more nimble, but she wouldn't hear of it. At last he gave in and, after he stripped the tack off the outlaws' horses, he shooed them away.

Their mounts saddled and packed and ready, Charity climbed up on Number Ten and waited. She had thought Jake was ready to go, but before he mounted Tico he opened his saddlebag and pulled out a sheet of paper and a thick piece of lead. Using his saddleseat for a support, he began to write.

"What are you doing?" she asked.

"Message," he said, and dropped the lead into his pack. He walked back to Briscoe's body, knelt, then felt along Briscoe's belt until he found a knife. He pressed the paper out flat on Briscoe's chest, and, without hesitation, plunged the knife into it, burying it to the hilt in the corpse.

Charity gasped, then swallowed hard. This was no mirage, no trick of the light, no detached execution of duty. It was hatred she saw on his face, cold and purely callous.

As they rode out of the camp, Charity swung Number Ten toward Briscoe's body and leaned toward the fluttering paper. Her breath caught in her throat when she saw what it said:

White King takes Black Knight.

Chapter Sixteen

Jake had slowed their pace from the initial, ground-covering lope to a walk. The land was flatter here, and the snow was patchy. Charity wondered if it might really be getting warmer. She had lost her hat the day she was captured, and was making due with two scarves. One wrapped her head; the other was tied across her lower face. She pulled it down and let it bag around her neck, then took a deep breath and blew it out through her mouth. There was some vapor, but not much. It *was* warming up.

They had ridden in almost complete silence for the hour since they left the outlaw camp behind. Charity hadn't minded. She imagined that Jake had some mourning—or loathing—he'd rather do in private. For her own part, she was still fairly stunned, and had spent the quiet time trying to sort it all out. But now she had begun to wonder whether he was so wrapped up in his thoughts, whatever they might be, that he was getting them lost. They were traveling in territory unfamiliar to Charity, but she could still tell direction by the rising sun. According to that, they were headed away from Fort Smith, not toward it. Jake was taking them deeper into the Indian Nations.

She cleared her throat. "We're going the wrong way."

Jake twisted in his saddle to face her. "That's the idea," he said, then, almost as an afterthought, "What are you doing clear back there? Come up and ride even with me."

He was taking them deeper into the wild country on purpose? She nudged Number Ten with her heels. "Why? Why, all of a sudden, do you want to go farther into the Nations when all you've been trying to do, ever since I met you, is get out of them? We keep going this way, we'll ride right through the Heartland and clear down to Texas!"

He raised an eyebrow. "Well," he said, with a certain degree of amused resignation, "you're still scrappy."

Charity sighed. "That's what *they* said."

"What?"

"Nothing. You didn't answer my question."

Palms pressed to his saddle horn, he shook his head slowly and sighed. "I'm tired of being the quarry. I don't like having Duval and those three boys on our trail. We tried to outrun Duval's men before, and look where it landed us. Me in the river and you . . ." He looked away for a moment. He rubbed at his face before he turned toward her again.

245

"My mistake," he said at last. "But this time I'm going to turn the tables. I don't like having you along for it, but you're here and I can't exactly leave you off anywhere."

Leave me off somewhere? Charity thought. *Leave me off? After everything we said and did, he wants to leave me off?* Suddenly she was so angry her hands were shaking.

She hoisted her chin. "Well, thank you very much! All I did was ask a simple question. I'm sorry to be such a blasted burden to you, *Marshal* Turlow."

It was Jake's turn to sigh and shake his head. "Don't go starting *that* again. Look honey, I only meant —"

"And don't you dare call me 'honey' !"

"What's the matter with you?"

"Nothing!" she snapped. "Nothing's the matter with me, except that I asked you a plain question and you yelled at me for no reason. You act like I'm some . . . some *duty!* Some cross you have to bear. Maybe you feel beholden to me because we . . . because of what you said back at the cabin. Well, I certainly don't mean to be a burden on you, Marshal, and you don't owe me a damn thing. I can take care of myself when I'm not being hounded by a bunch of mossy-toothed, foul-smelling polecats who only wanted you in the first place."

The cold intensity of his glare jolted her back to reality. How could she have started a fight with him after all he'd been through, after all they had *both* been through? They were exhausted, both physically and mentally. If they had any sense they wouldn't try to talk to each other for at least a week.

She started to open her mouth, intending to say she was sorry and that she hadn't meant it; but before she could, he spat, "Jesus! What am I to you, anyway? I thought you knew . . . I thought you felt the same as I did. I wanted . . ." He turned away and snorted.

"Jake, I—"

"Fine!" he snapped, cutting her off. "If that's the way you feel, *Miss* Caine. Bear with me, and I'll advise you of my plan. I intend to travel in a wide circle and let them follow us. We're going give them a nice, clear trail and then I'm going to cut back in on it and come up behind them. I fully believe it will be a success. I trust this meets with your approval, Miss Caine, but to tell you the truth, I don't give a damn one way or the other."

Charity wanted to die. His tone was so cold, so formal. When she thought of their last night together, the way they had lain together before the fire in Tink Maynard's cabin, the way his kisses had made her feel and the way she'd wanted to be with him, like that, forever, she wanted to cry. She had spoiled it, spoiled everything, just because she couldn't keep her mouth shut. Because she couldn't stop herself from picking at him when he was at his lowest ebb. She wondered if he had slept since the night before last. His eyes were red-rimmed, and he looked terribly haggard. "Oh, Jake," she said softly, her barely controlled tears making her voice catch. "Please, I didn't mean—"

"I don't intend for you to be involved in any of the actual capture. Or whatever it turns out to be," he added coldly. "I'll hide you out someplace nice and safe. Because you're quite correct, Miss Caine. This isn't your fight."

The way he said that last sentence flushed the remorse—and understanding—out of her system. Suddenly she was too angry to cry, and it didn't much matter to her that he was exhausted and had been through hell. He was back to treating her like cargo. She'd had more reverence from those cutthroats.

I'm a Caine, by God, she thought, *and I'll be treated with some respect!*

"Not my fight?" she snapped. "The hell it's not my fight! It might not have been in the beginning, but it is now. They tied me up and beat me, and that Wilford Rooney would have raped me if I hadn't bitten off his ear, and I've got a few accounts to even up with Arnie, too." She heard her own voice growing shrill, nearly hysterical, but she couldn't shut herself up.

"And your friend Rex?" she continued, powerless to stop. "Well, you weren't the only one that liked him. He was a good man, a real gentleman, and you know what they did to him? They—" Her breath caught, and she half-sobbed before she raced onward. "They crushed his legs

248

with a sledge hammer, that's what they did! He got gangrene and he was going to die, but he killed himself because he loved you and I think he liked me, and he didn't want us to die. That's brave, and the only way to honor that kind of bravery is to try to be just as strong. So if you have the guts to stay out here and try to bring down those pigs, then I do, too. I'll go along with you, *Marshal* Turlow, but not for the ride, and not to be left off in some nice safe place, like you'd park your poor defenseless grandma. I'm going to be there when it happens, and I'm going to have a hand in it. Claude Duval is all yours as far as I'm concerned, but Arnie and Wilford? They're as much mine as anybody's and I won't be cheated!"

Jake's only answer was to kick his horse in the flanks and jog ahead about four lengths, a distance which he maintained.

They rode in silence until well after mid-day. Jake's stomach had been growling and gurgling for hours, but he declined to mention it. It wasn't so much that he feared to lose the time— he'd already decided that Arnie and the others hadn't heard the gun battle, and that he and Charity therefore had plenty of time to lay down the nice looping trail he had planned. What held him back was that Charity had charge of the food, and he refused to ask her to stop and find him something to eat.

There had been a split second during that tirade of hers when he'd wanted to slap her; and that tiny moment of violence, confined though it had been to his thoughts, had made him more angry with himself than with anything she'd said.

She was right, of course. She'd been right all along. Because of him, she'd been put through hell, and she had a right to be testy. Testy? She had every right to be mad as sin. But then, he hadn't exactly been having a picnic these last few days, either. He was terribly tired, but the last few hours of sporadic dozing had taken the edge off it. He had learned, years ago, how to snatch short cat naps—five minutes or less—in the saddle on long rides. It wasn't as good as real sleep, but a man who could do it could travel twice as long as a man who couldn't.

Aside from the grief his stomach was currently giving him, he was no longer in any real physical pain. His shoulder twinged from time to time, but he largely ignored it. No, what really hurt was this last little surprise Duval's boys had handed him. It was disaster enough that they'd taken Charity. She'd been treated roughly, but it could have been a great deal worse. It could have been as bad as what the bastards did to Laura. Or Rex.

Dear Christ, he thought, for not the first time since Charity had spat that last gruesome bit of news at him. *Broke his legs. Crushed them. Oh, Rex, forgive me. Forgive me for ever being your friend, for getting you mixed up in this. Forgive me, Laura. Forgive me, Jesse and Cotton and Dennis and . . .*

The list was too long, and he choked before he could finish it. All their faces came to him, all the people who had died because, when he was eleven years old, he stood beside his father's grave and swore to get Duval, and had spent the rest of his life living up to that oath. The final image of Rex came into his mind once more— the smile on his gaunt, grayed face as he pressed Briscoe's finger down on the trigger and took his own life.

His eyes filled again with tears he could no longer suppress, and he longed to doze off once more. Those tiny naps had, at least, kept him from thinking about it or seeing the pictures. Who was it that had called sleep "tiny slices of death?" He couldn't remember, but whoever had said or written it knew what he was talking about.

He was glad Charity had held to the distance he'd established between them. *Of course,* he thought, *it probably hasn't a thing to do with a regard for my privacy. . . .* She despised him, and he couldn't blame her for it. He deserved to be despised. The last thing he needed was her pity.

Behind him and to the right, he heard the slow plod of hooves quicken, and turned his head just enough to glimpse Charity, gently urging her horse toward his. Hastily, he rubbed his face against his coat sleeve, then pulled his hat down low over his eyes.

Get hold of yourself, Jake, he thought. *You don't have time for this. Rex didn't sacrifice himself just so you could go off on some emotional tangent. You've got Charity to think of, and you can't let her be the next victim, even if she does hate you.*

The thought that she might *really* hate him, that it wasn't simply anger or nerves, frightened him more than facing an army of Duval's men. After all the grief he'd brought to so many people, he didn't know that he deserved happiness. But he realized that if he had one chance for it, that chance was Charity Caine. If he could be her salvation, perhaps she could be his.

He kept his eyes ahead as he heard her ride up beside him and settle Number Ten into the same walking speed as Tico. Then, hoping his face wouldn't betray the jag of self-pity to which he'd let himself fall prey, he turned toward her.

"I'm sorry."

They said it in unison, each looking more apologetic than the other. And then neither of them could think of anything to say. They smiled at each other—painfully, almost shyly—but with some new depth of understanding that Jake couldn't put a name to. He only knew that the sense of her forgiveness, as little as he deserved it, was balm to his wounds.

And then, still smiling, each looked away from the other to gaze at the snowy tract ahead. But they were both still grinning.

Like a couple of fools, Jake thought, and smiled all the harder. It was going to be all right.

They ate the mid-day meal in the saddle. By about three o'clock they had been through woods, open country, and now woods again. Only once had they seen any signs of other humans: a line of pony tracks, which they crossed just after noon. Jake said the trail was at least two days old, and had been made by a hunting party of Indians. Charity was tempted to ask him just how he could be so certain, but refrained. He was better at this than she.

Not long after that, she braided her hair and, after securing it with one of the narrow thongs she always kept in her pants pocket, elected to ride bareheaded in deference to the warm sunshine.

In the open places, where shade didn't block the sun, the ground was slushy rather than snowy. Even in the woods, they could hear the soft drip of water from the uppermost branches of trees, and bits of slush sometimes spattered them from above. They passed through a hollow that Charity decided would have been charming in spring—but was pretty even in winter—where an astounding number of cardinals flitted, bright red against the black and white of snow and trees.

Jake continued to curl their trail in a wide circle. He had led them down out of the hills, across gently rolling lowland, and across a wide, flat, treeless plain, then back up into a new range of hills. Several times, when they came to a high place with some degree of visibility, he stopped to scan the horizon with a small spyglass.

He seemed confident, almost happy. Charity was not quite sure how, but at that moment of apology, some sort of tacit agreement had passed between them, without discussion or negotiation. It seemed to her as if their souls had touched, momentarily, to form a new pact, or perhaps reaffirm a much older one. And although she wasn't certain what it was, exactly, that she'd agreed to, she felt quite certain that it was the most important thing that might ever happen to her. She would hold up her end of the bargain, whatever that might be.

"We've turned again," she said. They were back in rolling, hilly country, and were presently riding through a creek-centered valley, sparsely treed.

Jake nodded. "Almost closed the end of the loop." He pointed ahead, toward the crest of a tall hill. "We'll stop up there. Spend the night if need be. Remember that long stretch of plain we crossed this morning?"

"Yes."

"It's on the other side of that hill. I'll be able to watch it from the topside."

Charity thought this was quite a clever thing. She was about to tell him so when he grabbed her reins and pulled Number Ten to a halt.

"What is it?" She twisted her head, looking about quickly.

"You were about to take a sudden drop," he said, smiling. "Look."

Her gaze followed the direction of his pointing finger. About fifteen feet ahead, a ragged hole, about two feet across, yawned in the snow.

She looked back at Jake.

He said, "Listen."

The sound came clear to her, faint and thin: a scraping, a soft thump; another scraping; a tiny, muted whine.

"What is it?"

"Fox, probably," Jake said. He was already swinging down off Tico. "See those tracks over there?"

She did. The softly melting tracks of a rabbit, widely spaced to indicate the animal had been running full out, swerved crazily across the otherwise unbroken snow. The fox's prints came directly out of the wood to the left, cut straight toward the hare's path, then stopped abruptly at the hole.

Jake ground-tied Tico, then picked up a stout branch and started toward the trapped fox. He poked at the ground before him, testing it as he went.

"We'll see if we can't get this fella out of here," he said just as the stick broke through the snow, caving in another opening. "Unless he's hurt too badly. Least we can do then is put him out of his misery." He jabbed the branch down again. Another section of snow fell away, then another and another, until he had knocked down the debris that had covered a square, man-made pit at least eight feet across. Even with her high vantage point atop Number Ten, the angle was wrong; Charity couldn't see the bottom. Or the fox.

Jake squatted down on his heels and peered over the edge. "Well, he's not hurt, but I'll bet he's mad as hell," he said with a rather disarming grin. He began to kick snow down into one corner of it. "I think he'll just jump out if I can build him up a little platform to leap from."

"Who dug that hole?" Charity asked. "Does somebody live around here?"

Jake ripped a small, leafless shrub out of the earth, tossed it down atop the snow he'd already shoved into the hole, and proceeded to kick and push more snow on top of that.

"Not anymore," he replied, a little breathlessly. "But years ago there was a hermit, name of Lutie Jenks, who had a shack up here. Went crazy after a while, I guess. He thought the bears were after him. Thought they were evil spirits or something. I never did quite understand it. Lutie was dead and gone by the time I started working the Nations. My first partner, Cotton Beutel, told me about him. There, I think that's enough." He wiped his hands on his coat front, then came back and mounted Tico.

"He dug this hole to catch bears?"

"He dug a lot of 'em. They're all over these hills. Thought it was bad luck to trap or shoot them, though why it'd be any less bad luck to drop them in a pit is beyond—Look, there he comes!"

They heard a scrape and a scramble, and suddenly a fox, blinking and trembling, emerged from the gaping hole. It stood for a moment, staring at them, and then it wheeled and disappeared into the trees.

"I don't know that old Lutie ever caught himself a bear with one of these things," Jake said after a moment. "Probably a good thing. I don't know that he'd have known what to do with one if he caught it. But some of those pits are a good eight or ten feet deep. Brush gets knocked over them, the animals don't see them, and down they go. Funny. Outside of a puma, a bear's about the only critter big enough or nimble enough to get itself out of one."

He pressed his heels to Tico and started off at a slow jog. Charity rode alongside him. "How did you know there was a pit there?"

He pointed to the tree that stood nearest the hole. Carved into the bark, about five feet from the ground, were the words *BAR HOLE,* half-obliterated by snow.

"Cotton told me he marked 'em all after he rode his good saddle horse right into one back in fifty-eight," Jake said, "Trouble is, that little fox couldn't read the signs. So tell me. Did you really bite off Wilford Rooney's ear?"

They stopped and dismounted at the top of the next hill, tying the horses in the trees, then walking to the edge of the wood. There had been a landslide on one face of the hill, which created a clear view—a vista extending, unbroken by trees, for nearly as far as the eye could see—of the broad plain below. Jake sighted down on it, slowly twisting his head from right to left. "Nothing yet," he said finally, and handed Charity the spyglass. "Take a look."

He was right. Even at this distance, she could plainly see their trail. The twin pairs of hoof tracks, melted deep into the snow, looked like two dark wandering lines. But there were no other signs of disturbance except for the dainty pocks of deer track that wove out, and then back into, the edges of the woods on either side of the plain. She handed him back the glass. "Now what do we do?"

He stood up and led her back into the trees, toward the horses. "We wait. And watch." He stripped off Tico's saddle, then Number Ten's, and began the ritual of rubbing them down.

"And when they come? Then what?"

"When they start across the plain, I'll ride down the way we came and shortcut through the low woods. I'll be waiting for them above

258

that little hollow we went through this afternoon. The one where we saw all the cardinals."

Charity curled her hands into fists. "And what about me?" she asked; quite calmly, she thought, for a person who already suspected what the answer to that particular question would be.

"You're going to wait for me here," he said, and snugged a blanket over Tico.

"But—"

"No. No buts." He turned toward her and took her in his arms. "Charity, please don't argue with me on this. This is my job. My war."

She opened her mouth, but he gently pressed two fingers to her lips.

"No," he whispered, his voice firm, his eyes pleading. "Charity, you're my only hope to come out of this with any sort of anchor, any sort of peace or future. Please. I can't risk you."

Something warm and golden seemed to fill her spirit, gently reminding her of the unspoken pact they'd made. She pressed her face to his chest and hugged him tight. "All right, Jake. I'll do whatever you want."

Chapter Seventeen

They couldn't chance a fire, so they ate a cold supper of jerked meat and hardtack. There was no shelter except that of the trees, but they dared not take full advantage of it. They needed to stay at the top of the hill, right at the edge of the woods, in order to keep watch over the moonlit plain below; and could not afford to build any sort of shelter that might be spotted from afar. But it was not so bad as it might have been, for although the sunset had put a temporary end to the thaw and brought back a more serious cold, there was no wind. The weather, while still far from hospitable, was the best they had seen.

They sat, side-by-side, their backs against a wide tree trunk. Jake's deerskin cape had been thrown down to protect their backsides from the snow, and he'd shucked out of his wool coat. This tucked cozily about their outstretched legs, they were both bundled inside Charity's bearskin coat. If Jake had been a slightly bigger man, they could not have buttoned it; as it was, the fit was just snug enough to give them an excuse to cuddle.

Charity nestled her head against Jake's shoulder and smiled. It felt so good to be this close to him again, to feel the warmth of his body mingling with hers. His arm was about her. He gave her a little squeeze, and when she looked up, he smiled softly and brushed a kiss, light as a whisper, against her forehead.

She closed her eyes. That kiss, so tender, was not the gesture of a man filled with hatred. If his heart was so hard toward Duval's men, that blackness of spirit was aimed at them alone. It did not seep into any other part of him: of this she had become certain. He couldn't help the way he felt toward them any more than she could help loving him. If the demons of his past haunted him, she would help him exorcise them. If he would allow it.

But one thing I likely ought never to do, she thought dryly as she pictured, once again, Jake's expression as he knifed the note to Briscoe's corpse, is *invite him to a game of chess . . .*

She felt him cuddle her a bit closer. *Mine,* she thought with a tired smile. *That hand, this arm, the way he smells right after he's shaved, the sound of his laughter, the robin's egg blue of his eyes . . . he's mine. And I'm his, however and whatever he wants me to be. I'll go where he wants, I'll do what he pleases. I won't be headstrong anymore. I may be a Caine, but I don't have to act like one all the time. I can change. I will change. I'm Jake Turlow's woman now, and I'll be whatever he wants me to be.*

She lifted her head, whether to kiss his cheek or whisper something in his ear, she wasn't sure; and just then his head lolled back. He opened his mouth and began to snore.

Charity bit at her lip and tried not to chuckle. She was tired, too; but now that she'd had time to think about it, she realized that while she'd caught a few hours of sleep in Briscoe's camp, Jake had walked through the night to get to her.

She reached across the wide expanse of coat and gently pried the spyglass from his gloved fingers. She settled back again. She would keep the watch for now.

"Oh, damn."

Charity opened her eyes, then squinted against the first pale orange rays of morning light. "What?" she said sleepily. "What is it?"

Jake was unbuttoning the bearskin coat. A moment later he was on his feet, struggling into his own coat with one arm while he raised the spyglass with the other.

Charity couldn't understand his distress. Even without the spyglass, she could see that there were still but two lines of horse tracks crossing the plain. She had fallen asleep during her guard duty, but she hadn't missed anything. She stood up, yawned and rebuttoned her coat. It had always seemed huge, but now it seemed even larger, if that were possible, and terribly empty without Jake in there with her.

Then she realized Jake wasn't looking out over the plain at all. He was turned to the side, and he had the spyglass trained on the next forested hillside. A flock of crows, so far away that their black specks looked like a swarm of gnats, rose out of the trees, then settled again.

"Son of a bitch," he said softly, and collapsed the spyglass, jamming it in his pocket. His face was hard. "They figured it out. No, Arnie and Wilford are too stupid for that. Duval figured it out. He must be with them. Or close by." He turned on his heel, the snow squeaking under his boot, and started back through the trees, toward the horses.

Charity trotted after him. "What are we going to do?"

Jake was already saddling Tico. "I've got to get down the hill. They're coming round the back way. Got to be waiting when they come down into the valley. The one we rode through to get up here. They'll have to cross it." He gave his pistol a quick check, then reholstered it.

Charity rocked Number Ten's saddle into place and threaded his girth strap. "All right," she said as she snugged, then tied it off. "Just tell me what you want me to do."

Jake swung up on Tico, then reached over and snatched Number Ten's reins. "You're staying right here," he called softly over his shoulder as he rode away. "And I'm taking your horse so you don't get any ideas about following me. I'll leave him about halfway down the hill in case . . . in case something should happen."

"But Jake—"

He didn't reply. He had already disappeared into the maze of black and white tree trunks.

Charity stood, staring at the place he had been, her hands balled into fists and thumping angrily at her sides. He'd left her. He'd gone off to play hero and left her behind like . . . like what?

Like the woman he loves, she thought, immediately irritated with herself for forgetting all those promises of reform and unquestioning love she'd sworn the night before.

"All right, Jake," she whispered. "I'll wait. But please, please come back to me."

Slowly, she walked up through the trees to the vantage point where they'd spent the night. She turned and looked: not at the plain, but toward the next hill. She couldn't see anything out of the ordinary except the crows, a few of which were still circling. They could have been sent to the air by a passing cat or fox. But Jake had seen something: some flicker of movement or some sign. It struck her, for the first time, that he was probably very good at his job. And then she wondered how she had managed to ignore that obvious fact for so long.

"Because I was too busy being mad at him," she muttered. "I was too busy being a Caine."

She plopped down on the cape, which he'd forgotten in his hurry, and took a deep breath. *I'll wait, Jake,* she thought. *It won't be easy, but I'll do it.*

* * *

The first shots sounded less than a half-hour later.

Charity leaped to her feet. There was a pause after the first flurry of gun reports, and she held her breath. Moments later, the sharp explosions began again. She threw her arms around the tree and pressed her cheek to the cold bark. Her eyes were squeezed shut and her heart pounded so hard she could hear the blood thudding in her ears.

"Don't die, don't die, don't die, don't die . . ." was her whispered litany. And then, quite suddenly, the sounds of battle stopped.

Charity pressed a hand to her heart and waited. Silence. She stepped away from the tree, and turned, once again, toward the far hill.

Did he still live? Wouldn't he give her some sign? Call out her name, perhaps? She stood, listening. The only sound was the soft creak of tree limbs and the muted, unmetered spatter of water droplets from their sun-warmed upper branches.

"Jake?" she whispered, and took a tentative step forward. "Jake?"

She began to run. Back through the trees, then down the hill she followed his tracks. She skidded and fell, got up, slipped and stumbled, gained her feet again and kept running, her coat's thick hem dragging behind her like a train. And all she could think, as she slid into trees or tripped over their snow-covered roots or frantically pushed her way through slushy drifts that soaked her pantlegs was, *Please don't be dead.*

The woods were so thick that she couldn't see many yards ahead, and when she came to where Number Ten was tied, she nearly blundered straight into him. She debated for a moment whether to leave him tethered or hop up and ride the rest of the way down, but decided to leave him be. If something terrible had happened down there in the valley, she'd make all too convenient a target riding down there on that big old horse. In the end she left him where he was, but she slipped Grampa Zeb's Henry out of its boot and slung it over her shoulder before she took off running again.

She began to wonder if she would ever get to the bottom of the hill. Jake's tracks zigzagged through the trees, the trail sometimes steep, sometimes almost level before it would dip downward again. Several times she made tiny shortcuts, jumping down slight but sheer drops that he hadn't chanced on horseback, but that she could traverse on foot.

And as she took another of those shortcuts, and ran, full out, across a small open area that he had for some reason chosen to skirt, her feet went out from under her.

She expected to land on her hip or fanny, just as she'd already done more times than she could count. But this time she didn't hit the ground at all; she fell through it.

She landed with a bone-jarring thud that knocked the wind from her lungs and flooded her vision with dazzling white sparkles dancing in a black void. She closed her eyes, but the picture didn't change. She'd "seen stars" on numerous occasions, what with Grampa Zeb's propensity for punctuating his conversations with a shove that took her breath or a sharp hit to her head. Or both.

She knew what to do. She kept her eyes closed, pulled up her knees and tucked her head between them while she waited to breathe.

At last her lungs filled with a rush, and a few seconds later the concussive glimmers faded. She gave her head a shake and rubbed at the back of her neck, then got to her feet. A shiver raced up her spine. Walls. Sheer, dirt walls.

She was down one of Lutie Jenks's bear holes. She pressed against the frozen wall of earth, stood on tiptoes, and stretched her arm up as high as she could. Her fingertips missed the top by more than a foot.

She took a step back and tried to will her racing heart to slow; but it kept racing, and all she could hear inside her head, was her own voice, much younger: *Let me out, Grampa! Don't leave me down here!* She backed up and ran toward the wall, leaping as she did. Her gloved fingers brushed the rim, knocking down a meager clot of slushy, dirty snow that hit her in the face.

She backed up and ran at it again, but her feet slipped on the pit's snowy floor. She missed the rim entirely, skidded against the wall and fell. Something, buried beneath the snow, cracked sharply under her knee. She shifted to the side and dug fingers into the snow, thinking it might be a branch or limb. If there were more, she might be able to built up a little platform in the corner, as Jake had done for the fox.

Her fingers touched something solid and she tugged it free. It was a bone, old and dried out, and now broken. She dropped it immediately, lurched to her feet, and cowered in the far corner.

Not human, she told herself, *not human. It's a deer, that's what it is. How many deer carcasses have you helped dress out in your life? See, there's even the point of an antler sticking up over there. He probably broke his leg. That's why it cracked when you landed on it. It was probably broken already. Simple, so simple. Not human. A deer fell in here and couldn't get out.*

But she couldn't get out either. She forgot about Jake. She forgot about Duval and Arnie and the others. She forgot about everything except that single, paralyzing image from long ago: the cellar door locked, the little girl alone in the darkness for days.

Shaking, she slid down into the corner and curled herself into a ball. *Please, Grampa, let me out. I won't be bad again, ever.*

But Grampa wasn't going to come. Nobody was going to come, and she was going to die. She'd starve to death, just like the hapless, broken-legged deer, and no one would ever find her body. No one would ever know what happened to her or Jake.

Jake.

She remembered him with a start, shocked that she could have forgotten him, even for a few seconds. Was he lying bloody in the snow? Had Wilford and Arnie taken out their knives? Did Wilford have a new prize for his rifle scabbard?

That such a horrible thing could happen to Jake—beautiful Jake, who was so kind and good that he could even love a Caine—seemed far worse, and more hideously unfair, than her own fate. But she was trapped. There was nothing she could do except wait. If Jake was still alive, he'd come looking for her. If he was dead, then she'd die here. That was all there was to it. Too tired to cry, she snugged her knees to her chest and began to rock slowly, instinctively attempting to comfort herself.

It might have been hours or minutes later when she heard a sound above. Her head snapped up. If it was a catamount, she'd make easy prey.

She jammed hands into her coat pockets to grab Aunt Tildy's Colt, but came up with nothing more than two spent cartridges and some bits of straw. The Colt was in her pack, strapped behind Number Ten's saddle, just where she had stuck it before they left Briscoe's camp. She'd lost the Henry when she fell. It was up there, somewhere in the snow.

Another sound. Paws?

Cursing under her breath, she reached for and grabbed the deer bone she'd broken. It wasn't big, just a slender leg bone, but the break had left a sharp point on one end: a poor weapon, but the best she had.

Charity quietly shifted her position, readied herself to spring at—or away from—whatever sharp-toothed, hungry thing might hurl itself down upon her.

Another step, and another. But not a puma's tread. Hooves. With a soft snort, the horse stopped. The sound of the first boot alighting, then the second. Could it be? Joy and relief suddenly flooded through her, and without thinking she shouted, "Jake! Jake, I'm down here!"

There was no answer except the half-crunching, half-slushy sound of boots nearing her prison.

"Jake?" she whispered. It came out as a tiny, quavering squeak.

A shadow, long and narrow, fell across the pit. Charity shrank against the wall, the deer bone gripped in bloodless fingers.

From above, a deep, rumbling chuckle.

It was not Jake's.

For a split second she was certain it was Grampa Zeb, come up from Hell to laugh at her and throw a cover down over the hole so that she'd die without seeing the sun again.

"You been yourself having some bad luck, eh, *cher?*"

She felt as if all the blood in her body had suddenly drained away. She hadn't even the strength to hold her makeshift weapon. The deer bone dropped from her fingers. It thudded softly into the snow at her feet.

"Yes, you have plenty much bad luck, child. De marshal man, he not come for you no more."

Charity heard herself whisper, "Dead."

There was a pause, a rumbling chuckle, then, "Pretty soon enough. You and he going to die in de same way, some quite a bit alike. There can be poetry in death, eh *cher?*"

She couldn't see him. He was standing too far back from the pit's edge. But his shadow moved, waved over her slightly. She heard the pop of a match, saw the faint, foggy shadow of smoke as he lit a cigarette or cigar. A second later the match stub arced down toward her and bounced off her coatfront.

That single event, tiny as it was, served to snap her out of her fear.

"You bastard!" she shouted. "I'll see you dead if I have to come out of my grave to do it! I'm a Caine, by God, and that swamp magic of yours has got nothing on a Caine kind of mad. I'll *will* you dead!"

This time, laughter, barking and cruel, replaced the chuckle. "You no Caine, child. You best to know dat before you die. You no Caine a'tall."

"Liar!" she screamed. She batted at the air, wishing she could tie his damned shadow into knots.

He laughed again. "Only Caine 'cept Jabez what ever had de baby was Sam and his Garnet woman, and dat baby, she die. I know Sam, I there for de burying in ground. But Garnet, she take on bad. I give dem de mojo, but she not work so good for Garnet. So Sam he get her de new baby girl child. Buy dat baby off a Cherokee sportin' woman they call Hattie Feathers, what used to spread de sheets at Mule Creek trading post 'til de consumption kill her dead. You be no

Caine, *cher*. Why you think Sam and Garnet they call you 'Charity'? You whore's daughter. Don't got no daddy, no mama, don't got no name. Charity case. And dat's somethin' even de great and mighty Zebulon Caine not know."

Charity thought, *No!* but she couldn't make her mouth move. She heard a sharp hiss above, and knew that he'd tossed his smoke to the ground.

"So dat how you die. No kin, no man. No hope. But I think about you and dat marshal man of yours. I think about you for next day or so. Dat how long it take you to die, unless you strong. De stronger you are, de longer it take. You best pray weak you are, *cher*."

"Liar!" she shouted, finding her voice too late. His bootsteps were already retreating, alternately crunching and sloshing through the snow. "Liar! Take it back!"

She heard him mount his horse, heard the slow slushy meter of its departing hooves.

"I'm a Caine!" she called after him. "A Caine, I tell you! My father was Sam Caine, my mother was Garnet Trimble Caine, and I was born in Texas! My grandparents were Zebulon and Sweet Dove Caine! My uncles were Aaron and Odis and . . ."

She let the words trail off. She couldn't hear him up there anymore. He was gone, and she was alone and trapped and cold. Colder now that his words were beginning to sink in.

Gossip, she thought, *Dirty gossip*. But what if he was right? What if she wasn't a Caine after all? Snatches of conversations, spoken when she was very small, came to her. *Don't look Choctaw to me, Pap. Got more Cherokee bones.* Who had said that? Was it Uncle Jabez, the year he came to visit and made her the doll? And Aunt Tildy: *Don't know where you got them looks, girl. Too purty for a Caine. Too skinny and too tall. Don't look nothin' like any'a us, least of all your mam and pap. That Garnet must'a had some lookers hid away in her family, that's all I can figure . . .*

But did it matter now? And Duval had said Jake wasn't dead. Yet. *He said Jake and I were going to die the same way,* she thought. *Is Jake down one of these pits? Is his body broken and tormented? Is he waiting to die like that deer?*

"No!" She nearly shouted it. She wasn't going to let Jake die. There had to be some way to get out of this black, frozen hole and find him. She pushed the last pictures of her own younger self, terrified and trapped in that windowless cellar, from her mind. "I will do this," she muttered. "I might not be a crazy, wolf-blooded Caine, but they raised me, by God. That's got to count for something. Grampa Zeb always said there wasn't anything a Caine couldn't do if he put his mind to it."

She set to work.

She started at one side of the pit, and pushed and shoved and scraped up every bit of snow and debris, right down to the frozen mud floor, and piled it in the far corner. It didn't make as large a mound as she would have liked. When she stood atop it, teetering on the bones and sticks, she

273

could reach the rim of the pit; but it was slick and kept breaking away, and she couldn't get a grip on it. She slid back down every time she tried to pull herself up. Jumping didn't help; she only fell harder when her fingers slipped off the rim. She realized she'd have to get her elbows over the edge if she hoped to gain enough traction to pull herself the rest of the way up and out.

She hopped down off the mound and tore at it until she found one of the deer's antlers. She stared at it, biting her lip before she dug into her pants pocket. There was still one left. She tugged the thong from her pocket and, smiling a small, rather hard smile, she bound the antler to a stout stick and gave the leather tie a final, snugging jerk. It made a funny sort of rake and a fairly insecure one, but it was the best she could do.

She stepped up on the mound again. On tiptoes, she stuck the antler rake up and over, and began to pull snow into the pit. Most of it fell on her, but she didn't mind. She kept her mind on raking in what she could, and on Jake.

She had to stop twice to rewrap the thong that held her homemade tool together, but she managed to pull all the snow and slush within reach into the pit. She was sweating by the time she set aside her implement and began to shift the mound, taking away from the sides and adding to the top, then piling on the new snow she'd brought down from above.

She hopped up on it. It was a good deal higher. Leaning against the wall for balance, she held her arms over her head. Almost high enough.

She crouched, said a little prayer, then sprang straight up.

It was no good. She was still a few inches shy.

She jumped down off the mound, mopped the perspiration from her brow and began to pace. *Damn,* she thought. *Damn, damn, damn!* She had already raked down all the snow she could reach. She supposed she could move the entire mound to another corner, stand on it and rake down the snow from that side . . .

How many hours had she been at this? Her stomach was growling, she suddenly realized. It must be noon. But then, she hadn't eaten any breakfast. And she was so hot. Snow on the ground and she was hot. Now that was funny!

"Does it matter?" she muttered. "Does it really matter what time it is when Jake's out there somewhere, maybe half-dead, maybe worse? Does it matter that you're about to smother in this heavy old coat? Does it matter that—"

The coat. She fingered it thoughtfully. Of course she was hot, even if she could still see her breath fog the air. She had on Lord-knew-how-many layers of clothes under it. This damned old coat: big enough for two people, and at least twenty-five pounds in weight. It might, if it were folded up just so and put on top of the mound, make enough padding to raise her high enough to hook her elbows over the edge.

She scrambled out of it, and began to fold it into as tight and thick a package as she could.

Carefully, she set it atop the snowy hillock she'd built, and climbed up. She wobbled a little and it was still a few inches short, but . . .

She crouched once more, screwed her eyes shut and gritted her teeth, then sprang up with all her might.

Her forearms went over the rim, her elbows securely angled over the topside. Grunting, she began to hoist herself up, her boots kicking and scratching at the frozen mud of the pit's wall, her shoulders aching. And just when she thought that she wouldn't make it, that she'd surely fall back into the pit and break every bone in her body and die, her waist cleared the rim.

With a heave, she hauled herself forward, bent herself over it: her torso flat on the ground, her legs still hanging over the edge, her toes dug into the wall.

She lay still a moment, tensed and panting. And then, with great effort, she shoved herself to the side and brought up one leg. She rolled over in the snow, brought the other leg up, and lay limply. Her breath came in great gasps and her arms were throbbing, but the sun was on her face. There were no walls about her. She had not died. She has escaped the pit — and the cellar. She was free.

At last she sat up, still breathing heavily but with more ease. Directly across the pit from her, carved deeply into a tree she had only seen from the side when she first came running through the little clearing, was the message which might have been her epitaph: *BAR HOLE.*

She stood slowly, scowling as she brushed wet snow from her sodden shirt and trousers. "Thanks a lot, Lutie Jenks, wherever you are," she muttered. "Thanks for that sterling bit of information."

The Henry was easy to find, and when she gave it a quick check it seemed unharmed. She started down the hill, careful this time to stay right on Jake's trail. Without the coat she was beginning to feel the chill, but she would be all right. She was still so flooded with adrenaline that she doubted the cold could hurt her, anyway.

And there was Jake to find. That was first. For if she couldn't find him, then it wouldn't really matter to her if she froze to death.

Chapter Eighteen

The limb creaked again. *Break, you son of a bitch,* Jake thought, and, at the far end of the rope's swing, contorted his body against the ties that strapped his arms to his torso.

He succeeded in increasing the arc slightly, and twisted again at its opposite end. Back and forth he sailed, a little higher and more wildly each time. His ankles ached and his head felt bloated with blood, but he supposed that was only natural when a man gets himself hogtied and hanged, upside down, from an oak tree.

The limb wasn't going to break. He'd known it all along, but it was the only think he could think of to try. He relaxed. Slowly the arcs lessened until his body came to an uneasy suspended rest. He sighed, and that small movement started him swaying, spinning slightly like a lonely wind chime caught in a breeze. The limb creaked softly. The rope snugged over it complained with a muted grating sound.

His head hurt from the thump someone had

given it. Duval, of course. There hadn't been anyone else alive to do it. He wondered if Duval had sneaked up on him as he kicked Wilford Rooney's body with a savagery that had given him just as much remorse as gratification. Had Duval crept closer as he knelt over Wilford Rooney's body, ready to knife another note to it, or had Duval winged him from a distance with a well-aimed bullet or rock? That was more like it. Duval wasn't one to come in close.

He guessed he'd been hanging there for an hour, anyway; maybe longer. He'd been awake for the last thirty minutes of it, and able to form anything close to a coherent thought for only the last fifteen. Waking up strung from a tree with your head dangling five or six feet above the ground was, he found, a nauseating experience. If he'd had anything on his stomach, he probably would have thrown it up. That urge, at least, had passed, but the back of his head still pounded insistently with every beat of his pulse.

Go ahead, Jake, he told himself. *Feel the back of your skull and see if it's a graze or a lump. Or both. Use that invisible extra arm that isn't strapped to your side.*

He wondered how long Duval had taken to bind him in rope. He wondered why Duval hadn't just killed him. "Damn you," he muttered. "How long do you figure it'll take me to die, you son of a bitch? Two days? Three? Four? You just wanted to be able to take as much time as you could get to kill me. You want to savor it, you bastard! Did you laugh when you hauled me up here to hang like a butchered hog?" His voice had risen from a whisper to nearly a shout, and at the end, his cry of "Duval! Come back and finish it!" was a howl that echoed though the hills.

He took a deep breath. *Got to get a grip, Jake,* he scolded himself. *Got to think. Got to be calm.*

Damn Duval, anyway, and damn those notes. If he hadn't been bent over Wilford, intent on pinning a last message to his chest, Duval night never have crept up on him. If he hadn't started following Duval's lead years ago by retaliating with those bloody reminders of who had won each round, he wouldn't be in this mess. And he likely wouldn't be having to face the final humiliation of Duval's reply every time his body rotated toward the oak's thick black trunk.

There, affixed to the gnarled trunk with his own knife was the paper he had been about to peg to Wilford's corpse. His own lettering was still there. It said *Check.* But Duval had altered it with four simple letters that told the end of twenty years of brutality. Now the note read *Checkmate.*

Jake's body slowly twisted away from the tree and the note and toward the valley clearing. Wilford Rooney's still and rotund body lay not ten feet away. Arnie Denato and Theodore "Little Teddy" Turpin lay another five yards out, their limbs tangled as if, at the moment of death, they had been dancing and had fallen in a heap.

In truth, Jake had taken them quite by surprise. He had clipped Wilford first, and when Wilford went off his horse, Arnie's horse had reared, slipped, and landed against Little Teddy's. They both went off, but Arnie had his gun out already and was trying to fire as he spun through the air. Arnie had, quite by accident, killed his own man. Jake doubted if Little Teddy had time to notice whose pistol had fired the fatal bullet, and he doubted just as strongly that Arnie had time to realize what he'd done. Jake had shot him through the chest before he hit the ground.

They were all dead, now. He remembered standing up slowly and going to the bodies, making certain they were dead. He'd been thinking that it would be a good long while before he heard from Duval again. It would take the Cajun time to scrape up a new gang and find a ramrod he could trust. He had raised his arm to plunge the knife into Wilford's corpse. And then had come the jolt to the back of his head.

Lazily, the rope twisted him about. He could see the hoof tracks—closely spaced and leisurely—that led away, across the narrow valley clearing and up into the trees opposite. Duval's tracks.

The rope turned him past the Duval's line of retreat, and again the bodies came into his line of vision. First Wilford Rooney, then the other two, and then he slowly twisted back toward the tree trunk and its fluttering epitaph. *Checkmate.* Well, that was right. Or was it?

He had forgotten Charity, although how he ever could have was a mystery to him. She was still up the hill, waiting. She'd come. A man wouldn't die from just being dangled upside down from a tree, even if it did make his head feel big as a prize pumpkin.

But what if she didn't come? He knew she'd look for him eventually. *Hell,* he thought with a tiny smile, *she'll probably come charging down the hill on that old plodder of hers at full gallop, reins in her teeth, firing with both hands . . .*

It was an interesting picture and a chuckle escaped him before he realized that Duval's tracks headed up the hill, straight toward the campsite.

A chill traveled through him. Suddenly, finding a way to save himself didn't seem an end in itself — it was only one in a series of things that had to be done in order to get to Charity.

A twig snapped to his right, back in the trees. An image flashed into his mind: bags of suet and seed that, in winters past, Laura had suspended from the sycamore in the front yard. Food for the birds. Well, he was dangling just as surely as those little net bird feeders of hers, except he was more enticing to varmints of a larger, more carnivorous nature.

He wriggled against his ropes in an attempt to turn himself, just slightly, to the side. Instead, he began a slow arcing spin, but was relieved when that full circle didn't reveal a cougar or a wolf. It was only Tico back there in the trees, pawing up the wet snow up to uncover tufts of dead grass.

Jake held his breath, willing the sickening spin to stop. At last it was reduced to a lazy sway. *Good old Tico,* he thought. *Only horse that didn't run off. If I could just get him over here, maybe . . . maybe what? Have him chew through the ropes like a trick dog? Have him reach up there and untie you, or maybe pull out his handy-dandy pocket knife and cut you free?*

"Jake, old buddy," he said aloud, "you hang here upside down much longer, you're gonna go all the rest of the way crazy."

He eyed the note again. His knife was there, pinning it to the bark. If he could swing himself toward it, he might be able to get the knife between his teeth, and then . . . *and then what?*

Another sound. A thump, very near. He craned his head, the rope turning him as he did so. He didn't see anything, but Tico's head was up. The gelding looked out across the clearing, toward the opposite trees.

Another thump. This time he was spattered across the face by a thin spray of snow, and saw the culprit — a snowball, just rolling to a stop beneath him. The bastard was back, and that snowball was more humiliating than any bullet or brass-knuckled blow. Without thinking, Jake roared, "You son of a bitch! Why don't you just kill me and finish it!"

Another thud. This time it bounced off him, but it wasn't a snowball. It was a little blue drawstring bag which had once held peppercorns.

He twisted his head again, putting himself into a spin as he called, "Charity? Charity honey?"

On the second rotation toward the far trees, he saw her emerge from the wood. She'd lost her coat and her clothes looked soaking wet. On the next rotation, he glimpsed her as she stepped over Arnie's body, and around Wilford's. Two more turns and she was beside him. She put her hand on his shoulder and stopped his spin. Her head was roughly level with his. She said, "You look pretty silly, Marshal Turlow."

He was grinning so hard his face hurt. He said, "You look pretty damned beautiful, Miss Caine." He had never meant anything more than he meant that.

She said, "I suppose you'd like me to cut you down?"

Damn, she was better than beautiful. "Unless it'd keep you from something more important."

She put her hands on her hips and looked up toward the limb from which he was suspended. She clicked her tongue, then said, "Well, I reckon it won't hurt me to be a few minutes late to the Ladies Aid Society meeting." She went to the tree trunk and pulled his knife free. She stared at the paper, then crumpled it. "Your Mr. Claude Duval doesn't know all the rules," she said.

"What?"

"The last move took a knight. That means I get three squares on the diagonal with my rook."

Jake shook his head, and it started him circling again. Either she was crazy or he was. Maybe he hadn't heard her right. He decided to pretend he hadn't heard. He said, "I'll whistle up Tico. You can stand on him."

She steadied him again to stop his spin, then took a step away and stared up into the tree. "I'm not standing on any horse."

"He'll hold perfectly still, And you'll never be able to skinny up that oak. The lowest limbs are too far off the ground. Why don't you—"

She held up a palm to silence him, but she didn't look his way. She seemed transfixed by that damned limb. He wondered if she'd fallen and hit her head, and rather hoped she had—it would explain a great deal. He waited. He supposed he'd best humor her.

At last she said, "You know, Jake, my Grampa Zeb taught me a lot of things. Now, most of them aren't worth a hill of beans, but some of them come in handy from time to time. He taught me how to play chess, though Lord knows I never wanted to learn. He taught me how to deal from the bottom of the deck and how to mark cards, and just where on a fellow's head to hit him if you want to kill him and not just knock him silly. He taught me how to shoot, too, although I can't claim to be much of a sharp-shooter past about thirty feet. Grampa Zeb said it didn't matter much, though. He always claimed a gun wasn't much of a weapon for a woman. Said it wasn't 'underhanded' enough. I like to think he meant 'subtle,' but he probably didn't. Now, he said—"

"Charity! Honey, will you please just go get Tico? If you just sit on him you can reach high enough to cut my hands free, and then maybe I can pull myself up enough to—"

"Hush," she said, waving a hand.

"Charity, you've got to hurry!" he said, with more frustration than he intended to display.

"Duval could ride back in here any minute!"

She shook her head, although she still wasn't looking at him. She took another step back, cocked her head at the limb, then took another step to the side. "He won't be back. He's long gone."

Jake gritted his teeth. She was beautiful but, whether he loved her or not, she was crazy as a loon. Crazy as a Caine. As calmly as he could—which was none too calmly—he said, "How do you know that, honey?"

She wasn't looking at him, but he saw a smile flicker at the corner of her profiled mouth. "You don't need to talk to me like I'm six years old, Jake. I saw him. He stopped and had a little chat with me."

"What?" he practically shouted. The force of it started his rope twisting again, and he started into another slow spin.

Charity ignored it. She said, "I'll tell you about it later. When we go to get my coat."

She moved another three feet to her right. At her side, she absently swung the knife between her thumb and forefinger, rocking it back and forth like a little seesaw: blade end goes up, hilt goes down. "Anyway. As I was saying before you interrupted me, Grampa Zeb always held that the best weapon for a woman was either poison or a knife. Never taught me about poisons, likely because I did the cooking. He was mean, but he wasn't stupid. He taught me a few things about knives, though. Drilled me night and day for the solid year that I was sixteen." She looked down from the limb and at the long knife in her hand. She gave it a little toss into the air and Jake gasped, certain it'd slice her on the way down. It flipped three times before she caught it, deftly, by the tip of its blade.

She said, "Decent balance. Not wonderful, mind you. But decent."

Jake, swaying gently side to side as a result of the head-shaking, muttered, "You're enjoying this, aren't you?"

She said, "If I were you, I'd curl up some so I wouldn't land on my skull."

With that, she pulled back her arm, the knife's blade between her fingers, and sent it, spinning end over end like a blurred and sparkling wheel, toward the limb.

Jake jerked his head up just in time. He hit the ground jack-knifed, on his side. Above, the knife still vibrated, its blade embedded deep in the limb where the rope had been.

"Jesus!" he breathed, and before he could say anything else, Charity was on the snowy ground beside him, kissing him, pulling him up against her, kissing him again and again and laughing as she kissed him. Or crying? He felt her tears on his cheeks. Here he lay, trussed and helpless, unable even to hold her. There were dead men all about them. And she was laughing and weeping and kissing him, and he was so damned hard he was about to split his britches. *Jake, old buddy,* he thought as he squirmed against his bonds, *you'll never find another girl to match her, 'cause they only made the one.*

"Honey?" he finally managed. "Honey, untie me."

"Oh," she said, breathlessly, "the ropes," and stuck the tip of her tongue in his ear before she set to work on the knot at his wrists.

The first thing they did, after she got Jake free and he made a quick search of the outlaws' bodies, was to hop on Tico and follow Duval's trail. Although Charity had been hoping for a little more kissing and hugging, she knew Jake was right. She also knew, from the way his voice cracked and the way he held her tight to him after they double-mounted Tico—he with some difficulty—that had the circumstances been even slightly different he would have made rather emphatic love to her there and then.

She couldn't stop smiling.

When they reached the pit in which she'd been trapped, Jake found a long branch and fished her coat up out of the hole while she gave him a brief recount of her conversation with Duval. She omitted, however, what he'd told her about her parentage.

Jake bundled her in the coat, clucking over the sodden state of her clothes like a mother hen. "Got to get you out of those and into something dry as soon as we get up the hill, Miss Charity Caine," he said. "I just got you back. Don't you go and catch pneumonia on me!"

She promised that she wouldn't.

They followed Duval's track long enough to

make certain he'd headed off in the other direction, and then they retrieved Number Ten and went up the hill to their own camp. From the edge of the wood, they saw Duval's retreating track, and at the end of it, Duval himself: a tiny grey dot against the snow.

"You could go after him now," Charity said softly, hoping he would so they could be done with it forever and all; and hoping that he wouldn't, because she was afraid that Duval might be the one to end the game.

"No," Jake said. "There'll be another time for that, but for somebody else. Not me. I'm getting you out of the Nations. I did some thinking while I was riding down the hill to head off Wilford and his friends. I decided that if I made it through, I was going to quit. Turn in my badge."

"But what will you do?"

He shrugged. "Ranch. Farm, maybe. Maybe I'll go back east. Maybe farther west."

Charity bit at her lip, afraid to say anything. He'd said "I," not "we." Well, what could she expect? She was a Caine. No, she wasn't a Caine. She believed Duval on that count. But Jake still thought she was a Caine. She supposed she could tell him, but . . .

"What do you like better? East or west?"

"I . . . why are you asking me?"

His brow furrowed. "Well, you're coming, aren't you?"

She stifled a sigh. "If you want me, I don't care where we go."

A smile split his face. "All right, then." He just stood there, grinning at her as if he couldn't think of anything else to say and hadn't given himself permission to hug her.

Finally, she said, "Shouldn't we be moving?"

He shook his head. "No. We've only got an hour or so of daylight left. Not enough to get us to Tink's anyway, and that's the nearest civilized shelter." He poked a thumb toward the plain below. Duval had disappeared into the distance. "He's not coming back. We're as safe here as anywhere. Tell you what. I'll throw a lean-to together for us. It's going to get colder again tonight, and it'll be nice to be out of the wind. I'm not crazy about building a big fire, but I think we can chance a small one, at least long enough to make some coffee and a hot dinner. And in the morning we'll head out for Tink's. All right?"

She nodded. "I'm starving. Jake, do you think Tink's all right?"

He was already leading her back into the trees, toward the horses. "He's fine. Tink Maynard is hard to kill. They wouldn't have gone back after him."

They reached Tico and Number Ten, and Jake produced the little hatchet he'd confiscated back at Briscoe's camp. It looked like a toy, and Charity stared at it quizzically. "I hope you're not planning on hacking down anything very big with that."

He laughed and ran his thumb along the blade. It was steel and shiny and looked to be very sharp. "You'd be surprised what a fella can do with a hatchet this size if he's motivated enough. Tell you what. While I'm cutting us some shelter, why don't you tend the horses?"

He set off into the trees, and it wasn't more than two minutes before she heard him chopping.

She moved both horses deeper into the trees, where they would have the most shelter, then started on Number Ten, stripping off his tack and rubbing him down before she blanketed him. Tico was next, and when he was seen to, she dug out nosebags and grain and fed them both. She was not so quick at it as was Jake, and by the time she finished he had made several trips to and from this small area in the trees, each time depositing huge armloads of long, stout branches against the base of a thick pine a short way up the hill. He was presently standing before it, rubbing his hands together and blowing out steam through his mouth.

"Sun's almost down," he said, waving for her to join him. "Getting colder and the wind's coming up some. I'll get this thrown together in — Say, your teeth are chattering!"

She hadn't noticed until just then, but she was freezing.

"You've still got those wet clothes on under that coat, haven't you?" He appeared angry with himself, although Charity had no idea how he thought he could possibly have made her clothes dry for her.

He had brought kindling, too, and he kicked a clear spot in the snow before he stacked it in the bare spot. "Here, honey, you start a fire while I get this thing put together. And then you can get inside out of the wind and change into something dry."

She nodded. She didn't speak because she knew the words would come out chopped by chattering teeth, which would only make him feel worse.

She built the fire and warmed her hands over it, then set on a pot of coffee to brew. She made an attempt to sort through the foodstuffs, but by then she was too cold and too tired to care about cooking anything. She wondered if Jake wouldn't mind a dinner of hardtack and jerky, so long as he could wash it down with hot coffee.

"What do you have there?"

He was crouching beside her. She hadn't even heard him come up. "There's plenty," she said, trying not to stutter with the cold. "Cornmeal and jerky and b-bacon and—"

He took her elbow and stood up, bringing her with him. "Okay. I'll get dinner." He pushed her saddlebags into her hands. "You get in there and get changed before it gets any colder."

"In where?"

He turned her about toward the pine where, when she last looked, he had been sorting through a pile of cut saplings and branches. The pile was gone, and the pine tree had been transformed. One section of its lower limbs, which brushed the snow, had been cut away to make a pocket in the green boughs. Within this, he had cleverly placed and tied and woven all the wood he'd cut, to make a tiny and fairly solid A-framed

292

shelter, the one open end of which was draped with a blanket.

"Go ahead," he said, smiling, and gave her a little nudge. "It ain't fancy, but it's home."

Glancing back over her shoulder at Jake, who was still grinning smugly, she went toward it, knelt, and crawled inside.

It was not big enough to stand in by any means, but it was better than five feet long and perhaps four feet wide, just as high, and surprisingly snug. He had tacked a blanket along the inside of the wall that took what wind the pine tree didn't block. The rest of the blanket lay over the strip of floor that wasn't by his deerskin cape. The floor gave under her with a rather spongy spring; when she pulled back a corner of the deer hide to peek beneath, she found he had stripped the cut pine boughs of their smaller, needle-lush branches, and used them for mattress padding. All things considered, it was very comfortable. Inviting, in fact.

Suddenly, Charity didn't feel so cold. She felt, in fact, almost warm. And, just as suddenly, she had a sterling idea. She smiled, and began to tug at her boots.

Chapter Nineteen

It was almost dark when Jake tapped on the roof of the shelter. "Get ready for the cold," he said. "Gonna pull back the blanket for a minute."

She pulled the coat close about her and said, "I'm ready."

The blanket lifted, revealing Jake in silhouette against the graying sky. In one hand he carried the smoke-blackened coffee pot. In the other was the big iron skillet. He placed the coffee pot in the near corner, rocking it on the padded floor to make sure it was stable before he took his hand away. Then he set the skillet inside the door. "Don't touch that," he said. "It's hot. I'll be right back with dinner and some light."

He let the blanket fall again, leaving Charity in darkness. The rich, tantalizing scent of coffee was overpowering, and her stomach growled. It also seemed to her that the tiny shed had warmed quite a bit in just the minute or so since Jake had closed the blanket door. Much faster than just her own body heat could account for.

The blanket lifted again, and this time both Jake and the interior were brightly illuminated by the small torch he held. "Hold these, honey," he said, and handed Charity two long sticks, on the ends of which were impaled odd, tubular chunks of what looked—and smelled—like crusty cornbread. Next, he reached behind him and produced a single plate, layered with thick slices of bacon with most of the fat cooked away. "And this," he added, handing it to her.

The smoky, salty aroma wafted up over her and her stomach rumbled again. It was all she could do to keep from grabbing a chunk of bacon and stuffing it in her mouth.

Jake crawled inside, let the blanket fall closed behind him, and then pushed the skillet (which she could now see was laden with four rocks, each the size of a man's fist) nearer the door. He laid the torch down, resting its fiery head on the stones. What little smoke it gave off rose to disappear through the cracks in the shelter's construction.

He scooted toward the back of the lean-to and pulled off his gloves. "There," he said with a satisfied smile. "Already got those rocks hot all the way through. They'll help keep us warm for a few hours after we toss out the torch."

He reached across and retrieved the coffee pot before he produced a tin mug from each of his coat pockets. He began to pour. "Eat your bacon and sloosh," he said. "Don't wait for me."

He didn't have to say it twice. The first two

thick slices of bacon went down so fast that she was barely conscious of having chewed them. She took a gulp of coffee. "Sloosh?" she said belatedly, as she reached for more bacon. "What's sloosh?"

He took the two sticks from her hand. "This stuff you forgot you were holding." He gripped one long golden pellet, slid it off its stick and handed it to her. She took it. She sniffed it. "Cornbread?"

He nodded, and pulled his off its stick before taking a bite. "Not bad," he said, chewing. "Poor man's cornbread. We used to make it during the War. You take your bacon, cook it up pretty crisp so you've got most of the fat left in the skillet. Then you dump your cornmeal—and whatever else you've got in the way of seasonings, which was usually nothing—into the fat. Mix it up good, into a dough. Then you wrap it round the end of a stick and prop it over the fire to bake up."

She tried it, making certain to nibble around the burnt parts, and resisted the urge to make a face. It lacked flour and eggs and salt and honey; everything, in fact, except cornmeal. But she said, "S'good."

He laughed. "That isn't what your eyebrows are saying. Well, it's not in a league with your cookin', but it'll fill you up. And it's about the extent of my kitchen skills."

If the sloosh wasn't exactly tasty, it was, as Jake had said, filling. She finished hers before he did, licked her fingers, and poured herself another cup of coffee. She leaned back, fortified, smiling smugly, and ready to put her plan into action.

Jake lifted an eyebrow. "What?" he said, in between bites of bacon.

She smiled and pushed a stray strand of hair out of her eyes. "I didn't say anything."

He studied her for a moment, his expression quizzical. "You look like the cat that swallowed the canary bird, Miss Charity Caine." He tipped his coffee cup, draining it, then cocked his head. "Just what are you up to?"

She smiled as innocently as she could. "Marshal Turlow, you have a suspicious mind."

"Force of habit," he said after a moment. "It's just that . . ."

She lifted a brow. "Yes?"

He shook his head, then took the plates and cups and, leaning to one side, stacked them in the corner. "Nothing. Never mind." He pointed to her pack, which she'd shoved against the rear wall of the shelter, where it could be used as a pillow. "Did you have enough dry clothes in there to see you through?"

She nodded, still smiling faintly in spite of all her attempts to the contrary. She was feeling very warm again. He was so sweet and so concerned and so . . . attractive. She shifted her position slightly.

"Sorry you couldn't dry your wet things over the fire," he said, "but I didn't think we'd better chance it any longer than it took to make supper. I—where are your wet clothes, anyway?"

As she leaned to one side to let him see the rolled bundle of damp clothes behind her, her coat's hem slipped a few inches, exposing a bare foot and ankle. She pulled it back beneath her and rearranged the coat.

Jake said, "Were your boots soaked, too? I don't know how we can get them dry before—"

"They weren't wet through," she said, gently cutting him off. "They're fine." She wondered if her voice sounded as husky to him as it did to her.

Jake was staring at her coat's hem, just where she'd tucked it over her foot. He cleared his throat. "Oh." He unbuttoned his coat and glanced up at the peaked roof. "I must have built this thing snugger than I thought. Warm in here."

Charity smiled. "Yes, it is. Of course, with the torch and the rocks, and us being so close together. . . . Body heat. I suppose it all adds up. Take me for example. Now, I was so tired when I crawled in here that it was all I could do to get myself out of my wet things. I plain didn't have the strength to put on my dry ones." Jake's head jerked up, but she just kept on talking. "Even stark naked under this coat, I'm feeling a little warm myself."

Jake opened his mouth to say something, but she beat him to it.

"Well, it's early yet," she said, trying as hard as she could to appear bored. "Can't be much past seven. I don't suppose you've got a deck of cards?"

Both his eyebrows shot up. "What?"

"Cards. You know. King, queen, jack? Hearts, spades, clubs, diamonds? Little pieces of pasteboard with—"

"Thank you, Miss Caine," he said through clenched teeth. His brow furrowed a bit, though he still looked amused. "I know what cards are. And no, I don't just happen to have a deck on me. My cards are out in the saddlebags with the billiards table."

"Well then," she said pertly, as she reached into her pocket, "we'll use mine." She began to shuffle. It took all her willpower to keep from looking up when she heard him grumble and shift his position.

"Where . . . ?" He paused to clear his throat. "Where in God's name did you find a deck of cards?"

She riffled the deck, cut it one-handed, and reshuffled before she slapped it down in the small space between them. "Cut," she chirped. When he tapped the top with his index finger without looking at it, she added, "Same place you confiscated that little hatchet of yours. I picked them up back at Briscoe's cave and stuck them in my pack. Got a bag of rock candy and a beat-up dime novel, too. It's a Buffalo Bill one, I think. If you're nice to me, maybe I'll read some of it to you later." She began to deal: two face down, one card up. "Seven card stud, nothing wild.

They're not marked, in case you're worried."

Numbly, Jake picked up his hole cards. Charity stifled a giggle. He looked at them, then at his face-up card. His lips pursed, and then he looked her straight in the eye. It sent a flood of heat rushing through her. He said, "And what, Miss Caine, do you propose we bet?"

She took a deep breath. She had planned on being in control, but that look he'd just given her had made her a little woozy. She said, quite softly, "I have the high card showing. Queen of diamonds. And the queen bets . . ." She slithered one slim, bare leg out from under the coat, exposing it to the knee. ". . . one leg."

Jake leaned back. He checked his hole cards again. "I see," he said with a grin that was full of purpose. "Well, that's really only half a leg, you know, but I'll accept it. And I'll see that leg." He tugged off a boot.

Charity nodded. "That's fair." She dealt them each another face-up card. She pointed to the pair he had showing: two spades, the seven, and the deuce. "Possible flush. And the five of hearts for me. Nothing. But I'm still the high card. Let's see . . ." She pursed her lips, making as great a show as possible while she pretended to consider her bet. At last she reached down to her coat's hem and, plucking it up by the fur, slid it all the way up her thigh, stopping just before the hip. "I bet a thigh."

Jake exhaled loudly. He tugged off his other

boot and fairly threw it aside. It just missed hitting the torch. "I'll see that."

She shook her head. "I don't know that the house can accept a boot for a thigh, Marshal Turlow. Although we might call it even if you'd throw in a belt."

"Now listen, Charity—"

She held up a hand and solemnly shook her head. "Marshal, don't make me call the bouncer."

Sighing and cursing good-naturedly under his breath, he unfastened the buckle, then slid the belt free of its loops. He dropped it on top of his boots.

Charity smiled. "I knew you were a good sport, Marshal." She dealt out another pair of cards, face up. "Another spade for you. A flush looks imminent. And a jack of diamonds for me. My queen's still the high card. Let's see. I believe the queen will bet . . ."

She caught her bottom lip between her teeth, as if she was giving it great consideration, which in fact she was not. She had the deck neatly stacked, and each of her bets calculated to drive him to a delectable distraction. After a pause long enough to ensure Jake's continued frustration, she uncurled the second leg from beneath her fanny and slid it alongside the other, careful to expose it only to the knee. "The queen bets a leg."

"Miss Caine," Jake said quite seriously, "that queen of yours is a piker. But I'll see that leg with . . ." He looked down at himself. "I don't know that I have anything worth quite exactly a leg."

She tapped her chin with her finger thoughtfully. "How about a coat?"

"A coat's worth more than—"

"That or your pants."

He stared at her for a moment, then shrugged out of his wool coat. "Miss Caine," he said resignedly, "you would make a fortune on the river boats."

"Why, thank you," she replied, but before she could deal out the next set of cards, he took her wrist.

"A coat is definitely worth more than a leg," he repeated. "That coat covers the bet and raises it."

She lifted a brow. She hadn't counted on this. "Well, what do you suggest that I—"

"Something to warrant a more interesting call from you than another thigh," he broke in. "Not that I have anything against your thighs, mind. It's just that you're being far too limited in your betting. Be bold, Miss Caine, or you'll never sit at the better tables!"

And then his fingers went to the top button of her coat. He slid it free, looking into her eyes the whole time. Softly, he said, "May I suggest a breast?"

Charity tried to swallow and couldn't.

Very slowly, he eased one lapel of the fur aside and downward, uncovering the top swell of her left breast; then lower, until the nipple peeped

302

through the fur; then lower still, until the soft weight of her breast was supported and plumped by the coat's volume. She could feel it tickling her. She could also feel her nipple immediately tighten.

"Yes," he breathed, his eyes—those blue, blue eyes—still locked to hers. "I can see that you feel it's only fair." Jake skimmed his fingertips over the top swell, then took the nipple's bead between his thumb and forefinger. Holding it firmly yet gently, he gazed into her eyes. "I believe you do want to see my wager, after all."

And when he ran his thumb across it slowly, teasing at the budded tip with his nail, she felt the tingling heat of it shoot in a straight line from her breast to the base of her belly.

And then, quite abruptly, he sat back. Charity blinked. She couldn't quite catch her breath.

Jake grinned at her maddeningly. "Cards?" he said.

Suddenly aware of little more than her exposed breast and the effect it was having on Jake—and herself—she numbly dealt out the last face-up cards: an ace of diamonds to him and a deuce of clubs to herself. It was not the way the deal was supposed to have proceeded, but she was so flustered she'd carelessly reversed the deal, thereby giving him the high card that was supposed to top out her royal flush. *Grampa Zeb would not be amused,* she thought automatically.

When she looked up at Jake, he was smiling much too broadly. She swallowed hard. She forgot all about Grampa Zeb.

"Well," Jake said. "My, my. What does this little old ace of diamonds of mine bet, I wonder?" He crossed his arms over his chest and stared Charity up and down, from the top of her head to those bare legs sticking out from beneath the fur, with a lingering pause in the middle, at her exposed breast. She felt hot color rise in her cheeks.

Jake's fingers went to the buttons on the front of his pants. "Tell you what," he said brightly. "The ace of diamonds bets a pair of britches. Nice britches, homespun, hardly worn for more than a year, only been in need of patching on two occasions."

He managed to get out of them without thrashing around too much, although he nearly kicked out the torch. At last, his Union-suited legs poking from beneath his shirt tails, he handed the trousers to her. Smiling with a rather ominous pleasantness that made Charity's blood fairly bubble in her veins, he whispered, "Would you like to see that bet, Miss Caine? Perhaps . . . raise it?"

Her breath was shallow, but she managed to say, "You have the advantage of me, sir. I have no pants."

He leaned forward and murmured, "I am more aware of that than you can begin to imagine. May I make a suggestion?"

She opened her mouth, but nothing came out. She nodded.

He rubbed at his jaw. "Pants are a valuable commodity, you know. Can't match the value of a man's pants with just any old thing. Has to be something precious. Yes, something precious." He leaned forward again and gently laid back her coat's other lapel before, with excruciating deliberation, he eased it down until both her breasts were completely exposed and cradled in fur.

He cupped a breast in each hand, then slowly circled the puckered and swollen crests with the flats of his palms so that Charity could feel every crease and line in them through her pounding nipples. Without wanting to, she arched her back and pushed forward. He leaned in toward her, raising slightly on his knees. She parted her lips, eager for his kiss, but his mouth merely brushed her cheek.

He dipped his head, and just as his fingers released one nipple, he took it into his mouth to quickly swirl the tip of his tongue around its tip. She gasped as he took his lips away, leaving the cool air to tease her newly moist skin and tighten it all the more.

He took his hands away, took his lips away, and sat back, leaving Charity open-mouthed and breathless. Quietly, he said, "I believe there's one more card to play, Miss Caine."

Hands trembling, she dealt the last cards, face-down this time. She didn't even watch her hands.

It was no use. She had long since lost control of the game, and now she had nearly lost control of herself. She'd wanted to be the one to tease him and hold him off until he couldn't bear it anymore, but now she realized she'd be lucky if she could last another thirty seconds before she threw herself into his arms.

Jake picked up the last card and fanned it in his hand along with the first two. Charity couldn't understand how he could appear so calm when she was burning with want. He laid his hole cards, facedown, next to the four exposed pasteboards. "Seems I'm still the high man, so it's my bet. Now let me think a minute . . ." He gazed at her breasts again, and this time Charity flushed so intensely she felt the heat of it spread to her bosom. A flustered squeak escaped her lips. As she bit down on her lip, Jake looked into her eyes. "Oh, don't worry, Miss Caine. You've still got plenty left to bet."

He took off his shirt and laid it over his coat. And then, with an almost lazy deliberation, he unbuttoned the top of his Union suit, then shrugged out of it so that it bagged at his hips. Charity couldn't stop staring at his chest. She had forgotten how broad it was, and how rich was its pelt of reddish hair. She wanted to press herself against its furry warmth, to feel her breasts being tickled by it. And just below his waist, she could see the distinct outline of his shaft, fully erect, eagerly straining against the fabric. Just the tip—dark, sleek, and glinting with a single bead of moisture—peeked above the white cloth.

"You haven't even looked at your cards," came his low, baritone murmur. A blur.

She felt for them without looking. She couldn't seem to take her gaze away from Jake. She found the pasteboards and picked them up, held them before her without focusing. Jake leaned forward. Charity dropped her cards.

He whispered, "And what's worth a man's shirt and half his long johns, I wonder?" He put his hand on her calf and slowly slid over her knee, then up her exposed thigh. "A bared fanny, do you think?" His hand traveled upward, under the coat to her hip, then behind her to cup the swell of her buttock. "Miss Caine, I'd delight in a long, long look at your naked bottom. The problem is that if you turned to let me have my fill of the sight of it, I'd lose my perspective on your beautiful face and those lovely breasts." His hand still cradling her buttock, he dipped his head to brush a kiss across her shoulder.

Her breath was coming in such short, shallow pants that she feared she might lose consciousness. *Get control of yourself!* she thought, but how could a girl get control of herself when every cell in her body was sizzling like water on a hot griddle?

"What we have here," he said, sliding his hand back down her leg and from beneath her coat, "is a monumental dilemma." He sighed and sat back, leaving Charity wobbling. He crossed muscle-belled arms over his chest. "Fair is fair, Miss Caine. Why don't you just slide that coat off to, let's say, your waist?"

I will get control of this, Charity thought. *I will get control of myself.* She took a deep breath, then she managed to say, "A-all right, Marshal Turlow." Her fingers, still shaking, went to the next buttons and fumbled them free. "I'll call that bet," she said, her voice so throaty and thick that it felt not at all her own. She let the coat slip from her shoulders and arms, then opened it completely to sit before him, naked in the torchlight, as she added, "And I'll raise you."

He leaned forward, sweeping the cards from between them as he reached for her. "Oh, you already have, Miss Caine," he whispered, just before he kissed her. "You already have."

Chapter Twenty

Although Jake knew Charity was passionate, he hadn't expected her to be quite so ferocious. He had reached across to take her in his arms, but within seconds after their lips met, Charity had pushed him onto his back, tugged his long johns down over his hips and straddled him without once breaking the kiss.

Now she was slithering over him, kissing his temples, his brow, his nose, his chin. Her hair fanned and looped upon his chest and arms, curtaining her sinuous torso as she rubbed her lush breasts against his chest; sliding up and down, first moving forward to dangle one breast above his face just long enough to let him catch the dark nipple in his mouth before she tugged it away and offered its twin; then sliding lower to rub her belly back and forth along his erection until he was barely able to think.

He'd wanted to take it slow this time, but she'd made that impossible. He wove his fingers through the hair at the back of her head, tightened his hand into a fist, and turned her face toward his. Her eyes were slitted, her lips parted, her cheeks flushed.

She looked like he felt.

He pulled her face to his and kissed her hard, begging her wordlessly to get on with it before it was too late. He felt her draw her knees up to hug his sides, and when he felt her position herself over him, then ease down to envelop him completely, they both let out sighs that bordered on groans.

They moved together perfectly. She rode him, born to his rhythm; he thrust up into her mindlessly, with no coherent thought in his head but the syllables of her name.

It was over quickly, in an explosive climax that came to both as one. She collapsed upon him, still impaled, panting, her internal aftershocks clutching him in the most intimate and subtle of embraces. And as she nestled her head on his shoulder and tucked the crown of her head just under his chin, Jake realized that his face was wet with tears.

His arms went round her to stroke her bare back, moist with sweat in the chilled air, and rub soft circles on her backside.

Her tangled hair fanned over his shoulder and arm like a cloud of fine black lace. Her breathing grew easier: deep and regular. He kept rubbing her back. "Baby?" he whispered. "Charity honey?"

She gave no answer except a low, vibrating "Mmm" that he felt as much as heard. That, and a slight snuggling of her head against his shoulder. She was asleep.

He grinned. All that intensity had worn her out. In his case, it had purged. He hadn't realized how much anger and frustration he'd been carrying these last few days. Charity kidnapped; the carnage that was all that remained of the Lightfoot family; Rex suddenly alive, and just as quickly dead; and then that last little trick of Duval's. . . . Perhaps the jag of self-pity he'd fallen into after the shootout at Briscoe's cave had skimmed the top of it, but he'd forced himself to cap his feelings. If he hadn't, he might have broken down.

But at this moment, after this nearly violent bout of love with Charity, he felt cleansed. Was it over, he wondered? Was he really clean, finished with it?

Yes, he thought, *it's finished for good and all.* Duval was on his way back toward the heartland, and there'd be no more trouble out of him until long after Jake and Charity were out of the Nations for good. *I'll forget about him,* Jake promised himself. *I'll make myself forget about twenty years of poison. Charity is the antidote. Charity will set me free.*

Slowly, so as not to disturb her, he cocked an arm up and pillowed his head on it. Where would they go? Louisiana? He'd been to New Orleans once and liked it, aside from the sticky air and the mosquitoes. Maybe Kansas City. Just as many mosquitoes in the summer, but at least you had a true winter. Or all the way up into Iowa. Now, there was good farm land!

He tried to picture himself out in the fields, walking behind the plow with the long reins thrown over his shoulder, and Charity coming out to him, carrying a pitcher of lemonade. He saw himself wiping his brow and accepting a glass from Charity. Then he realized she didn't look happy. And he didn't either. He shook his head and pushed the vision away. No, not Iowa. Or Missouri or Minnesota or Kansas. He was no farmer, and Charity was no farmer's wife. No city girl, either. He couldn't see her putting up with whalebone or bustles or high-button shoes for more than about five minutes. But there were other places, plenty of them. Millions, probably.

He thought of Charity and that damned knife toss of hers, and stifled a chuckle. *Good Lord, Jake,* he thought, smiling with a more complete joy than he'd felt for years, *Better keep on your toes. Put your elbows on the table one too many times, and she'll nail you at thirty yards with a butter knife.* He chuckled under his breath. *What have you gone and got yourself into?*

For one thing, it looked like he'd gotten himself into a night with the lights burning bright. The torch showed no signs of guttering, and it was at the foot end of the lean-to. There was no way he could toss it out into the snow without disturbing Charity, which he had no intention of doing. In addition, he couldn't straighten his legs without putting them into the fire or through the blanket and into the cold.

On any other occasion these facts might have disturbed him greatly, but at the moment they only made him grin. Charity shifted on him slightly, making a tiny sound as she did so, and he felt himself stir and stiffen within her. *Oh, no you don't,* he lectured himself happily. *Let the lady sleep. Just calm down.*

But his body wasn't listening, and the harder he worked to control himself the worse it got. At last he reached for Charity's coat and arranged it, as best he could with his limited range of movement, over them both. Then he felt above his head for her pack. He freed the buckle one-handed, then groped inside until his fingers settled on what he wanted. He drew it out, angled it so the light hit it, and stared at the cover.

Buffalo Bill Cody: Grit Makes the Man was the title.

Oh, hell, he thought, and thumbed it open to the first page.

Charity woke to dark, silvery light and a cramped leg. It took her a moment to realize she was lying across Jake's chest. She smiled sheepishly as she remembered why she'd fallen asleep that way. During the night she'd managed to scoot herself up his torso a few inches and to cant herself enough to one side to drop her left hip to the ground and straighten her leg. The right knee was still crooked, at a fairly extreme angle, across his belly and over his hip.

She lay still for a few minutes, ignoring the discomfort in her knee and focusing, instead, on the deep rhythm of his breathing and the way his chest carried her up and down with each breath he took. How strong he must be, to sleep the night with what amounted to a one hundred and ten pound blanket on his chest!

Slowly, she lifted her head to look at him. He was still sleeping, lips parted slightly, his face sweet and relaxed. Next to his head, her pack's contents were half-spilled out over the deer hide floor. The purloined dime novel, winged open, lay under Jake's hand.

She craned her head up and toward the shelter's doorway. The torch had long since burnt out, but dawn light made two luminous strips on either edge of the blanket. She blinked and looked away.

Slowly, she began to ease her right leg down along Jake's side. Her knee was so stiff she could fairly hear it crack, and she wiggled a bit more than she intended. Jake squirmed beneath her just slightly, and as he did so, she felt his shaft press against the inner joint of her thigh. She paused before she moved again. He grew a little larger, a little harder. He made a small sound, deep in his throat. Charity smiled.

Her leg was less contorted by this time, although still crooked. And she was still straddling him, although she had slipped to one side. Jake had slept with his knees cocked up—likely, she realized, because he was a good bit taller than the shelter was long. So she couldn't climb off of him without making a ruckus.

Beneath her, Jake shifted his torso and hips. He was very hard now, and pushing at her inner thigh insistently. That wonderful sensation, newly familiar, tingled between her legs and made her want him back inside her. She wondered if they had fallen asleep that way. The thought of it excited her all the more. She touched his chin with her fingertip. *Maybe,* she thought with a smile, *a ruckus is just the right way to start off a day* . . .

Slowly, she eased her hand between them and wrapped her fingers about his length. She whispered, "Oh, Marshal? Marshal Turlow?"

His eyes didn't open, but one of his arms came up under the coat to hug her. "Baby," he whispered, his voice lowered by sleep to a rumbling, scratchy bass. "Charity."

She squeezed him slightly, then relaxed her grip. "Good morning," she breathed, and kissed his ear. "How was your book?"

He opened one eye. "Book? My . . ." He opened the other eye. He smiled sleepily. "Not nearly s'good as my poker game." Beneath the fur, he rubbed her shoulder. In reply, she squeezed him again, slowly moving her hand up and down, and rather firmly; then gently swirling her palm across the head. It was moist, and

315

slick as wet silk stretched over steel. He swallowed hard and said in a raspy voice, "You're asking for trouble, Miss Caine."

She nipped at his chin. It was whiskery, and the edges of her teeth slid along the short beard hairs rather interestingly. "I think I can handle just about any trouble you care to hand out, Marshal Turlow."

"Is that so?" Quite suddenly, he hugged her tightly to him and rolled to the side so that they lay face to face, still covered by the fur coat. His hand slid down her back, tickling at her spine until it reached her buttock, then her thigh. He pulled it up to rest atop his hip. His member was still in her grip, caught between their bellies. "*Any* trouble that I care to hand out?" he said softly, and kissed her.

Their loving was slower than the previous night, but not by much. Charity couldn't wait to feel him ease his way inside her, to be once again perfectly connected to him. She writhed against him, whispering, "Now, Jake, now," between his kisses until, after what seemed to her like forever but was probably less than five minutes, he slipped his hand between their bodies and placed it upon hers. Together, they guided him in one long, slow motion that nearly drove her mad.

The position, coupled with the close confines of the lean-to, held their lovemaking to a less frenetic level than the previous night's, and it took all of Charity's willpower to keep from shoving Jake over onto his back so that she could be in control and speed the pace. Not that she could have pushed him if she'd tried: he obviously had no intention of altering anything, and held her firmly against him, kissing her brow and eyelids, his stubbly whiskers tickling her face as he thrust up into her over and over.

She moved with him as best she could, all the while hugging his hip with her leg and twisting toward him, meeting his every thrust. Very quickly she felt that most wonderful of sensations begin to well inside her, then suddenly flood over and through her. She craned her head back. She thought she felt Jake's lips at her throat. She thought she heard him speak her name just before he bucked into her even more deeply.

And then they were still. He remained inside her as he relaxed. His arms were about her and he was holding her, just holding her: no words, no caresses, no kisses. And the simple fact of just being held seemed to her even more precious than what had come before it.

She would have gladly stayed in his arms forever.

Too soon, she felt him kiss her temple. She lifted her head and looked into his eyes. *Oh Lord,* she thought, *how can any eyes be that color? You can see into forever in that blue.* Without thinking, she twisted her belly against his.

He smiled and rubbed her back. "My dear, beautiful Miss Caine," he said, his eyes glinting, "you are insatiable. But one of these days I'm gonna have to get you to slow down. We keep going at this rate, you're liable to kill me before I'm forty!"

With that he gave her a playful smack on her bare bottom and pulled himself from within her. When she made a small noise of disappointment, he grinned at her maddeningly. "C'mon, honey. If we get started now, we'll make it to Tink's by noon. And I don't know about you, but I could use a bath and a shave and a real roof."

He sat up, the coat falling away from his torso. He immediately rubbed at his arms, then grabbed for his longjohns. "Be warned, baby. You don't know how warm that old coat of your is until it's not on you anymore."

The shelter wasn't big enough to allow two people to dress within it simultaneously, so she huddled beneath the coat until Jake was back in his gear and had crawled outside to tend the horses. As she dressed in dry clothes, then braided her hair, she wondered how anyone could bear to take things any slower when it came to making love. She thought back to that first night she'd spent with him in the cave on Whiskey Ridge. How on earth could she have ever thought that he'd made love to her without waking her? It seemed so silly. It seemed years ago. Had it only been five days? And six—no, six and a half—since they'd fled her cabin.

She finished plaiting her hair and tied it with a leather thong. Less than a week, and her life had been changed forever by a man who symbolized the thing she had been trained to hate the most.

Grampa Zeb, she thought as she pulled her coat back on, *you were full of Grade A, certified horse manure.*

She picked up her pack and the bundle of wet clothes, and by the time she reached Jake, who was saddling the horses, she was humming.

Chapter Twenty-one

It was just past eleven in the morning when they rode in sight of Tink's cabin. Most of the snow in the yard was melted away to islands of white, and the avalanche at the cabin's front had melted down to knee level slush, through which had been shoveled a neat path. Smoke rose from the chimney. Charity, riding just behind Jake, sighed with relief. Tink was safe.

As they dismounted, Jake called, "Hello the house! You in there, Tink?"

The front door swung wide almost immediately. Accompanied by the rich, seductive smell of roasting venison, Tink Maynard, dressed in britches that bagged at the legs but strained about his belly, emerged to fill the doorway. His left arm was in a sling that covered most of his undershirted front.

"Jehoshaphat, Turlow!" he bellowed. "I'm heartened to see them villains didn't finish you off!" One-handed, he pulled up his red suspenders, thumbing them over his shoulders with a *snap*.

320

"Is that that Charity girl you got with you?"

Charity slid off Number Ten and planted her boots on the muddy ground as Jake, laughing, replied, "Can't slip anything past you, Tink."

"You folks get on in this house, then! That is, 'less you plan on bustin' up my furnishin's for more firewood. Just got a set of legs back on my poor ol' table this very mornin'." He looked Charity up and down. "Can't say neither of you look the worse for wear."

"Good to see you, too," Jake said to Tink as he took Charity's elbow. She supposed he was just making sure she didn't slip in the slushy mud, but the gesture made her feel rather grand.

"Glad you were still here and not up at your new place," Jake went on. Without letting go of Charity's elbow, he slapped their horses' reins around Tink's hitching rail, then gestured out toward the trees. "Don't know as I'd have had the first idea where to look for it."

"Hell, boy." The old trapper stepped aside as Jake steered Charity through the door. "After them ya-hoos chased you off and left me lyin' in the snow, was about all I could do to crawl up the damn hill."

"You look fit now," Charity offered, although she was staring not at Tink, but at the shoulder of venison roasting on the fireplace spit. A lidded black kettle was suspended over the fire, too.

"Well, I sit more'n I used to."

Charity opened her mouth, but before she could ask Tink what that had to do with how he looked—or could inquire as to what was simmering in the black kettle—Jake whispered, "You have to speak up."

"Got company, darlin'!" Tink announced as he closed the door.

"He's not just deaf," Charity whispered, "he's crazy as a—" Just then she heard a giggle, decidedly feminine, from behind the corner curtain.

"Tink, you old rapscallion!" Jake boomed. "Is that the Widow Pritchard back there? Cora? That you?"

"I should say it ain't," Tink replied. Charity wished they didn't have to shout at each other. Much more of this and she feared she'd go deaf. "Cora Pritchard picks younger bucks than me to shack up with. I don't know how she finds 'em out here in the middle of—"

Another giggle came from behind the curtain, and a chubby hand pulled it slightly to the side. An eye peeked round the edge. Charity grinned.

"Well," Tink said, "I do believe me and you has had this particular confab before, Turlow. Thats there is Two Turtles Lightfoot. C'mon out, honey."

As Two Turtles emerged, giggling and blushing, Tink said, "She come draggin' in here late that same night. Oh, we was a pair to draw to, I can tell you. But she got me patched up good." He patted his belly, then stroked his

322

whiskers. "She's nigh on near as good a cook as the Widder Pritchard, too, I'll wager."

Behind her hand, Two Turtles giggled again and looked at the floor. Charity went to her and rested her hand on the woman's shoulder. "I was worried about you," she said softly. "I saw the place where . . . where you were ambushed."

Jake turned toward her. "You . . . ? I hoped you hadn't seen . . ." He looked as if he wanted to throw his arms around her and comfort her. She wished she was standing by him so he could give in to the urge. She didn't actually need the comforting, but she would take advantage of any reason to feel his arms around her again.

"Speak up, Turlow!" Tink roared. He looked a little irritated. "Where you folks headed? Still of a mind to shoot for Fort Smith? I'd ask you to bide the night, but this, uh . . ." Tink cleared his throat and looked toward the door, Two Turtles giggled again. Jake winked at Charity, who bit at her lip.

"Well," Tink went on at last, "this here's a small house. Only got the one, uh . . ." He started to point to the bed, then thought better of it and grabbed his coat off a nail beside the door. "C'mon along, Turlow, let's tend them horses a'yours while you tell me just what the hell happened after them fellers chased you outta here, and then you folks stay on for midday supper."

Once Tink and Jake closed the door behind

323

them, Charity took Two Turtle's hands and drew the woman to sit with her beside the fire. "Are you all right?" Charity said, expecting to play the role of comforter. "I saw what they did to your family."

Two Turtles shrugged. "I am fine," she said at last. Her voice, which did not at all match her physical shape and size, was high and flutey and so soft Charity wondered how in the world Tink would ever hear a word she said. It was almost a child's voice, except that her words were formed quite crisply. "It was very bad, what they did. But Lightfoot and those boys?"

She made a face, then turned her head and spat into the fire. "Lightfoot was bad to me, and those boys, they were from his first wife, a long time ago. They beat me, too, with sticks. Lightfoot, he thought that was funny. He worked their mother to death. Would have worked me to death, too. When we got to the clearing, he saw that a package was gone from the travois. He sent me back along the trail to find it. That was good for me. I was far behind, going back through the woods. Those men, they didn't see me. They killed Lightfoot and the boys fast."

She snapped her fingers three times. "So my life is saved because of a package. Ten pounds of sugar. That is what it was."

She sat back in her chair and rubbed hands over her face. "It is not good to speak bad of the dead. In some things Lightfoot was a good man, I think. He had friends. It was just not a good thing to be one of his wives. You want to take off your coat? This is a strong fire."

"What? Oh. Of course." Puzzled, Charity shrugged out of the heavy coat and laid it across the bed. She didn't know which surprised her more: that Two Turtles seemed so philosophical about the recent tragedy, or that she was talking so much. After her only other meeting with Two Turtles, Charity had been convinced the woman was the next thing to mute. "What will you do?" she asked. "Do you have people to go to?"

Two Turtles shook her head and smiled softly. "My mother and father are gone. My people . . . my mother was Creek. My father half white, half Osage, but lived white, mostly. Nobody quite sure what to do with me." She studied Charity's face. "Who are your people?"

Charity cocked her head. "The Caines."

"Zeb Caine?" Two Turtles sat back suddenly, her brows alternately raising and furrowing. "That one is your people?"

Well, Charity thought, *at least she didn't hit me.* "He raised me," she said at last.

"Not blood?"

"No."

Two Turtles relaxed again and leaned forward slightly. "I am glad to hear this. My father, he rode with that wolf's head, Zeb Caine, many summers ago. They have an argument over some small thing. I heard it was about who owned a

325

Spanish spade bit. And Zeb Caine kill my father with an axe handle. I don't like my father very much. He was not good to my mother. But still, he was my father."

Charity opened her mouth to say how sorry she was, but Two Turtles stopped her before she got the words out.

"It is nothing to do with you," she said. "What I meant before was, who are your people? You are not white."

"Oh. My grandmother was Choctaw . . . no, Cherokee. No. My mother was Cherokee." It was, at least, what Duval had told her. "I don't know who my father was."

The woman made a small gesture with her hands. "I think your family has a hard time making up its mind."

Charity didn't quite know how to answer that without going into too many details, so she said, "Where will you go?"

"I stay here for now. Tink asked me. I know him a long time. He knew my family, when I was just little. He likes my cooking, he talks to me, and he's a good man, even good to women. He pillows me fine," she added brightly, then blushed.

They lapsed into silence. Two Turtles stared into the fire, a smile playing at the corners of her mouth; Charity surreptitiously scented the air, trying to determine what was cooking in the black pot.

After a few minutes, Charity felt Two Turtles's

hand on her arm. "Do you wish to go with Turlow?" she asked. "Before, when we met you, I thought you were a prisoner. You frowned very much. But you don't wear irons. Does Turlow take you to Fort Smith, to the jail?"

Charity smiled. "At first I didn't want to go with him. But no, I'm not his prisoner. I want to go with him." *Anywhere,* she added silently. *Anywhere on this wide green earth.*

"Ah!" Two Turtle's face broadened with a grin. "You love Turlow! I was stupid before, but I see it now. I think Turlow would be good to love. He would not hit you or work you too hard." She leaned closer. "How does he pillow?" she asked, quite seriously.

Charity suppressed a laugh, but found herself blushing furiously. "He . . . he pillows fine," she finally managed.

Two Turtles nodded sagely as she bent forward to give the spitted venison a half turn. "Important thing," she said.

"Well," said Jake as he pushed back from the table, "that supper sure beat anything I've had for the last couple days, Two Turtles."

Charity was inclined to agree with him. The melange in the black pot had turned out to be a sort of stew, made from tubers and onions and canned tomatoes and a few things she didn't recognize, and frankly didn't care to. But it had been well-seasoned and filling, and after two

327

servings of it plus a thick slice of meat, she couldn't imagine that she'd be hungry again for days.

"Plan to head for the Widder's?" Tink asked. He reached for his coat, dipped into the pocket and pulled out a fat cigar, which he laid on the table and chopped neatly in two with his knife. He handed half to Jake.

"Don't mind if I do, Tink," Jake replied loudly. He nipped off the other end and stuck it in his mouth before he offered Tink a light. "Yes," he said finally, after he lit his own and took a few puffs. "Imagine we'll bide the night there, then head on to Fort Smith in the morning. Got any letters to go in? Happy to take them for you."

Tink shook his head. A small clot of ash fell into his white beard, but he didn't notice. "Nope."

Two Turtles noticed, though, and reached over to brush it away. As she did, she muttered something in that tiny voice, and Tink burst out laughing, then patted her on her wide fanny.

That's how it had been throughout the meal. Charity and Jake had to shout at Tink just to get his attention, but Two Turtles could whisper from across the room and Tink understood her every syllable. Charity supposed love must be a powerful thing indeed.

Jake stood up and stretched his arms. "All right. Don't mean to be rude, Tink, but if Charity and I are going to make it to the

Widow Pritchard's by nightfall, we'd best be on our way."

Charity gestured toward the dirty dishes, but Two Turtles waved her hands. "You go. Tink will help me." She turned to Jake. "You men get the horses. I want to talk to Charity."

After Jake and Tink had pulled on their coats and closed the door behind them, Two Turtles went to the edge of the bed and, motioning to Charity to join her, sat down.

"You have no pretty things," Two Turtles said. Her hands were folded in her lap.

"Beg pardon?"

"I do not think you have pretty things. If I was so pretty as you, I would wear pretty things all the time."

Charity thought for a moment. Two Turtles was right. She didn't own one frilly thing. The most feminine object she owned was her nightgown, and she'd sewn that out of flour sacks. "I guess I never had the need," she said at last.

Two Turtles shook her head sadly "You have need now. I give you a present." She turned, stuck her hand beneath the pillow, and pulled out a deerskin pouch, plain except for a double row of beads sewn just above its fringed bottom. She settled it on her lap, drew open the drawstring top, and began to rummage inside. "Good thing I have this with me when Lightfoot sends me back for sugar," she whispered, then giggled softly.

At last she extracted a smaller leather pouch

and teased open its pursed top. "Yes," she said with a smile. "This is for you."

Charity leaned toward her but couldn't see anything.

"Hold out your hands."

Charity did.

From the pouch and into her cupped palms tumbled a thing so beautiful that she gasped. Eyes wide, she glanced up at Two Turtles again, who smiled at her and nodded, before she allowed herself another look at the treasure.

It was a necklace, four strands deep and quite long, made of tiny beads of soft coral. Every three inches or so, the four strands came together to thread a fixed smooth bead of turquoise, barrel-shaped and about the size of her thumbnail. Charity let it drape over her fingers, then held up her hand. The necklace swung lazily, its hundreds of richly hued beads softly catching the light. She had never held anything so beautiful, let alone owned it.

She felt Two Turtles's hand on her shoulder, heard that little-girl voice whisper, "Why you cry? You don't like?"

She hadn't realized that she was weeping. She sniffed, then rubbed at her eyes. "It's a happy cry, Two Turtles. They're beautiful. I never . . . nobody ever gave me a present before."

Two Turtles smiled. "I bet Turlow give you lots of presents. He looks like a man with many gifts in mind. But you will wear these sometimes, too, and think of Two Turtles and Tink."

She reached down into her bag again, this time pulling out another pouch which contained a handful of turquoise beads, similar to those on Charity's necklace, but larger, and with a larger bore. She held out her hand. "Choose three," she said.

Some were bright, some were greenish, and some were mottled, with streaks of black or splotches of white. Charity picked three of the clearest blue.

"I thought so," Two Turtles said, and put her pouch away. "You pick the color like Turlow's eyes." She closed Charity's hand over the beads. "Those are for your hair. You should have things of beauty about you when you are loved."

They both turned toward the door at the sound of the men's voices drawing near. Charity stood up and dropped the necklace over her head. The turquoise beads went into her pocket. Two Turtles picked up her coat, but before she could hand it over, Charity threw her arms about the woman.

"Thank you," she whispered. "Thank you so much. I won't ever forget you."

Chapter Twenty-two

Jake pulled his muffler a little closer. *I wonder how long,* he thought, *it'll take before I can forget about him.*

The night before he'd been certain he'd permanently exorcised the demon of Claude Duval from his system. He'd felt so clean, so new, after making love with Charity that he was certain he could start fresh. But today Duval's specter was back, and he couldn't shake it from his thoughts. He knew Duval was far away. He knew he'd never see him again. But at each snapping twig, at every soft *plop* made by a clot of snow dropping to the ground from a high branch, he thought, *Duval*.

There was no such thing as a clean break for him, as much as he'd wanted it, and as certain as he'd been that he'd accomplished it. How far away from the Nations would he have to go, he wondered. How many weeks or months or years would it take to be truly free of the old hates and fears?

"How much farther is it?"

Jake grinned, relieved that Charity had intruded on his thoughts. "Finally decided to talk to me, eh?"

Riding beside him on Number Ten, her face tipped downward, Charity looked up at him through her lashes and smiled almost shyly. She'd been quiet since they'd waved goodbye to Tink and Two Turtles: preoccupied, he decided, with her thoughts. They must have been happy ones, since she'd been smiling rather enigmatically during the two hours they'd been traveling southeast. It reminded him of that painting by da Vinci. He'd seen a copy of it once, in a book.

The Mona Lisa, he thought, finally remembering. *That's it. Except Charity is miles prettier. And the way that smile curls over her face makes me want to do more than just lean her up against the wall and look at her . . .*

"Sorry," she said softly. "I was just thinking." She pulled the front of her coat a bit more snugly about her. "Is it much farther? Might be my imagination, but I think it's getting colder again."

"Another couple of hours," Jake replied. "We ought to make it just about dusk. And you're right. I wouldn't be surprised if we had a hard freeze by nightfall. We'll be in for some icy riding tomorrow."

"Two more hours," she said rather vacantly, and then looked over at him quickly, blushed, then stared down at her gloved hands.

I will never understand women, Jake mused

happily. How different this Charity was from the wildcat he'd practically dragged through the blizzard. She looked so shy: she seemed almost flustered by his just having smiled at her. It was amazing to him that this was the same girl he'd had to slug in the jaw—and hogtie—in order to get her to allow him to save her life. She seemed to him, at the moment, like a schoolgirl who has just realized she's about to receive her first kiss. He knew Charity's catamount side was still there—if something tipped her the wrong way, her claws would clear their sheaths in a big hurry, and that was part of why he loved her—but at the moment she was closer to a purring tabby than he believed he'd ever seen her. It worried him, although in the nicest sort of way. He wondered what she was daydreaming about. He hoped it was him.

He twisted in his saddle slightly, then thumbed back the brim of his hat. "Honey?"

She peeked at him from the corner of her eye. "Mmm?"

"What were you and Two Turtles talking about in there?"

She looked down at her hands again. "Just things ladies talk about." She acted as if the word "ladies" gave her a special sort of satisfaction. "She gave me a present," she added after a moment.

That surprised him. He said, "What was it?"

"A necklace. A beautiful necklace." She touched the front of her coat.

"Well, say! That was nice of her. I, uh . . ." He twisted to dig into his saddlebag, wondering all the while why he hadn't remembered this sooner. "I've got a present for you, too."

"A present? *Another* present?" She looked as if she could hardly believe her good fortune. "What is it?" She reined in Number Ten and leaned toward him, her head shifting as sweetly as an eager ten-year-old's as she tried to peer at his hand.

"Nothing as pretty as you got from Two Turtles, even though I have yet to see the damned thing . . ." He shoved things around in the bag, making little clinks and thunks, until he found what he sought. "Here it is. It's more on the order of utilitarian."

He turned toward her again and handed her a knife in an intricately tooled leather sheath. She took it and drew out the blade. "Where'd you get it?" she asked, fingering the hilt.

"I took it off . . . that is, Arnie had it. I imagine he stole it off somebody. It was too nice to leave behind. I mean, I know you can handle knives, and this one looks to be well made. Handsome, too. Almost pretty with those flowers on the hilt, and . . ." He sighed. It wasn't a very good present to give the woman you loved. He wished he'd had perfume to gift her with, or jewelry. "Damn. You hate it, don't you?"

Without glancing his way, she flipped the knife straight up. It spun three times in the air before she caught the flat of the tip of its blade between her thumb and index finger.

"What did you say?" She turned toward him, and he guessed he must have looked as crest-fallen as he felt, because, quite quickly, she smiled and shook her head. "Oh. Oh no! I don't hate it at all! It's a beauty!"

He relaxed a little. "The sheath's got a boot clip."

"Oh yes, I see." Grinning, she slid the knife back inside it, then hiked up her coat's hem and leaned over to slip the whole business down the inside of her boot top.

"Thank you, Jake," she said after she let the coat fall back. "I like it fine."

As they started forward again, the horses' hooves crunching through the patchy snow's newly frozen crust, she added, "I think I like presents a lot."

"You going to let me see what Two Turtles gave you?"

She shook her head. "Not now. When we get to that Widow's house."

"But—"

She held up a hand and languidly waggled a gloved finger. "Later, Jake. It's not pretty with these dirty old clothes."

Jake sighed. "Whatever you say, honey," he said, but he thought, *Never. I will never understand women. But I'm going to try to figure this one out if it takes me till Judgment.*

* * *

She had it fairly well planned, and just going over it in her head again had her squirming on her saddle seat. She was glad of her big old coat. She could move around inside it quite a bit without Jake noticing. And the closer they rode to the Widow Pritchard's place, the more anxious she was to make love to Jake once more.

Maybe two or three times, she thought happily, and scootched forward in her saddle, just a fraction of an inch. *Aren't we ever going to get there?*

Back at Tink's, someone—she couldn't remember who—had mentioned that the Widow had a nice big cast iron bathtub at her place. It had sounded like Heaven. *I'll take a real bath, with all of me in the water at the same time,* she thought, *and I'll wash my hair. And then . . .*

She peeked at Jake, then bit at her lips to keep from breaking out in a big, silly grin. She'd been thinking about the way he'd loved her on the tabletop back at Tink's house on the morning they were snowed in, and again, she'd felt a surge of warm tingles. She wondered if the Widow Pritchard had a nice big sturdy table.

In between giddy thoughts of making love and imagining new ways she might try it with Jake, she had also been wondering when might be the right time to tell him that she wasn't a

337

Caine, after all. It seemed to her that her name was the one thing that made the difference between her being Jake's mistress and his wife. There was a particular fantasy in which she'd indulged over the last day. In it, she was wrapped in Jake's arms. They were naked and sweating, having just made rather strenuous love, and she would "confess" that she wasn't a Caine. Jake would then sweep one arm out to the side and intone, "Ah, darling! Then we can be wed!"

It was stupid, she knew. For one thing, Jake Turlow would never talk like that. But it made a fine picture in her mind.

On the other hand, she had begun to wonder if perhaps she shouldn't just keep her newfound heritage a secret. What if Jake wouldn't marry her either way? By keeping the barrier of the Caine name and reputation intact, she could give him — and herself — an effective excuse for the lack of matrimonial vows. Or commitment.

It was a perplexing dilemma, and she soon pushed it to the back of her mind and returned to thoughts of wide sturdy tables and warm beds and bathtubs, which were not only happier things to think of, but more stimulating.

She was so lost in conjuring up new and exciting ways to make fast and almost violent love to Jake that when she heard him say, "There it is," she was startled.

The Widow Pritchard's cabin was better than twice the size of Tink's, and looked a good deal more civilized. It was L-shaped, with a wide, tidy porch in front, and had two chimneys, one at each end. There was a well in the front yard and, at the side of the house, between it and the little barn, Charity could see the outlines of what, when it wasn't snowed under, was likely a vegetable garden.

They rode on into the yard and, after Charity slid off Number Ten, Jake tied both their horses to the porch rail. "She doesn't look to be home," he said, gesturing toward the snowy porch. "Cora's a real particular lady. She'd have that swept off." He pounded on the front door. "Cora?" he called. There was no answer. "Nope. Nobody home," he said. "Always pays to check first, though." He tried the front door. It opened with no argument, and he ushered her inside.

Charity's first inclination was to go right back out and take off her dirty boots. Cora Pritchard's cabin was the neatest, tidiest place she'd ever been inside. There were pretty gingham curtains at the windows, and between them, glinting against the closed shutters, were real glass panes. The floor was scattered with rugs: some hooked, some braided. At the far end, its headboard towering, was a high, wide bed, deep in comforters and bright, busy quilts. There was a tablecloth on the table, and pretty bric-a-brac— china figurines and empty vases—lined curio shelves on either side of a long breakfront. There were even pictures on the walls. Wherever

Cora Pritchard had gone, she hadn't been away long. There wasn't a speck of dust anywhere.

"Honey? Charity? Are you all right?"

"What?" She wondered how long she'd been standing there with her mouth open. Jake was across the room, crouched before a pot-bellied stove that was bracketed by two overstuffed red chairs. He already had the kindling going, and was adding logs from a hammered brass bin.

"I was just . . . it's so pretty!"

Jake smiled and stood up. "Cora keeps it nice, even if most of the stuff is second or thirdhand. But you're going to live someplace much nicer." With that cryptic remark, he walked out of the room.

Careful not to walk on the rugs, Charity followed him back into the cabin's "L." Here she found a kitchen area, which she guessed had probably been the entirety of the original cabin. At one end was a large stone fireplace, whose heat would not only warm the kitchen and provide a place for cooking, but would also heat what else of the cabin the stove didn't reach.

At its side, tucked into the corner at an angle, was the bathtub she'd heard about. It seemed huge to her after so many years of taking baths standing or crouched in a tin washtub, and she thought, *Why, I could almost get Number Ten in there!* There was a sink with a pump, a large work area, and row upon row of cupboards, all with matching fronts that didn't look the least bit saggy or jerryrigged.

By the time she finished gawking, Jake had already started a tiny but rapidly growing blaze in the hearth. He gave the pump a few experimental cranks. "Prob'ly frozen, but—" Water gushed forth: brown at first, then clear. He grinned. "That's lucky," he said, grabbing two buckets from beneath the sink. These he filled before he hung them over the fire.

"C'mon," he said, taking her elbow before she had time to realize he was at her side again. "Let's unload the horses. While I'm getting them settled in, you can make us some supper. I'm starved!"

"Me, too," Charity mumbled. She was still staring at the pictures and the rugs but mostly at the table and the bed. Those big, soft red chairs looked interesting, too. *I wonder* . . . she thought. He took her arm and steered her gently toward the kitchen. "Starved," she said. *But not,* she added mentally, *for food* . . .

Jake was whistling when he finally left the barn and walked up toward the cabin. It was as good as dark. The western horizon showed only a feeble glow of grayed pink through the trees, but that wouldn't last much longer than a few minutes.

He stepped up on the porch and stomped the snow off his boots. The ground, which had iced up enough to be crackly under the horses' hooves by mid-afternoon, was now hard and slippery between the crusted patches of snow.

341

He debated, for a moment, if perhaps he and Charity shouldn't just hole up here at the Widow's for a few days, until it warmed up again. But then, it might just decide to stay cold for a while, and they'd end up cleaning out the Widow's larder. Cora was a fine woman and didn't mind one whit that passing friends used her place while she was out gallivanting. Jake had stayed at Cora's—both when she was there and when she wasn't—at least two dozen times in years past, and she was always tickled to be of help. However, he didn't think her hospitality extended to folks who tried to move in for the duration.

No, he decided, they'd best start out again in the morning. It was only another day to Fort Smith. He wanted to get back to town. He wanted to walk into the courthouse and turn in his badge before he had time to think better of it. He wanted to pack up his things and put the house up for sale and spirit Charity off to someplace far away, someplace safe. Someplace without Claude Duval.

He shook his head hard, as if he could rattle the thought of Duval out his ear. But it wouldn't go away.

At last he put his hand on the latch and pushed it down. *Not tonight, Jake, ol' buddy,* he thought. *Tonight the whole wide world is safe and warm, and you are not going to think about one blasted thing but the lovely Miss Charity.*

"What's that I smell?" he boomed as he kicked off his boots, then walked toward the kitchen.

Charity's coat was heaped on a chair in the corner, her extra clothes, still wet from the day before, hung from the backs of chairs and the edges of open cupboard doors. Charity herself was crouched before the fireplace, stirring something in a black pot. She was barefoot.

"Do you think she'll mind?" she asked. "Mrs. Pritchard, I mean. I found her canned goods, and she had so much . . ."

Jake knelt beside her and peered into the vessel. "Peas with little bitty onions? No, Cora won't mind at all. Cora's a peach. What else you find?" He reached to take the lid off another little pot, but Charity tapped the back of his hand with her spoon.

"You'll see," she smiled.

"All right." He stood up and licked the back of his hand. It tasted good. "Then I'll do the bucket brigade for the bath tub." He wrapped dish towels around his hands and took the first pails from their hooks over the fire, poured them into the tub, then refilled and replaced them. "Where's your necklace?" he asked before he went to set the table. "The one Two Turtles gave you."

Charity put a hand to her throat rather absently. "I took it off. These clothes . . ." She looked down at herself, then smiled up at him almost apologetically. "I'll show it to you later."

343

By the time she finished with supper, he'd filled the old cast iron tub nearly half full with near boiling water. *Ought to be just about right by the time dinner's finished,* he thought. He'd set the table and found two pretty candles for it. He'd also raided Cora's stash of homemade wine. He carried in bowls and covered dishes from the kitchen, arranged everything just so, and when Charity was finished slicing the meat—a goodly chunk of roast venison that Tink and Two Turtles had pressed on them as they left—he walked her out into the main room, his hands over her eyes.

"Oh!" she breathed, when he took his hands away. He had to admit that the table did look nice. He'd dug out Cora's good lace tablecloth, and between the candles he'd placed a pretty vase from the curio shelf. He wished there had been flowers for it, but a fellow could only do so much.

He seated her, pulling out her chair and sliding it back in, just so. He was feeling rather courtly anyway, for some reason, but he had other things in mind. He'd been watching Charity, although surreptitiously, for the better part of the afternoon—he was well aware that if he didn't watch out, she'd be apt to practically rape him the first chance she got. Well, he wasn't going to let that happen again, as much fun as it was. No, he was going to show her that there were other ways, ways that had likely never crossed her mind. Tonight things were going to be slow and romantic, and he was going to be in control.

He hoped he could live up to his own expectations. Just the way she was looking at him, the candlelight flickering warmly across that beautiful face, was enough to make him want to take her there and then, right in the middle of the peas and onions and roasted new potatoes and gravy and candied beets and creamed corn.

Back off, Jake, he scolded himself. *Tonight, you're going to act like a civilized man.*

He smiled at Charity as he lit the candles, then opened a bottle of Cora's best wild raspberry wine. "This looks wonderful," he said. "I know you're not fond of spirits, but I think you'll enjoy this. Your glass, Miss Caine?"

Chapter Twenty-three

Never had Charity had more trouble getting through a meal. All through it Jake barely said a word that wasn't gentlemanly. But he never stopped staring at her, never stopped watching her. And she couldn't wrest her gaze from him for any longer than it took to make certain she was cutting her meat and not her napkin.

The wine, which was delicious but heady, seemed to warm her more than either the fire or Jake's presence could account for. The food in her mouth took on new meaning. It wasn't just nourishment. It was more than taste. Its texture and substance took on almost sexual qualities as she slipped bites of this or that between her teeth, chewed and swallowed, licked salty juices or crisp bits from her lips.

"Well, then," Jake said at last. He folded his napkin beside his plate.

Were they finished? She didn't know if they'd only been at table for a few minutes, or if she'd been sitting there her whole life, staring at him across the candles and feeling so many waves of yearning flood through her body that she had nearly forgotten it was possible to feel anything but this need, this overpowering desire. The ache inside her, welling since mid-day, had grown to a nearly physical pain.

He came to stand behind her and rested his hand on her shoulder for a moment before he pulled out her chair. She stood up on legs she feared were too wobbly to hold her, and turned toward him. She wanted him now, this minute. She wanted him inside her here, on the table; on the rugs; on the bed: anywhere, everywhere.

But instead of reaching for her, he reached past her and picked up a stack of dirty dishes. "I'll help you clear, honey."

Numbly, she began to stack plates as he walked from the room. *Is it just me?* she managed to wonder. *I know I had two glasses of wine, but that couldn't account for . . .*

"Coming, Charity?" he called.

She piled the plates on top of the roast's platter, picked up the stack, and followed him. *I can't stand this anymore,* she thought, and when he took the plates from her, she wrapped her arms about his waist.

"Not yet," he said with a smile that left her panting, and gently peeled her arms away. "All in good time, my sweet Charity." And then, leaving her to sway in the middle of the room, he went to the bathtub and flicked at the water with his fingers.

"Perfect," he said softly. "The dishes can wait 'til later. Until morning. Let's have you out of those clothes."

It wasn't as romantic a speech as she might have wished for, but it was enough to set her fingers to quickly unfastening the buttons on the front of her shirt. She had freed them halfway to her waist before Jake's hand closed over hers.

She looked up. His face was inches away. She would have stood on tiptoes to kiss him, but his other hand was on her shoulder, pressing her firmly back down on her feet.

"Slow down," he whispered. "I'll do it for you."

He began to free the buttons, slowly, one at a time. She tried to reciprocate by opening the front of his shirt, but he brushed her hands away without a word. By the time he had stripped her to the waist, she could bear it no longer and reached for his belt buckle.

Again he eased her trembling fingers away. "Not yet," he whispered.

And then she was naked. Her breath came in little shudders. He had undressed her completely, but without so much as one stroke of her skin, one fondle, one caress. Didn't he realize that he was driving her mad?

Apparently he didn't realize any such thing, because his next act was to turn his back on her and reach up into the end cupboard. He brought out a box, bent up the already opened end with his thumb, then sprinkled pale, lilac-colored powder into the bath water. Immediately a strange new scent, subtle and sweet, rose into the steamy air.

"Lavender," he whispered, before she could ask.

"Jake, please . . ." It came out as a whimper.

He took her hand and led her to the edge of the tub. "And now I'm going to bathe you," he said softly. His voice seemed to rumble through her body, to vibrate through her soul.

"Bathe," she whispered, her eyes locked on his. Before she realized how she'd gotten there, she found herself sitting in the tub, warm water cradling the undersides of her breasts while its steam bathed her in fragrance.

Jake was quickly out of his shirt and the top half of his Union suit. She reached to touch his chest, but he blocked her hand. "Shhh," he said, and began to slowly lather a cloth against a fat yellow bar of soap.

He began with her face, washing it gently, careful to keep the soap from her eyes, and rinsing it just as meticulously. All Charity could do was stare at him and try not to squirm. Next, he played the washcloth, nubby and thick, along her throat and shoulders, sweeping it over her tingling skin in slow, firm strokes; then lower, across her shoulders and down her back as he lifted her hair out of the way; then beneath the water's surface and down her spine, rubbing slowly in firm circles.

Charity had leaned forward for him, and when he laid his hand against her shoulder, pressing her to recline against the tub's backrest, she realized she'd gripped the tub's edges so tightly that she nearly had to pry her fingers away.

"Jake?" she whispered as he ran the cloth over her collarbones, then down to float across the top of one buoyant breast.

"Shhh," was all he said. She felt it as much as heard it. The sound of it, mixed with the fire's lazy pops, seemed one with the washcloth's texture as she felt its pressure, formed to his wide hand, circle first one breast and then the other, over and over, abrading her hardened nipples so gently that she would have cried out if only she could have remembered how.

"Relax," he murmured as the cloth slipped lower, making spirals over her midsection, then her belly.

Lower it went, and all she could think was, *Touch me, Jake, touch me there, please* . . . But he moved along, down the length of one thigh, then calf, then foot; slowly laving every inch before he moved to the other leg. Her foot and ankle, her calf, knee, and thigh were all carefully massaged and tickled as he leisurely worked his way back up. By the time he reached her hip, Charity's yearning has gone past desire, past discomfort. And just when she knew she couldn't stand it another second, that she would surely die or go mad, she felt the cloth slip round her hip and between her legs.

A tiny whimper escaped her lips as Jake, his eyes locked to hers, began to slowly move his hand, and the cloth in it, up and down. She whimpered again when he let go of the cloth. It floated to the top of the water, a white island between her parted knees, as she felt Jake's finger slip between her outer lips and begin to pet her slowly, delicately.

She opened her mouth, tried to say his name, but before she could, he hushed her again. The long, sibilant, "Shhh," was a physical thing, vibrating her flesh and merging with the tremors that were already shaking her, buzzing to the inexorable rhythm of that slow hand beneath the water.

Again, her fingers locked to the tub's wide rim. Her head began to crane backward. She took in tiny gasps of air between clenched teeth and closed her eyes without wanting to. She heard Jake's resonant whisper: "Slow, Charity. Slow." And as the deep timbre of his voice rumbled through her, her hips and then the rest of her body suddenly seized into a spasm of pure perfection.

She felt her spine flex and arch, and was half-conscious of lifting nearly out of the water. She was light and heavy all at once, and for a moment she thought she would surely faint. But then she became aware of Jake's hands as they steadied her and eased her back down, and then his lips pressed against her open mouth: brush-

351

ing softly, sweetly, against one lip, then the
o   t   h   e   r   .

"Relax," he whispered against her cheek, as if,
in that uncertain span of time, she could have
done anything else.

A moment later she felt his hand on her arm.
"Mmm," was all she could say. It didn't seem
her eyes would open.

"Scootch forward a little," he murmured.

Dreamily, she complied, and felt him step into
the tub behind her, then sit, his knees cocked
up on either side of her torso. She felt him fid-
dling with her braid, saw him toss its leather tie
to the floor. She wrapped her arms around his
lower legs. "I want to wash you, too," she said,
her voice throatier than she had expected. She
could feel him easing the plaits from her hair,
straightening it with his fingers.

"Tip your head back," he said.

"But—"

"Tip it back, honey."

She did, and smiled as she felt warm water
being poured over the crown of her head. He
was dipping it with something, she couldn't see
what, but he was careful not to let it run into
her eyes.

"Jake?"

"It's all right. Just relax and watch the fire."

She felt too wonderful to argue or even ask
what he was up to, but in a moment she knew.
There was the sound of a bottle being un-
corked, then set aside, and immediately he be-

352

gan to lather her hair with the most wonderful soap she had ever smelled. It was like roses mixed with some other flower she couldn't name and, combined with the fragrance of lavender, it made her feel as if she were immersed in a sea of blooms.

As the firelight made soft orange patterns on the inside of her lids and the steamy fragrance of flowers surrounded her, she listened to the soft sounds of his fingers, working the suds through her hair. He was so careful. Never did she feel him pull at a tangle, never did he scrub too roughly. Never had she felt more feminine, more alive, or more adored. Too soon, she heard the sound of water being dipped and felt Jake rinsing the soap away.

And then his hands were gone from her. Not at all abruptly; but it affected her that way, for she had grown, in these last few minutes, so accustomed to his constant touch that it seemed a part of her own body had been taken from her. But then she heard the little telltale slosh of water behind her, and knew he was bathing himself.

She wished the tub were bigger. She wanted to turn around to face him. She wanted to bathe him as wonderfully as he'd bathed her, and then she wanted to make love to him. She wondered if it were possible to do it in the water. The thought of it made her squirm anxiously, and in doing so, she backed up a fraction of an inch: enough so that she felt his erection thump against her back.

"Jake?" she whispered, twisting, trying to see his face.

His arms came round her before she could turn far enough to catch a glimpse. His soapy hands encompassed her breasts and his thumbs played over her nipples as he hugged her back against his damp, pelted chest. The slight movement pressed his swollen member even more insistently against her back.

"Just a second, baby," he breathed against her ear. "Stay still. We're not done yet, but we're going to do this my way."

His hands slipped away. She heard rinse water being scooped and poured, and then his hands were on her shoulders. He stood up, then helped her to her feet. She turned toward him immediately, intent on throwing her arms about him. They could make love standing up, she thought, the way they had at Tink's. She slid her hands about his neck, but instead of lifting her up and nestling her down upon himself as she'd hoped, he eased her arms away.

"Jake? Jake, please, I need . . ."

"Just wait," he said with a wink.

He picked up the rinse water bucket and slowly poured it over them both, washing away the last of the soap, then took her hand while she stepped over the edge of the tub after him. She clung to his hand, hoping to pull him to the floor where she might have the advantage, but he wasn't having any of it.

He wagged a finger at her. "No, my darling, beautiful, anxious Miss Caine. Slow."

With that, he pressed her, still naked, to the edge of the raised hearth, and sat beside her. She swiveled toward him to kiss him, but he turned away, reaching over his head to the mantel. After a second or two of groping, he produced a silver-handled hairbrush that bore the monogram *CCP.* Cora Pritchard's.

"What are you—?"

He waggled a finger at her. "My rules tonight, Miss Caine," he said. A smile tugged at the corners of his handsome mouth, pressed his dimples into his cheeks more deeply. "Don't make me use this on your pretty bottom."

With a sigh, Charity let him position her so that her back was toward him and the fire. He began to brush her hair.

It occurred to her, as the minutes wore on, that in the span of her life she had brushed her hair dry more times than she could begin to count, but never had she suspected that it might be such a stimulating experience. He worked her tresses gently and slowly, as if he were taking a great deal of pleasure in their feel and texture. He fanned her damp hair in his hands as well as with the brush, sweeping a section out to one side or the other so that Charity could see every strand and catch the scent that still clung to them as he allowed them to slowly slip from his fingers to tickle her shoulders and breasts or skim against her back.

She bit at her lips, trying to hold back the little sounds she felt forming deep in the back of her throat. But she couldn't control the muscles in her buttocks and thighs, which had begun to clench and twist with every sweep of that brush through her hair, every touch of his fingertips upon her temple or scalp.

Just when she was certain she could stand it no longer, he laid the brush aside and turned her to face him. "My beautiful Charity," he whispered, and kissed her.

It was a deep kiss, as lingering as what had come before. Lips met in ways old and new; tongues danced, intertwined, searched, tasted; heart beat against heart.

"My Jake, my Jake," Charity whispered as, at last, he stood and lifted her into his arms. "My Jake," she murmured against the warm strong flesh of his shoulder as he carried her to the other room and, through the faint candlelight, to the bed.

The mattress was deep and soft, and just as she thought, *Feathers, they're feathers, a down mattress at last,* Jake kissed her again and came to hover over her. Charity's arms went round him. Her legs parted to receive him, but he did not enter her. Instead, he began to kiss his way down her throat, then her torso, his lips traveling a line that took him to her belly, and then, as he crouched between her legs, to the still-damp thatch at their juncture. She could feel his breath, hot upon her; and when he kissed her, she gasped as much in astonishment as pleasure.

His hands slid under her hips, buoying her, lifting her, angling her just so, and then he kissed her again. Her fingers clutched at the quilts, knotting them in her hands as she felt his tongue, hot and silky, slip within to taste her.

"God," she said. A tiny squeak. "Jake."

It was unimagined magic. His tongue, his lips, teased and pleasured her as he explored. His arms slid round her hips, encircling them, and as his shoulders angled her thighs more widely, his fingertips slipped to the place his mouth played to open her so that they might play alongside his tongue.

She felt herself rising, as if she had become weightless and would float to the ceiling if not for Jake's arms, Jake's mouth. She didn't know if she was breathing. She couldn't remember how. She didn't care if she never remembered.

And then it happened. A burst of heat on top of heat, of the fire that burns fire. She cried out as tongues of flame raced through her limbs, surged through her to gather in a molten, overpowering wave that left her limp and exhausted. Small, breathy sighs issued from between her parted teeth as she felt Jake relax his grip on her hips and kiss, quite sweetly, the inside of her thigh.

"Jake," she breathed.

She reached for him, her hand limp and feeling not at all her own, and laid it on his shoulder as he began to kiss his way back up her body. His lips wandered her flesh in circles wide, then tight, then wide again. His hands swept up her sides, then down again, leaving gooseflesh in their wake. He stopped at her breast to kiss a ring about her nipple before he took it into the warmth of his mouth and suckled it, teasing the tip with his teeth while Charity laced her fingers through his hair. He stroked her skin, feathering here, massaging there. And by the time he reached her throat, her jaw, and then her lips, Charity's need had returned in full measure.

He lay atop her, propped on his elbows, his chest suspended a whisper above hers, his lips a moment away. One side of his face was faintly gilded by candlelight. His thighs, hard with tensed muscle, were between hers. His shaft pressed a hard, insistent line into her belly. And as, at last, he kissed her lips, she slid her hand between them, half afraid he'd push her away and mumble something about "his rules." But he didn't, and when she took him into her hand, he made a soft groaning sound.

She wondered how he could stand having gone so long without a release. She raised her hips, twisting them slightly, trying to position herself so that she might guide him up inside her.

"Shhh," he breathed, and the rumbling hiss of it once again bored into her. She stopped wiggling.

He kissed the tip of her nose. "All right, Miss Caine," he said softly, his voice still teasing, but deep and burred with passion. "But slowly, mind."

With that, he shifted his hips and allowed Charity to guide him. As he slowly, gorgeously, buried his full length, she let out a small sob of relief. But when, after several seconds, he hadn't moved, she began to twist her hips against him.

His hand slipped down her side to curl about her hip and hold her still. Chuckling, he kissed her eyelids, then whispered, "Slow. Let me, all right?"

She sighed, nodding.

He chuckled again. "You have to do more than just say so. Relax, my impatient darling. Let yourself go limp."

She took a deep breath and tried. It was difficult to relax when Jake was inside her and the thing she wanted most in the world was to roll him over on his back and ride him as wildly and furiously as she could; but she tried her best to comply.

After a few moments, he murmured, "That's my girl," and then, his elbows planted firmly on either side of her, he began to rock within her. He moved with excruciating deliberation. Several heartbeats passed with each sure, languid stroke, and all the while Jake kissed her: her lips, her brow, her eyelids, the line of her jaw.

It was torture for her to stay still, but she did; and as he moved within her, she began to realize that she was tensing around him, caressing him with internal muscles she hadn't known she owned. As she returned his kisses and her fingers combed his hair and played over his shoulders, she began to concentrate on what was happening inside her. She began to pull upon him, push at him, to caress him with tiny experimental patterns of rhythm and pressure, to cling to his length by design instead of instinct; and as she did, she found herself riding along a new plateau of bliss, one which she had traveled before, but at which she had never been able to linger.

She clung to this sublime state, this hazy twilight place where flesh and the heavens were one, where time was eternal, where a woman could float forever and feel nothing but effervescent wonder.

And then she heard Jake's raspy whisper, "Yes. That's it, Charity."

She felt hot tears steaming down her face, although she wasn't conscious of crying, and hugged him inside her all the tighter.

And then, without Jake's changing that steady, maddening, excruciating rhythm, she reached the end of the plateau to slide, then spin into euphoria. On and on it went, Jake clinging to her, never faltering in his pace as she spasmed against him. Just as she felt the inner convulsions ease, just as the world began to swim back into focus, she felt herself lifted again and swept upward to a loftier rapture than before. *Impossible* was the only word that came to her as she hovered for what seemed forever. *Impossible.*

Again she began to slowly drift down toward reason, only to be inexplicably caught on the crest and carried upward. Her flesh was aflame and freezing all at once. Her limbs jerked wildly, beyond her control. Blood pounded in her ears and at her temples as tiny points of light danced on the insides of her eyelids, sparkling with colors too exotic and miraculous to have names. She was barely aware that Jake had shifted to angle her shivering thighs wide, but she knew that his tempo changed abruptly to one of unbridled, mindless frenzy. And this last thing, this wonderful wild animal madness, lifted her helplessly toward the ultimate explosion of senses.

As he jolted into her with one final, fierce thrust to spill himself, she cried out something: his name, perhaps. Her lungs emptied with it to leave her with no body, no form which she was able to command. She had nothing left but sensation, the most miraculous and sublime imaginable.

All this, she thought later, still tingling and limp. Jake lay beside her, his arm about her, his legs tangled with hers, both of them too exhausted for anything but dreamless sleep. As the

361

last candle guttered, she nestled her head against Jake's chest, its thick fur still damp with sweat. In the darkness, as the clean male scent of him filled her nostrils and her eyelids fluttered closed, she smiled wearily and thought, *To have all this, and love, too.*

Chapter Twenty-four

Charity woke to the sound of whistling and the smells of brewing coffee and frying potatoes. Her eyes still closed, she smiled softly in memory of the night before, then snuggled down into her pillow.

"Oh no, you don't." Jake's voice: low, and near her ear. "Rise and shine, Charity, m'love."

The smell of coffee was suddenly stronger, and she opened one eye. Freshly shaved and already dressed, he grinned as he waved the coffee cup under her nose.

"It's almost seven-thirty," he said, when she took it and sat up. There was a star-patterned quilt covering her. She supposed he must have put it there. She pulled it up under her chin, for the cabin was chilled.

"I bailed out the bathtub," he continued. "Wouldn't do for Cora to come back and find it all rusted up. And I did the dishes. And I've already had my breakfast."

He leaned over her and held the coffee away from her lips just long enough to kiss her. There was a hint of salt on his mouth, from the potatoes. "Yours is on the stove, lazy bones," he whispered before he ruffled her hair. "I threw together some hash out of the leftovers from last night. Well, all right, just the venison and potatoes—mostly potatoes. All that noise I made, and you didn't stir an inch. Why, a body'd think you were all tuckered out!"

She aimed a half-hearted punch at his shoulder, but he ducked to the side. "That's my girl," he said smugly. "Go ahead and have your breakfast while I get Tico and Number Ten ready to travel."

She was enough awake that she was wishing he wasn't quite so antsy to get back on the trail. She wondered if she could talk him into putting it off, say, an hour or so. Long enough for him to get back out of his clothes and warm the other side of the bed back up. Perhaps long enough to try out another piece or two of Cora's furniture. She said, "Jake, couldn't we—?"

His laugh cut her off. "Oh, no," he said. "I'm not going to let you get me started all over again, you greedy little wildcat, or we'll be here till nightfall."

She cocked her head. "Would that be so terrible?" It sounded like a wonderful idea to her. She couldn't for the life of her imagine a more splendid way to spend the day than in this snug and lovely cabin with Jake. Preferably naked and in his arms.

"It wouldn't be one bit terrible," he said. "But

we need to get back to Fort Smith. I need to, anyway." He went to the door and opened it as he tugged on his coat. Frigid air pushed its way across the room, and Charity quickly hiked up the quilt to cover her shoulders.

Jake chuckled. "If that didn't wake you up, nothing will."

After he closed the door behind him, she wrapped herself in the quilt and went to the kitchen. There was a note, in Jake's hand, propped on the mantel. It said:

Dear Cora,

Thanks for the hospitality. I tried to put everything back where it came from. I split some wood for you. I'll leave it on the porch.

Tink Maynard sends his best.

> *Cordially,*
> *Jake Turlow*

P.S. That raspberry wine of yours still has a kick. I owe you a bottle.

Smiling, Charity ate her breakfast and dressed, washed the few dishes she'd dirtied, and threw the rinse water into the hearth, dousing the fire. Then she carried her things to the other room. Heaping them casually on the table, she reached into the coat's pocket and brought out the necklace Two Turtles had given her. She put it on, then took it off again. *I'll wait,* she thought. *I'll wait until I have something pretty to wear it with. That, or I'll wear it with nothing at all.* She smiled. She was fairly certain of Jake's reaction to that picture.

Next, she retrieved Cora Pritchard's silver-handled hairbrush and brushed her hair. Automatically, she began to braid it down her back, then stopped and brushed out the first plaits. *Not today,* she thought with a smile. Turning the coat over, she dug into the other pocket and found the three turquoise beads. She parted her hair in the middle, then separated a small section toward the front of her head, to the right of the part. She had a hard time threading even a third of it through the first bead, though the hole bored through it was a large one, until she dug a slim leather thong from her pants pocket. This she looped through a section of her hair before she poked the thong ends through the bead. One little tug, and the leather pulled her hair through, neat as you please. In this manner, she made a long, slender braid—studded, at intervals, by the three beads and secured, at the end, by the thong—which hung down one side of her head and swung down over the rest of her hair. She held the brush in front of her face and tried to study her reflection in its ornamental back.

"Oh well," she said finally, when all she could see were blurry snatches of random color reflected on lumps and bumps of cast silver. "I probably look fine. I know I look different, at least I *feel* different. I might even look pretty, and I'm going to Fort Smith today. I'm not a Caine anymore, I'm going to see a real town, and Jake Turlow loves me."

She wrapped her arms about her shoulders and gave herself a hug. "And I love Jake Turlow," she added softly. She wondered what kind of place he'd find for her to live in. She couldn't move in with him, of course: that would cause too much gossip. But she knew he'd find someplace nice. Maybe even someplace with gingham curtains, like Cora Pritchard's.

I'm Turlow's woman, she thought, and startled herself by giggling. She didn't know how often he'd be able to come visit her, but she was fairly certain it would be often. With a happy sigh, she picked up her saddlebags and packroll, intending to take them out to the porch. But before she did, she remembered something.

She dropped the saddlebags back on the table and opened the nearest pouch. Inside, jostling about with a box of cartridges and another of shells, a spare pair of longjohns and a large number of other odds and ends, was a cloth sack. She pulled it out. As hurriedly as she'd packed the night Jake spirited her away from her house, she had managed to gather up all the Caine family treasures: everything that had been in that old strongbox of Grampa Zeb's.

She went to the potbellied stove and sat before it in one of the red chairs, the sack in her lap. Then she leaned forward and opened the stove's door. Jake hadn't fed its fire this morning, but there were still a few coals glowing inside.

She opened the sack and slowly, one at a

time, began to feed the last of the Caines into the fire. In went the wanted poster for Uncle Odis and the pictures of Uncle Jabez. In went the lock of hair, which sizzled and popped and stank as it burned. Next she tossed in the medals and the Confederate bonds. She almost chucked in the twenty-dollar gold piece, but thought better of it and tucked it in her shirt pocket. She wasn't sure how much things cost in town, but she was fairly certain it would pay her room and board until she found a job.

The rest of the photographs went into the tiny blaze. She watched Aunt Vena, Uncle Aaron, Cousin Dirk, and all the others blacken and curl and turn to ash. But she saved the blurred daguerreotype of Sam and Garnet Caine until last, and finally decided to keep it. A person might say—and rightly so—that it was their fault she'd been brought up a Caine: that she'd been beaten and locked up and snarled at for nineteen years. But if they hadn't adopted her, if Sam Caine hadn't paid off her mother and taken her along, how would she have been raised?

She stared at the picture. "How much did I cost, Sam?" she whispered. "Five dollars? Ten? A bottle of whiskey? How much is a halfbreed baby worth, I wonder?"

She supposed it didn't matter. All in all, living with Grampa Zeb, even considering all the hitting and yelling, had likely been superior to growing up a whore's child in some godforsaken trading post.

She tucked the photograph back in the sack, closed the stove's door, and went back to her open pack. The hilt of the knife Jake had given her peeked from its flap, and she brought it out, smiling. She cradled it in her hands. A present. A present from Jake. It was quite beautiful: bone handled, with a rose carved into each side of the hilt. The blade—narrow, bright steel, honed sharp on both sides, and about eight inches long—was more dagger than hunting knife. Grampa Zeb would have called it a "gentleman's pigsticker." It was the most elegant thing she had ever owned.

She had gone a whole, lifetime without even one gift, and now it seemed that every time she turned around, someone gave her something remarkable. She wondered if this was what Christmas was supposed to be like, and then she wondered if Jake would spend Christmases with her once she was officially installed as his mistress.

She slipped the blade back in its sheath, then clipped it inside her boot top. The picture of Sam and Garnet went back into her pack. As she buckled it, she heard Jake outside. He was leading the horses up, whistling as he came.

She smiled. Yes, better a Caine, even a temporary one, than a trading-post whore, probably pressed into service by the age of eleven or twelve. Better a Caine than that. Better anything than that.

And if she hadn't been a Caine, she might never have met Jake.

A moment later he was standing in the open doorway, stomping the snow off his boots. "Colder'n a sombitch out there," he said happily.

Charity hurried into her coat. She started to wrap a scarf over her head, but he stopped her. His fingers stroked her hair, then went to the section she'd braided.

He touched one of the beads and smiled. "Pretty," he said.

She felt herself blush. "Two Turtles gave them to me."

"These, too? When do I get to see that new necklace of yours? String of beads?"

Again, a picture came into her mind: a picture of herself, standing before him in the firelight, wearing nothing but those beads; and a picture of the look she knew would be on his face. Her cheeks felt hotter. She looked at the floor and mumbled, "Yes. A string of beads. Four strands of coral and turquoise. I'll show you when we get to Fort Smith."

Jake chuckled, then said, "Women. They'll tell you about it, but they won't let you look." He bent to brush a kiss across her forehead. "All right, sweetie. Let's get on our way."

The horses were packed, the cabin was secured, and they were nearly out of the yard and into the trees when Jake said, "When we get to town, I'll get you something nicer."

"Nicer? What are you talking about?"

He rubbed at his jaw. "Well, nicer than a thirdhand knife, I mean. Something more fitting for an engagement gift."

She yanked on her reins, spinning a surprised Number Ten toward Jake. "W-what?"

Jake's eyebrows arched halfway up his forehead. "Jesus!" he gasped. "What'd I do?"

"Nothing!" She could hardly breathe. "I mean . . . what did you say?"

"I said I wanted to get you something nicer than . . . you know, something frilly, like a dress or some earbobs, or some feminine geegaw like that. Hell, I don't know. We're out here in the middle of nowhere. And I never got engaged before, let alone married! How in tarnation am I supposed to know what kind of—"

She started to cry, and all she could think was *Christmas. Christmas in March!*

He reined Tico up next to her and took her hand. "Honey, whatever I did, I'm sorry. Really. Just tell me what you want, and I'll get it. Well, I'll get it if it doesn't cost more than a hundred and forty dollars or so. That's about all I'm worth according to my last bank statement. You're not exactly marrying a rich man."

She rubbed her face, and the only thing she could think of to say was, "I don't care if you've only got fourteen cents. I love you, Jake."

He cleared his throat and looked down as he

squeezed her hand. "Well hell, honey," he said at last, and rather thickly, "I love you, too, but that's no reason for the two of us to sit out here and cry icicles all over each other."

"Yes, Jake," she said, and nudged Number Ten with her heels. "And I love my present. I love it better than anything I ever had."

They rode on in silence. Charity was happy to simply sit in the saddle and smile. Jake, riding abreast of Number Ten, seemed content to do the same. She wondered what he was thinking. Her own thoughts flitted between trying to imagine herself as Mrs. Jake Turlow and debating as to the best way to tell him she wasn't a Caine. It didn't really matter, she supposed. Didn't he want to marry her anyway?

Marriage. Every time she thought of the word she felt her insides turn over in the most wonderful way. She thought she should tell him, though, about the Caine business. He'd probably be relieved to find out there was no chance of one of his children—*our children,* she added with a smile—being throwbacks to Zeb or one of those cutthroat uncles.

Mrs. Jake Turlow. If she'd had a piece of paper, she would have written it a thousand times.

"Jake?" she said at last. They had just emerged from the woods, and were riding across a flat clearing. All around, the dark tree branches were dotted blue and red by jays and cardinals. Faintly, she could hear them

372

scolding.

"Yes ma'am?" He grinned at her, and she wished she were close enough to kiss him.

"There's something I think you ought to know. It's like this. See, Grampa Zeb really wasn't my—"

Tico reared and crashed into her a split second before she heard the shot. She screamed as Number Ten bolted. She glimpsed Jake's body arcing through the air as she hauled on her reins, trying to get Number Ten's attention. It seemed that he'd never stop, but she was only thirty feet away when he finally skidded to a stumbling halt. By then, Duval was jogging his ghost-grey horse into the clearing.

Jake lay crumpled, face down, on the crusty snow. Duval rode up to the body. His rifle was still out, its barrel casually pointed down at Jake's back.

Duval gestured to her with his free hand. *"Cher, cher, cher.* How many lives you got, anyway?" He shook his head, as if she were a favorite child who had greatly disappointed him. "You get down off dat plow horse critter, child, and keep hands away from de rifle boot."

When she hesitated, he pulled back his rifle's hammer and wiggled the barrel at Jake.

"Do it now, *cher.*"

She did.

"Now you smack dat dog meat on the rump and get him—and dat rifle and de shotgun I see stickin' out your pack—far away gone."

She slapped Number Ten across the flank. He turned his head and snorted at her far too lazily for a horse that had just given his best impression of a mustang bronc.

"Get the beast gone, child, or I shoot him where he stand."

Charity smacked Number Ten on the rear as hard as she could, then waved her arms and shouted, "Git! Go on! Shoo!"

He trotted off toward the trees, although by the time he reached them he was down to a walk and nosing the broken patches in the snow for something to eat. Charity turned back toward Duval. He had already dismounted.

"Dat good enough. Open your coat."

She unbuttoned it.

"Hold it wide, let me see if you carry the pistol." She complied, but he wasn't satisfied. "I think you better take it off, *cher*. Big old coat like dat can hold many surprises. How many bears you sew together to make dat thing, anyhow?"

She was too frightened to cry, too angry to feel the cold when she pulled the coat off and let it drop to the ground. Why hadn't she thought to stick Aunt Tildy's Colt into her belt?

"You're a good child, *cher*. Now over there you go, stand quiet." He pointed, with the rifle's barrel, to a place several yards to the side. "You stay put, don't move a finger or a toe, you un'erstand?" He turned back to Jake and kicked him in the side. "You dead yet, Turlow?"

374

Jake groaned: a weak, broken rattle. Charity's breath caught in her throat. Duval twisted his head toward her long enough to say, "Don't move, no-name child," then planted a boot against Jake's side and rolled him onto his back. "Marshal, you are one plenty hard man to kill."

Charity watched as Jake tried to move, tried to prop himself up on one elbow. It slid out from under him. Charity took a step forward. Her boot crunched the brittle snow. Without bothering to look at her, Duval swung his rifle her way. "Stay put," was all he said.

She heard Jake's voice. He seemed to be gasping for breath. He said, "How . . . how'd you . . . ?"

One-handed, Duval opened his coat and brought out something tiny and golden, something that glistened in the sun. A locket on a fine golden chain. It was the one she'd seen him toying with back at Briscoe's cave. He held it up and let it dangle from his fingers.

Charity heard Jake wheeze, "Laura's."

"I bring you back dis, Turlow. An afterthought. I think you might like to look at it while you hang there dying upside down. But you are gone. Imagine how I am disappointed." He let the chain slip from his fingers. The locket landed on Jake's chest. One faltering hand came up to cover it.

Charity heard herself say, "You're no better than he was."

Duval's head swiveled toward her. He raised an eyebrow. *"Cher,* you have something important? You want to plead for dis man? For yourself, maybe? I tell you dat you waste your words. You got no hope. You got no hope since day you get born in de dark back corner of dat whore's crib."

She shook her head. "You're just the same," she said flatly. "You talk different, you look different, but you're just like he was. You're filth. You're disease."

"What you talk about? Me and Turlow, we not one bit de same alike. De prime example of which is dat Turlow is about to be killed dead."

She held his gaze. She wasn't afraid of him anymore. She'd gone past fear and into something cold and hard. "Not Jake. Zeb Caine."

He shook his head. *"Cher,* I don't know who your true daddy was, but you sure crazy. 'Bout crazy enough for Caine."

He turned his back, dismissing her.

Just exactly the same, she thought as slowly, her heartbeat steady, her hand calm, she began to slide her hand down her hip, down her thigh, toward her boot.

"I don't think dis time I'm gonna take no chance wit you, Marshal," Duval said. "You just too damn lucky."

Charity's fingers touched the rose-carved hilt, slid the blade free.

Duval rested the tip of his rifle's barrel against the center of Jake's forehead. He said,

376

"Is still checkmate, Turlow."

Charity threw the knife.

It spun through the air, a sparkling blur, and, with a small *pop,* sank half-way to the hilt into the side of Claude Duval's neck.

He twisted toward her, blood rapidly staining his collar and coat, his bony features caricatured in surprise. He swung the rifle around. He brought the barrel up.

She held her ground. She stared directly into his cold grey eyes, straight down into his black and barren soul. She said, " 'On days with an 'R', the white queen gets an extra turn.' That's a Texas rule. Don't you know anything?"

His mouth moved, formed the word *cher,* but no sound came out. He fired, the shot going wild, just as he crumpled to his knees. He swayed there a moment, blood streaming from his neck, and then he fell forward.

He didn't move again.

She stood frozen for a moment, staring stonily at the body, feeling the hatred wash one final icy wave through her before it drained away more quickly than she would have thought possible; and then, with a whispered "Jake!" that grew to a scream, she ran forward.

She skidded to her knees beside him and cradled his head in her lap. Tears streamed down her cheeks, steaming faintly as she wiped the snow from his face. "Oh, Jake, Jake, please don't die, please be all right!"

He opened his eyes and looked up at her.

Wonderful eyes, she thought. *Beautiful, wonderful, impossibly blue eyes. Please God, don't let the life go out of them . . .*

"Charity?"

"Yes, Jake. It's me, I'm right here. Where are you shot? Can you sit? Is it bad?"

He motioned weakly and she helped him sit up. There was a new hole in the back of his coat, near the shoulder. He tried to move his arm. He grimaced but it moved, and he rasped, "Jesus, I wish somebody'd shoot at the other side for a change."

Charity slumped back on her heels and let go of him. He fell back into the snow with an, "Oof."

"That's all?" she shouted. "He just shot you in the shoulder? I thought you were *dead!*"

He grinned at her lopsidedly. "Kinda thought I was for a minute there, myself. Knocked the wind clear out of me when I landed."

She helped him to his feet and waited while he whistled for Tico, who, looking confused, trotted toward them out of the trees. Number Ten, probably for want of anything better to do, followed him in. After Charity bandaged Jake's shoulder, rigged him a sling—and pronounced that he'd likely be able to lift an anvil inside two weeks, considering the rate at which he healed—she helped him hoist Duval's body across the grey horse's saddle.

She watched as Jake, one-handed, snugged up the ropes that would keep the corpse from slipping off the saddle. His face was different now, somehow. When they had first turned over the body and he'd looked down into Duval's dead eyes, she'd seen on Jake's countenance the same hatred he'd shown for Briscoe. No, not the same. This was worse, much worse, and for a moment, she'd been afraid. But then his features had softened, the poison gradually draining from them. She could see no trace of hatred now. He was quite businesslike as he tightened the ropes and secured the blanketed corpse.

No, there was no malice left in him, and she felt none in herself. It was gone forever, all played out. Jake looked calm, and although he was neither buoyant nor deliriously happy at putting a final end to this feud, he seemed, at least, at peace.

All in all, she decided, he looked pretty damn fit for a man who, in just the last week or so, had been the next thing to dead more times than she could count. *Duval was right about that part,* she mused happily. *We're both hard to kill. Between the two of us, we'll likely live forever.*

"Here, honey," Jake said when she joined him, ready to mount up. There was a small, bright red feather in his hand. He tucked it into the leather thong that secured her braid. When she swung her head, she could see it from the corner of her eye. It danced over her black hair like a tiny tongue of fire. "There," he said.

379

"That's almost as pretty as you are. Those birds scattered out of here so fast they left half of themselves behind."

She hadn't noticed until just them. A few birds — magpies and jays, mostly — were returning to their roosts; but the trees, which had been thick with winter birds when they first entered the clearing, were for the most part barren of life.

"Oh. This, too." He handed her back the knife. He'd cleaned every speck of blood away. "You know," he whispered as he circled her shoulders with one arm, "I'm awful glad I didn't give you earbobs or a dress."

She couldn't stop smiling, even when he kissed her.

As they rode out of the clearing and toward Fort Smith, Duval's grey horse — and its cargo — trailing behind, he said, "What's the first thing you want to do once we hit town?"

"Get you to a doctor."

He smiled. "After that, I mean."

She thought for a second. "I think I'd like to go to the jail."

Jake arched a brow. "The jail?"

She poked a thumb over her shoulder. "Well, don't you suppose there's a reward on him?"

"Of course there is! Last I heard, he was worth thirty-five hundred. But Charity, I'm in no big hurry to collect—"

"Hang on there a minute, Turlow," she replied, trying her best to sound haughty, though she didn't succeed as well as she would have liked. "You'd better not try and collect it. That's *my* bounty you're talking about."

He threw his head back with a laugh, then grabbed his shoulder, grimacing. "So it is," he said at last, smiling and wincing all at once. "So it is. Hell of a dowry, Miss Caine, I do declare. And since you got to pick the first two things to do, I get to pick the next two. Fair?"

She nodded. "Fair."

"All right. After we run your errands, we're going to the courthouse."

"The courthouse? Is that where we pick up the money?"

"It's where you put in your voucher. But that's not the main reason we're going there. I want to marry you, remember? I'd've married you first thing, but you've got these silly notions about doctors and rewards."

She couldn't have budged the grin from her face if she'd used both hands. "And your second thing?"

"The second thing starts with you naked," he said with a wink, "and is going to turn into a whole list of things just as soon as we sign that license and get back home."

Her cheeks went so hot that she was surprised when steam didn't rise from them. "Yes, Jake," was all she could think of to say.

He nodded. "That's settled, then. Weren't you in the middle of telling me something back there? Just before he showed up?"

She heard it then: a familiar birdsong, long missed through the bitter winter. She looked up, quickly scanning the branches overhead, and then she saw it: the first robin. Spring was coming after all. She turned toward Jake, smiled softly, and said, "It'll wait until after I show you my beads."

FEEL THE FIRE IN CAROL FINCH'S ROMANCES!

BELOVED BETRAYAL (2346, $3.95)

Sabrina Spencer donned a gray wig and veiled hat before blackmailing rugged Ridge Tanner into guiding her to Fort Canby. But the costume soon became her prison—the beauty had fallen head over heels in love!

LOVE'S HIDDEN TREASURE (2980, $4.50)

Shandra d'Evereux felt her heart throb beneath the stolen map she'd hidden in her bodice when Nolan Elliot swept her out onto the veranda. It was hard to concentrate on her mission with that wily rogue around!

MONTANA MOONFIRE (3263, $4.95)

Just as debutante Victoria Flemming-Cassidy was about to marry an oh-so-suitable mate, the towering preacher, Dru Sullivan flung her over his shoulder and headed West! Suddenly, Tori realized she had been given the best present for a bride: a night of passion with a real man!

THUNDER'S TENDER TOUCH (2809, $4.50)

Refined Piper Malone needed bounty-hunter, Vince Logan to recover her swindled inheritance. She thought she could coolly dismiss him after he did the job, but she never counted on the hot flood of desire she felt whenever he was near!